She remembered so clearly that long ago day, when the Yankee visited her father.

At the time, Letty assumed the visitor would come and go without making the least difference in her orderly if restricted life. How wrong she had been. Thorn Bradley came to the plantation of White Pines that day, and from the moment she looked into his eyes, he took possession of her heart.

Try as she would, Letty had never been able to forget him. As long as she lived, Thorn Bradley would be in her thoughts, because she loved him. It was that simple. Not that she believed for one second that Thorn returned her feelings.

Suddenly aware that she wasn't alone, Letty turned slowly to look behind her. As if the mere thinking of his name had caused him to materialize, Thorn stood at the base of the knoll.

"Hello, Letty," he said.

The Magnolia Tree

MARTHA KIRKLAND

JOVE BOOKS, NEW YORK

THE MAGNOLIA TREE

A Jove Book / published by arrangement with
the author

PRINTING HISTORY
Jove edition / September 1998

All rights reserved.
Copyright © 1998 by Martha Kirkland.
This book may not be reproduced in whole
or in part, by mimeograph or any other means,
without permission. For information address:
The Berkley Publishing Group, a member of Penguin Putnam Inc.,
200 Madison Avenue, New York, New York 10016.

The Penguin Putnam Inc. World Wide Web site address is
http://www.penguinputnam.com

ISBN: 0-515-12361-7

A JOVE BOOK®
Jove Books are published by The Berkley Publishing Group,
a member of Penguin Putnam Inc.,
200 Madison Avenue, New York, New York 10016.
JOVE and the "J" design are trademarks
belonging to Jove Publications, Inc.

PRINTED IN THE UNITED STATES OF AMERICA

10 9 8 7 6 5 4 3 2

To my husband, Tal Kirkland, . . . with love

*In appreciation to Mr. Richard N. Kennedy, Jr.,
of The Gun Room in Atlanta for his kindness and
invaluable help*

Prologue

Letty Banks lifted the Colt .44 Dragoon from the wash-stand. She hadn't touched the revolver since she'd loaded it three hours earlier and laid it beside the small leather pouch that held the powder and ball, but now she heard the sound she'd been waiting for.

Resting the barrel of the heavy weapon across her lap, she held the wooden handle firmly with her right hand, then pulled the hammer back carefully with the heel of her left hand. Her heart pounded against her corset stays. She knew nothing about guns; God help her if she hadn't primed it properly and it exploded in her face. She hoped she wouldn't have to shoot it, but she would if she had to.

She had warned the timid shadow of a woman who was her mother, and soon she would warn Abner Banks: Nobody would touch that baby. Nobody!

While the newborn slept beneath the mosquito-netted canopy of Letty's four-poster bed, unaware of the chain of events her birth had set in motion, Letty sat ramrod straight in the small, petit-point rocker she'd dragged over to the bedroom window. She'd been sitting there most of the afternoon listening for her father's return.

A rivulet of sweat trickled down the young girl's backbone, adding to the clinging dampness of the linen chemise beneath her yellow cambric dress. Though a gentle breeze wafted through the open window, lifting the hem of the white lace curtains, it brought little relief to her heated body. She ignored both the heat and the breeze. Nothing mattered now except the confrontation that was about to take place, a confrontation as unavoidable as the heat itself.

Above the usual plantation sounds of servants returning from the fields, chickens cackling for their evening feed, dogs barking, and Minna's goose threatening one and all, Letty heard Diablo's hooves on the hard-packed Georgia red clay. She held her breath. The stallion needed only twenty seconds to gallop the distance from the carriageway to the front steps of the veranda.

While Letty mentally counted off those seconds, she ran the tip of her tongue across her lower lip. She winced. The metallic taste of dried blood reminded her a moment too late of the deep cut at the corner of her mouth—a cut left there by the ornate design of her father's signet ring. Dismissing both the memory and the pain, she returned her attention to Diablo's arrival.

"You! Whoever you are," her father shouted at whichever one of Minna's twins had been unlucky enough to come from the stable to take his horse, "you tell Caleb that stirrup broke when I put my weight on it, and if it ever happens again, he'll find himself doing the smithing at night and picking cotton with the field hands during the day!"

"Yes, Marse Abner," the frightened child answered.

Letty grasped the Dragoon with both hands and rose from the petit-point rocker. She wished she hadn't cocked the revolver so early. She needed to wipe the sweat from her palms but wasn't certain she could ease the Dragoon's hammer back onto the safety without making the weapon go off. Her hands had grown so slick she was afraid her finger might slip off the trigger if she had to pull it. Not *pull*, she reminded herself, *squeeze*.

She heard the echo of her father's boots as he stomped across the wooden veranda, then silence as he tread upon the thick, oriental carpet in the foyer. The silence was followed by rhythmic thuds as, two at a time, he took the polished heart-of-pine stairs leading to the second story. For a man well past his fortieth birthday, he moved quickly, and within seconds she heard him in the hallway just outside her bedroom door.

Knowing it would only delay the inevitable, she hadn't bothered locking her door . . . everyone in the county knew that Abner Banks went where he wanted, when he wanted. This time was no exception. Without bothering to try the handle, he kicked the door open, making it crash with a loud thud against the bedroom wall. Letty willed herself not to react, but the sudden clamor awakened the baby, who howled with all the strength of her day-old lungs.

Abner stopped in his tracks at the unexpected sound. "What the—"

Glancing at the swaddled infant for a mere second, he dismissed the child and gave his full attention to his daughter. He looked first at the Colt Dragoon she pointed at him, then at the washstand where the leather pouch lay alongside the tin container that held the percussion caps. He smiled lazily. All who knew him feared that smile.

"So, Loretta," he drawled, "you know how to use a Dragoon, do you?"

She forced her voice to sound as casual as his. "I'm willing to find out, Papa. Are you?"

Ignoring her question, Abner pushed the lapels of his bottle-green frock coat aside and hooked his thumbs behind his galluses. Though he relaxed his tall, wiry body against the doorjamb, his seeming indifference didn't fool Letty into relaxing her guard; she knew from the hint of Yorkshire that slipped into his carefully cultivated southern drawl that he was seething with anger. She'd known he would come home mad as a snake, just as she knew without a shadow of a doubt that he would make her pay for this latest piece of defiance. He wasn't called Old Canebrake for nothing.

Legend had it that once, while Abner was hunting on the banks of the Ochlockonee River in south Georgia, a cane-brake rattler had bitten him on the arm. Those who claimed to have witnessed the incident swore that Abner became enraged and chased the rattler as it slithered through the thick underbrush at the river's edge. When he finally cornered the snake, he put the heel of his boot on the reptile's head and mashed until only a bloody pulp remained. Not yet satisfied, Abner picked up the headless body and threw it to Priam, his body servant.

"Cook him for dinner!" Abner ordered. "When something takes a bite out of me, I mean to have the last bite!"

Letty didn't question the legend; it was too true to form for doubt. Old Canebrake always got the last bite. Dragging Mary off to the slave auction this morning was one of those last bites, and there would be more to follow. But not for Mary's baby. Not for Mary's little Ocilla. Abner would keep his heel off that little head, or he would die. Letty had made that vow to God!

As though he heard her thoughts, Abner glanced once again at the infant on the bed. "You would defy me for a slave's whelp?"

Letty felt tears sting her eyes, but she willed the salty droplets not to fall. "Mary is like my own sister. We've been together since we were babies. All her life she slept in my trundle bed. Now I know why you made her leave me and move down to the cabins. It was so you could—"

"You are a stupid, ignorant girl who knows nothing of a man's needs and—"

"And you are an abomination! Not even fit to be called an animal."

Abner straightened and took one step toward her, but when she raised the revolver even higher, he stopped. A hint of anger flashed in his pewter-gray eyes. "Don't be a fool, Loretta. They are slaves. Nothing more."

"Mary is my friend. And her baby is your child!"

Letty said no more, for she was obliged to swallow to

prevent the bile from rising into her throat—bile that threatened each time she thought of Abner Banks crawling into Mary's bed night after night, forcing the sixteen-year-old to submit to him. "How could you do it?"

Choosing to misunderstand her, he said, "I lay this day's work at your feet, Loretta. The fault is entirely yours."

In his own twisted way, her father was correct. She had brought the final tragedy down upon her childhood playmate. Letty had triggered today's disaster, even though Mary had begged her not to say anything, to pretend she didn't know who had fathered the newborn.

Letty hadn't listened.

All during the winter and spring months, while Mary's belly grew bigger and bigger, she adamantly refused to tell who had gotten her pregnant. But the moment Letty saw the newborn, she knew. In addition to its pale skin, the infant had Abner's chin, and only one other person had a chin that square, that obstinate. That person was Abner Banks's other child, Letty.

Angry and sickened by the discovery of her father's debauchery, Letty had rushed out of Mary's cabin and run to the house. She found Abner sitting on the veranda entertaining two men who had come out to White Pines to celebrate the news of the end of the Mexican War.

"To Young Jimmie Polk!" one of the visitors cried, lifting his bourbon-laced swizzle in toast to the President.

"To Winfield Scott!" the other added, almost smashing his glass against that of his crony. "And the Halls of Monte-what's-iz-name."

Paying no attention to the two swizzle-guzzling visitors, Letty sped up the steps of the veranda and stormed across to the shaded corner where her father sat nursing his own drink. Unmindful of anything but her own outrage, she clamped her foot down on the rocker of her father's chair, stopping it in mid-motion and making his swizzle slosh out of the glass onto his coat sleeve.

Her eyes blazing and her hands clenched into fists, Letty cursed him. She called him a lecher and a satyr, leaving the smirking guests in no doubt as to the reason for her outrage.

Abner got the last bite for that public insult, of course. A shudder ran through Letty's body as she relived the horror of his vengeance.

In the silence that followed her insults, she watched a lazy smile pull at the corners of her father's mouth. The two visitors saw it, too. Suddenly sobered, the men recalled forgotten appointments in town and made a hasty retreat.

With the dust from the visitors' buggy wheels still swirling, Abner Banks roared for someone to fetch his horse. Still without saying a word to Letty, he marched out to Mary's cabin. Within minutes he reappeared, dragging the terrified, whimpering young girl behind him in the dirt like a half-filled sack of cotton. Mary's wrists were tied together with one of his galluses.

Letty ran toward him, her face sheet-white with terror. "Papa! What are you doing?"

"I'm going to town," he answered coldly, "to Moss's auction."

"Papa, no! Don't do it. Please don't!"

She tried to pull Mary's wrists free of his iron grasp, but Abner pushed her aside as though she were a pesky gnat.

Desperate, Letty dropped to her knees in front of him, her hands beneath her chin like a supplicant. Tears streaked her face. "I'm sorry, Papa. I'm truly sorry. I apologize for everything I said. It's all my fault. Punish me if you must, but please don't make Mary pay for what I did."

He pushed her aside again.

Still on her knees, Letty threw her arms around his legs and held on with all her strength. "Papa, please, I'm begging you. Don't sell Mary. I promise I'll never interfere again . . . not about anything. I promise on the Bible that as long as I live I will never again—"

Abner slapped her across the face with the back of his hand, and the force of the blow sent her sprawling in the red dust. While Letty lay there dazed, blood running from the corner of her mouth, her father tossed the sobbing Mary across the front of Diablo's saddle, then mounted behind her and galloped down the carriageway.

Long after the *clop, clop* of the horse's hooves had faded into the distance, Letty could still hear Mary's screams.

"The fault is entirely yours," Abner repeated, bringing her thoughts back to the present. "You meddled once too often in things that were none of your concern." He jerked his head toward the canopied bed. "And now you are doing it again. When will you learn you can't stop me from doing what I want with my own property?"

Fury surged through Letty. She was no longer the young girl he'd left lying in the dirt. Listening to Mary's screams had aged her, changed her from a girl into a grown woman. Stepping to within a foot of her father, she pressed the muzzle of the revolver against his chest. When she spoke, her voice was clear and calm.

"I want you to understand me, Papa. That baby over there is my sister. I couldn't stop you from dragging Mary away, but I promise you, if you lay a hand on her child, I will kill you."

Father and daughter glared at each other for what seemed like hours, the silence between them broken only by the furious buzzing of a bumblebee trapped in the folds of the lace curtain. Letty could almost see Old Canebrake's mind working, plotting. Finally he turned and walked from the room. Just as he stepped into the hallway, he paused, looking back over his shoulder.

"I understand you, Loretta. Now you understand me. You want the brat? Take her. Do whatever you will with her. Her destiny is entirely in your hands. You have my word as a gentleman that no one will lay a finger on her." He paused, letting the significance of his next words sink in. "No one will touch her . . . not as long as you remain on the plantation.

"However," he continued, giving her a smile that sent sweat gushing down her back, "if you set so much as a toe outside the boundaries of White Pines, never mind your reasons for doing so, all bets are off. The moment you leave the place—this year, next year, twenty years from now—I will personally hang that brat from the oak tree beside the stable, where she will remain until you return. And when you return, you may watch me remove her rotted carcass and throw it into the hog trough.''

A strangled sound in Letty's throat betrayed her.

"At last," Old Canebrake said, smiling once again, "I believe we truly understand each other."

One

November 1855

"Auntie. *Auntie!*"

The little girl's soft voice interrupted Letty's chaotic thoughts, making her jump as though she had been caught doing something reprehensible. Happy to abandon even momentarily the complicated plans that ran helter-skelter through her brain, she pushed the silver jewelry casket—the initial cause of her confusion—to the back of her dressing table.

"Yes, Ocilla, what is it?"

"Will you wind your new music box so it plays that song again? I forgot how it goes."

Letty removed the small winding key from the casket, then turned to the child who sat on the far side of the bedroom at the drop-leaf table where the two of them ate their morning meals. She was a beautiful child, with soft brown eyes and a smooth, olive complexion, but she was small for her eight years, her bone structure delicate. Letty dangled the key back and forth as though it were bait. "I'll play it again, Ocilla, but only if you finish your breakfast."

The little girl glanced from her own half-eaten egg to the

twin, hand-painted china plate that held the remains of
Letty's breakfast. "But you didn't finish yours."

"True, my love, but I am not a growing girl. You are.
When I was eight years old, I always ate everything Verona
put on my plate."

Having uttered such a boldfaced, though well-intentioned
lie, Letty had the grace to lower her gaze. How could she
blame the child for having no interest in the meal when *she*
had been unable to force more than a few bites down her
own throat? She had done nothing but push the food around
on her plate the entire time she sat at the table. She couldn't
eat, not while her brain was in such turmoil.

She needed to think, to plan. So much had happened
since yesterday, so much that could change hers and
Ocilla's lives forever.

For such a momentous day, yesterday had begun as all
their days began. She and Ocilla had enjoyed a breakfast
of ham with buttered grits, plus hot biscuits dripping with
some of Verona's gooey fig preserves. Then after they took
the breakfast tray down to the butler's pantry and left it on
the walnut worktable for Priam, they went out to the cookhouse to discuss the dinner and supper menus with the
cook.

An ordinary beginning to an ordinary day. Or so Letty
had thought at the time.

Verona had left the top half of the cookhouse door open
to let in the cool autumn air and let out the heat from the
massive stone fireplace, so as Letty and Ocilla neared the
brick building, the smell of cinnamon and bubbly hot sweet
potatoes filled their senses.

They didn't go inside the cookhouse. Since the single-
room kitchen had little space for visitors, they propped their
elbows on the ledge of the bottom half of the door, a ledge
worn satin smooth by several generations' worth of elbows,
and leaned toward the interior.

"Hey in there, Verona," Ocilla greeted.

"Hey, yourself, sugar dumpling," the fat, middle-aged
woman replied.

The cook hunched over a thick, unpainted worktable

where she guided a water-filled glass rolling pin across a thick mound of pastry dough. Her sleeves were rolled up past her dimpled elbows, and with each rhythmic lift of the rolling pin, flour danced through the air and landed on her soft ebony arms. She paid no attention to the wayward flour, for her mind was obviously on other things this morning. Her obsidian eyes shone with excitement.

"Morning, Miss Letty. I didn't think y'all was ever going to come out this morning."

"What's happened, Verona? You look like the fox that swallowed the prize laying hen."

Verona had two talents—cooking and gossip—and she liked nothing better than to combine the two. To heighten the drama of her information, she let the question remain unanswered until after she'd reached behind her to the wall hung with pots and cooking utensils and selected a deep tin dish. Finally, as though she had just thought of it, she jerked her head toward the pot of sweet potatoes that sat on a trivet inside the stone fireplace.

"I be fixing sweet potato cobbler for supper. You reckon that'll do for company?"

Letty's slightly lifted eyebrows identified her to the cook as fresh ears. "Company? What company?"

Verona shrugged her plump shoulders as though the entire subject was of little interest to her. "I don't know, Miss Letty. Don't nobody tell me the names of the company, just how many mouths to fix for. Last night Priam come down to my cabin and say fix for two extry today. And that's what I be doing."

Unable to maintain the pose of disinterest another moment, the cook laid her rolling pin down and leaned forward, the better to tell her story. "Priam say Marse Abner go to town yesterday to see that lawyer man, that Mr. DuBose. Then when Marse Abner come home, he tell Priam two gentlemen coming today. Mayhap they be here by dinnertime, but definitely by supper. They's coming by boat."

"Boat? Now, Verona, you know as well as I do that our river is too low for a traveling boat."

"They ain't boating all the way up to here, Miss Letty. Priam say they leaving the boat downriver a piece and coming on up here by land."

"Hmm."

Both women remained silent for a short spell, each lost in her own speculation about the two gentlemen. Of course, the visitors were of interest only because they offered a new topic of conversation in a place where new topics were scarce. It was highly unlikely that either woman would meet the men face-to-face. Verona wouldn't see them because she never entered the main house, and Letty wouldn't see them because she would avoid them as she did all visitors to White Pines.

For the past six years the only visitors who had come to the plantation had come to see Abner. Shortly after the death of Letty's mother—a shy woman whose spirit had been subdued to nonexistence by her husband—the ladies of the neighboring plantations stopped visiting White Pines. They had never liked Abner Banks, considering him a parvenu, but they had visited Amalie Llewellen Banks because she was one of their own. And they would have continued to visit Letty for that same reason if she had not insulted them by refusing to leave White Pines to visit in their homes.

In the years that followed Amalie's death, all Abner's guests came for the same reason, to drink his whiskey and to pit their card-playing skills against his. Since these visitors exhibited little character and breeding, it was an accepted practice for Letty to stay out of sight as much as possible when Abner entertained. Today would be no exception.

"The visitors are probably coming to see that new foal of Papa's."

Verona considered this possibility. "Likely you hit the nail on the head, Miss Letty. Mens surely do like horses."

While she talked, Verona took a large pinch of pastry dough and rolled it between her palms until it was about the size and shape of a new crabapple. Without saying a word, she reached across the table and dipped the dough ball into a bowl containing a mixture of brown sugar and cinnamon.

When the ball was coated to her satisfaction, she turned to Ocilla, who had listened quietly while the women talked. As if knowing what was coming, the child grinned from ear to ear, then scrunched her eyes shut and opened her mouth wide.

"Lordy, Miss Letty," Verona said in mock displeasure, "did you ever see such a spoiled young'un? She think just cause she the only little girl on the place, folks ain't got nothing better to do than fix treats for her. She think old Verona done fix this here sugar tit just for her, don't she?"

Letty chuckled. She had heard those same teasing words hundreds of times when she was a child. She recalled the way her mouth used to fill with saliva while she watched Verona roll the dough ball in the sugar and spice. She remembered as well the way she had waited expectantly with her eyes squeezed shut and her mouth agape, knowing the treat was meant for her. Now she watched Ocilla duplicate her actions of years past by leaning closer into the kitchen so Verona's short arms could reach her.

The cook shook her head, making her extra chins flap against her neck. "Well, I reckon what can't be helped got to be endured." Having said her piece, she leaned her bulk across the worktable and stretched her hand toward the child. "All right, Ocilla, open your mouth and close your eyes, and I'll give you something to make you wise."

Ocilla couldn't open her mouth any wider, so she closed it and opened it again instead. Verona put the entire sugar-coated dough ball into the little girl's mouth. "There you go, lambie pie, sweets to the sweet."

While Ocilla savored the treat that puffed her thin cheeks out like those of a courting bullfrog, Letty asked Verona if she had made up her mind about the calico swatches Caleb brought her from town the week before.

"The red and blue check is the one, Miss Letty. I knowed that the first time I set eyes on it. Sudy's a plumb fool about red, been that way since she was a baby. She probably pitch a hissy fit if she knowed I could have chose red for her birthday dress and didn't.''

They discussed the calico for several minutes. When that topic ran its course, Letty reminded Ocilla to thank Verona for the sugar tit, then they left the cook to her sweet potato cobbler and went on their next errand.

They followed the pine-bark-strewn path that led to the whitewashed stable and beyond, and just before they reached Caleb's blacksmith shed, Ocilla slipped her hand into Letty's. "I'm glad *Maître* is having guests, Auntie. That means you can eat your supper with me in the pantry. I like it so much better when you eat with me instead of him."

Letty stroked the delicate-boned hand tucked in her own. "I like it better, too, my love. Much better."

That settled, Ocilla expressed her desire to spend the afternoon sitting by the bedroom window where she could see the visitors when they arrived. "So I can tell Verona all about them," she said.

As it turned out, the child didn't get to see the visitors; they arrived before she and Letty got back to the house. Nor did she get to have supper with Letty in the pantry. Later that afternoon Priam informed them that Letty was expected to dine with her father and the unknown visitors.

Letty and Ocilla were in the bedroom when they heard the news. Letty had finished her work for the day—the inventory of dry goods in the storehouse was counted and the records brought up to date, and the list of things for Caleb to bring from town tomorrow was compiled and the money counted out. With her own chores done, she sat in the petit-point rocker by the bedroom window perusing a schoolroom slate that held the arithmetic problems she had set Ocilla for the day. She was about to point out an error to the child when Priam scratched on the bedroom door.

"Miss Letty?"

Ocilla jumped down from the ladder-back chair she had pulled up to the rosewood writing desk and hurried to the door. "Hey, Priam."

"Hey to you, too, sugar," he said, giving the child's

thick, brown curls a gentle tousling. "Miss Letty, Marse Abner say to tell you he fixing to have company to supper."

"Thank you, Priam, but we have already heard. Verona told us. I'll have my supper in the pantry with Ocilla if it's not too much trouble."

The old man shook his head. "That ain't never too much trouble, Miss Letty, you know it ain't, but Marse Abner say this time you got to hostess."

Not certain she'd heard him correctly, she said, "Hostess? Are you sure that's what he said?"

"Yes'm. Marse Abner say tell you this particular company be 'specting a hostess." Priam looked down at his white-gloved hands and kept his attention there. He cleared his throat. "And Marse Abner say tell you if you know what's good for you—"

"Never mind, Priam," she interrupted to spare the old man the embarrassment of repeating her father's threat. "I can guess the rest of it."

Her first impulse was to ignore the command. Her father hadn't required a hostess for years, and he could darn well do without one now. She had no desire to sit at the table with Abner and watch a pair of louts bolt their dinner and throw back glasses of wine, as though it were well water, just so they could hurry to the library for hands of whist and decanters of bourbon. Her nose wrinkled at the thought.

Within seconds, however, memories of other small rebellions and their repercussions cooled the heat of her first impulse. Perhaps she would do well not to flout Abner unnecessarily; there would be time enough to defy him if the guests proved too disreputable. Having decided on a course of action, she pushed her misgivings about the guests aside and agreed to join her father.

Later, while Ocilla ate her solitary meal in the butler's pantry, Letty prepared herself for the evening meal in the dining room. She washed her face and hands and rebraided her waist-length, light brown hair, then wound the single braid around her head in its usual coronet, securing it with a plain, mother of pearl hair clip.

Wanting her father to understand that she was not pleased at his summons, Letty chose the least attractive of her two woefully unmodish dinner dresses, a fading pink silk whose only embellishments were an ecru lace bertha and a row of tiny rosebuds embroidered around the hem of the organ pleated skirt. Spurning the crinoline that would have given the dress some slight pretensions to fashion, she stepped into an outdated horsehair underskirt.

Once all the tabs were tied, and all the buttons done up, she added one piece of jewelry, a gold locket containing a lock of her mother's hair. Her sober toilette completed, Letty turned back the cover on the trundle bed, leaving it ready in case Ocilla grew sleepy before she returned. With no further excuse for delay, she went down to the parlor to confront her father's guests.

Defiance turned to chagrin when Letty entered the parlor and discovered not the louts she had expected but two fashionably dressed gentlemen of impeccable breeding. The shorter gentleman, his yellow hair stylishly combed and pomaded, was by far the handsomer of the two guests, but it was his companion who made Letty curse herself for not wearing her burgundy dress, and for not putting her hair in ringlets or dabbing lilac water behind her ears.

A tall man in his late twenties, the gentleman had dark straight hair that brushed his coat collar at the back, and thick, black eyebrows that framed the clearest blue-gray eyes Letty had ever seen. One look into those eyes and her heart began to race as though she'd just run several miles.

While her brain leaped from a wish for bouncing curls to a fear that she hadn't laced her corset tight enough to enhance what little womanly roundness she possessed, the blond gentleman rose from his chair by the fire and made her a gallant bow. "Your servant, ma'am."

To keep from staring at the tall gentleman, who made her a perfunctory bow, Letty concentrated on the shorter man's evening tailcoat and black, shawl-collared waistcoat, which did not quite camouflage the fullness around his middle.

"Miss Banks," he said, "allow me to introduce myself.

My name is Andrew Holden, and I am the legal adviser to your maternal grandfather, Mr. Horace Llewellen. I have come all the way from Charleston, bearing you a birthday gift from your grandfather.''

The gift, a chased silver jewelry casket, had been delivered into Letty's hands after supper. And now, twelve hours later, with the morning sun streaming in her bedroom window and the remains of her breakfast growing cold on the plate, Letty's senses still reeled from the possible consequences of the gift.

She turned back to the dressing table to touch the cool silver, to reassure herself that the casket with its hidden music box was not a figment of her imagination. It was real. She hadn't imagined it. Slowly she lifted the lid and looked for the hundredth time at the letter that lay upon the red velvet lining. It, too, was real. Letty didn't touch the letter. She didn't need to read it again; she already knew its contents by heart.

''I've eaten the entire egg, Auntie,'' Ocilla sang out, interrupting Letty's recollection of the shock she had felt when she read her grandfather's letter the first time. ''Will you wind the music box now and let me hear the song again?''

''Here,'' she offered, holding the key toward the child, ''you may wind it yourself.''

Ocilla skipped over to the dressing table and pulled the jewelry casket toward her so she could slide the back panel aside. Once the base was open, she fitted the looped end of the two-headed key into a keyhole and wound the mechanism.

The job completed, she folded her thin arms and placed them on the dressing table, then she rested the square chin that was a small replica of Letty's on her forearms. The child watched mesmerized as a six-inch-long cylinder covered with little protruding pins revolved past a metal comb consisting of eight tuned teeth. The protruding pins plucked the teeth, and the result was a tinny rendition of ''Old Dan Tucker.'' Ocilla hummed along, her high, reedy notes enthusiastic though offkey.

The song went through numerous choruses, each one playing slower than the one before it, until the cylinder finally sounded only the occasional *plink, plink, plink.* The child rewound the mechanism three times and was about to wind it a fourth time when she was distracted by the sound of voices coming from the veranda. The music forgotten, she dashed to the window and pulled the curtains aside for her first glimpse of the visitors.

"It's them, Auntie!" she said in an excited whisper. "They're down there, I can see them. One of them is walking down the carriageway, and he's taking giant steps like he's angry."

The child pressed her face against the windowpane in an effort to see the veranda steps. "Now here comes the other one. He's hurrying, trying to catch up with the first one. Oh, no!"

"What is it?" Letty asked, embarrassed by the breathless quality she couldn't keep out of her voice at the thought of the wide-stepping visitor.

"They've already put their hats on, and I can't see which one has the yellow hair. Priam said it looks just like corn silk." Ocilla's lower lip pouted in disappointment. "And I so wanted to see a man with corn-silk hair."

"The shorter gentleman has the blond hair. The other gentleman has dark hair."

"What's his name?"

"Thornton Bradley," Letty replied, enjoying the feel of the syllables on her lips. "But the gentleman with the corn-silk hair calls him Thorn."

Ocilla giggled. "Auntie, I *meant* the gentleman with the corn-silk hair."

"Oh." Mortified at the heat she felt creep from beneath her stays to climb unimpeded up her throat to her face, Letty cautioned herself not to act like a foolish old maid. To keep the child from seeing the color that tinted her cheeks, she examined a small spot on the neck ruffle of her lawn wrapper. She really would have to get hold of her wayward thoughts, for she was dangerously close to pinning her heart on her sleeve for everyone to see.

"The blond gentleman is Mr. Andrew Holden. He is employed by the law firm that handles my grandfather's cotton business. He is—"

Ocilla jumped back from the window and let the curtain fall from her fingers, the giggles of a moment ago dissipating like smoke in the wind.

"What is it, my love?"

"It's . . . it's *Maître*," Ocilla whispered.

Opening her arms, Letty beckoned to the child, who came immediately and snuggled against her side. "Never mind about *Maître*, my love. He won't hurt you. I've told you that before. Don't you remember?"

Ocilla nodded her head. "I remember. But his shoulders looked all angry. And he wadded up a piece of paper and threw it on the ground like he hoped it would break."

"A piece of paper?" Letty glanced at the silver jewelry casket, almost as though she could see through it to the letter that lay within. "Perhaps *Maître* has received some bad news. I wouldn't be at all surprised. I suspect our visitors delivered a letter to him not unlike the one they delivered to me." Letty felt a cynical smile tug at her lips. "No wonder the gentlemen felt the need for such an early-morning walk."

"Did they come to White Pines to deliver letters? I thought they came to look at *Maître*'s new foal."

"No, the gentlemen did not come for that reason. Knights in shining armor aren't interested in foals."

Ocilla's eyes were wide with wonder, her voice hushed. "Is that what they are? Knights in shining armor?"

"They just may prove to be so, my love."

"Do they have swords and do they use them to slay dragons to free the beautiful princess?"

Letty pulled Ocilla even closer into her arms, then rested her chin on top of the little girl's head, her softly spoken words making the child's curls bounce. "The only sword I know of lies in the silver music box, and those modern-day knights in shining armor have brought that sword to me. I pray with all my heart that I can use it to free you and me from our dragon."

Two

Thorn Bradley's giant steps put distance between him and
the veranda, but not enough distance to suit him. He needed
more than a long walk to dispel his distaste for White Pines
and its owner. He wished he could keep on walking until he
was past the entrance gate he knew was just down the
carriageway. He wanted to feel his boat beneath his feet,
smell the fresh, clean water as it dipped beneath the hull
and lapped softly against the bow. He would need days of
fresh air in his nostrils to banish the unpleasant odor of the
scene they had just endured with Abner Banks.

Jamming his hands down into the pockets of his snug,
fawn-colored breeches, Thorn hunched his shoulders forward, straining the material of his blue frock coat. Swearing
beneath his breath, he called himself all kinds of fool. He
wished he had never given his friend's brother a berth on
his boat. The reason he had taken the waterways survey job
in the first place was to get away from people and their
machinations.

Hearing Andrew's hurried footsteps on the carriageway
behind him, Thorn pulled his wide-brim hat down low on
his forehead. Pulling the hat down to obstruct his view of
Andrew was as close as he was going to get to being alone.

Of course, the hat also kept him from seeing anything other than the red earth that passed beneath his boots, but that didn't matter. He hadn't come outside to admire the beauty of the ancient oak trees, their leaves awash in red, orange, and gold, any more than he had come for the crisp, autumn air or the sweet aroma of the sugar cane being ground in one of the plantation's unseen outbuildings. He had come outside to keep from putting his fist through Abner Banks's face.

"Thorn, wait up!" The unaccustomed exertion of trying to overtake his long-legged companion made Andrew pant between each word. "Dammit, Thorn, wait for me. I can explain."

Thorn stopped so Andrew could catch up with him, but he did not push the hat back from his forehead.

"I wanted to tell you everything before we left Charleston," Andrew said between gasps, "but my brother was afraid you might not bring me here if you knew the whole story."

"William was right, I wouldn't have. I try to keep out of other people's feuds, especially when they involve two men who will stop at nothing to have their own way."

"That's what William said you would say." Andrew cleared his throat as though something were stuck in it. "But he also said that when y'all were at school together you would never let the older boys knock the freshmen around."

Thorn noted the embarrassment in the other man's voice and relaxed the angry set of his shoulders. "You are hardly a freshman, Drew."

"I am when it comes to dealing with the likes of Abner Banks. William was afraid Banks might go into a rage when he read Llewellen's letter and kill the messenger. But William knew he could trust you to get me back home to Charleston in one piece. He said you would be able to handle Banks."

"I'm afraid that trick would require one of those Indian snake handlers."

"Phewwee, ain't it the truth!" Andrew's brow relaxed

at Thorn's little joke. "Lordy, Thorn, did you see the way that man smiled? Made my skin crawl like somebody'd just walked over my grave. William says folks call the fellow Old Canebrake, and now I see why."

Thorn pushed his hat back. "How well does your brother know Abner Banks?"

"He knows Banks mostly by reputation. Runs into him every so often at the cotton exchange. That's the only reason he knows him personally—doesn't socialize with him. And he doesn't trust the fellow two bits' worth. Of course, my brother doesn't trust old man Llewellen, either, or the old man's reasons for wanting those letters delivered in person."

Andrew took a spotless white lawn handkerchief from inside his dark blue coat and wiped the perspiration from his pudgy hands. "Mr. Llewellen claimed that he couldn't be certain his granddaughter would get his letter, not unless I put the jewelry box into her hands myself. He also said he wanted me to nose around—make sure that Banks wasn't holding Miss Loretta prisoner here at White Pines."

"Prisoner? Absurd. Not even a snake like Abner Banks has the power to force a grown daughter to remain where she doesn't want to be."

Andrew shook his head. "I don't know. The old man claims he's been trying for years to get her to come to Charleston, but for some reason she won't leave the plantation."

"Perhaps," Thorn suggested, "she finds little to choose between her father's company and her grandfather's." He stared down the length of the carriageway. "Whatever the story, I wouldn't worry about her if I were you. Even if there has been some kind of coercion, once the word gets around that Mr. Llewellen has deeded White Pines plantation to his granddaughter, hordes of would-be bridegrooms will come galloping down this path. I predict that Miss Banks will be leaving on her honeymoon trip by spring."

Thorn looked around him, as though recalling the vast fields they had passed when they arrived yesterday. "There must be more than a thousand acres of cultivated land at White Pines. Quite a dowry.''

''A thousand and four hundred acres,'' Andrew corrected somewhat wistfully.

Thorn observed his friend's brother. ''Perhaps it was part of Mr. Llewellen's plans that once you saw the place, you would get the jump on the horde and marry his granddaughter out of hand.''

Andrew puffed up like a partridge. ''I'm no fortune hunter!''

Thorn touched the brim of his hat in salute. ''Beg pardon, sir. No offense intended.''

Peaceable by nature, Andrew inclined his head in an abbreviated bow. ''In all honesty, I can't say the idea of putting my luck to the touch didn't flit across my brain for just a moment. I'm not entirely without prospects, and I would make Miss Loretta a dang sight better husband than some, for I truly like her.'' He took a quick look over his shoulder to make certain no one could hear him. ''Even though she's a bit long and lean for my taste. Not to mention being older than the ladies I usually—''

''What rubbish! Miss Banks's face and figure are quite pleasing. Furthermore, she can't be a day over twenty-four. That hardly brands her as past praying for.''

At the rather impassioned reply, Andrew stared at Thorn, a speculative look in his eyes. ''Maybe I'm not the only one tempted to join that horde of would-be suitors. Though I thought my brother mentioned something about a Miss Delia Lewis back in Connecticut.''

''Lowell,'' Thorn muttered between clenched teeth. ''Miss Delia Lowell.''

Thorn concentrated on a giant oak he could see down near the entrance to the carriageway. He didn't want to think about Delia. Not now, not here. Not at this place, where two bitter men warred for dominance over one another, caring little about the young woman caught in the middle of their feud. The situations were too similar.

Angrily he jammed his hands into his pockets. *Be damned to all those who interfered in other people's lives!*

He had left Connecticut because Delia's father and his father were pressuring her to set the wedding date. The two old cronies had planned this union of families and property for years, both of them seemingly blind to Delia's reticence. Thorn loved her, but he wanted her only if she loved him. And if the two fathers would stop interfering, perhaps Delia would realize— No! He didn't want to think of her here.

Pushing thoughts of Delia to the back of his mind, Thorn returned to the subject at hand. "Believe me, Drew, I have no interest in joining the hordes, no matter how tempting the dowry or the bride. But if you are entertaining even the slightest thoughts of paying your addresses to Miss Banks, I advise you to think the matter over carefully. You and I might agree that Mr. Llewellen has a right to do whatever he wants with his land, but I doubt that Abner Banks sees it that way. I've known men like Banks before, and believe me, that man would kill for a lot less than a thousand plus acres."

Having warned his friend's brother, Thorn considered he had done enough interfering of his own, so he turned and continued his walk down the carriageway. Andrew fell in beside him, taking short, quick steps to keep up with Thorn's longer strides, and for a time they strode quietly, neither feeling the need for further conversation.

Just before they reached the entrance gates they veered off to the left and followed a rough path across a still-green meadow. Beyond the meadow stood a two-story cotton house, and beyond that a newer building Thorn assumed was the gin house. Choosing not to go where he might encounter other people, Thorn detoured through a pine thicket then let his nose lead him to a fragrant herb garden.

It was a small plot, the bed raised to let the water drain, and it was laid out to resemble a patchwork quilt. Someone had taken pride in the simple plantings, for the foliage of the herbs formed perfect squares of yellow, green, red, purple, and gray, with each pattern repeated four times.

Taking care where he put his feet, Thorn wandered through the zigzag rows, pausing now and then to sniff the various bouquets. With each new smell he seemed to lose himself, to be carried farther and farther away, to a place and time long forgotten.

When he came to a row of shrubs just beginning to show small lavender blossoms, he leaned forward and picked one of the flowers, then crushed it between his palms and breathed in the pungent aroma. "This is savory," he said, the words spoken softly, almost as though he were in a chapel. "My mother used to make tea with this when I was a child. It's good for bellyaches."

Andrew snorted, breaking the quiet spell. "Then we'd better take a handful of the stuff back to the house, for Abner Banks is sure to need it by now." He bent forward to pick a blossom but jumped back when he disturbed a bee. "On second thought, better not pick any."

When Thorn gave him a questioning look, Andrew said, "Banks married thinking the land would be his, but for some reason, his father-in-law reneged on the original marriage agreement. Now, after running the place for twenty-five years, probably waiting all the while for Llewellen to die and leave White Pines to him, Abner Banks is going to need something stronger than weed tea to cure what ails him."

Thorn put a savory blossom in his coat pocket, then stepped over the shrub. "I imagine losing everything would give any man a powerful bellyache."

"Oh, Banks hasn't lost everything. Just the land. He owns the slaves. He owned them even before he married Miss Amalie. Folks say he won them in a card game, but I don't know if that's so. Anyway, he has more than a hundred slaves. Being from Connecticut, you may not know this, but the total cash value of a hundred slaves comes to considerably more than the value of the White Pines land."

Thorn stared at him, struck by the importance of this piece of information. "If that's the case, then Banks is nowhere near to being checked. Even without the land, he still has the wherewithal to fight his father-in-law, not to mention anyone else who crosses him." He put his hand on Andrew's shoulder. "Do you want to be that one?"

Andrew shook his head. ''Not me. There's nothing worth crossing Abner Banks over. Nothing.'' He shivered as though a cold wind had touched him. ''And God help the poor fool who thinks there is.''

Three

While Ocilla resumed her place at the window, still hoping for a glimpse of the cornsilk hair, Letty took the letter out of the silver jewelry casket and read it one more time. When she came to her grandfather's signature, she closed her eyes and pressed the letter to her heart. "Yes!" she murmured. "It will work. It must!"

After several moments she folded the double sheets of paper, returned them to their envelope, then went to the writing desk and pressed a spring that released a shallow drawer only she and Ocilla knew about. As she put the letter in the drawer, then closed it, she fancied she could hear her own heartbeat, and as her fingers caressed the smooth wood that guarded hers and Ocilla's future, her entire body tingled with anticipation.

After taking a deep, steadying breath, she turned toward the window and beckoned for the child to come to her. "My love, you and I have things to do. Important things."

As though Letty's excitement transmitted itself to the child, Ocilla came to her, her eyes alight with curiosity. "What things, Auntie?"

"First, I want you to go down to the wagon shed and

see if Caleb is ready to go to town. Tell him I need to add one more item to his list.''

''Is that all?'' she asked, disappointment in her tone.

Letty cupped her hand under the child's soft chin, wishing she could share her plan with the only person she loved, yet afraid to utter a word lest Abner should somehow find out before she had everything arranged. ''That is all for now, sweet thing, but perhaps by this evening I'll have something exciting to tell you. Until then,'' she added, pretending to turn a key to lock her lips, ''we'll both be as silent as a pair of bunny rabbits. Agreed?''

Ocilla turned her own pretend key. ''Agreed.''

As soon as the child went to find Caleb, Letty withdrew a marbleboard accounts ledger from one of the pigeonholes of the desk. It was the book in which she kept the slaves' personal accounts—their meager earnings and their debts—and she opened the ledger to the page bearing Verona's name. After double-checking the amount, she wrote PAID IN FULL below the cook's name. Next she took a cigar box from the drawer and rummaged through a mixture of shillings, tokens, pence, cents, and half cents until she found two Spanish dollars which she put in the deep, seamed pocket of her mauve merino dress.

With the money tucked securely in her pocket, she took the breakfast tray down the narrow back stairs and left it in the butler's pantry. Priam was nowhere in sight, but he must have been there only moments before because the linen press stood open, and the napkins that would be used for today's dinner lay on the corner of the small, hand-rubbed walnut table where Ocilla ate her evening meals.

The moment Letty stepped out onto the back porch, the aroma of fried chicken and cracklin' cornbread coming from the cookhouse informed her that it was almost noon. Verona had perfect timing, so at White Pines a person's nose was as reliable as a timepiece.

As usual, the top half of the cookhouse door stood open, and though Verona was not immediately visible, the table loaded with platters of crusty chicken, thick pones of corn-

bread, and four or five bowls of boiled vegetables testified
to her presence in the kitchen.

Letty leaned way over the door until she saw the cook
sitting on a short, plank stool in the far corner; on the floor
in front of her was a large cook pot containing water and
picked-over rice. Sweat glistened on Verona's round, black
face, and dirty water stained her apron and the front of her
dress as she leaned over the pot, washed the rice by rubbing
it between her hands, then set the clean rice in a second
pot filled with cold water.

Verona's attention was focused on the wash pot, so when
Letty spoke her name, she jumped, sloshing brown water
across her feet and the hard earthen floor. "Lordy sakes,
Miss Letty! You just took ten years off my life!"

"Sorry, Verona. I didn't mean to frighten you, but I
needed to ask you how many yards of that checked calico
you wanted. I have the money you earned, and I am on my
way down to the shed to give it to Caleb so he can make
the purchase today."

Verona had grabbed a cloth and begun drying her feet,
but she stopped her mopping-up and stared at Letty, her
interest caught. "How come Caleb got to get the calico so
early? Sudy's birthday ain't for weeks yet."

Letty looked at the spilled water rather than into the alert,
black eyes that never missed anything. She couldn't tell
anyone about her plan, especially not an inveterate gossip
like Verona. Not before she spoke to Mr. Thorn Bradley.

"Oh," she said, trying for a casual manner, "I just
thought I would order the material now while I was thinking of it. I know how long it took you to save enough
money for the dress, and I got to thinking how awful it
would be if I forget to order it for you."

"That 'ud be awful, sure enough," Verona murmured.

The old cook stared long and hard at the young woman
who had run the domestic business of the plantation for
more than six years and had never forgotten so much as a
spool of thread. When Letty said nothing, the question in
Verona's watchful eyes turned to speculation.

"Mayhap you right, Miss Letty. Best to do things before

they get forgot. Only thing is, Minna ain't told me yet how much yard goods it'll take for the dress. She wanting to figure it to the last jot and tittle, 'cause I promised her that howsomever much money Caleb bring back when he fetch the calico, that be hers for doing the sewing.''

"Then I'll go ask Minna."

Happy for an excuse to leave before Verona started asking questions, Letty left the cookhouse and hurried down the path that led to the stables. The crunch of the pine bark beneath her new kid boots disturbed a wood thrush who fled from his perch atop a spindly quince bush to settle on the ledge over the door of the smoke house. Once he felt safe, the bird filled the air with his flutelike notes, reprimanding Letty for provoking his flight.

"Heavenly Father," she whispered as the bird continued his reproach, "I ask only one thing. Please let Ocilla and me flee from White Pines as easily as that little bird deserted the quince bush."

Having learned from experience that spiritual help did not necessarily come when bidden, Letty hurried her steps so she could finish this business of the calico and seek some human help—human help in the form of Mr. Thorn Bradley and his boat.

If White Pines had been any other plantation, she wouldn't have given a thought to the purchase of the calico. On other plantations, slaves who kept laying hens or grew extra vegetables to sell in town got to keep the small sums of money they earned to spend as they chose. It didn't work that way on White Pines.

Abner Banks wouldn't let his slaves handle money; he said it made them envious of one another, that it caused fights. The only reason he permitted their simple enterprises at all was because Letty promised to record and keep all the earnings and arrange all the purchases. She had been happy to do it for them and had never minded the extra work, but now that would have to end.

If her plans went as she hoped, she would soon be hundreds of miles away from White Pines, and there would be no one here to do the bookkeeping and the ordering. For that reason, she wanted to make certain Verona got her calico today, for who could tell what Abner Banks might do after Letty was gone.

She didn't stop at the large, double doors of the white-washed stable but continued around to the side of the building where an outside flight of stairs offered access to the second story. The weaving room was located above the stable, and at this time of day Minna and her two helpers would be inside, working at their barn looms, busily shooting their shuttles to and fro to weave the coarse osnaburg they would later make into trousers and dresses for the field hands.

If she could avoid it, Letty didn't climb the stairs, for their steep grade and open steps were a waking nightmare for her. Even the thought of high places made her light-headed, so she stopped at the bottom of the stairs and called Minna's name. Her only answer was the muffled sound of the weaving harness moving up and down.

Cupping her hands on either side of her mouth, she called a second time. Still receiving no answer, she took a deep breath to still her fears, then lifted her skirts and climbed the first two steps.

"May I be of service, Miss Banks?"

At the sound of Thorn Bradley's voice, Letty jerked around, very nearly losing her balance in her haste.

"Whoa," he said, catching both her arms to steady her. "I didn't mean to startle you."

Letty felt the heat of Thorn's strong hands through the soft wool of her dress sleeves, and the warmth sent a surge of pleasure up her arms and straight through to her madly beating heart.

Because he stood on the ground and she on the step, she looked directly into his eyes. They were the most beautiful eyes she had ever seen—the clear blue-gray of the icehouse creek on a crisp December morning—yet there was sadness in their depths. Something inside Letty made her long to reach out and touch the thick, black brows that arched above the cool blue-gray, to let her fingertips smooth away the sadness. It would have been easy to touch him, for his face was so close to hers she could smell the clean, soapy scent of his skin.

His warm breath fanned a wisp of hair that had worked loose from her braid and fallen across her flushed cheek, and at the gentle movement, her own breath seemed to stop. She had never been this close to a man before. It was heady business.

Last night she had allowed herself only a few quick glances at his face, but now she studied him as though she had asked and been given permission to do so. His features were ill-assorted—his long nose too slender and his mouth too wide—they robbed him of any pretensions to classical male beauty. Yet she found the odd combination spellbinding.

Letty let her gaze rest on his lips. The slim upper lip was well defined, but the symmetry of the full lower lip was broken by a small scar at the left corner. She stared at the little scar, mesmerized. It did something strange to her senses, and for the first time in her life she wondered how it would feel to have a man's lips pressed against hers.

Almost as though he had read her thoughts, Thorn released her and stepped back. Immediately Letty felt the warmth of embarrassment creep up her neck to her cheeks, for Thorn Bradley's eyes had asked no question about lips pressing against lips.

"I apologize, ma'am, for frightening you. We were just turning the corner of the stable when we heard you yell, and we thought you might need some h—"

"The fellow walks on cat's feet!" Andrew interrupted accusingly, making Letty jump a second time. "You would expect a man of his size to make more noise. If you ask me, it's dashed impolite for a fellow to be so soft-footed. And he doesn't care pea turkey who he creeps up on, either. I tell you, Miss Loretta, I've lost count of the number of times he's snuck up on me."

Letty forced a smile to her lips.

"One night," Andrew continued, "he nearly made me jump off the boat." His tone invited her to share his incredulity. "And me in a spanking new pair of boots!"

Appreciating Andrew's attempt to smooth over an awkward moment, Letty followed his lead and made her tone as playful as his had been. "My boots are not *spanking* new, Mr. Holden, but I assure you I cherished my landing place no more than you did the water. And for my part, I will offer my thanks to your cat-footed friend for saving me from an unpleasant fall." She curtsied to Thorn. "I am in your debt, sir."

Although Thorn acknowledged her curtsy with a slight bow, he did not join in their teasing banter.

Remembering too late that she hoped to be even more in the man's debt, Letty cursed herself for having stared at him like some lovesick ninny. Now, with no option but to follow Andrew's lead and ignore the incident, she took a steadying breath and stepped down to the ground.

Letty wished she knew how to sweet-talk a man into doing what she wished, but she'd had little experience in such feminine arts. All she knew was the direct approach. Hoping that would do, she got right to the point. "You helped me a few moments ago, Mr. Bradley. Will you help me again?"

Something in her voice told Thorn that this was no idle request. "Again, ma'am?"

"Yes, sir. I . . . I realize the favor I am about to ask may seem somewhat forward, but I assure you I would not ask it if it weren't important."

In her rush to get it said, the words seemed to tumble from her lips. "When you leave White Pines tomorrow, sir, will you give me and another person passage to New Orleans aboard your boat?"

For an instant, Thorn wondered if he had heard her correctly. *Take a female downriver?* Never!

He hadn't supposed Loretta Banks to be a fool, yet how could she possibly think he would agree to such a request? Perhaps she thought *him* the fool. He would be if he agreed. He might as well propose marriage on the spot and be done with it, because once such a trip was completed, he would be forced to marry her.

"I'm sorry to disoblige you, Miss Banks, but I cannot do as you ask."

She seemed surprised at his refusal. "But, sir—"

"I am on a working trip," he interrupted, "not a pleasure cruise. Furthermore, the boat isn't mine. It belongs to the Revenue Marine Service. I am remapping areas along the intracoastal waterways that have changed due to erosion or meandering, and I have no way of judging ahead of time how involved the task might be. It could take as long as a month before I reach New Orleans. So you see, passengers are out of the question."

"Sir, I wouldn't care how long it took. Believe me, you would hear not one word of complaint from me."

"Miss Loretta," Andrew said, his voice kinder, more conciliating than Thorn's, "I'm afraid you don't understand the situation. The accommodations onboard the boat are not suitable for ladies. You and your chaperon would have no privacy. Furthermore, the man who doubles as crewman and cook is not fit company for decent females."

Something akin to panic seized Letty. She had been so concerned about her father's reaction that she hadn't prepared herself for the possibility of Thorn refusing her passage. She had pinned all her hopes of success on his taking her away from White Pines as soon as she made the deal with her father. Experience told her that she must act while the element of surprise was still in her favor. She knew better than to give Abner Banks time to devise a counterplan.

Perhaps she had been too quick with her request. Too abrupt. "Please, Mr. Bradley, don't refuse me out of hand. This is far too important. Possibly I failed to convey the urgency of the situation."

While she talked, Thorn Bradley stared at the hat he held in his hand, giving his full attention to the removal of a speck of lint from the brim. To keep from screaming at him for his seeming lack of interest in her plea, Letty balled her hands into fists and gouged her fingernails into the soft flesh of her palms.

Did he think it was easy begging favors of a stranger?

After a silence that lasted for interminable seconds, seconds in which Thorn continued the inspection of his hatband, Letty felt Andrew reach over and take one of her hands between his pudgy ones. She didn't resist, nor did she look at him as he touched the angry marks her fingernails had made in her palm.

"Please forgive my frankness, Miss Loretta," he said, "but all the proprieties would be offended if you traveled on a boat with two bachelors." Embarrassment made him mumble the last two words. "Perhaps I should mention a conversation I had with your grandfather just before I left Charleston. It might have some bearing on your wish to leave."

Letty continued to watch Thorn. "I am listening, Mr. Holden."

Andrew cleared his throat. "To put it in a nutshell, Miss Loretta, your grandfather suspects that you might not be free to come and go as you please." He cleared his throat again. "If this is the case, you have only to tell me, and I will inform him. He is prepared to send his traveling coach to White Pines—with armed escorts if necessary—to bring you to his home in Charleston."

Letty eased her hand from Andrew's. "I know you mean to be kind, Mr. Holden, but that plan will not serve. When I tell you that I must leave tomorrow, believe me I do not overstate the case. I cannot wait. And I cannot—will not—go to my grandfather."

"But I assure you, Miss Loretta, your grandfather will welcome you with open arms."

Letty shook her head. "My mother married to escape my grandfather's house, and I am not fool enough to reverse that action. Besides, he would never welcome my si . . . my niece. And I will not leave White Pines without her. Where I go, she goes."

Something in her voice made Thorn look up from the scrutiny of his hat. She was staring at him, her blue eyes wide with anxiety. *Niece?* He had heard nothing about a niece. And why on earth would her grandfather not welcome the child?

As he returned her stare, his attention was caught by the sound of childish laughter. The stable doors swung open, and a little girl stepped out, her small, tawny hand lost in the callused one of a tall, loose-limbed black man in his late thirties.

"Oh, Caleb," the little girl said between giggles, "you're such a jokester. Auntie told me to take everything you say with a grain of— Oh!"

Thorn watched the laughter that had bubbled so freely from the child die the instant she spied him and Andrew. Her soft brown eyes widened with surprise, then she gasped and jumped behind the man she called Caleb. Unfortunately the man provided little cover.

Skinny did not aptly describe the black man. He stood several inches past six feet, yet he probably weighed no more than one hundred and fifty pounds. Despite his lack of bulk, however, Thorn guessed he must be strong, for he wore the leather apron of a blacksmith.

Like the child, the black man stopped the moment he saw the two men. Eyes downcast in studied deference, he waited quietly for someone to acknowledge his presence.

"Ah, Caleb," Miss Banks said, "you've come at just the right time." Though her voice sounded normal, Thorn thought he detected a slight tremor in her strong chin.

The man called Caleb put his hand to his bare head as though tipping a hat. "Morning, Miss Letty. Gentlemen."

Though Andrew responded pleasantly to the greeting, Thorn merely nodded his head; he couldn't take his eyes off the child. He watched her peep around the black man's legs, almost as if stealing a look at Andrew's hair. When she caught Thorn watching her, however, she hid her head again.

"I've got Verona's money here, Caleb," Miss Banks said, reaching inside the deep pocket of her dress and pulling out two Spanish dollars. "She has decided to get the blue-and-red-checked calico, but you'll have to go up and ask Minna about the yardage."

She handed him the money. "And for goodness' sake," she warned, putting her finger across her lips, "don't forget it's a surprise. Sudy isn't supposed to know."

"I'll remember to forget, Miss Letty."

The black man smiled, and it occurred to Thorn, looking from the blacksmith to Miss Banks, that there was a respect between the two.

While he spoke, Caleb reached behind him where the little girl remained hidden and took her by the shoulder. "Come on out now, sugar," he coaxed. "I'm fixing to go to town, and I can't climb aboard the wagon with a little girl hanging on my shirttail."

When the child did not come out as he bid her but buried her face in his bony back, Miss Banks held her hand out to her. Thorn noticed that the hand shook slightly.

"Come to Auntie, my love. You've no need to be frightened of Mr. Holden and Mr. Bradley. They won't eat you. Though I imagine that after their long walk they are ready for some of Verona's fried chicken."

Andrew laughed nervously. "Word of a gentleman, I never eat pretty little girls when there is fried chicken waiting for me."

Thorn watched the child exchange the security of the blacksmith's back for the fullness of Miss Banks's skirt, wrapping the folds of the mauve merino around her so she was hidden once again. He exchanged looks with Andrew.

From the color that suffused Andrew's face, the two men were of the same opinion: Miss Banks's slender nose and square jaw were obviously the originals for this mixed-blood child's small copies. No wonder the lady had been so certain that her grandfather would not welcome this "niece."

Remembering also that she had vowed she would not leave White Pines without the child, Thorn's expression softened. He understood a mother's love for her child; his own mother had been that way.

Almost reverently he slipped his hand inside his pocket and touched the small, lavender savory blossom he had taken from the herb garden. Yes, he knew about a mother's love. Though he had known it for only a few short years, he had never forgotten.

And he also knew about snakes!

Thorn could only imagine how that delicate little girl fared under the same roof with a man like Abner Banks. After crushing the savory blossom so that the fragrance filled his nostrils, he came to a decision.

Brushing past Andrew, he took Miss Banks by the elbow, surprising both her and the little girl, and began leading her up the pine bark path toward the house.

"Sir! What do you think you're doing?"

At first she tried to pull her elbow free of his strong grip, but she stopped her struggle when he leaned down and spoke very softly in her ear.

"Space aboard the boat is limited to the barest necessities," he said. "You and the little girl will have to make do with one small valise each."

Four

Letty couldn't remember ever having enjoyed a meal as much as she enjoyed the one they all shared that bright fall afternoon. Perhaps it was because she was excited about leaving the next day, or maybe she enjoyed it simply because Thorn and Andrew were there and her father was not.

"Marse Abner say he don't want no dinner, Miss Letty," Priam informed her when she came down for the afternoon meal. The old servant's voice was hushed, and he looked behind him before he spoke again. "He gone to town. Rode off while them gentlemen was in the parlor sipping sherry and waiting for you to come down."

His rheumy old eyes clouded. "I ain't seen Marse Abner that mad in a long time, Miss Letty. Cold-as-ice mad he was. Something bad sure to happen when Marse Abner get that way. He make somebody pay."

Letty's mouth went cotton dry for a moment before she reminded herself that Abner Banks could never hurt her again. In a matter of hours, she would be free. Her grandfather had given her a powerful bargaining tool, and Thorn Bradley had promised her passage to New Orleans on his boat. Tomorrow she and Ocilla were leaving White Pines for good.

Her confidence restored, she patted the old man's stooped shoulder. "Don't worry, Priam. Papa is mad at my grandfather, and my grandfather knows how to take care of himself. Besides," she added, the knowledge that all her dreams would soon come true making her lighthearted, "he would have to ride all the way to Charleston to get even with my grandfather, and you said he'd only ridden into town."

When Priam did not smile at her little joke, she patted his shoulder once again and opened the doors to the parlor.

"Ah, Miss Loretta," Andrew greeted, rising from the cream upholstered slipper chair and making her a bow. "Thorn was just telling me about a balloon ascension exhibition in New York City. Can you believe it, ma'am? He actually went up in the thing. Just him and the engineer. And when the wind picked up and blew them past the outskirts of the city, they had to set down in a farmer's potato patch."

Thorn leaned against the mantel, the polished brass of the mantel clock reproducing his chiseled profile. "It wasn't as slapdash as Andrew makes it sound, ma'am. The engineer was in control the entire trip."

Letty felt her stomach contract at the mere thought of drifting willy-nilly through the sky. "You sound as though you enjoyed it, sir."

"I did. And I hope to go up again. Balloons are the travel of the future."

"Well, they're not in my future," Andrew said. He set his wineglass on the mahogany piecrust table beside his chair and offered Letty his arm. Priam had just opened the mahogany pocket doors that connected the parlor and the dining room and indicated that the meal was served.

"For my part," Andrew added, once they were seated at the table, "nothing could induce me to float around in the sky in a basket. Why, I'd as soon subject myself to another confrontation with that crazed goose we met this morning."

"Oh, no!" Suppressing a giggle, Letty said, "Don't tell me you ran into Minna's goose."

"I assure you, ma'am," Thorn answered, a smile lighting his eyes in a way that made Letty's breath catch in her throat, "we did not run *into* the goose. We ran *away* from it."

"As any sane person would," Andrew added. "The most vicious bird I've ever encountered."

When Letty and Thorn both laughed, Andrew launched into an exaggerated version of his encounter with the goose, an account so outrageous that Letty soon had to wipe tears of laughter from the corners of her eyes.

"Word of a gentleman, ma'am," he declared, "I feared for my life."

The meal continued in this light vein, progressing through the fried chicken and vegetables to the molasses-covered rice pudding, and while they finished their dessert, Andrew asked if Letty would favor them with a selection on the clavichord.

She hadn't played for anyone for years, but she agreed to his request. This had been the most wonderful day of her life, and if Andrew and Thorn wanted to hear a few songs, then she was glad to oblige. It was the least she could do.

Their meal completed, they returned to the parlor, and while the gentlemen made themselves comfortable in the upholstered chairs that flanked the front window, Letty ran through a trio of Scottish aires. Within a few minutes she overcame her initial shyness at performing and gave herself up to the joy of the music.

"You play well," Thorn commented when she finished the aires.

"Damned with faint praise!" Andrew insisted. "Miss Loretta, you are an accomplished musician."

Letty flushed with pleasure, unaccustomed to compliments. "It is the instrument, sir, it will not make a false note." She ran her hand across the polished wood with its small, inlaid squares. "My mother received it as a wedding present. It is reputed to have been played upon by Mr.

Mozart, and Mama maintained that Mozart's touch rendered it forever incapable of a bad performance.''

Andrew's pale brows lifted skeptically. ''Forgive me for disputing a lady,'' he said, getting up and going to stand beside her where he could watch her fingers, ''but I insist it is the musician.''

Inclining her head in a half bow, she said, ''Thank you, Mr. Holden.''

''Please, Miss Loretta, it's Drew. My friends call me Drew.''

''Thank you, Drew.''

He smiled and leaned against the clavichord. ''Do you know any of the new songs?''

For just a moment Letty mentally ran through her repertoire, then she burst into a spirited rendition of ''Buffalo Girls.'' Though hardly a new song by Charleston standards, Andrew did not correct her but began clapping his hands and tapping his foot to the music. His unself-conscious enthusiasm made Letty laugh, and when she glanced across the room at Thorn, he, too, was smiling at his friend's antics.

''I need a partner,'' Andrew said, looking around him as though expecting a young lady to materialize out of thin air. ''This music makes me want to dance.''

He held his arms out as though they encircled a young lady's waist, then he twirled around the room.

''A partner! A partner! My kingdom for a partner!''

Though Thorn laughed, he bid the fellow behave himself and quit wearing out the carpet. ''Miss Banks can't play and dance at the same time, and the only other female in the house is the little girl who's going with us tomorrow. You saw for yourself what a shy child she is.''

Drew merely twirled faster. ''Bring her out,'' he said. ''Once she sees what a fine dancer I am, she'll forget about being shy. Where is the little lady?''

Letty's fingers slowed on the keys, her smile gone. ''Ocilla is in the butler's pantry, Drew. My father will not allow her in the front of the house.''

Embarrassment heightening his color, Andrew stopped

his foolery. "Beg pardon, Miss Loretta. My mouth some-times runs away with me."

Thorn's face was unreadable. "Do you mean the child isn't even allowed to come hear you play?"

Unwilling to let him see the bitterness she was sure must show in her eyes, Letty studied the yellowed ivory keys beneath her fingers while she modulated into "Jeanie with the Light Brown Hair." "I usually leave the doors open so she can hear."

While the red-faced Andrew resumed his place at the clavichord, his attention once again on Letty's fingers, Thorn walked over and slid open the heavy pocket doors. No one said anything when he didn't return to his chair but disappeared into the dining room.

Much later, after Letty had exhausted her repertoire and closed the front of the clavichord, she and Andrew went looking for Thorn. They found him in the butler's pantry.

He sat in one of the two stiff, ladder-back chairs the room boasted, with his booted feet crossed at the ankles and propped in the woven cane seat of the other chair. Muffled snores escaped his parted lips, stirring the soft curls of the little girl who sat in his lap, her sleeping head resting against his chest.

Abner Banks returned while his daughter was upstairs put-ting Ocilla down to finish her nap. Unobserved, he walked to the door of the parlor where Thorn and Andrew were discussing their departure the following day. Choosing not to make his presence known, he stood in the doorway, a sneer of contempt curling his lips.

Since Andrew's back was to the door, Thorn was first to realize that Banks watched them. He didn't like the bright look in the man's eyes; it put him in mind of a feral cat who had spotted prey.

To let Andrew know they were being watched, Thorn stood and bowed to their host. "Good afternoon, sir."

"Possibly," Abner Banks replied coldly.

Andrew jumped as though he had been caught in an in-discretion. "Mr. Banks! You missed the music," he added nervously. "You are to be congratulated, sir, for your daughter is an accomplished young woman."

Without even looking in Andrew's direction, Abner spoke to Thorn. "It is a universally accepted fact, I believe, that all heiresses are accomplished."

Before anyone could reply to this derisive remark, Thorn heard the swish of Miss Banks's skirts as she came down the stairs. Her father must have heard it, too.

"Loretta," he said without even turning around, "I wish to speak with you. In the library." He gave Thorn one last sneering look. "But only if our guests can spare you, of course."

Not waiting for her answer, Abner brushed past her and strolled across the carpeted foyer. The library door closed softly behind him.

Letty hesitated only long enough to smile an apology to the visitors, then she crossed the foyer and knocked at the door her father had just shut.

"Come in," he answered.

She had thought she was prepared for this moment. Several hours ago she had even wished for time to pass quickly so she could have the encounter with her father and be done with it. But now she noticed that the hand she rested on the doorknob shook ever so slightly, and the tongue that should have moistened her lips was so dry it threatened to stick to them instead.

Not wanting to give her father the upper hand by acting cowed, she took a deep breath, pushed the door open and entered the book-lined library, closing the door softly behind her.

Her father sat in a red leather-covered wing chair, his booted feet stretched toward the fieldstone hearth. Priam had lit a fire to ward off the chill of the late afternoon, and Abner Banks stared into the flames that licked at the stacked pine logs.

When the silence that stretched between father and daughter was broken by the pop of bursting resin, Letty abandoned her stance by the doorway and walked over to the fireplace. "You wanted to see me, Papa?"

"Sit down," he ordered, hooking his foot around the leg of a small stool and shoving it toward her. "I don't plan to strain my neck by looking up at you."

She would have preferred some place other than the footstool, but not wanting to alienate him over trivialities when the realization of her dream was so close, she did as he bid her and sat down. Her full skirt billowed around her like a mushroom, making her feel gauche and clumsy, but since that was probably why he had chosen the stool for her, she ignored it.

"So, Loretta, you are to be married at last. I always pictured you withering into old maidhood, but I guess the deed did the deed, so to speak. Anything can be purchased if the price is right. Even a husband."

Clenching her teeth, she resolved to crack every last molar rather than give her father the satisfaction of knowing his insults had hit a nerve. She knew better than to hand him a weapon to use against her.

"I can't say I think much of your choices," he continued, "but if you can stomach either of those fortune hunters your grandfather sent down here, it's no skin off my nose which one of them you take." He studied a minute scratch on the toe of his left boot, as though that small blemish were of more interest than their discussion.

"Since the matter of your dowry was settled years ago by your mother's portion, that leaves only one piece of business we need to resolve: your occupancy of White Pines. If you will furnish me with the approximate date you and your new husband expect to conclude your wedding trip, I will make certain that I and my slaves are off your property before you return."

With what she hoped was an air of assurance, Letty folded her hands in her lap and squared her shoulders. "You misunderstand the situation, Papa. No matter what my grandfather's motives for giving me White Pines, I have no wish to use it to purchase a husband. I do, however, have plans for the deed."

Abner scrutinized her with eyes as cold and watchful as those of a serpent watching a mouse he means to have for dinner. "What plans are those, if I may ask?"

"I propose to swap you the deed for Ocilla."

After only a moment's hesitation, her father threw back his head and roared with laughter. "Damnation!" he said finally, still smiling. "It would be worth a trip to Charleston just to wave the deed in Llewellen's face. The old buzzard would probably have a stroke!"

Letty could barely swallow. "Then you'll do it, Papa?"

"Do what?"

"Give me Ocilla for the deed."

"Why would I want to do that?" The smile vanished from Abner's face, as though it had never been. "It is immaterial to me which one of us holds the deed."

"But—"

"You are a fool, Loretta, and you haven't the least idea how to play the game."

To control the sudden trembling of her fingers, she laced them together. Something had gone awry here, only she didn't know what. "I don't want to play games, Papa. All I want, all I've ever wanted, is to take Ocilla and leave this place."

"Remaining here was your choice," he said lazily. "You are free to leave White Pines at any time. You always have been."

"But what about Ocilla?"

"Ocilla?" Her father moved his feet away from the hearth, then he stood and walked over to the French windows that opened onto the veranda. "Ocilla's fate was sealed years ago. You sealed it yourself."

He opened the windows and stepped outside. "Perhaps you would like to see how I entertained myself while you entertained our guests with your Scottish aires and minstrel tunes."

All Letty's instincts told her to run from the room. But like a child who can't keep his tongue from probing a sore tooth, she followed her father to the veranda, clutching the silver handle of the French window for support. Her hand felt like ice. She didn't need Abner's pointing finger to know where to look.

Her gaze swept to the left, across the breadth of the side lawn and down the pine bark path to the stables, then it finally stopped at the large oak tree beside the stable. From one of the tree's thick branches hung a brand-new rope, its end looped into a noose. It swayed in the November breeze as though beckoning someone to come try it on for size.

To halt the scream that threatened to erupt from her throat, Letty bit her lips until she tasted blood. As she turned to run back into the house, Abner caught her wrist and twisted it behind her, pulling it up between her shoulder blades. Ignoring her cry of pain, he pushed her to her knees, then grabbed her braid and forced her head back, compelling her to look once again at the swinging noose.

"That," he said, "is the way the game is played."

When he let go of her arm and her hair, Letty slumped to the veranda floor like a rag doll.

Abner smiled. "One last thing, Loretta. As the new owner of White Pines, you'll soon be getting this year's tax bill. Since you don't have that kind of money, you'll need to write to your grandfather to ask him for a loan. I advise you to pay the taxes promptly, for it would be a shame if either you or I were forced off the property. Either way, the outcome for Ocilla would be the same."

Without waiting for her reply, he walked back inside the library and shut the French windows.

Unwilling to give Abner the victory of her tears, Letty cradled her injured right arm with her left and struggled to her feet. Once down the veranda steps she sped across the front lawn and down the carriageway. She didn't stop running until several minutes later when she reached the solitude of her herb garden.

Alone and sheltered from prying eyes, Letty fell face-down across the delicate plants, crushing their intricate patchwork design beneath her trembling body. Helpless, hopeless tears mingled with the rich, black soil; Old Canebrake had inflicted the last bite once again.

Letty had no idea how long she lingered in the stupor that followed her bout of tears. She hadn't even noticed Thorn's arrival, nor the fact that he had laid down beside her on the damp ground and wrapped his arms around her. Insensible to his offered comfort, all she felt was stiff and cold and empty, and nearly nauseous from the pungent smells of the crushed herbs. She wondered why she had ever thought their aromas pleasant; they smelled like death. If she didn't move away from them soon, she felt certain she would vomit.

Pushing away from Thorn, she rolled onto her side and sat up. Her hands and sleeves were wet, and when she reached up to brush a strand of hair from her eyes, she discovered that her face was streaked with mud.

"Take this," he said, offering her his linen handkerchief.

Letty ignored his offer, choosing instead to lift her skirt and wipe her face and hands on the hem of her bleached flannel petticoat.

"You must be freezing, Miss Banks. Let me give you my coat."

Having slipped his arms out of his jacket, Thorn was about to drape it across her shoulders when she stopped him. "No," she said. "I am so cold it wouldn't help. I need more than a coat."

He didn't ask her to explain. Instead, he said, "When you didn't come back after your talk with your father, I became worried. Is there anything I can do?"

"Help me up," she said. "I don't think I can get up unaided."

Once he had helped her to her feet, she took a step back, putting some distance between them. "My offer was for more than a hand up, ma'am. If it will help, I can take you to my boat right away. You needn't even return to the house if you don't want to. I'll go find the little girl and—"

"No!" The panic in her voice made her sound like a lunatic even to her own ears. She grabbed his sleeve. "You mustn't."

Realizing that he hadn't moved an inch, she let her arm fall to her side and made herself speak more calmly. "He won't let Ocilla go. New Orleans was just a foolish dream. A dream that can never come true."

"Is there no way I can help you, then?"

She shook her head. "No one can help me. Not now. Not ever."

A delayed shudder surged through her body, and a hiccough crept up the back of her throat. When she was in control again, she told him he could help her most by leaving White Pines. "Today. Right now, while there's still enough light for you to make it to your boat."

He didn't argue. "You're sure that is what you really want?"

When she nodded, he reached out and took her hand and lifted it to his lips. Ignoring the mud stains, he kissed her fingers. Then he turned her hand over and pressed his lips against her palm.

"God keep you, ma'am. You and the little girl."

Letty turned her back until he was out of sight, then she waited in the pine grove just beyond the herb garden until she heard their horses on the carriageway. She gave them time to pass through the entrance gate before she marched to the stable.

While she walked, the westering sun slashed the sky with awe-inspiring reds and violets. She neither saw nor cared. She had a job to do, and her mission blinded her to everything else.

She passed by dozens of cabins on her way to the stable—cabins that at this time of day were usually filled with the sounds of tired field hands and the smell of cook fires. All was dark and ominously still. With the exception of a few unfed chickens who scratched the dirt for bugs, the yards were deserted. No people. No dogs. Not even Minna's goose.

When Letty finally reached the stable, that too seemed uninhabited. Nothing moved. Nothing except that obscenity that hung from the oak tree. Against the breathtaking backdrop of the red and violet sky, the noose swayed slowly back and forth.

Letty went directly to the base of the tree. She wouldn't look up, she decided. It would be easier that way. If she concentrated on where she put her hands, maybe she wouldn't feel the height.

Her skirt! How was she to control her skirt? If it got in the way, she would surely fall.

At the thought of falling, her stomach threatened to disgorge her dinner, but she refused to let her fear deter her. Resolutely she swallowed and made herself relax. If she panicked now she might as well get a gun and blow her brains out; her father would make her life a nightmare from here on out.

"You don't have the least idea how to play the game," he had said. Well, she was learning fast. And this next move was hers.

She pictured Ocilla's precious face, concentrating on it as though it were a talisman, and in a few moments the impossible seemed possible again.

First she tackled the problem of her skirt. After stepping out of her petticoats, she reached between her ankles and caught the back of the skirt, then pulled it between her legs and up to her waist. When she pushed the hem securely through the big silver buckle of her belt, then looped it over and tucked it inside the belt, the skirt resembled a pair of balloon-legged britches.

The obstacle of the skirt out of the way, Letty turned back to the tree. She was searching for a foothold when she heard someone hiss at her from behind the stable.

"Hsst! Miss Letty!"

She stood very still. "Caleb?"

"Yes'm, it's me." He moved closer but remained in the shadow of the stable where he couldn't be seen from the main house. "What you fixing to do, child?"

"I'm taking down that noose."

She heard his quick intake of breath. "You sure you want to do that? Marse Abner hung that rope up himself. Reckon he'll be powerful mad at anybody takes it down without his say so."

"I'm taking it down," she said.

Without another word, she wedged the toe of her slipper into a fissure in the bark and hoisted herself up a few inches. She was searching for a second toehold when Caleb grabbed her arm and pulled her away.

"Come away from there, child. You'll fall and kill yourself. You know you ain't got a head for high places. Never did have, even when you was just a little girl."

When she turned and put her hands on the tree once again, Caleb drew in a deep, ragged breath. "If you plumb set on having that rope, best let me climb up and get it for you."

Letty shook her head. "No. Papa would make you pay, and pay hard."

Caleb's face was grim. "Most likely it's for me anyhow. Everybody on the place in hiding, scared it's for them, but I'm the one made Marse Abner mad last."

"The noose is for Ocilla," Letty said quietly.

Caleb stared at her as though unable to credit his own ears. "What you say?"

"It's for Ocilla."

"No. That can't be right. That little angel baby ain't never done nothing but bring joy to—"

"The noose is meant for Ocilla," Letty repeated.

Where Caleb's eyes had been dulled with fear, now they blazed with anger. Mumbling something beneath his breath, he moved Letty aside as though she were still the little girl he had put on her first horse. "I'll have that noose down in two shakes."

It took him considerably longer than two shakes, but finally the rope fell to the ground. For such a lethal weapon, it made little noise.

"Silent as a snake," she muttered.

Letty picked the would-be weapon up and carried it to the blacksmith shed just behind the stable. Caleb had banked the fire in the forge so that it burned low, but Letty took the bellows and puffed it back to life. Once it burned to her satisfaction, she held the end of the rope to the blaze until the hemp caught fire. While she watched the orange and yellow flame eat its way up the rope to the noose, fury hotter than the consuming fire ignited inside her, burning away her earlier feelings of despair and searing her heart forever.

When the noose began to burn, she tossed it onto the forge. She watched until there was nothing left of the hemp but ashes, then she turned and walked away.

For several minutes Letty stood in the shed doorway and stared into the gathering dusk, trying to conquer the rage that still gnawed at her insides. She needed to be calm before she returned to the child she had failed once again. When she saw a light appear in the window of her father's bedroom, her body stiffened, and her hands clenched into fists.

"Be warned, Old Canebrake," she whispered into the quiet twilight, "this game isn't over yet. And snakes don't live forever. One day someone's going to put their heel on your head, and that someone just might be me."

Five

Letty eased the warped door of Verona's cabin open and stepped out onto the porch. It had been a long night, and the closeness of the dim cabin had been oppressive. With a sigh, she stretched her muscle-weary arms above her head, twisting her body to the left and then the right until her bones cracked, then she filled her lungs with sweet, dew-freshened air.

Though the morning sky still clung to the last vestiges of darkness, Verona's rooster, Chanty, upon detecting the first gray shadings of dawn, loudly announced the beginning of a new day. Inside the cabin all was still. Sudy was finally asleep after an all-night ordeal of on-again-off-again labor.

"Morning, Miss Letty."

Her nerves already strained, Letty jumped.

One of Minna's young helpers stepped out of the dimness beyond the cabin. "'Scuse me, Miss Letty, if'n I frighted you. I come the back way so's I didn't have to pass by Minna's cabin. That new goose of hers be even meaner'n her last one. Yesterday, for no good reason, he up and took a plug right out the back of my leg.''

Letty put her finger across her lips. ''Shhh, Theda. I gave Sudy something to help her sleep, but I had to cut the dose so it wouldn't hurt the baby. She'll wake up real easy, and she needs all the rest she can get.''

The young girl tiptoed around to the front of the porch and whispered her message. ''Minna say for me to come sit with Sudy a while so's you can go up to the house and rest.''

Letty nodded, then reached inside the cabin for the mahogany herb box she'd set by the door.

''Sudy'll sleep for a while, Theda, unless the contractions start again. If they do, send someone up to the house for me.''

''Must be a man child, Miss Letty. My mama say as how a girl child, she slip out nice and quiet like, but a man child, he always put up a fuss.''

Too tired to dispute the pros and cons of old wives' tales, or explain about thirty-five-year-old women who were delivering for the first time, Letty propped the herb box on her hip and adjusted the leather strap across her shoulder.

''Just send for me if Sudy needs me.''

''Yes'm, I'll sure do that.''

Chanty crowed again, reminding Letty how much she wanted a bath and a few hours of sleep. She had been up all night mopping Sudy's brow and trying to calm both Sudy's and Verona's fears. Now her clothes were plastered to her body, and her eyelids ached as though there truly was a man who threw sand in people's eyes. Happy at the prospect of even a short nap, she slipped the leather strap up a little higher on her shoulder and stepped off the porch into the well-swept yard.

As she passed the blacksmith shed, Caleb hurried out, almost as if he had been watching for her.

''Morning, Miss Letty.''

He fell into step beside her. ''I'd be happy to tote that old herb box for you. I reckon you must be tired.''

''Thank you, Caleb, but I think it has become part of my shoulder. With so many of the people coming down with dysentery this summer, I seem to be carrying it around all the time."

"I know that's right."

He trailed one bony finger across the top of the box. "That wood is mighty scruffy after all the use it's been put to lately. It needs a good sanding, and that's a fact." He held his hands out. "Won't take me no time to do it. I can take care of it while you up at the house. I'll bring it along later all nice and shined up."

It finally penetrated Letty's fatigue-dulled brain that Caleb, the most straightforward person she had ever known, was trying to be wily. "What are you up to, Caleb?"

Ignoring her question, he put one hand under the box and would have lifted the strap off her shoulder with his other hand if she hadn't stepped back.

"Why were you laying in wait for me, Caleb?" She smiled to take the sting out of her words. "And why do you want my herb box?"

He looked over his shoulder as though checking to see if anyone might overhear him. "It ain't my secret to tell. All I can say is Ocilla got something planned for your birthday, and I got to have that herb box before it happens."

"I'm thirty years old today, Caleb. What do I need with any more birthday surprises?"

"You may be thirty, child, but Ocilla only fourteen, and to her a birthday's a mighty fine thing to have. And so is a birthday surprise."

The truth of his words was unarguable, so with a sigh of resignation, Letty let the strap slip from her shoulder and offered the scuffed container to the conspirator.

Caleb took the herb box with great care. Since he had nothing more to add to the conversation, he returned to the blacksmith shed to complete his secret task, while Letty trudged up the path to the back of the house.

As she drew close to the back porch, she saw Priam waiting for her. The old man sat in a rocking chair, his head slumped forward revealing a balding spot amid the cotton-white hair, and all the while loud, irregular snores spilled over his drooping lower lip. It wasn't difficult to guess why he was there. He must have a message to relay. Letty hadn't spoken directly to Abner Banks since she'd burned the noose six years ago, and the unenviable job of go-between had fallen to poor Priam.

Though she tried to sneak past the old man's chair without waking him, a floorboard squeaked beneath her foot, betraying her. Priam jerked his head up and almost choked on a half-swallowed snore.

"Miss Letty!"

For a moment, age and sleep befuddled his brain, then he yawned and rubbed his knuckles back and forth across his eyelids. "I been waiting for you."

Putting her hand under his elbow, she helped him stand. "You shouldn't be out here in the morning damp. You know what it does to your rheumatism."

"I know, Miss Letty, but Marse Abner give me a message for you last night."

"Didn't you tell him Sudy was having trouble?"

"Yes'm, I told him you with Sudy. He say give you the message soon as you come in."

Quelling her anger at her father's cavalier disregard for the aches and pains of such an old man, she said, "Well, I've finally come in. What does he want this time, Priam?"

The old man pulled a blue calico handkerchief from inside his coat and wiped his damp chin. "Marse Abner say tell you it's your birthday today, and he want you to eat supper with him in the dining room tonight."

Letty bit back the sharp retort that sprang to her mind; there was no point in flailing the hapless go-between. "You tell my father my answer is the same as always, Priam."

An unhappy messenger, the old man twisted the calico handkerchief between his gnarled fingers. "Marse Abner say tell you, case you say the same thing as always, that he got you a mighty fine present for your birthday. Had it sent all the way from Savannah."

Too tired for all this now, she merely shook her head. "I'm sorry, Priam, but you will have to tell him I said no. My father knows exactly what present I want—the only present I will ever accept from him. You tell him if he is ready to give me that present, he can let me know. Then I'll come down to supper. If not, I'll have my meal in the pantry with Ocilla as I always do."

Having said all there was to say, Letty turned and went inside the house.

The late-morning sun woke her. It streamed through the bedroom window, landing on the mosquito-netted four-poster and making it uncomfortably warm, too warm for sleeping. Still tired from the long night with Sudy, Letty didn't sit up immediately but lay quietly, watching Ocilla, who sat at the writing desk, her small, slippered feet hooked around the legs of the chair. Ocilla might be fourteen, Letty thought, but her delicate arms and legs and her still undeveloped figure made her look like a child several years younger.

The young girl's back was to the bed, so she didn't look up from her task. The only sound was that of the scratchy pen as she entered figures in the servants' ledger.

Letty couldn't see Ocilla's face, only the long, thick curls that hung down her back—curls tied with a blue grosgrain ribbon to keep them in order. She could imagine, however, the serious brown eyes and the pink tongue that peeped out the corner of the small mouth as the young girl concentrated on her task.

First she counted out Confederate graybacks and merchant's tokens, then she entered the money total in the ledger. After writing the final entry, Ocilla rolled a wooden-handled blotter over the page, then blew for good measure. She closed the inkpot carefully, then slid the inkstand back into its cubbyhole and closed the little door. While she wiped her quill clean on one of the pen wipers she had embroidered for Christmas gifts last year, she looked up and caught Letty watching her.

"You're awake at last! Happy birthday, Auntie!"

Letty yawned and turned her face to the wall. "I am not awake," she muttered. "It was a figment of your imagination. I am still asleep, and I plan to stay asleep for hours yet."

Ocilla giggled. "If it was *my* birthday and Caleb had just brought *me* a letter from town, I would want to be awake."

Her interest piqued, Letty pushed the mosquito netting aside and sat up. "A letter from whom?"

Ocilla aimed her gaze at the ceiling, as though considering a weighty question, then she tapped her chin with the end of the freshly wiped quill. "I wonder, are figments of the imagination the same as haints? Verona says one must never speak to haints, so if I speak to a figment, do I risk being whisked away to some horrid, frightening place, where—"

The pillow hit the young girl on the shoulder, then fell to the ground.

"Save me! Save me!" Ocilla yelled between giggles. "I'm being attacked by a figment of my imagination."

Quickly retrieving the pillow, she threw it back with greater accuracy, hitting Letty on the side of her head. "Take that, you figment."

Letty raised her hands in surrender. "I give up!"

"Then you'll stay awake? You won't go back to sleep?"

"No, my love, I won't go back to sleep. I am awake for the day."

"And ready for a birthday surprise?"

"I suppose so," she said, yawning again, then stretching her arms over her head. "As ready as I will ever be."

"Good."

Ocilla stood, set the chair she had been using against the wall beside the desk, then flew to the bed to throw her arms around Letty's neck and rain kisses down upon her cheeks. The exuberance of her display forced the birthday girl to fall back among the pillows. "Happy birthday again, Auntie."

"Thank you," Letty replied, extricating herself from the thin arms. "But if you cut off my breathing, I may not live to another birthday."

Her captor giggled but released her, allowing her to sit up once again.

"As a reward for your being so cooperative," she said, reaching inside the pocket of the apron that covered her pale yellow dress, "here is your letter. The envelope says it is from Mr. Holden, but it does not bear his Charleston address. It has an army return."

Curious, Letty took the letter and slipped her finger beneath the flap to break the seal.

"While you read, Auntie, I'll go down and get you something to eat. You are such a sleepyhead that it is almost time for our tea, so I'll just bring you a cup of buttermilk and cornpone so you won't starve."

Letty looked up from the letter she had just removed from its thin envelope. "I am already starved, young lady, and I need something more substantial than cornpone and buttermilk. And what is this about a tea?"

Ocilla closed her lips tightly and pretended to turn a key. "I'll never tell," she mumbled, trying to keep her lips closed. "Never. Not even if you tickled me with a dozen feathers. Not if you tortured me with—"

The *clopity, clop* of hoofbeats interrupted her foolishness and sent her scurrying to the bedroom window to investigate. "Auntie, two men are coming up the carriageway. One of them is a soldier."

Letty joined Ocilla at the window, but because she wore only her chemise and drawers, she was careful to keep behind the lace curtains. The two riders galloped up the dusty carriageway, dismounted, then waited for someone to come take their horses.

"Who are they?" Ocilla whispered.

"I've never seen either of them before."

The horses were beautiful purebreds—the kind one seldom saw anymore, since the army had requisitioned most of the animals—and judging from the sweat that glistened on their hides, they had obviously been ridden out from town. The riders were less distinguished.

Both men were in their early thirties, and both sported full mustaches and thick side whiskers. While they waited, the taller man busied himself with straightening the sleeves of his well-tailored Confederate gray uniform; while his companion, a stockily built civilian, concentrated on adjusting the gathered bunting secession rosette he wore like a boutonniere in the buttonhole of his gaudy checked frock coat.

For some reason, Letty shuddered just looking at the man with the rosette.

"What's the matter, Auntie?"

"That man makes me feel as though someone just walked over my grave." She stepped back and tugged Ocilla along with her. "Come away from the window, my love. Don't let them see you. You don't want strange men gawking at you."

Ocilla came away, though she obviously hadn't satisfied her curiosity. "I wonder what they want."

"Since one of them is in uniform, my guess is they have ridden out to see about purchasing provisions and livestock for the army. But no matter what they want, you and I will do well to keep out of their way. You never know about men like that; they could be trash."

Still very shy, Ocilla promised to stay out of the men's way. "But only if you will promise to hurry up and get dressed."

Letty sighed dramatically. "I promise, I promise."

While Ocilla went down to get the milk and bread, Letty retrieved Andrew's letter. Over the years she and the lawyer had carried on a correspondence of sorts, and she was interested to know what had happened to him since last he wrote. As well, there was always the hope that he might mention something about Thorn Bradley. Settling herself on the edge of the unmade bed, she smoothed the pages out on her lap.

Dear Miss Loretta,

I am in receipt of yours of the 12th June and am happy to hear that you and the little girl are both well. These are trying times. As you will see by the envelope, I have joined my brother's newly formed regiment. By the time you receive this letter, I will be gone from Charleston. For that reason, I have taken the liberty of assigning the handling of your dowry to Mr. Daniel Thompson, Esq., of our office. I hope this meets with your approval.

On a personal note, I am pleased to inform you that I am recently betrothed to a young lady whose family has long been acquainted with my own. Our nuptials must, of course, bow to the necessity of the *Cause*.

As my friend, I know you will share my concern when I tell you the young lady lives in Savannah. I am sure you have heard of the infamous attack by Yankee troops on Fort Pulaski. Their occupancy menaces that lovely city, as well as the home of my betrothed.

And speaking of Yankees, I wonder if you recall my brother's friend, Mr. Thornton Bradley, the gentleman who accompanied me to White Pines six years ago. When last William heard from Thorn, more than a year ago, he had become a hot-air balloonist for the United States Weather Service. Now I hear that both sides are using balloonists in their armies, and I wonder if Thorn is in the Union Army. If so, I sincerely pray that I am never asked to fire upon any balloonist. It would distress me to think I had injured a friend.

Please accept my sincere felicitations on your coming birthday. And if I may ask it, please remember me in your prayers.

Yr. obdt. servant,
Andrew Holden

Letty's fingers trembled as she returned Drew's letter to its envelope. That task completed, she was obliged to clutch the edge of the bed to stop her entire body from shaking. "Thorn," she whispered, the mere saying of his name making her heart ache for what might have been.

Thorn, who had been so kind to her, comforted her. Who had held her close in his arms as she lay in the mud of her herb garden. Thorn, who had left White Pines, but never quite left her thoughts. Thorn in one of those hot-air balloons!

She prayed it wasn't true. She had read stories of those things, with their flimsy woven baskets. The balloons were forever catching fire or crashing into treetops. Sometimes they even tossed their hapless passengers out of the basket to plummet hundreds of feet to their death.

Her breath caught in her throat. Even the wind that carried the balloonists was their enemy! Wind changes could make a balloon drift off its course. When Thorn was at White Pines he had laughed about drifting off course once and landing in a farmer's potato field, but there was no war then and no enemy lines. What if his balloon drifted over Confederate territory and he was shot from the sky by someone like Drew?

The thought of Thorn's body plummeting to the ground made Letty's vision blur and her head swim woozily. She lay back on her bed to keep from fainting.

"Auntie!" Ocilla called from the doorway. "Don't go back to sleep. I've got your buttermilk and cornbread here, and our tea will be ready soon."

Letty sat up, but she didn't take the cup and spoon. She didn't trust her shaking hands to hold the lumpy concoction without spilling it. "Set it on the washstand for me. I'll eat it in a moment."

When Ocilla put the cup on the washstand and peeped through the lace curtains again, Letty realized there were voices drifting up from the veranda, and they had been doing so for some time without her paying attention to them.

"*Maître* is down there with those two men," Ocilla whispered over her shoulder. "If I stay out of sight may I listen? They're talking about something called a Confiscation Act."

"Confi—" Letty gasped, then rushed to the window, her heart pounding. "Shh," she warned. "Let's be very quiet. This could be important."

While Ocilla crouched on the floor, her elbows resting

on the windowsill, Letty sat on the edge of the petit-point rocker. When she reached over and placed her hand on Ocilla's shoulder, her fingers still trembled, but now they trembled from excitement.

The men sat in rockers on the shady side of the veranda, but Letty could hear them without any difficulty. And she could smell them. Her nose wrinkled at the sweet, heavy aroma of rum swizzles.

"Have another," Abner Banks offered.

"Thankee kindly," replied an unctuous voice. "Don't mind if I do."

"What about you, Lieutenant?"

"No, thank you, sir. One is my limit."

Abner yelled for another round of swizzles, then he cautioned his visitors to say nothing more until after Priam brought the drinks and returned to the back of the house.

"Now, Lieutenant," Abner said after the drinks were replenished, "continue what you were saying about this latest Yankee outrage."

"About this new Confiscation Act, you mean, sir?"

"Act?" roared the other visitor, his voice slightly thicker than it had been before the second round of drinks arrived. "Thievery is what I call it! Freeing the slaves in areas them damn Yankees overrun, as well as confiscating Rebel property. What would you call that but thievery?"

"Mind your volume," Abner warned. "These days even the walls have ears."

"Lincoln's a fool," the man continued, his volume diminished, but his anger still roused. "Wants to let the 'freed' slaves join the Union Army."

Letty leaned her head back against the rocker and closed her eyes, though she was anything but relaxed. The man was obviously getting drunker by the minute, and Letty knew better than to put much stock in the words of a drunk, but what if he had the story right about the Confiscation Act?

Were the Yankees truly freeing slaves?

She laced her fingers together to still their trembling. *God in heaven,* she thought, *there might still be hope for me and*

Ocilla. If what the man said is true, then please*, God, let the Yankees get here soon!*

Though she and Ocilla listened at least half an hour, she heard nothing more about the confiscation of slaves. The conversation went from the speaker's incredulity at anyone believing Negroes could fight to the latest in Yankee jokes.

"Say," he began, laughing as he spoke, "d'ya know how many Yankees it takes to unhitch a mule?"

Letty could only guess at the answer, but not wanting to expose Ocilla to who-knew-what kind of crudeness, she stood up and slammed the window.

"I was right, my love, the man is trash."

"How many Yankees does it take, Auntie?"

She was spared the necessity of an answer by someone scratching at the bedroom door. It was Theda.

"Is it Sudy?" Letty asked, her concern renewed for Verona's daughter. "Have her contractions started again?"

"No'm, Miss Letty. Sudy still asleep. Minna be sitting with her now, so I come back to help Verona with the birthd—"

Ocilla rushed forward and clamped her hand over the young seamstress's mouth, then as soon as she let her go, both girls were overcome with a fit of giggles, their eyes alight with excitement.

" 'Scuse me, Miss Letty," Theda said between giggles, "but I got to tell Ocilla something out in the hallway."

The two girls stepped out into the hall and shut the door behind them, leaving Letty to her contemplation of the conversation she had overheard from the veranda. After several moments of whispers and smothered giggles, Ocilla returned to the bedroom. She tried to look serious, but her lips kept pulling up at the corners.

"Our tea party is almost ready, Auntie. You've got just time enough to freshen up."

Letty had trouble with her own lips. "Oh, it's a tea *party* now, is it? And just how freshened should I get for this tea party?"

Ocilla went over to the washstand and tipped the pitcher so that cool water splashed into the bowl. After sprinkling the water with lemon verbena, she stepped back and bowed with an extravagant gesture. "Wash your face," she instructed saucily, "then touch up your hair. And don't even *think* of putting on that old green rag you wear when you work in your herb garden. Wear the new blue gingham. The one that matches your eyes."

Having issued her orders, she went to the door and opened it. "And when you finish, Auntie, meet us up at the springhouse."

"The springhouse? Why?"

"Because the creek is there, silly, and I like my watermelon cold." Ocilla pretended to turn a key to her lips again. "And that is all I'm going to say."

As soon as the door clicked shut, Letty did as she had been instructed and washed her face and hands in the scented water. Obediently freshened, she combed and rebraided her hair, then removed the blue gingham from the chiffonnier.

Though she gave the thirty-year-old spinster in the looking glass a deprecating smile for succumbing to the notion of dressing to match her eyes, she spent a few more seconds than were necessary admiring the snug fit of the new yoke waistline and the flattering fullness of the double-flounced skirt. Pleased with the effect, she pinned a satin rose to the bodice to add a festive touch.

Her toilette completed, Letty grabbed her straw leghorn to keep the afternoon sun off her face then hurried down the narrow back stairs. She had almost reached the bottom step when she heard someone talking in the butler's pantry. It wasn't difficult to recognize the slurred voice as belonging to the man who wore the secession rosette in his lapel.

As she drew closer, the sour stench of unwashed male stung Letty's nose, and since she had no desire to encounter the lout—especially after he had been imbibing half the afternoon—she tiptoed back up a few steps to wait until the man returned to the front of the house.

"Aw, come on," she heard him plead, his voice syrupy. His words were so garbled by drink that she wasn't certain she had heard him correctly.

"I got money," he said.

Letty closed her eyes in disgust as she heard the muffled sound of coins jingling in a pocket. He must be showing off in front of Priam.

"One li'l bitty old kiss ain't gonna hurt you none. C'mon, gimme. You treat old Felix right, and he'll give you a penny for a hair ribbon for them pretty curls."

White-hot anger followed close on the heels of realization, and by the time Letty heard Ocilla's whimper, she had already raced down the remainder of the steps and around the corner to the pantry.

At first all she saw was the man's back, his checked coat straining across his thick, squat body. Then she saw a bit of Ocilla's pale pink skirt and realized he had the young girl pinned to the wall, his body pressed against hers. He was trying to pull her shielding hands away from her face.

"Filthy pig!" Letty screamed. "Get away from that child!"

Blinded by fury, she dropped her hat and flew at the man, her hands balled into tight fists and her arms swinging. He turned just as she reached him, and she hit him a stinging blow across the side of the head.

"What'n hell!"

Before the lout could raise his arms to protect himself, Letty hit him again. This time the blow only glanced off his shoulder.

"Hey, lady! Stop!"

When he tried to scramble past her, he stepped on the leghorn hat she had dropped, and he and the hat skidded on the polished pine floor. Too drunk to save himself, he lost his balance. With his arms flailing, he fell back, hit his head on the corner of the linen press, then crumpled to the floor with a resounding thud. The instant he was down, Letty began kicking him in the back. The arms. The ribs. Whatever she could reach.

Out of her mind with rage, she was about to kick the man in the head when her father and the lieutenant arrived, their breath coming in gasps, a result of their quick sprint from the veranda to the rear of the house.

"What in blazes!" Abner yelled. While he grabbed Letty's arm and dragged her away, the stocky man scurried from the pantry on all fours.

"Dirty swine!" Letty called after his retreating form.

She tried to pull free of her father's iron grasp, but he twisted her arm behind her back and forced her to be still. Labored breathing echoed in the sudden quiet of the room.

"Get hold of yourself," Abner hissed close to her ear. "Have you lost your senses?"

Letty's eyes burned into his. "Take your hands off me," she ordered.

They glared at each other for several seconds before Abner loosened his hold on her arm. Pulling away from him, she ran to Ocilla, who was huddled on the floor in the far corner, shivering, her face turned to the wall. "Come, my love," she whispered softly, putting her hands beneath the child's arms and helping her to stand. "Auntie is going to take you upstairs."

"May I be of assistance, ma'am?" the lieutenant offered.

She looked at him as though he were a slug in the garden. "Stand back, trash."

"Loretta!" Abner warned. "Apologize to this gentleman at once. This is Lieutenant Warren Nesmith, one of the Chattanooga Nes—"

"*Gentleman*, Papa? *Gentleman?* What would you know of gentlemen?" She put her arms around the shivering Ocilla. "You gave me your word as a *gentleman* that no one would touch Ocilla. As long as I stayed on the property, you said, no one would touch her."

Abner took a step toward her. His back was to the lieutenant, and he spoke through clenched teeth. "You will apologize, Loretta. I will not tell you again."

Lieutenant Nesmith assured him that no apology was necessary, as did the stocky man who now stood just behind the lieutenant.

"No, sirree, Mr. Banks, ain't no 'pology necessary. Why, if I'd've knowed that there little gal was your daughter's, I never would've laid a hand on her."

Abner ignored the men. "You heard me, Loretta."

Letty pushed past her father and led Ocilla toward the stairs.

"Never would've touched your gal, ma'am," the stocky man repeated. "No, sirree bob."

"My daughter does not own that slave, sir."

Though he spoke to the man, Abner glared at Letty, his eyes cold. "The *property* is mine. *Mine.* To do with as I wish."

Letty stopped, her foot on the bottom step, and glared back at her father. The loathing she felt for him almost choked the breath from her body.

Abner moved close to the stairs. "It seems we have come full circle, Loretta." Angrily he caught her wrist and yanked her toward him, his face so close she could smell his liquored breath. "It is time you learned that *I* am master here. Time you showed me the respect that is my due."

"You want the respect you're due?" Yanking her wrist away, Letty leaned forward and spat in Abner's face.

The wind ruffled the leaves of the oak trees and sent a hot breeze through the bedroom window. In the distant sky a bright flash of lightning was followed by the muted rumble of thunder, and when Letty pushed the curtains aside to search for the moon, it seemed to be in hiding. The night was as dark as her thoughts. And as turbulent. She had given Ocilla a mild potion to make her sleep, but her own nerves were taut, her stomach in knots from the encounter downstairs.

How much more must we endure?

While she knelt beside the window, her head resting against the cool sill, someone scratched at the bedroom door. Though she knew the door was locked, she jumped, hitting her forehead against the window sash.

"Who is it?"

"It's me, Miss Letty. It's Theda. Verona sent me. She say for you to come quick. Sudy be in a mighty bad way."

Letty closed her eyes; she had forgotten all about Sudy and her complicated pregnancy, as well as her promise to return. But how could she go down to the cabins and leave Ocilla here alone?

Slowly she got up off the floor and lit the lamp, keeping the flame low so it didn't disturb Ocilla. She unlocked the door, but opened it only a crack. "I can't go to Sudy right now," she whispered. "I can't leave Ocilla. I've given her a potion, and I want her to sleep for at least another hour. Tell Verona I'll come as soon as Ocilla wakes."

The young girl's chin quivered. "Verona say I ain't to come back without you, Miss Letty. She say if you don't come, Sudy and that little unborn baby both fixing to die."

Letty slumped against the doorjamb. *Why must everything happen at once?* She was afraid to leave Ocilla, yet she couldn't let Sudy die.

"I be glad to stay with Ocilla for you, Miss Letty. I can sit with her just like I sit with Sudy this morning. Soon as Ocilla wakes up, her and me'll come on down to Sudy's cabin."

Letty looked at Ocilla for a full minute, watching her breathe; watching her thin ribs move silently beneath her cotton gown as she inhaled and exhaled. Unbidden, a picture of Sudy, moaning and writhing in pain, intruded itself upon Letty's reverie. Finally, reluctantly, she agreed to let Theda stay with Ocilla.

"But you are not to unlock the door for anyone. You hear me? I mean anyone. No matter who they are."

"I won't, Miss Letty. I won't open this door for nobody."

After assuring herself that Ocilla still slept, Letty left the room, waiting until she heard the key turn in the lock before she tiptoed down the back stairs and out the door.

On the way to Verona's cabin, Letty stopped by the blacksmith shed to get her herb box from Caleb. Unfortunately the shed was empty. Caleb must have gone out to the pasture acreage to help round up the sheep and cattle before the storm hit. Where he'd put her box was anyone's guess. When a quick search of the shed proved fruitless, Letty was forced to go to Sudy's without her herbs.

As it turned out, by the time Letty got to the cabin, Sudy had progressed to hard labor.

"Praise the Lord," Verona said the instant the cabin door was opened. With trembling hands, the old cook brushed the tears from her drawn face, then moved away from her daughter's bed to give Letty access. "Please help her, Miss Letty. I done everything I know, and don't nothing work."

Sudy, her eyes glazed with pain, lay in a pool of sweat, desperately clutching a length of rope suspended from the ceiling. Alternately writhing and moaning, the woman seemed unaware of Letty's presence.

A quick examination confirmed Letty's worst fears: the baby was in the breach position, and it was too late to turn him. Though it took all Letty's skill and all Sudy's strength to deliver the baby, in just under an hour Sudy's son was born.

Holding the newborn in her arms, Letty marveled at the tiny miracle. The boy was tan, perfect, and already sporting a full head of nappy hair. When he didn't breathe on his own, she flicked the bottom of his foot to make him gasp. Once he let out a healthy protest, she cleaned out his mouth and nose, then laid him on Sudy's stomach so the new mother could see that her baby was perfectly formed.

Sudy didn't see the baby, however; she had swooned with the last push.

When Letty finished with the umbilical cord, she lifted the child off Sudy's stomach and handed him to Verona. The old cook's arms trembled with fatigue, as though she had birthed her grandson herself, but she took the newborn and held the naked, screaming baby to her heart.

"You'll have to oil and swaddle him, Verona. I'm not finished with Sudy. I've got to massage her stomach. She's too exhausted to deliver the afterbirth without help."

Much later, as Letty prepared to leave the cabin, Sudy caught her hand and pressed it to her dry lips. "Thank you, Miss Letty," she mumbled. "I won't never forget what you . . ." In mid-sentence, the weary mother slipped into a much needed sleep.

With a final nod to Verona, Letty opened the door. The instant she stepped out onto the porch she was assaulted by wind-whipped dirt. She gasped as the grit stung her face and forced its way into her mouth. While she had been busy with Sudy, the storm had moved closer. The rain hadn't come yet, but thunder rumbled almost continually, and lightning flashed every few seconds, turning late night into day and revealing angrily swaying trees.

Where were Ocilla and Theda?

Letty had assumed they were waiting outside on the porch, but there was no sign that they had even been here. Recalling Ocilla's fear of storms, Letty assumed the wind and lightning must have frightened the child. Was that it? Had she been too scared by the storm to come outside? Or perhaps the two young girls hadn't even left the bedroom. Perhaps they were afraid they might encounter the lout who had accosted Ocilla.

"White trash," Letty mumbled as she stepped out into the yard. "I wish I had kicked your brains out."

Wanting to get back to Ocilla as quickly as possible, Letty picked up her skirt and walked as fast as she dared in the dark. As she hurried past the stable, lightning struck a tree in the distance, making the earth tremble and almost knocking her off her feet. For a short time the entire area was bathed in an eerie brightness, and in the momentary light Letty thought she saw someone standing in the doorway of the stable, holding the reins of a saddled horse. She stopped and stared.

When the light was gone, and it was pitch dark again, she decided this evening's chaos was taking its toll on her, making her imagine things. Caleb was out at the pasture, and no one else would be in the stable at this time of night. Certainly no one would be fool enough to ride out with a storm of this magnitude about to set in, not unless he had a mighty compelling reason to do so.

The rain began to fall in large, battering drops, reminding Letty that she had a compelling reason for hurrying home. Dismissing the apparition in the stable, she picked up her skirt again and ran up the pine bark path. She was still several yards from the house when a flash of light revealed the back porch.

Something, or someone, sat on the steps. And this time it was no apparition.

Letty stopped and waited for the next flash of light. When it came again it revealed Theda, her face buried in the crook of her arm, and rain pelting her shaking shoulders like pebbles.

Letty sped the last few yards.

"Theda! What are you doing here? Why aren't you with Ocilla?"

The young girl's eyes were big with fear. "He made me go away, Miss Letty. I told him I supposed to stay with Ocilla, but he—"

"Who?" Letty's heart beat madly against her ribs. "Who sent you away?"

"That white man, Miss Letty. He say if I don't open the door, Marse Abner going to beat me with a whip. He say the whip going to tear the skin right off my back, and I—"

An animal sound she didn't recognize shrieked from Letty's throat. Almost choking on her own fear, she dashed past Theda and ran up the back stairs. Something had happened to the hall lamp; it was no longer burning. The hallway was so dark Letty had to grope her way to her room, and when she finally reached it, the bedroom door stood open.

The stench of man sweat filled her nostrils.

"Ocilla!"

There was no answer. Letty's chest hurt with the effort to breathe, and fear made her knees turn to India rubber. She held to the doorjamb, waiting for the lightning, and when it finally flashed, her heart almost stopped at what she saw.

The room was a shambles. Debris littered the floor, the mattress lay drunkenly half on, half off the bed, and the mosquito netting hung in torn shreds like ghostly cobwebs. There was no sign of Ocilla.

"Ocillaaa!" Her scream echoed like a clap of thunder.

The answer was little more than a whimper. "Auntie."

Letty crashed through the darkness to the far side of the bed, where her foot touched something soft huddled between the bed and the wall. "Ocilla?" she whispered. "Is that you, love?"

The next lightning flash revealed the young girl, her eyes wide with pain and bewilderment. She was trying to shield her nakedness with the tattered remnants of her cotton nightgown.

Letty gripped the post at the foot of the bed, and, pushing with a strength she didn't know she possessed, she moved the massive bedframe far enough to allow her to crawl to Ocilla's side. Wanting to take the child in her arms to comfort her, Letty slipped her hand beneath the delicate, trembling shoulders. As she did so, her fingers brushed something stiff that lay on the floor.

Revulsion shot through her. Even in the dark Letty knew what her fingers had touched. It was the gathered bunting of a secession rosette.

Six

May 1863

Letty stretched her stiff arms above her head, and while she twisted first to the right and then to the left, the cane-bottom chair squeaked, protesting almost as loudly as her bones. Smothering a yawn, she pinched her earlobes to keep herself awake. She hadn't slept for two days, not real sleep, only catnaps. But now she was afraid to do even that. She was afraid if she dared close her eyes for too long, Ocilla would slip away from this world, leaving Letty with no one to love, nothing to live for.

"Please don't go," she whispered into the dimness of the quiet cabin.

She had whispered that same phrase every few minutes for the last hour. She didn't know anything else to say. She had said it all, and more.

At first she had prayed. Then she had begged. At last she tried bargaining. If God would only let Ocilla live, the earth would know no more obedient Christian than Letty Banks.

When bargaining with God didn't work, she even tried to summon the devil. What good was an immortal soul if the one person she loved in this world was taken away?

The devil hadn't answered her call, either.

"Please don't go," she whispered again.

She stood up and stretched until bones popped up and down her spine, then she set the chair beneath the table that held her herb box and her Colt .44 Dragoon. The chair and the table were the only pieces of furniture in the cabin, except for the hand-rubbed pecan cradle Caleb had brought yesterday and the narrow wooden bed on which Ocilla lay.

The corn husk stuffing in the mattress crackled, and Letty rushed over to the bed. "Ocilla," she whispered. "Are you awake?"

"Auntie?"

"I'm here, my love."

She held Ocilla's limp, almost lifeless hand and tried to will some of her own robust health into the young girl's tired body. Impotence and rage gnawed at Letty's insides. Rage that had not lessened in the nine months since she had brought Ocilla—battered and bleeding—to this cabin.

Kitten-like mewing sounded from the pecan cradle, but the cries went unanswered. There would be time enough for that child later. It was this child Letty must hold onto now; this child she must keep from the gates of heaven. She pressed the thin, feverish hand to her lips and kissed it.

Without taking her eyes off Ocilla's face, she got down on her knees and begged God once more. "Please, Lord. Please let Ocilla live. She's only fifteen. That isn't near enough time for—"

"Auntie?"

At the softly spoken word, Letty put her ear close to Ocilla's mouth. She wasn't certain she hadn't imagined the sound. "Auntie's here, my love."

The hand she held, the hand she had tried to infuse with life, moved slightly. It moved only once, then it was still.

Pain like a hot knife stabbed through Letty's heart, and she whispered for the last time, "Please don't go."

•   •   •

For a long time Letty sat on the edge of the narrow bed, clutching Ocilla's hand to her heart and slowly rocking to and fro. Silent tears rolled unheeded down her face and neck, dampening her heaving chest. She was aware of nothing but the unbearable pain in her chest and the delicate hand she held, the hand she couldn't bear to let go.

Eons later, when the flood of tears abated, Letty stood, tucked Ocilla's cold hand beneath the faded patchwork quilt, then gently pulled the cover up over the child's shoulders. With slow, gentle strokes she smoothed all the wrinkles from the quilt, straightening the edges just so, then she leaned forward and pressed her lips against Ocilla's thin cheek. When she could delay it no longer, Letty placed a fresh linen cloth over the now lifeless face.

Moving listlessly, as if in a dream, she walked over to the cabin door, lifted the heavy bolt, then opened the door and stepped out onto the porch. It was the first time she had been outside since the night of the storm—the night she brought Ocilla to the cabin.

The sun hurt her eyes. It was too bright. Too warm upon her face. All around her the trees sported fresh, new green, and in the distance the pink buds of the wild azaleas were just waiting to burst open. Letty looked away. The sight of burgeoning new life sickened her.

As her gaze spanned the empty yards of the cabins down the row, she spied Minna and Theda sitting in the shade of a tulip poplar near Minna's cabin. They were quilting. Minna always quilted in the spring. Because the quilting frames were too large to fit inside her cabin, she had to wait for balmy weather when she could work outside in the open.

Letty watched the seamstresses with dulled eyes. They had already stretched the plain fabric backing across the frame and laid the stuffing material over it, and now they concentrated on pinning the first quilting pieces into place. They didn't look up from their work.

She wished she could go back inside the cabin before they saw her. She wished she didn't have to speak to them.

She didn't want to speak to anyone, but she knew she had no choice.

Minna must have felt Letty watching her, because she suddenly looked up from her work. The woman seemed to know why Letty was on the porch. Removing the pins she held pressed between her lips, Minna whispered something to Theda. Instantly Theda jumped up, knocking over her three-legged stool, and ran across the swept yards.

"Can I fetch something for you, Miss Letty?"

Letty's lips moved, but she couldn't make the words come out. Her throat felt as though someone had squeezed it shut. Accepting the reprieve, she turned to watch a noisy squirrel scurry halfway up a sapling pine tree, circle it, then turn and run back down.

"What you need, Miss Letty? You just tell me, I'll get it for you."

Letty still watched the squirrel. She couldn't look at Theda. The memories were too painful. "I need Caleb," she said finally, though the husky voice didn't sound like her own. "Tell him to . . ." She cleared her throat. "Tell Caleb to bring a coffin."

Theda began to cry. "Yes'm. I'll go tell him."

"And, Theda," she added as the young girl turned to walk away, "find Sudy for me. Tell her Ocilla's baby will need to be nursed before nightfall."

Twenty minutes later Caleb knocked at the cabin door. Letty flinched at the sound. She had thought it would take him longer. Caleb always kept three coffins stacked and ready—one each for a man, a woman, and a child—but Letty needed more time. She wasn't ready for the exigencies of death. Not yet. She hadn't even begun to say her goodbyes.

He knocked again. "It's me, child."

When she didn't answer, Caleb pushed the door all the way until it touched the wall. He didn't step inside the cabin but remained just outside the door. Balanced against his long, bony body was a pine casket.

Letty closed her eyes at the sight.

After swiping the sleeve of his shirt across his own eyes, Caleb lifted the casket and brought it into the small room. As quietly as possible, he set the casket on the table beside the herb box and the Dragoon, then he opened the lid, revealing the lining of bleached osnaburg he had tacked into place.

Moments later, when Verona and Minna entered the cabin, Caleb went back outside. The seamstress carried a wooden tray containing freshly hemmed washcloths, and the cook held a cruet of rose-scented oil; the women had come to perform the last act of friendship. No one said a word, and while the women prepared Ocilla's young body, then wrapped her in the white shroud Minna had put by for her own burial, Letty stood quietly in the corner and watched.

When all was completed except the placing of the shrouded body in the coffin, Caleb came back into the cabin. Letty seemed not to know he was there, so he stepped in front of her so she was obliged to look at him.

"It be best if you go now, child." His voice was hoarse, and he had to clear his throat before he could continue. "You don't need to worry none. I'll lift that sweet angel as gentle as a little bird."

As though in a trance, Letty left the cabin.

Without stopping to speak to any of the people who waited in the yard outside the cabin, she walked straight up to the house. She needed to freshen up and put on clothing appropriate for the funeral. She already knew which dress she meant to wear, for she had made that decision as she listened to Caleb set the coffin on the table. It was the only dress she owned with pockets deep enough for her purpose.

After she washed, she brushed and rebraided her hair, then circled it into a coronet and pinned a small, lace handkerchief over it like a cap. Passing up the blue gingham dress that Ocilla liked, she reached to the back of the chiffonnier and pulled out the old mauve merino she had not worn in years. When all the buttons were fastened and the pockets checked for holes, she opened a drawer of the writing desk and removed the little white Bible her mother had given her for her twelfth birthday.

Without glancing toward the looking glass, she hurried from the room. At the bottom of the back stairs, Priam waited for her, resplendent in his dark gray company livery and fresh white cotton gloves. He had aged years in the months since she had last seen him.

"Miss Letty, I—" His voice quivered. "I be proud if you allow me to help tote the coffin to the tree."

Letty jumped as though he had slapped her. "The tree! What do you mean the tree?"

Priam studied the floor. "Miss Letty, you know what tree I mean. The burying tree. All the White Pines colored folks be buried at the tree. The spirits that live in the tree give comfort to them that passed, and—"

"No!"

Letty brushed past the old man and ran to the door. "Not the tree! I thought Caleb understood."

"Miss Letty!" Priam called after her. "Wait! What you fixing to do?"

She didn't answer. After hurrying down the porch steps, she ran as fast as she could toward the path. When she arrived at the cabin, her breath was coming in gasps, and she held her hand to her aching side; yet she did not stop until she stood directly in front of Caleb, who waited just inside the doorway.

At first he seemed not to understand her breathy instructions. Then when she repeated them, he looked as if he might argue. After a moment, however, he nodded his head. "You sure about this, child?"

"Positive."

While she leaned against the door and caught her breath, Caleb went over to speak to two men who stood at a respectful distance. Both men carried shovels. It being late afternoon, and everyone having finished their daily jobs, several dozen men and women had gathered. Like Verona and Minna, they waited quietly for the funeral to begin.

Letty heard whispered mutterings as the word spread through the crowd just what Caleb wanted with the two men. Several people glanced over their shoulders as though afraid of what or who might be listening, then with eyes downcast they slowly walked away, returning to their cabins. The two men looked as though they might follow suit, but finally they agreed to do Caleb's bidding. Shouldering their shovels, they followed Caleb in the direction of the family burial plot.

Twenty minutes later Caleb returned alone. He led a mule hitched to a two-wheeled farm cart; over the bed of the cart he had spread a sheet of fresh osnaburg. "Everything's the way you want it."

"Thank you," she said, then she turned to Priam, who stood on the porch beside her, wringing his handkerchief. Laying her hand on the old man's arm to still the nervous gesture, she called his attention to Verona and Minna, the only people who remained in the yard. "Please thank the women for me, Priam, then send them to their cabins. The fewer people involved in this the better."

The old man nodded his agreement. "I'll tell 'em for you, Miss Letty. But don't you go trying to send me away, 'cause I ain't going." His wrinkled face was set. "I'm fixing to see that child buried, and that's all they is to it."

Letty looked deep into Priam's rheumy old eyes, then nodded her head. "I won't send you away."

He stuffed his handkerchief back into his pocket. "I reckon Marse Abner be mighty angry when he find out, Miss Letty. No telling what he—"

"Ocilla was my sister!"

Letty's words cut through the old man's prediction with a prediction of her own. "Before this day is over, Priam, one of us—if not Ocilla, then I—will be buried in the family plot."

Priam said no more. While he went to send the women away, Letty stepped back inside the cabin to have a last moment alone with Ocilla.

The fire in the grate, like the fragile girl it had tried to warm, had gone out. The room felt cold and empty, as empty as Letty's heart. The coffin was already sealed, so all she could do was lay her trembling hand on the unvarnished pine lid. She closed her eyes. When she opened them a few moments later, she walked around to the other side of the table and picked up the Dragoon. Her hand no longer trembled as she checked to make sure the chambers of the revolver were loaded.

Letty had only just slipped the weapon into the deep pocket of her merino dress when Caleb scratched at the open door. At a nod from her, he and Priam entered the cabin. Carefully, reverently, they carried the coffin outside and set it across the farm cart. Priam rode in the cart to hold the coffin secure, while Caleb led the mule by the harness. Letty followed behind.

At a snail's pace they crossed the gently rolling pasture behind the cabins until they came to the fenced knoll where the Banks family dead were buried. Hundreds of pale yellow jonquils grew on and around the graves of Amalie Banks and the three ill-fated infant sons she bore Abner before the healthy Loretta was born.

Flush with the low picket fence, and distanced as far as possible from the other graves, was a mound of freshly turned earth. Letty's knees buckled when she saw the mound, but she picked herself up and kept walking.

Caleb stopped the mule, then he and Priam lifted the coffin off the cart and carried it up the knoll, setting it beside the freshly dug grave. While they bowed their heads, Letty opened the white leather Bible and read the Twenty-third Psalm. When she finished reading, she laid the Bible on the coffin and stepped aside to let Caleb secure the ropes needed to lower the pine box into the ground. He was making the final adjustments when the peace of the place was shattered by the thud of a horse's hooves.

Like a man possessed, Abner Banks galloped across the pasture on his latest stallion, using the whip to force the bay to further speed. Without stopping, he rode right up the knoll, reining in the spirited steed just before the powerful hooves trampled Amalie Banks's grave. His face crimson with rage, Abner dismounted, then pushed the horse out of his way.

With his booted feet wide apart and his hands on his

hips, he demanded, "What in hell is going on here?"

Letty slipped her hands into her pockets. "I am burying my sister."

"Not in this plot you're not!"

Abner pointed his riding crop at Caleb. "Boy, if you want to keep the skin on your back, you'll take that slave back to the burying tree this instant!"

Letty stepped between her father and Caleb. When she spoke, her words were hushed, her voice cold. "Abner Banks, this is your last chance to behave as a human being. Leave me in peace while I bury my kinswoman."

Her father's eyes flashed with hatred. "Will you never learn?"

Stepping toward her, Abner raised the arm that held the riding crop. But as he moved to bring the crop down across Letty's shoulders, an explosion rent the air. At the loud report, screaming birds fled to distant trees, while the stallion, his eyes rolled back in fright, reared, then galloped away.

For a moment, Abner Banks stood as if frozen in time, a puzzled expression in his eyes. Then, without a word, he fell face forward to the ground.

Caleb and Priam, their eyes wide with horror, stared first at the fallen man, then at Letty's smoking skirt. She hadn't taken the Dragoon out of her pocket; she had simply pointed it at her father's chest and fired.

Now she withdrew the revolver and tossed it over the low fence where it landed with a dull thud. The westering sun struck the mottled gun barrel, making it shimmer like a dead indigo snake lying in the grass, but Letty paid no more attention to the discarded revolver than she did to her fallen father. Instead, she returned to the far side of the knoll and Ocilla's coffin.

After kissing her fingertips, she touched the pine one last time. "Lower her gently, please, Caleb. There's no rush. We'll have no more interruptions."

Seven

After the last shovelful of red earth was placed on Ocilla's grave and Letty had knelt and said a simple prayer, she bid a final farewell to her beloved sister. When she stood, she motioned for Caleb and Priam to follow her to the bottom of the knoll. She didn't even look down as she passed the body of Abner Banks.

"First," she began, none too steadily, "I want to thank you both for helping me bury Ocilla. I couldn't have—"

"Now, Miss Letty," Priam interrupted, his voice sounding offended, "you hush about that."

"You got that right," Caleb added.

Letty swallowed with difficulty. "All right," she agreed, "I'll hush about that, but we've got to talk about my father's death. I got you both involved in the shooting, and I regret that more than I can say. This wasn't the way I planned it. I had planned to shoot him at the house, after the funeral was over."

The two men exchanged uneasy glances.

"Don't worry," she said. "I haven't lost my senses. I've merely kept a vow."

As though needing to gather her thoughts, she watched as a reddish-brown butterfly hovered over the farm cart before abandoning the drab vehicle for one of the bright yellow jonquils. "When Ocilla was only one day old," she continued, "I vowed to God that I would kill anyone who hurt her. Papa let someone else hurt her, and that's the same thing."

Letty watched the butterfly for a moment longer, then she sighed heavily, tiredly. "The sheriff has to be told about this." She shaded her eyes so she could look up at the sun. "There are a couple of hours of daylight left. If you hitch up the wagon now, Caleb, you'll have time to reach town and return before nightfall."

"Now, Miss Letty, ain't no need for me to go to town just yet awhile. First we got to—"

"The sheriff will want to know what happened. You just tell him that Papa is dead. When he comes out here, I'll admit the whole thing. I killed Old Canebrake. This time I was the one who got the last bite."

"But, Miss Letty," Caleb said, "we don't—"

"Here's what you say," she continued, unaware of his interruptions. "When the sheriff asks for your story, you tell him that I ordered you and Priam to leave me alone on the knoll with Ocilla, and while I was here alone, Papa rode up. You tell him you didn't know a thing until you heard the gunfire. You two came running to investigate, and that's when you found Papa on the ground and me standing over him with the revolver. You can both swear that you didn't know I had the gun in my pocket."

She glanced up on the knoll at the freshly packed earth of Ocilla's grave, and as she looked, her lips began to tremble. "I'm a murderer," she said, as though the enormity of the act had just registered, "and a murderer can never enter the gates of heaven." Tears choked her voice. "Ocilla is in heaven now, and I'll never see her again."

With purposeful stride, Caleb walked over to where the Dragoon lay in the grass and picked it up. After checking to make sure it wouldn't go off, he walked back over to Letty and handed it to her. He spoke softly, reasonably, the way he used to when she was a little girl and afraid to get up on a horse. "You best take this here gun up to the house, child, and put it in a safe place. I reckon the sheriff will want to see it.''

Once she had put the revolver back in her pocket, Caleb took her by the elbow and led her over to the farm cart where he helped her up onto the dirty plank seat. After Priam got up on the seat beside her, Caleb took the mule by the reins as he had done earlier, and in a very few minutes they were at the back porch of the house.

"While I ride to town," Caleb said, helping Letty out of the cart, "you go lie down on your bed and rest a spell. You ain't slept for a long time, child, and you plumb wore out."

Like a sleepwalker, she let Priam lead her into the house; then, after placing the Dragoon on the table in the pantry, she climbed the back stairs to her bedroom. Without removing her clothes, she lay down on her bed and fell asleep instantly. She didn't awaken until almost twenty-four hours later when Priam scratched at her door.

"Miss Letty? You awake yet?"

Slowly, heavily, she raised her head and looked around the room. She couldn't figure out why she was lying across the foot of the bed, nor why she had slept in her clothes. And the trundle bed wasn't pulled out. *Where was Ocilla?*

When she sat up, ready to call the child's name, she saw the hole in her skirt pocket and smelled the burned cloth, and the horrors of the previous day pierced her sleep-induced forgetfulness. Like a knife, the memory cut right through her chest to her heart. Tears flooded her cheeks.

Priam scratched on the door again. "Miss Letty?"

After wiping the tears away with the tail of her skirt, she willed herself to stand. Though her legs wobbled like those of a new colt, she managed to walk to the door. When she opened it, Priam came into the room with a loaded breakfast tray, its contents covered by a starched white protective napkin.

"I brung you some sweetmilk, Miss Letty, and some hot biscuits, just this minute out of the oven. Verona opened a jar of her fig preserves to go along with the biscuits, and she say tell you they's plenty more where that come from."

Averting his gaze from the little table where she and
Ocilla always ate their breakfasts, he set the tray on the
desk, then drew up the ladder-back chair. "You come on
and set down now, Miss Letty. You ain't eat since I don't
know when."

She didn't move. "Priam?"

"Yes'm?" he answered politely, though he kept his attention riveted on the chair he held.

Letty put both her hands to her forehead. "I can't seem
to think straight. My head feels like it's stuffed with cotton,
as if I've been asleep for a long time. Why didn't you wake
me?"

The old man wiped a speck of dust from the back of the
chair, then he offered it again. "Yes'm, Miss Letty, you
slept a mighty long time. You surely did."

"Don't toy with me, Priam. What happened when the
sheriff came? Didn't he want to question me about the murder? I thought surely I would be locked in one of those
cells in the basement of the courthouse by now."

"Now ain't the time for studying about sheriffs, Miss
Letty. Now's the time for eating." He removed the protective napkin, revealing the food and the sparkling china and
cutlery. "You sit down here and eat them biscuits and drink
that sweetmilk, you hear? When you done, Caleb got something to say to you. He setting on the back porch waiting
for you."

Disregarding the fact that the very thought of food made
her stomach churn, Letty sat down and ate and drank
enough to give her some energy. She knew she would need
strength to face the ordeal of the sheriff and his questions.

The moment she finished eating, she went down the back
stairs and out to the porch where Caleb sat in Priam's rocking chair watching smoke rise from the cookhouse chimney.

He stood up as soon as he heard her come out and
walked over to the porch rail, his gaze still fixed on the
chimney. "Afternoon, Miss Letty."

"Caleb, why did the sheriff leave without speaking to
me?"

As if considering his answer, Caleb leaned forward and rested his long arms on the porch rail, his work-scarred fingers curved around the whitewashed wood. His attention was still on the curling smoke. "The sheriff ain't been here. I didn't fetch him."

"Didn't fetch him? But why?"

He finally turned and looked at her, his expression mulish. "I didn't fetch the sheriff 'cause we didn't have no call to fetch him. Not when Marse Abner fell off that new horse of his and broke his neck."

Letty stepped beside him where she could look up into his face. She thought she must have misunderstood him. "What did you say?"

"Me and Priam saw the whole thing. We was both nearby when Marse Abner fell. It happened just after you went up to rest, and that's how come you didn't know nothing about it."

Warming to his story, he continued. "Marse Abner come home riding that skittish new stallion of his. Look like he been riding it hard, too, the way that poor horse was all lathered up and wild-eyed. Then when they was crossing the stableyard, something scared that stallion, and he throwed Marse Abner. Marse Abner dead time me and Priam got to him."

"But—"

"Priam and me ain't certain what scared that horse, but we think it was most likely that nasty-tempered goose of Minna's. Everybody afraid of that goose. I reckon somebody ought to tell Minna to sell the fractious old thing before anybody else gets hurt."

Letty stared at Caleb, unable to credit the story he had invented. "But Papa's got a bullet hole in his chest. No one who sees him will believe—"

Caleb put his finger across his lips and took a quick look around. He spoke in a whisper. "Ain't nobody fixing to see nothing, child. We done buried him."

"What!"

"Shh. We hid him until it got dark, then we took a casket up to the knoll and put him in it. When we was sure wouldn't nobody see us, we carried him down to the tree, put him in the grave that was already dug there, and then we piled the dirt back on.''

He glanced toward the cookhouse. ''This morning I went by Verona's cabin and told her how Marse Abner died falling off his horse. By now I reckon she told the story to everybody on the place.''

''But he's got a bullet in—''

''You don't need to worry 'bout that. Ain't none of the White Pines folks fixing to dig up a grave to see if Marse Abner's neck is broke. And if any town folks come around asking questions, you can show them the new grave in the family plot. I don't reckon they would bother a grave in a family plot.''

''I appreciate what you're trying to do, Caleb, but we can't hide the fact that I committed murder.'' Lifting her hands, she spread the fingers and turned the palms up for him to see, as though her hands alone would convict her. ''I did more than murder. I killed my own father. That's two of God's commandments broken. I'm guilty and I will have to be punished.''

Neither of them spoke for a long time. Caleb resumed his contemplation of the cookhouse chimney smoke, and Letty watched a busy dirt dauber smear mud just above the door frame in preparation for a new nest.

Eventually Caleb cleared his throat. ''I been thinking about them commandments. The way I see it, if they're God's commandments, then it ain't none of the sheriff's business if they was broke. The Lord knows everything that happened here, and He don't need no sheriff poking into His business. And as for punishment, the way I reckon it, there's been more than enough punishment to go around.''

He gave her a chance to mull over what he had said before he added his clincher. ''And now I got just one question, child. It's a question I reckon Ocilla would want to have answered. If the sheriff comes and takes you away, and they put you in jail for the rest of your life, what's going to happen to Ocilla's little baby girl?''

Eight

The lawyer made himself comfortable in Abner Banks's red leather chair before he unfolded the will and laid it on the desk. The stiff new paper crackled under his liver-spotted hands.

"Now, Miss Banks," he said, looking at her rather than at the will, "it's been my experience that ladies do not understand the complicated legal terminology of a Last Will and Testament. For that reason, I submit that in the interest of time, I should just tell you in my own words how your father disposed of his property."

Letty simpered and lowered her gaze to the hands she had clasped demurely in her lap. She wished the old charlatan would get on with it. The black dress she had donned as a mourning gown had belonged to her mother, and the bodice squeezed so tightly against her ribs and waist that she was afraid to breathe.

Furthermore, she wasn't sure how long she could keep up this pretense of stupidity, a pretense vital to her future welfare. If she had learned nothing else from Abner Banks, she had learned how to play the game. She had learned not to disclose her strengths too early, and she had learned to follow her instincts. Her instincts told her to play this hand close to the vest.

She didn't trust the lawyer. She had met him only once before, but she knew that he and her father were partners in some kind of deal with a Confederate purchasing agent. She had overheard that much. And since Abner had always looked like a cat who'd been in the cream pot after the purchasing agent came and went, Letty assumed the deals benefited him and the lawyer more than they helped the hungry Confederate soldiers.

After Priam had served them refreshments on the veranda, she and the lawyer had retired to the library for the reading of the will. Mr. DuBose Maynard, properly decked out in funereal attire of well-sponged black frock coat, black vest, black cravat, clean white linen, and no jewelry other than his gold pocket watch, immediately assumed the position of authority behind Abner's desk. Letty chose the unyielding parson's bench so she wouldn't need to bend at the waist and challenge the black dress.

"Before I begin, Miss Banks, I feel it my duty to inform you that the entire town is outraged at the way you handled this affair. In my thirty-six years as a lawyer, I have learned that there is a right way and a wrong way to do everything." He stressed his next words by pointing his finger at her. "You chose the wrong way."

Letty lifted a wisp of handkerchief to her dry eyes. She even managed a couple of sniffs. If the old humbug meant to see her sufficiently cowed before he got down to the business of the will, she didn't mean to disappoint him.

He clicked his tongue at her as though she were a recalcitrant child. "When the army procurement officer came back to town and told us he hadn't been able to talk with Abner because he was dead—had been dead for almost a week—well, you can imagine the rumors and suspicions. No one has seen you in town in years, Miss Banks, so speculation ran rampant as to your sanity. Believe me, only your sex kept the townspeople from forming a party of investigation."

He had been leaning across the desk to emphasize his

remarks, but when she hid her face in her hands, he relaxed in the chair and crossed his arms over his ample middle. "Of course, when Sheriff West came back from his official visit to you, he told us how grieved you were. He remarked how tenderly you had cared for the grave, how flowers covered all the family plots, and how the tears welled up in your eyes when you looked upon the new mound of earth. After his report, we all understood that it was your bereavement that clouded your judgment."

Letty would not let herself think of the grave. She refolded her hands in her lap and concentrated on her fingers.

Maynard cleared his throat. " 'Sheriff West,' I told him, 'you may depend upon it. Miss Banks didn't know she was supposed to contact anybody about the death. Females never know the logical thing to do.' Naturally West agreed with me."

"Naturally."

The lawyer accepted her comment at face value. "Anyway, what is done cannot be undone. The death was recorded as accidental." He bowed his head and put his hand over his heart. *"Requiescat in pace."*

"Rest in peace," Letty repeated softly, remembering the child she had loved and cared for and buried.

"And now," Maynard said, shifting the papers on the desk, "let us get to the business at hand, the will. The plantation, of course, is not mentioned in this, your father's latest will."

He looked over his pince-nez glasses. "I believe your grandfather's lawyers handled that matter seven years ago." He waited for her answer with what Letty considered unseemly interest, his gimlet eyes reminding her of a water rat's, a rat who had spied a likely fish.

"I am in possession of the deed to White Pines," she replied.

Now his eyes narrowed with speculation, though he tried to cover the lapse by grumbling about the inadvisability of placing property in the hands of unschooled females.

Letty ignored the remark. She had seen that look in his eyes. DuBose Maynard had plans, and those plans included the deed to White Pines. She would have to be on her guard.

Having just warned herself to be on guard, she ground her fingernails into her palms when she realized that Maynard had returned to the salient points of the will, and she hadn't heard a word he had said.

"And though I advised him against it, that was his final decision."

She raised her hand to stop him. "Excuse me, Mr. Maynard, my mind must have wandered. What did you say just then?"

"I was merely explaining your father's instructions as to the dispensation of the slaves. Their new owner is referred to in the will only as a Mr. Smith."

"What!"

"Your father left a letter, written in his own hand, with instructions for the delivery of the slaves to their new master. That letter has been given to Sheriff West to carry out."

Letty grasped the edge of the parson's bench to keep from screaming.

"I told your father, 'Abner,' I said, 'Miss Banks cannot run White Pines without slaves.' But Abner would not be swayed by my words."

Letty felt as if she had been turned to stone.

Maynard shuffled through his papers until he found the page he wanted. "One hundred and twenty slaves are listed, and every one of them is willed to Mr. Smith. With only two exceptions. Abner was most particular about what became of one slave."

The lawyer ran his finger down the page. "Yes, here it is: a female quadroon known as Ocilla. Your father stipulated that this particular female was not to be sold. He instructed that she be sent directly to Mr. John Denholm, a gentleman who oversees a sugar plantation in the Caribbean. 'To do with as he wants' were your father's exact words."

Letty clenched her teeth until her jaw ached. *Damn him! Damn Abner Banks!* She hoped he was suffering the eternal fires of hell. She hoped he was writhing in agony this very moment.

"I will need to take the quadroon with me when I return to town."

Letty forced herself to answer calmly. "The female named Ocilla died not long ago. She died in chi . . . of dysentery. Many of our people suffered from it this summer, although everyone recovered except her."

Maynard made a note on the paper. "No offense, Miss Banks, but I will need some kind of proof of her death."

With only a slight quiver in her voice, Letty said, "There is a new grave by the tree where the servants bury their dead. I will have someone take you there if you like."

"That will do fine. I take it there were no issue from this female."

Letty's words were barely audible. "Ocilla was little more than a child at the time of her death. She was much too young to be having children."

The lawyer made another note on his paper.

"Sir, you said there were two exceptions. What was the other?"

"Your father stipulated that you might choose one slave to remain with you. He said you could choose any slave you wanted, except the quadroon called Ocilla, of course. All the others will go to Mr. Smith."

"*All* the others?" Letty pressed her lips together to keep from screaming. "Surely there were Deeds of Manumission in the will. Priam, my father's personal servant, is in his seventies, and the cook—"

"Madam, Deeds of Manumission were banned by the Legislature in fifty-nine. With more than three thousand freedmen roaming loose in Georgia, the gentlemen of the Legislature had no choice. It was the only solution. In fact, the *Georgia Citizen* had an article just last week about some freedmen being picked up for vagrancy and sold back into slavery. These are troubled times, Miss Banks."

He picked up the papers again, as though weary of the entire subject. "So you see," he added, "even if Abner had willed any Deeds of Manumission, the law would not have granted them. Of course, it's a moot point, as the subject never came up.''

Letty stood and walked over to the French windows. She needed some air. He had freed no one. Her father had been cruel to the end. Giving her the power to choose only one from among so many who were dear to her was his final cruelty. She leaned her head against the cool panes of the window.

''There is one further bequest, Miss Banks. A bequest to you.''

Letty opened the window and stepped over the threshold. She wanted to hear no more from Abner Banks.

Maynard cleared his throat to get her attention, and when she didn't return to the room, he muttered something and got up to follow her. ''Madam, my time is valuable. Let us finish this and be done with it.''

She didn't turn around.

''Abner said you were ungovernable.'' The lawyer's voice said he agreed with the assessment. ''It was because of your intractableness that your father made out his will as he did. I warned him that if you happened to be married at the time of his death, your husband might feel he had just cause to take the will to court and have the entire document set aside. Abner assured me that you would not be married. But after further reflection, he added a codicil to insure that the body of the testament was carried out as he wished it.''

Maynard flipped to the last page of the will. ''To Caroline Loretta Banks,'' he read, ''I bequeath my hunting lodge near the Ochlockonee River.''

Three days after the reading of the will, DuBose Maynard returned to White Pines. Getting down to business as soon as Letty invited him to be seated in one of the rocking chairs on the veranda, the lawyer informed her that wagons would arrive the following afternoon to transport both field hands and house servants to their new owner.

Gripping the arms of the rocking chair so hard her

knuckles turned white, Letty said, "But where will they go?"

"That, madam, is none of your concern."

Letty stood up and walked to the end of the veranda. *Tomorrow*. Tomorrow was too soon. She needed more time. Her plans were still too sketchy.

She made herself return to the rocker. "I'm afraid tomorrow is impossible, sir. The servants cannot be ready in so little time."

"Then make them ready."

"But they have livestock and crops they have raised on their own. They'll lose them if they leave so soon."

"That is not my concern."

"No, sir," she said, "I don't suppose it would be."

He cleared his throat. "What you should be thinking about, Miss Banks, is your own future."

As though he had nothing more on his mind, he removed the pince-nez from his vest pocket and wiped the spectacles with a white linen handkerchief. "I don't suppose you've had time to bring in *your* crops."

"No, sir, I have not. The cotton is nowhere near picking time, and I have more than two hundred acres of corn that is not yet in full ear."

Maynard appeared displeased with the cleanliness of his spectacles and breathed onto the left lens and then the right one. "Miss Banks," he said, wiping the glass as though smudges were his sole interest, "I am aware that you have a lawyer in Charleston who handles your interests, but Charleston is a long way from here. If I may make a suggestion, *in loco parentis,* so to speak, I think you should sell White Pines."

Letty licked her dry lips. He had made his move at last. "How interesting that you should suggest it. I have been thinking of moving to Charleston. I have a distant cousin there who has offered me the protection of her home and family."

He smiled wide enough to reveal a missing bicuspid. "A wonderful plan, ma'am!"

She returned his smile. "Perhaps you know someone who wishes to buy my property?"

He shook his head. "Times are hard, Miss Banks, and money is dear. But I will keep my eyes open for you. You will, of course, wish to remove to Charleston as quickly as possible, so if you care to leave the selling of the property in my hands, I will insure—"

"Oh, I couldn't possibly leave until the property is sold, sir. My cousin plans to use my money to open a blacksmith shop."

The lawyer was visibly surprised. "A blacksmith shop! Two ladies? But how—"

"I will be taking the White Pines blacksmith with me. My father's will said I might choose one slave to remain with me."

Anger darkened his beady eyes. "I feel sure your father meant for you to choose some female."

"Is there some difficulty with my choice, Mr. Maynard? Perhaps I should contact my lawyer in Charleston. He could come here and handle everyth—"

"No, no, Miss Banks. I assure you there will be no need for that." He returned his spectacles to his vest pocket and rose. "If the blacksmith is your choice, then so be it. I will send you his papers when the wagons come tomorrow."

He stepped off the veranda into the yard. "If for some reason you should change your mind and wish to leave for Charleston immediately, my offer still stands to handle the sale of the plantation for you. I am at your service."

As soon as the lawyer left, Letty walked down to the blacksmith shed. Caleb looked up expectantly when she opened the door and released the mule's forefoot he held in his hand. He was putting fresh shoes on Jacob and Esau, the well-matched mule team whose existence Abner Banks had managed to conceal from the War Procurement Committee.

"It's done," she said. "He's sending your papers tomorrow."

Caleb closed his eyes, then leaned his forehead against

Esau's smooth withers. "Thank you, Jesus," he whispered. "Free at last."

"It was like you said. He wanted me to choose someone else."

He nodded. "A blacksmith brings a higher price than most."

Letty stepped close to him so she could speak quietly. "You know the state of Georgia won't let me set you free legally. Even if I gave you a Deed of Manumission, the first night rider who challenged your status could claim you as his own and sell you."

"I know won't nothing be legal till the Yankees come," he said. "Still, you done give me your word I'm a free man, and your word's good enough for me."

"Are you still with me on the plan? If you aren't, just say so. I'll understand."

"I done give you my word, child."

"I know, but you've had a couple of days to think about it. I suspect old Maynard will be sending me a buyer for White Pines any day now, and once I sell, I'll have some cash money. Enough money for us to travel to New Orleans and take a boat to Mexico. You could be legally free in Mexico."

He examined a rough spot on Esau's fetlock. "You know how to talk Mexican?"

She shook her head.

"Me, neither. We best stick with the plan we agreed on and let the Yankees take care of the legal part when they get to Georgia."

Stepping over to the anvil, he picked up the tongs that held Esau's new shoe. "I don't know nothing about Mexico. Me, I'm for the Ochlockonee."

They spoke for a few more minutes, then she told him she was going down to Sudy's cabin. "To get Ocilla's baby."

"About time," he said. Then without another word, he returned his attention to the mule.

Letty was more shaken by the walk past the row of cabins than she had imagined possible. Everyone knew of Ab-

ner's will, for she had sent Priam to inform them of the
facts the day the will was read. Because they knew they
would be uprooted soon, no one had gone to the fields the
past two days. People filled the porches and yards, visiting
and enjoying some unexpected time with their friends. She
didn't blame them for taking a little vacation, but knowing
the wagons were coming tomorrow, and not some day in
the distant future, she couldn't look anyone in the eye. She
felt both guilty and helpless.

She breathed easier when she spotted Sudy sitting on the
front stoop of her cabin, a child at either breast. An inveterate gossip, like her mother, Sudy was enjoying a visit
with one of the field women, but when Letty arrived, the
field woman nodded and went away.

"Afternoon, Miss Letty," Sudy said.

"Sudy."

She joined Sudy on the stoop, staring with amazement
at the enthusiasm of the two suckling infants. "They seem
to know what they're supposed to do."

At just that moment, Sudy's boy, a roly-poly lad of ten
months, let go of his mother's breast and vented a burp
worthy of a full-grown man. Both women laughed.

"This here young'un would eat all day long if'n I let
him," Sudy bragged.

She watched Sudy nuzzle her face against the boy's
thick, tight curls. He was a completely healthy baby, despite
his difficult birth, and his skin, though not as dark as
Sudy's, showed every indication of achieving that same
hue. By contrast, Ocilla's little girl, at about seven pounds,
looked pale and shriveled. Her head was covered with soft,
feathery wisps of fuzz, and her skin reminded Letty of a
pink-tinted, ivory cameo she'd worn when she was a child.

Letty lifted the newborn's hand and brought it to her lips.
The instant she released it, the arm curled back to the
baby's body. Intrigued, she repeated the act several times.
The baby hadn't been swaddled, so each time her little
tightly curled arm was stretched out and released, it immediately retracted to its fetal position.

After a moment she reached over and stroked the little

boy's straight, plump arm. She'd spent the first nine months of the boy's life sequestered with Ocilla, so she hadn't seen him grow. "He's a fine boy, Sudy. What did you name him?"

"I call him Henry." Sudy looked at the tiny girl at her breast. "What you fixing to call this little motherless baby?"

"I don't know. I haven't given it any thought." She reached down and gently extended the tiny arm again. The moment she let it go, it folded back to the baby's chest. She and Sudy both laughed.

"Know what she puts me in mind of, Miss Letty, her arms and legs all curled up that way?"

"Uh-uh, what?"

"She puts me in mind of one of them cinnamon ferns that grows down at the creek. You know the ones I'm talking about? They all tight curled when they new, and you can take your finger and uncurl 'em. But soon as you let go . . . p'toinngg . . . they all curled up again."

Letty stroked her finger across the little fist. "I believe you're right, Sudy."

"And her hair near 'bout the same color as them ferns, too. If she was my baby, Miss Letty, I reckon I'd call her Cinnamon."

Both babies finally suckled their fill and fell asleep. Assured of his mother's continued sustenance, Henry released his hold on Sudy's nipple and let his head fall to the side, his lips relaxed. Not so Ocilla's baby. She clung to the breast even though she slept, her lips making little pseudo sucking movements as though she needed more.

Letty watched the tiny lips pucker and relax and experienced a longing in her own bosom that was almost painful. Maternal possessiveness overcame her, and she reached down and lifted the sleeping infant out of Sudy's arms.

She cuddled the baby, its downy head close to her face, inhaling deeply. "Babies smell so good."

Sudy laughed. "Yes'm. Most of the time they do."

Letty smiled at the joke. "Well, this little cinnamon fern

smells wonderful, Sudy. I thank you for taking such good care of her.''

Balancing the baby in one arm, Letty reached inside her dress pocket and pulled out a small roll of Confederate graybacks tied in a white handkerchief. "This is for you," she said. "I wish it could be more."

At the sight of the money, Sudy's mouth dropped open, and while she was trying to frame words of thanks, Letty reached into the pocket again. This time she pressed something smooth and shiny into Sudy's hand. "And this is for Henry. It's my father's gold watch."

Sudy looked from the watch to Letty, then tears spilled down her cheeks. "I tell him you give it to him, Miss Letty. And I tell him how you keep him and me from dying the night he born." She snuffled, then dashed the back of her hand across her wet cheek. "I won't never forget about that, Miss Letty."

Letty took the woman's hand in hers. "There is one thing I would like you to forget, Sudy."

Brown eyes stared into blue eyes. "Yes'm."

"Will you forget all about Ocilla's baby? If anyone should ask what became of it, will you just say you have no idea?"

Sudy's eyes held a thousand questions, but she nodded her head in agreement. "I do that, Miss Letty. I forget all about her. Anybody ask me, I say I ain't never seen no baby. Don't you worry none, won't nobody hear about that little cinnamon fern from me. Not nobody. Not never."

Squeezing Sudy's hand, Letty mumbled something about sending someone for the cradle, then she hurried away before her own tears fell.

Since she didn't want to go back past all the other cabins, Letty followed a well-worn path that led from behind Sudy's cabin to the springhouse, where milk and butter were kept. She didn't let herself think of the birthday tea party Ocilla had planned for her at the springhouse; she thought only of the footpath that led from there back to the house.

As Letty walked carefully down the sloping terrain, she

felt the temperature drop. It was always cool at the spring-house because the creek flowed both above and below-ground, and because the trees grew so thick they formed a canopy of shade all summer long. To shield the baby from the unaccustomed coolness, Letty lifted the tail of her skirt and wrapped it around the sleeping infant; then, as she held the tiny body close, sweet, poignant memories of another baby tugged at her heart.

"Hello, Ocilla's little girl," she whispered, looking into the small, pink face.

Suddenly it seemed fitting that she and the baby should come to this place. Especially since she might never come this way again; might never again see the large, mossy boulder Ocilla used to climb to proclaim herself Queen of the World.

While Letty held this new baby close, she thought of all the things she had wanted for Ocilla, things her father had denied her for no other reason than spite. Resolutely she pushed thoughts of Abner Banks from her mind. She didn't want to think of him—not here, not now—not while she held Ocilla's child in her arms.

With a love she thought she would never feel again, she lifted the baby's tiny fingers to her lips. "Little angel, I'm going to give you everything I couldn't give Ocilla. And I'm going to keep you safe. I promise. No one will ever hurt you, not if I have to sleep with the Dragoon under my pillow for the next fifty years."

As she pondered the possibility of spending the rest of her life shooting at white men who thought they could do anything they wished with females of color, another possibility occurred to her. An idea so daring it left her panting as though she had run the distance from the cabins to this cool, verdant place.

There was a way to keep this baby safe, at least as safe as any white female, but only if Letty had the nerve to carry it through. She examined the little pink fist she still held in her hand. "And I do," she whispered, "I have the nerve!"

Once she'd voiced the words, all her fears vanished like night shadows before the sun, and her breathing resumed its normal rhythm. She felt confident. Never again would she wait passively while fate played cruel tricks on her. This time she had chosen her own destiny.

Kissing the little pink fist once more, Letty began the slow ascent toward the house. "Let's go home, little cinnamon fern," she said. "Your mama's got things to do."

Nine

"You'll have to step aside now, ma'am," the young wagon driver said. "I can't wait no longer."

Letty ignored the driver perched on the rough-hewn seat, the mules' reins held loosely between his supple fingers. She stared at Priam, or rather at the wrinkled hand she held in hers, the leathery knuckles gnarled with rheumatism and years of work. She kept her attention focused on his knuckles, for looking at the old man's face had proved too painful. Since he had climbed into the wagon, she had looked at him only once, and it had almost been her undoing.

She hadn't seen his eyes, only his profile. He'd held his head high and proud, but his chin had quivered uncontrollably while rivulets of tears stained the front of his best livery. Pain racked Letty's chest as though someone pounded it with a mallet.

"You got to let me go now, Miss Letty." Priam's voice was so soft she almost didn't hear it.

"Priam. I . . . I . . ."

The old man pulled his hand free of hers. "You go on back to the house now, you hear? I done fixed your dinner on a tray and left it on the——"

"Gee-yup!"

The driver cracked his whip in the air above the mules' heads, and the wagon wheels began to roll. Letty had to jump back to save her toes.

She followed the wagon down the carriageway to the gate, then watched until it was out of sight. Unwilling to leave the spot, she remained by the gate for more than an hour, until the last of the wagons had lumbered past her and turned onto the dirt road. Unshed tears nearly choked her. Saying goodbye to her lifetime companions—Minna, Verona, and especially Priam—had cost her more than she had imagined possible.

The final wagon turned the bend in the road and disappeared from sight, and in time even the squeaking sound of the axles faded into the distance. When nothing remained but wagon tracks in the dust, Letty turned and ran back up the carriageway. She had only one thought, holding little Fern to her heart for consolation.

When she reached the steps of the veranda, however, the *clippity clop* of hooves on the carriageway penetrated the noise of her sobs. Letty turned toward the sound. Someone tooled a horse and a bright yellow sporting buggy at a spanking pace, and though the man's ill-timed arrival was an affront to her loss, it was also a blessing. If not for the interruption, Letty might have cried herself sick. As it was, she was forced to pull herself together and focus her energy on dealing with whatever scalawag DuBose Maynard had sent.

Not for one instant did she doubt that the lawyer had sent the man, or that he had come to buy the plantation.

Schooling her features, she watched as the driver reined in a showy bay gelding, fitted his driving whip into the bracket, and stepped down from the buggy. Then while he turned his back to scotch the wheel, she quickly swiped the sleeve of her dress across her tear-stained face.

If the man noticed her tears, he gave no indication, but greeted her with overblown bonhomie and a smile that didn't quite reach his small, furtive eyes. "Afternoon, ma'am. Have I the pleasure of addressing Miss Banks?"

When she nodded, he removed his tan derby, revealing

wavy, orange hair turned brassy by the liberal application of Macassar oil.

Letty took him in instant dislike. From his grass-green and burnished-gold checked suit to his diamond pinkie ring, everything about his appearance repulsed her. Though probably not more than thirty-five, the man appeared older than his years, probably because of the deep grooves etched on either side of his mouth, plus the broken capillaries in his large nose.

Enduring fully five minutes of Mr. Dozier Braithwaite's commiserations on the loss of her father and the resulting loss of the luxurious lifestyle to which she was accustomed, Letty finally lost her patience and interrupted his soliloquy.

"Mr. Braithwaite, may we get to the point of your visit? I assume you have come to make me an offer for my plantation."

A look of cunning replaced his obsequious smile. "Well, now, Miss Banks, the gentleman I represent isn't all that sure he wants to buy White Pines. You may not appreciate it, but there are drawbacks to purchasing property at this time."

She waved him to silence. "Suppose we dispense with pussyfooting, sir. I realize that many people have been forced to economize. This war that was supposed to last only a few weeks has already lasted two years, and because of the war, money is scarce. Real money, that is; I understand that bogus money is flowing freely in these parts."

"I assure you, ma'am, the gentleman I represent—"

"And then there's the condition of my land. Though White Pines is good land, it has been worked for a number of years. Even so, we average twelve bushels of corn to the acre and five bales of cotton to the hand. With seven hundred and fifty acres under cultivation, the owner can expect—"

Braithwaite waved her to silence, his smile as oily as his hair. "You said five bales to the hand, Miss Banks. What hands might those be? The way I understand it, all you have here is a blacksmith."

Tears threatened Letty's composure at the recollection of

the wagons that had only just left White Pines.

"To be honest, ma'am, the lack of slaves is a major drawback. The gentleman I represent is worried he'll have trouble finding enough field hands to bring this place back into shape." Braithwaite hesitated a moment for effect. "Of course, if your asking price is reasonable, perhaps I can convince him to rethink his stand."

Letty wasn't fooled by the man's tactics. "We are pulling hen's teeth, sir. Do you or do you not have an offer for me? If you do, let's hear it now. If you don't, then I have work that needs my attention." Placing her hands on the arms of the rocking chair, she leaned forward as if ready to stand.

"The buyer says he'll go as high as five dollars an acre."

"Five dollars! Mr. Braithwaite, you must think me an idiot. That total wouldn't even cover the price of the house and its furnishings. Fifteen dollars an acre is a fair price for the land, and you know it. As for the hundreds of acres of cotton, corn, and other food crops still growing in the fields, I had hoped to strike a deal with the buyer to let him harvest the crops and split the net profits fifty-fifty with me."

Braithwaite leaned back in his chair and stretched his legs out in front of him. The tone of his voice was as insulting as his posture.

"The gentleman I represent has no slaves to harvest those crops you mentioned, so there wouldn't be any profits to split. And as for the house, he doesn't want it. It'll cost him extra to have it torn down. He plans to build a grand mansion a little farther back from the entrance gates. So you see, five dollars is a fair price after all."

To control her anger, Letty took a deep breath, then let it out quietly. The man really thought she was stupid enough to believe his story and hand him the land, the crops, and the house on a silver platter. "We obviously have nothing more to discuss, sir, so I'll bid you good day."

This time she stood up and walked to the door.

Braithwaite scrambled to his feet. "The buyer says not

a cent over ten dollars, and that's his final offer!''

She paused for a moment, then returned to the chair she'd just vacated. "No credit. The amount is to be paid in full, and I want the gold in my hands before I sign the papers."

"Gold!"

Braithwaite's assumed airs deserted him. "Listen here, girlie girl, ain't nobody said nothing about gold. The buyer would be dealing in graybacks. There ain't no gold to be had in these parts."

"But there is bogus paper currency to be had in these parts, sir. It's gold or nothing."

When he made no reply, she bid him good day and went inside the house. For good measure, she closed and locked the door until she heard him drive away.

As soon as the carriage passed through the gate, Letty went down to the blacksmith shed to talk to Caleb. With all the people gone, as well as their dogs and livestock, there was an eerie, ghostlike silence about the place. After her meeting with Braithwaite, Letty found the quiet nerve-wracking, making her want to look over her shoulder every few seconds.

She breathed a sigh of relief when Caleb opened the stable doors and stepped out into the late afternoon sunshine. "I heard him leave. He want to buy the place?"

"He wants to steal it."

Needing to give vent to her feelings, Letty paced back and forth. "He pretended it was worth less because his anonymous buyer would have to pay to have the house torn down. Like I didn't know that DuBose Maynard wouldn't tear this place down in a million years. Maynard has always wanted to move up in the world, and I'm sure he believes he'll be accepted by the planter families if he lives in an old, established plantation house."

"I think he already got the slaves."

She stopped in her tracks. "What do you mean?"

"You know them wagons that took everybody away?" He looked in the direction of the carriageway, almost as if he could still see the wagons. "Well, there was only four

of them. I studied 'em special. The same wagons kept load-
ing up and driving away, then coming back for another
load. Same wagons, different drivers.''

Letty didn't question his assessment. If Caleb said a thing
was true, it was true.

"Wagons is scarce. And mules is even scarcer.
Wouldn't've been nothing special about using the same
wagons over and over. But using different drivers was just
to make us think they was all different wagons, and that
they was going a long way off when they wasn't.''

"Where do you think they took everybody?"

"Don't know. The wagons didn't have time to get to
town and back, so they must be keeping everybody someplace close by.''

Letty thought about this for a moment. "It makes sense,
especially if my suspicions are correct and Maynard is the
mysterious Mr. Smith named in Papa's letter.''

She started pacing again. "He's trying to cheat me at
every turn. Braithwaite said the buyer wouldn't be able to
split the money from the sale of the crops because there
wasn't anyone to harvest them. But I'll bet the moment I
sell, he'll have the workers back in the fields so fast their
heads will swim.''

Caleb shifted his weight from one thin leg to the other.
"Why don't we just leave? Now.''

"Leave? And let those thieving vermin have the land,
the house, and my mother's beautiful things all for free?
Never! This is all Papa's doing; it's his final move in the
game, and I refuse to let him win it.''

For a few moments, Caleb studied a callus on the inside
of his thumb. "You mighty brave, child, don't nobody need
to tell me that, and you fought some mighty hard fights in
your life. But Marse Abner dead. He can't win nothing no
more. You the only one got anything to lose. You and that
little baby up at the house.'' He cleared his throat. "You
thought about what would happen if that lawyer was to
send them wagon drivers back here? Mayhap in the middle
of the night. Ain't nobody to stop them from killing us and
taking what they want.'' His next words were spoken

softly. "You willing to die just to prove something to a dead man?"

It was mid-morning the next day when Braithwaite returned. Letty had just fed the baby and put her in her crib when she heard the horse and buggy. She hurried down to the veranda.

Even before the man climbed down from the buggy, Letty smelled the Bay Rum. He had obviously discovered the location of the barbershop since yesterday's visit, because his orange hair looked cleaner, and his face appeared freshly shaven. Unfortunately he wore the same checked suit he'd worn yesterday and, if wrinkles were any proof, the same shirt. The combination of Bay Rum and stale sweat assailed Letty's nose as he approached the steps.

"I know you like plain speaking," he began, "so that's what I've come to give you. You want to sell this plantation, and the gentleman I represent wants to buy."

"Payment in gold," she stated.

"Payment in gold," he replied.

Without being invited, he stepped up onto the veranda and sat in the rocking chair he'd occupied the day before. "The thing is, Miss Banks, the gentleman can lay his hands on *some* gold, but nowhere near the amount you're asking."

As if to whet her appetite, Braithwaite took a twenty-dollar gold piece from his vest pocket and laid it on the backs of the fingers of his right hand. He let it sit there for a moment, its brilliance competing with the morning sun. Then without appearing to move his fingers, he made the coin travel from one finger to the next and back again. "Fourteen thousand dollars in gold. Whooee! Now that's a lot of gold."

"Fourteen hundred acres is a lot of plantation, Mr. Braithwaite. Not to mention a good, solid house. The furniture, the carpets, and the paintings all came from Europe and are worth several thousand dollars. I won't bore you with a catalog, but I assure you everything is of the finest, down to the sterling silver doorknobs."

"I already told you the buyer ain't interested in the house. And he ain't paying for something he don't plan to use."

It was all Letty could do not to reply. But she'd promised Caleb she wouldn't antagonize the man.

"And so," he continued, "since all the buyer wants is the land, and since he's probably the only man in these parts with the gold you require, I've come to make you another offer."

With amazing dexterity, he flipped the twenty-dollar gold piece into the air, caught it without looking, and put it back in his vest pocket. "Three thousand in gold for your land."

"Three thousand! You must be joking. That's just a little over two dollars an acre. Your final offer yesterday was for ten dollars an acre. What makes you think I would accept less today?"

Braithwaite brushed an imaginary piece of lint off the sleeve of his checkered coat. "The ten-dollar offer was in Confederate graybacks. In gold, the offer is three thousand. Take it or leave it."

A cold stare was her only answer.

After several moments of silence, he leaned toward her, his voice menacing. "If I was you, I would take the offer. Who knows what might happen?"

Licking his thin lips, he continued. "The papers are plumb full of stories about gangs of army deserters roaming the countryside looting and burning. And a fellow was telling me just the other day about a band of thieves who've been committing the kind of acts a man don't mention in front of a decent female."

He let his gaze slide over her from her shoulders to her knees. "Except for that blacksmith, you're all alone here. I think you'd be smart to get out while the getting's good."

Letty suppressed a shudder. At that moment she was more afraid of the man sitting on her veranda than the alleged bands of marauders. Listening to his thinly veiled threats, she wished for the Dragoon she hadn't seen since the day of Ocilla's funeral.

"I will think about your offer, Mr. Braithwaite."

"If I was you, I'd think real hard."

He stood up and set his derby on his orange locks, then he strolled out to his buggy and removed the scotch from beneath the wheel. "Yes, sirree," he said just loud enough for her to hear, "it would be a real shame if deserters should happen by this place."

Not wanting to give Braithwaite the satisfaction of knowing how his threats had disturbed her, she kept her face impassive while he turned the buggy and headed down the carriageway. Caleb had guessed correctly; these men would take the land by force if she put up too much resistance, and they wouldn't care who they hurt in the process.

As soon as the buggy was out of sight, she went inside the house to find the Dragoon. Although she wore the revolver the rest of that day, it did her little good late that night when the acrid smell of smoke filled her senses and roused her from a fitful sleep. Her heart pounding with fear, she threw the mosquito netting aside and ran to the bedroom window.

A full moon revealed the stable and blacksmith shed to her left. They were intact. Trees and darkness obscured everything else, but she scanned the distance in the general direction of the cabins. Just beyond the cabins, not too far from the cotton house and the gin, she saw the glow of fire. Its source was the corncrib.

The pounding in Letty's chest eased somewhat. Since the corn crib held only a small amount of seed corn left over from last year's crop, its loss was of minor importance; however, any fire was a serious threat, endangering the remaining buildings as well as the crops in the fields.

Quickly she stuffed her feet into her boots then grabbed the Dragoon and sped into the hallway and down the steps. With no time to adjust the wide leather of the holster so it would stay around her hips, she put her head and one arm through it and wore it across her chest like a sash. The sheathed revolver slapped against her side as she ran across the lawn.

By the time she got to the crib it was gone, consumed

by the fire. Nothing was left but charred wood, ashes, and the sickening smell of smoke.

Caleb was already there. He had tried to fight the blaze with a shovel, but it had been too much for him. Now he leaned against a pine tree, coughing and sputtering from inhaled smoke. While he caught his breath, Letty took the shovel and beat out the few remaining embers. When she was satisfied that no threatening spark remained, she joined Caleb by the tree. They stood silently, staring at the destruction.

"Could it have been an accident?" she asked finally. "Lightning, maybe?"

He looked up at the clear, star-filled sky. Without answering her question, he reclaimed the shovel and went back to the rubble. Circling it slowly, he poked at pieces of wood and mounds of ash as though looking for something. At one such mound he found what he was looking for. Carefully he scooped up something in the shovel, then brought it out into the moonlight and dumped it on the ground near her feet. "There's your lightning."

Letty bent forward to examine the still-smoldering object. "It's just an old jug of some kind. I don't—"

"It's a kerosene jug. They sell 'em like that at the mercantile in town."

Anger almost choked her. "Kerosene! Then someone did this. And they didn't even try to hide it."

"I 'spect they left the jug on purpose so we'd find it. They wanted you to know they set the fire. This here was a warning."

"It's extortion! It's . . . it's . . ." The heat of her fury burned like the flames that had consumed the crib, and Letty grabbed the shovel and struck the jug with all her might, shattering it into a dozen pieces. Still angry, she smashed the pieces again and again until nothing remained of them but minute bits of pottery and dust. Finally, her rage spent and her breath coming in gasps, she tossed the shovel to the ground.

She wiped her sooty hands down the sides of her sweat-soaked nightgown. "They just *had* to threaten me! They just had to show me who was boss, try to force me to knuckle under.''

"Weasels always act like weasels, child. They don't know no other way."

"But I had already decided to do as you suggested. I meant to tell you in the morning to start packing the wagon, that I was ready to leave. Ready to just drive away. They could have had everything, the entire place, for nothing.''

Letty stared at the charred remains of the corncrib, and as she looked at the destruction, her hot anger cooled into resolve. She adjusted the holster that circled her torso; her fingers touched the handle of the Dragoon. ''But they can't have it now. They went too far! I've been bullied enough for one lifetime.''

"What you fixing to do?''

She turned to look at him. ''Do? I'm going to show them they can't—'' The words died on her lips. ''Caleb! Your hands! You've been burned.''

Twenty minutes later, Caleb sat at the table in the butler's pantry, sipping from a steaming cup. Letty had brewed him a tisane of goldenrod and betony with honey to soothe his smoke-irritated throat, and while he held the cup with one hand, she dabbed a salve of Balm of Gilead on the back of his other hand. Her face was stony. Caleb wasn't burned as badly as she had feared, just a few spots on his hands, but she felt guilty that he had been hurt when it was her DuBose Maynard had meant to frighten.

She looked at the soot that still clung to his hair and clothes. ''I'm so sorry.''

"Don't pay it no mind, child. I been hurt worse than this lots of times.''

"I know that. But you shouldn't have to pay the price for my pigheadedness.''

"Mayhap I'm paying my own price.'' He set his cup down on the table. ''Mayhap I been bullied enough for one lifetime, too.''

While Letty considered his words, she reached for her herb box. She closed the small salve pot and fitted it into the metal tray with its twelve cut-out circles and its twelve hand-painted pots—the birthday gift Ocilla never got to present to her—then she pushed the box to the other side of the table.

She pulled out a chair and sat down so that she could look Caleb directly in the eyes. "Are you sure? Is half a farm on the Ochlockonee truly worth the risk we'll be taking?"

Caleb didn't answer her right away, and when he did speak, it wasn't what she had expected to hear. "I was born on a plantation," he said. "The same one where my mama was born and her mama before that. Everybody on the place born on that plantation or some plantation just like it. Everybody 'cept for one old man."

He studied the salve that glistened on the back of his hand. "When I was a boy, that old man used to tell me stories about where he come from. It was someplace a long ways off, and I done forgot the name he called it, but it wasn't a plantation. He wasn't born a slave. He was born free."

Caleb pulled a piece of ragged cloth out of his pocket and wiped some soot off his palms. " 'Course that old man wasn't free no more, he was a slave same as all the rest of us. Only he wasn't like the rest of us. Somebody'd give him whippings aplenty, you could tell that from his back, but they hadn't ever been able to make him knuckle under.

"In that old man's heart he was still a free man. In his head he knew there was that far-off place that belonged to him, the place where he belonged. He was an old man, been a slave a long time, but he hadn't forgot his real home and he hadn't forgot how it felt to be free. Couldn't nobody take that away from him."

In all the years she'd known him, Letty had never heard Caleb say so much all at one time. As he talked, she studied his face; she could tell it was important to him that she understand his feelings.

"Before I die," he said, "I want to feel what that old man felt. I want to feel what it's like to be free. And I want to have a home. A place that belongs to me. You offered me that, and I ain't letting some bullying white trash take it away from me. Not without a fight, I ain't.''

He shoved the ragged cloth back into his pocket. "I'm still for the Ochlockonee, child, so let's start planning what we do next.''

Neither of them slept any part of what remained of that night; they were too busy. They had things to do and little time in which to do them.

The first thing Caleb did was take the sturdiest of the two farm wagons to his blacksmith shed and examine all its metal parts for flaws. Once he was certain the parts were in good repair, he transferred the wagon to the stable, shut the door where he couldn't be seen, then used the lumber he kept for coffins and plantation repairs to build up the sides of the wagon.

While he worked in the stable, Letty went through every room of the house choosing the items they would take with them. The selection proved more difficult than she had imagined. Even a wagon with built-up sides could hold only so much. There was no room for sentimentality; they could take only those things needed for the job of living.

Letty dared not look at her mother's portrait—that study in blue and magnolia white that hung over the dining room mantel—so she went immediately to her father's library. She climbed the ladder to the topmost shelf and pulled down all Abner's childhood schoolbooks. To that dusty pile she added a book on animal husbandry, one on agriculture, one on Georgia wildlife and flora, an instructor in cooking and housewifery, *Green's Almanac*, the Bible, and finally a collection of the works of William Shakespeare.

From the bedrooms she gathered a minimal amount of linens and quilts and some of Ocilla's old baby clothes for Fern. Any small items of value, such as her father's silver letter opener and his gold cigar scissors—items she might use in lieu of money—she put in her sewing basket.

In the parlor she paused beside the beautiful clavichord with its inlaid front panel, where, for a moment, she recalled the afternoon she'd played for Thorn Bradley and

Drew Holden. It had been a happy afternoon. Letty remembered laughing. Opening the instrument, she brushed her fingers over its sensitive keys, filling the room with a soft chordal hum. But as soon as the hum faded into oblivion, she closed the lid forever. There was no room for clavichords, family portraits, oriental carpets, silver epergnes, or any of the accoutrements of the old lifestyle.

"We can't eat clavichords," she said with a sigh, "and we need the space for the chickens."

After her perusal of the rooms, she went out back to the cookhouse where she chose a few utensils. Beneath the cookhouse was the root cellar, and from that cool storage place she removed piggins of onions and carrots and buckets filled with yams and turnips. The vegetables were of twofold value: She and Caleb would eat them during their first weeks on the Ochlockonee, then at the proper time they would plant the slips they'd saved in their new garden.

At daybreak Caleb closed and locked the stable to conceal the loaded wagon. Then, while he hitched one of the mules to the spare wagon, Letty returned to the main house to get ready for the trip to town where she would carry out the plans they had made several hours earlier while they sat at the table in the pantry.

"Three thousand dollars is a lot of gold," Caleb had said, a worried look on his face. "What if that lawyer don't really mean to give it to you? Could be another one of his tricks. Once you sign the deed, what's to keep him from shooting you right there in his office?"

"I think he'll have to let me leave the office, because other people will know I've been there. But you're right about his tricks. My guess is he'll send some of his men to waylay me on the road and steal the gold; that way he'd be in the clear."

Since waylaying her seemed the likeliest scheme, she and Caleb devised a plan of their own. To carry out that plan, however, she needed a special article of clothing.

Once she fed and changed Fern, then laid the baby back in the pecan cradle, Letty walked over to her own bed where she'd left her sewing basket, one of Abner's vests, and five neatly cut strips of velvet. The strips—each thirty inches long and two inches wide—had been cut from an old dress of her mother's, and now she positioned them on the back panel of the vest.

Laying each strip horizontally, she sewed only the bottoms. The tops were left open. When all five strips were in place, Letty made vertical stitches across each of them at two-inch intervals. After she double-looped the last stitch and snipped the thread with her embroidery scissors, the result was a vest with seventy-five miniature velvet pockets.

With no time to waste admiring her handiwork, she stepped out of her blue gingham dress, tossed it across the room, then reached for the gray chambray skirt she'd laid at the foot of the four-poster. It being almost June, she knew she would swelter if she wore anything as concealing as a cape, so she'd chosen the chambray with its full skirt and jacket bodice.

As a concession to common sense, she wore only one starched lawn petticoat over her pantaloons, corset, and chemise. And in the place of the under-bodice she usually wore beneath the jacket, she substituted the vest with the seventy-five velvet pockets.

She'd just fastened the last of the tiny, pearl buttons that ran from the jacket's snug collar down to its softly flounced peplum when she heard Caleb drive the wagon to the veranda steps. She checked herself in the looking glass to make certain the vest with its velvet pockets was undetectable beneath the jacket, then she set a simple, outmoded straw hat over her braids and tied it beneath her chin with a gray, satin bow. She carried neither parasol nor purse, only the deed to White Pines.

After one last peek at the sleeping infant, she hurried down the front steps to the veranda where Caleb waited beside the wagon. "Fern should sleep at least another hour, but if she should wake before I—"

"Time's a wasting, child."

Nodding her agreement, she let him hand her into the

wagon; then she put the deed beneath her on the weathered seat and picked up the reins. "Giddyup, Esau," she called to the mule. "Let's see if one of us remembers the way to town."

Ten

DuBose Maynard showed no surprise at Letty's sudden appearance, but ushered her into his office and offered her the visitor's chair that faced his massive, leather-covered desk. "How may I help you, Miss Banks?"

Refusing to dignify the charade of an unnamed buyer, Letty asked him outright if he still wanted White Pines at three thousand dollars gold.

Silently the lawyer opened his desk drawer, withdrew two copies of a purchasing agreement, and handed them to her. "The papers are filled in, they need only your signature."

While she read through the document, Maynard opened the door and motioned to someone across the street. In less than a minute Dozier Braithwaite entered the room followed by a nervous little man who carried an oversized ledger beneath his arm. Braithwaite carried a small, red-and-brown carpetbag. Neither man acknowledged Letty's presence, so after giving them the briefest of looks, she returned her attention to the papers in her hand.

"Mr. Maynard," she said, placing the document on the desk, "I want to be certain I understand this correctly. The three thousand dollars you are offering me is for the purchase of the land only. The agreement says nothing about paying me for my house and its furnishings. Nor is there any mention of compensating me for the crops in the fields.''

"That is correct, Miss Banks, I pay only for the land.''

Pushing the document across the desk to him, she said, "There at the bottom—where it says 'For the property known as White Pines'—please write in 'no improvements and no crops.' ''

Dozier Braithwaite sucked in his breath as if about to say something, but Maynard shook his head.

"An odd rider, to be sure, Miss Banks. Have you a reason for wanting it added?''

Letty opened her eyes wide, in what she hoped would pass for naïveté. "The day you read my father's will, sir, you gave me a piece of advice. You told me there was a right way and a wrong way to do everything. I am merely taking your advice.''

Without another word, the lawyer wrote the phrase she'd asked for on both copies and handed the document back to her. She took the quill he offered and signed Caroline L. Banks in the places he indicated.

"Mr. Braithwaite will sign as witness,'' he said, "then the county clerk can record the sale.''

While Braithwaite labored over his signature as witness, Letty turned to look at the little man who sat in the corner, the oversized ledger resting on his knobby knees. Now she understood why he was there; he was the county clerk.

DuBose Maynard took the signed documents, put one in his desk drawer and handed the other to Letty. "Now all we need, ma'am, is the deed.''

"I stipulated money up front, Mr. Maynard. I'll count the gold before I hand over the deed.''

"But of course,'' he answered.

Braithwaite set the carpetbag he'd brought with him on the desk and withdrew a tin box from its depths. The box contained twenty-dollar gold pieces, which he counted out fifteen at a time and stacked in neat, even columns. The county clerk's eyes grew more owlish as the columns grew.

"Three thousand," Braithwaite announced as he placed the final coin on the tenth stack. "Test 'em if you like."

His invitation may or may not have been serious, but Letty had every intention of checking the coins. She was no more interested in bogus gold than in bogus paper money. Removing her gloves, she chose several coins at random, and scraped her fingernail across their surfaces to make certain the coins were real gold and not brass plugs dipped in gold paint.

Satisfied the coins were genuine, she asked Braithwaite if he would lend her his tin box. "As you see, I have forgotten to bring a purse with me. I have nothing to carry the money in."

"Take the carpetbag, too," he offered, making her an exaggerated bow, "if you have need of it. Or better still, I'll carry it out to your wagon for you."

"Don't bother. I'm taking the money straight to the bank."

"Bank!" Braithwaite looked like a fox who'd found the chicken coop locked.

"Yes, sir. I wouldn't dream of taking so much money home with me. Not after all those stories you told me about deserters and bandits roaming the woods. I was so frightened by what you said that I decided to leave the gold in the bank overnight and retrieve it tomorrow before I leave for Charleston. I'll rest easier knowing it's safe in the bank strongbox. That way I can spend all my time deciding which of my clothes and personal mementos I want to pack on the wagon. I should be back in town shortly after the bank opens tomorrow."

Braithwaite's eyes darkened with malice, but after a few moments, moments in which Letty could almost see his brain concocting a new scheme, he forced the unctuous tone back into his voice. "A wise move, ma'am. A lady can't be too careful."

Maynard jerked his head toward the door. At the unspoken order, the nervous little man took his oversized ledger and scurried out of the office. When the door was shut, the lawyer stepped forward and held his hand out to Letty. "I probably won't see you again, ma'am, so my best wishes for a good life in Charleston.''

She ignored the hand he offered. "I have one more piece of business, sir. It concerns the property my father left me—the hunting lodge on the Ochlockonee River. I've sold the lodge and its sixty-five acres to a business associate of my grandfather's, and he wants proof of ownership. Unfortunately, I can't find the deed among my father's papers. What should I do?''

The lawyer sat back down at his desk, then rolled his chair back a few feet and turned to search through the wooden cabinet behind his chair. In less than a minute he had Abner's will in front of him. On a clean piece of paper he copied the legal description of the property, then wrote a note at the bottom of the page stating the date of the will and the names of the witnesses.

He handed the paper to her. "You should have said something before the county clerk left. He'll have to affix the proper stamps to make this legal.''

"That's all right. I'll go by his office after I finish at the bank.''

The lawyer escorted Letty to the door, mumbled some platitude about her new life in Charleston, then more or less pushed her out of his office. She heard him lock the door behind her.

Out on the scarred and much-spat-upon boardwalk, she stood alone, clutching the tin box to her bosom. Aware of the vulnerability of her position, she hesitated only a moment before dashing across the manure-strewn street to the single-story, redbrick bank building.

Letty showed the tin box to the bank clerk, a slim gentleman not yet old enough for service in the Army of the Confederacy, and explained to him that she wished to leave the box in the bank's safe for one night. "I'll be happy to pay whatever the fee is for such a service.''

Before the lad could state the fee, however, she raised her hand to her forehead. With a soft moan, she swayed forward, grasping the mahogany partition that divided the public area from the area off limits to all but employees.

"Ohhh," she cried pitifully, "I think I'm about to faint."

The young clerk left his post and ran around the partition to offer her his arm. "Please, ma'am, don't faint. I'm all alone here. Maybe you'd like to sit down on the divan, it's very comfortable."

She waved the suggestion away. Rolling her eyes up under her lids, she asked if there wasn't some place she could have a moment of privacy. "Any place will do. A cloak closet, a storeroom. Ohhh!"

Her renewed moans spurred the clerk to suggest the small box room where he ate his noon meal.

"Yes, please," she muttered weakly.

Accepting the support of the frightened lad's arm, she leaned on him, letting him lead her to the airless cubicle. As soon as he closed the door to give her privacy, however, her health returned miraculously. She listened at the door to make certain he had returned to his place behind the mahogany petition, then she set the tin of gold coins on an upturned box.

She lost no time in unfastening the buttons of her gray chambray jacket, peeling it off, and dropping it to the floor. Next she removed the vest and stretched it out flat beside the tin box. As quickly as possible, she slipped the coins two at a time into the miniature velvet pockets of the vest.

When all but three of the coins were tucked inside the quiet velvet, Letty lifted the vest carefully and slipped it back on. It weighed about nine pounds, but to her nerve-wracked body, it felt more like ninety.

She had just secured the last of the tiny pearl buttons on the jacket when the clerk knocked at the door.

"Ma'am," he called, "may I offer you a cup of well water?"

Five minutes later the empty tin box lay inside the bank's safe. Letty paid one dollar for the banking privilege. The nineteen graybacks she received in change from the gold piece she stuffed inside her half boot, and the two remaining gold coins she slipped inside her glove.

From the bank she went directly to the county clerk's office just two doors down. The clerk didn't hear her come in. He sat on the office's one stool, his back to the door, and wrote in a small ledger. As he reached across the table to dip his stylus in the ink pot, his oilcloth sleeve protector slipped down on his arm and almost tipped over the ink.

"Dammit!"

Letty cleared her throat before he could say more.

At the sound, the clerk nearly fell off the stool. "How long you been standing there?"

She forced her lips into a smile. It would not serve her purpose to make the clerk angry; he might question the validity of the paper the lawyer had written out for her and refuse to record the sale until he could check it out.

Stepping forward, she placed the paper on his worktable, then laid one of her twenty-dollar gold pieces next to it. The man's eyes lit up as they had in the lawyer's office.

She edged the coin an inch closer to him. "I need to record the sale of this property, and I'm willing to pay extra to have it done while I wait."

The clerk picked up the paper and scanned the writing, then from under his table he lifted the oversized ledger he'd written in before. He placed the large ledger on top of the small one and opened it to the appropriate page. As he recorded the information from her paper, he kept glancing back at the gold piece.

"I need the name of the purchaser," he said.

"Monsieur V. de Bonheur and wife."

He made the proper entries in his book, then wrote across the bottom of her paper, *Foregoing conveyance herewith grants, bargains, and sells to V. de Bonheur and wife, to have and to hold for their heirs and assigns.*

When he finished writing, he folded the paper and affixed four half-dollar conveyance stamps on the blank side, then wrote his name and the date across them. He held it out to her. "There you go, all right and tight."

Letty pushed the gold piece toward him. "I don't have any Confederate money, sir. I hope this gold coin will do."

As though he'd just been offered something juicy and delicious, the little man licked his lips. "Yes, ma'am. Gold is fine, just fine." He lowered his voice. "I haven't seen gold since before the war began." He touched the coin to his tongue, then smiled. "It's real all right. No bitter, brassy taste."

She lowered her voice as he had done. "Gold makes me nervous. I'm afraid to show it around, afraid of what might happen if the wrong kind of people found out I have it. I prefer paper money that I can take out a dollar at a time." She looked over her shoulder then lowered her voice even more. "When I took my other coins to the bank, I forgot to ask the clerk to swap me some for paper money. I've still got one coin left."

The man caught his breath; a nervous tic pulsed just below his right eye. "I'll be happy to change it for you, ma'am."

He reached into his pocket and removed a clip containing a mixture of Confederate and railroad bills. While he counted out twenty bills, Letty peeled her glove back and withdrew the last of her three coins.

After she slipped the paper money inside her other half boot, she picked up her legally recorded and stamped proof of ownership, thanked the clerk, then left the office. As she climbed into the wagon, she breathed a sigh of relief.

Everything was going just as she had planned. She had changed the name of the owner of the property on the Ochlockonee River, and she had managed to get almost forty dollars in paper money so she wouldn't leave a trail of gold coins for anyone to follow. Although she was sweating profusely from the weight of her golden vest, Letty smiled as she turned the mule in the direction of White Pines.

She and Caleb waited only until it was dark, then they stowed the last of the items on the built-up wagon. To the things they'd loaded the evening before, they added thirty yards of osnaburg, the best plow, a grindstone, and as many of the smithing and carpentry tools as they could wedge into the nooks and crannies. Finally they loaded a crate containing five hens and a rooster, plus a slender, flat crate that held Letty's herb plants.

Caleb hitched Esau and Jake to the wagon, tied the cow securely to the back, then drove into the woods about four miles from the house. At a sheltered area, he secured the wagon, then returned to the house by the same route he'd taken, using a brush broom to obliterate the trail left by the wheels.

Letty waited for him on the front veranda, the baby asleep in her arms. "I don't know why I didn't think of this before, Caleb, but if you'd like, you can go through my father's closet and see if there's anything in there you want."

He stayed upstairs only a few minutes, and when he came down he wore Abner's heavy hunting boots, some black britches, and a brown felt hat. Across his arm he carried a wool hunting coat. He also carried a rifle.

"You take Fern," he said, taking her arm and helping her down the steps, "and start walking to the wagon. Don't look back. And don't wait for me. I'll do what's got to be done here, then catch up with you."

Readily agreeing, Letty shifted Fern more comfortably in her arms, then walked across the lawn toward the pine bark path. Though the moon was full and bright, she didn't need its light to show her the way down the familiar path to the stable and blacksmith's shed. As she cut across the pasture behind the stable, she looked straight ahead, not even allowing herself one last glance toward the knoll where her beloved Ocilla lay beneath a blanket of fragrant, purple thrift.

Five minutes later Caleb caught up with her. He had run the distance, so his breathing was ragged, but he shifted the coat and rifle to his right arm and took the baby from her so she could walk faster. They walked swiftly and word-lessly. Neither of them looked back, but somehow they knew when the first of the flames began licking their way up the inside walls of the house.

"What about the cotton fields?" she asked.

"I soaked 'em good this afternoon. They'll catch soon as the sparks start flying."

"And the kerosene jugs?"

"I done just like you said. I left the jugs out in plain sight, where old Maynard would be sure to find 'em."

Eleven

Caleb shifted his weight on the hard plank wagon seat. They had traveled all of last night and most of the day, and now, after a short rest in a heavily wooded area, they were traveling again. His muscles felt as stiff as the plank beneath him, and the cool evening air he had welcomed after the hot June day had changed from refreshing to downright chilling. To add to his discomfort, the dew was settling on his clothes.

If he was feeling tired, he reckoned Miss Letty must be exhausted, for she'd had the baby in her arms for most of the day. A few moments ago she had put the little one in the crib, and now she was leaning forward as far as she could with her arms stretched out in front of her.

"It's no good," she said. "No matter how I twist, there is no way to ease the muscles in my back. And I think my tailbone has fused permanently with this board."

Muttering something that sounded like an answer but really wasn't, Caleb clicked his tongue to encourage Esau and Jake to keep moving.

He felt her looking at him. "Sorry, Caleb. I know I shouldn't complain. You have traveled every mile I've traveled and must be every bit as tired. In addition, you must be heartily sick of struggling with those cantankerous mules.''

"They ain't used to traveling at night, is all.''

"You're defending them? I don't believe it. Not half an hour ago I heard you refer to them as a pair of devil spawn.''

"Was that only a half hour ago?''

He heard her chuckle softly. Unfortunately her amusement vanished all too quickly as she shifted her weight from one buttock to the other, trying for a more comfortable position. "How much farther do you think it is?''

"I ain't persackly. It's been five years or more since Marse Abner took me down to the lodge to fix the shingles on the roof. And we didn't travel through the woods that time.''

Having exhausted that subject, they rode in silence for a while. Something was fretting her; he knew that because she was sucking on the side of her bottom lip. She used to do that when she was a little girl and couldn't figure something out. "You ain't worrying about that scallywag Braithwaite catching up with us, are you, child?''

"Braithwaite? No. If he's fool enough to follow us and try to mess up our new lives, I'll just have to shoot him. I'm done forever with letting men get away with anything they want. If he comes, he dies.''

Caleb didn't bat an eye. "If that ain't it, then what you thinking about? You got so much busy stuff going on inside your head, it's practically dribbling out your ears.''

"You know me too well, old friend. I was thinking about my name.''

"The old name or the new one?''

"The new one. The more I think about it, the more I realize that Madame Violette de Bonheur is more name than I care to spend the next forty or fifty years with. Which is unfortunate. Since that is the name on the ownership papers for the lodge, I am more or less stuck with it.''

"So what you fixing to do about it?''

"I was thinking maybe I could shorten it a bit. If anyone should ask, I could say that after my husband died, I decided to use an American pronunciation. That way, if either you or I stumble over the name, we'll have a ready excuse.''

She cleared her throat, then said the name as though she were introducing herself to someone. ''Hello, I am Violet Bonner. *Mrs*. Violet Bonner.''

At just that moment, as though she had spoken to him, a horned owl perched in a tree just ahead of them barked, *Who, hoo-hoo, whoo, whoo?* For some reason, that struck Caleb as unbelievably funny, and he laughed till he thought his sides would burst.

Joining in the fun, Letty replied as though answering the owl's question. ''I said I am Mrs. Violet Bonner.''

Whoo, hoo-hoo, whoo, whoo?

This time they both laughed, and as Caleb listened to her soft chuckle, he thought how good it was to hear her laugh again after all the tears she'd shed these last few weeks. Not that he'd actually seen her cry, of course, that wasn't her way. But he knew she had. He'd seen her eyes all red and puffy in the mornings and after she'd come back from planting the flowers on Ocilla's grave. She was a strong wom—

''. . . So, of course, when my little girl and I left Savannah, I—''

Help me, sweet Jesus! What was she saying? He hoped he hadn't heard her right. ''What was that again?''

''I was practicing my story. I was saying that after my husband's death, I decided to bring my little girl to the Ochlockonee to get away from the threat of war. And that's why we—''

''*Your* little girl?''

''*My* little girl.''

''Surely you ain't fixing to pass Fern off as—''

''As Fern Bonner,'' she said, the tone of her voice telling him she'd made up her mind on the subject some time ago. ''Fern is the image of her father, Monsieur Verne de Bonheur,'' she continued, picking up the threads of her story. ''Monsieur de Bonheur was French Creole. Originally from New Orleans. Fern gets her chin from my side of the family, but she gets her coloring from the de Bonheurs.''

As her words floated past him, Caleb felt an almost over-whelming sadness. There was an emptiness inside his chest; it felt hollow, like somebody had stolen something important out of there while he'd been asleep and couldn't defend himself. And he felt confused, for the thief was his only friend in the world, the last person he would have suspected.

''Creoles,'' she continued, ''are usually darker than those of us of English or Scottish ancestry.''

He wished she would just hush. He didn't want to hear this story she was so proud of inventing. Of course, it wasn't his place to tell her what to do with the child, but this plan stole some of the joy out of their new beginning. She'd told so many lies, necessary lies, lies that couldn't be helped, and he'd been proud of her for it. He'd been proud of the way she fought back and fooled all those would-be cheaters.

But this lie was different. In a way he couldn't put into words, this lie robbed him of something. He'd expected better from her.

As she continued to talk, he concentrated on the reins he held between his hands, and though he tried to stop his ears from hearing, they wouldn't cooperate. In time, she finally hushed, yet the hollow feeling in his chest remained, and every so often he was obliged to swallow a lump that kept creeping up into his throat.

The silence stretched between them with only the chirping of the crickets and the occasional call of a night bird to fill the void. It was a strained silence. And Caleb was almost glad when they came to a shallow creek and the weary Jake balked, braying loud enough to reveal their whereabouts for miles in any direction.

Gratefully Caleb climbed down from the wagon, caught Jake by the cheek strap, and alternately yanked and pulled the team through the water. Once they were on the other side of the creek, he led the mules for a longer distance than was necessary. He needed to be alone.

Some time later, when he got back up on the wagon and

took the reins, he'd come to terms with the subject of Fern's supposed ancestry. He didn't like it, but decisions about the child weren't his to make.

"I been thinking," he said quietly, "about getting me a new name. Caleb's a slave name. Marse Abner give it to me, and I want to get shed of it."

"Good idea."

Letty cleared a frog out of her throat, more grateful than she could say for Caleb's olive branch. She had been dreading telling him of her decision about Fern, but it was only after she began to speak that she realized why she had dreaded it. That awful, awful silence. It didn't matter that she hadn't meant to hurt him. She'd done it. And like so many things in life, once done, it couldn't be undone.

Since she couldn't make herself look at Caleb, she concentrated instead on Esau's broad rump. She watched the moonlight shine through the leaves of the trees, making mottled patterns on the mule's backside, patterns that danced and changed as he clumped over the rough ground.

"Do you have a name in mind?" she asked.

He shook his head. "I don't know no names. But I think I'd like one that belonged to a hero. You know any hero names?"

After a few moments of thought she said, "Georgia was settled by men and women who came here under the leadership of General James Oglethorpe, I guess he would qualify as a hero. How about James?"

"No. I don't hanker for no white man's name. Even if he was a hero."

"Of course." Letty took the rebuff; she figured she'd earned it and then some.

"Ain't there no colored heroes? There's lots of colored folks. Surely one of them was a hero."

"I am sure lots of Negroes have been heroes, Caleb. Unfortunately white men write the history books. Negroes, Indians, women, if any of them do something heroic, I reckon the men who write the books just leave it out."

"Hmm."

The subject was momentarily dropped when Caleb said

he felt certain the path to the lodge was close by. Yet, even while they busied themselves searching the overgrown area on both sides of the wagon for signs of the path, Letty mentally searched her limited knowledge of history for a Negro hero.

All of a sudden she snapped her fingers. "I've got it! I do know a hero. He is in a play written by William Shakespeare." She jerked her head toward the wagon bed. "In fact, that very play is in one of the books I packed in the wagon. The man's name was Othello, and they called him the Moor of Venice. According to the story, Othello was a black man."

Caleb mouthed the name silently a few times, then he said it softly. "Othello. Othello."

"Well? What do you think"

"It slips off the tongue easy enough. Othello," he repeated, "Othello Moor. Yes, it's a good name. I could be Othello Moor." He paused, staring at her as if to assure himself that she was being totally honest with him. "You sure he was a hero?"

"Positive. He was a great warrior, and he conquered somebody or other with a fleet of ships. I don't remember exactly who, but I can look it up. Maybe you would like to hear the entire story."

When he nodded, she continued with the few facts she remembered. "The people Othello saved couldn't do enough to show their gratitude. Fine clothes, a big house, they lavished gifts of every kind upon him. Finally they made him their ruler and let him marry the prettiest lady in the land."

Caleb laughed deep in his chest.

She laughed, too. "What?"

"With these gray hairs starting to come in my head, ain't nobody fixing to give me the prettiest lady in the land!"

"Oh, I don't know about that." She studied him for a moment. "How old are you, Ca—I mean, Othello?"

He shrugged his bony shoulders. "Nobody never told me. Mayhap nobody knew. When Marse Abner bought me and took me to White Pines, I was near about as tall as I am now, but I hadn't started growing whiskers yet. You was just a baby then, not even old enough to walk.''

For a moment she pondered the puzzle. ''I'm no expert on men's whiskers, but I don't believe anybody could grow as tall as you in less than fourteen or fifteen years. Since I will be thirty-one in a couple of months, that would mean you are somewhere around forty-five, give or take a smidgen. That's not too old. You still might find a woman who would appreciate . . .''

She let her voice trail off as Caleb reined in the plodding mules, who obeyed gladly.

Slowly he climbed down from the wagon, his pace not unlike that of the tired mules. First he looked closely at the ground, then after walking forward several yards, he looked again. The night sky had already begun its transition from black to blue, and in its pale light she saw him prod a clump of weeds with the toe of his boot, then walk a little farther.

''Miss Letty,'' he called, causing some nearby night creature to squeal its protest before scurrying noisily through the brush. ''It's all growed over with weeds and scrub, but I think this is the path.''

After giving it one last, cursory examination, Caleb walked back to the wagon. ''Yes, ma'am,'' he said, his voice and bearing suddenly charged with renewed vigor. ''This is it!''

His excitement was contagious; it swept away Letty's own fatigue, prompting her to sit up straight, energized at the thought of nearing her new home. As the wagon began to roll again, even Jake and Esau seemed to move at a spryer pace.

Looking all about her at the thick, wild vegetation, Letty inhaled deeply, savoring the heady aroma of the moist, rich soil. ''Smell that? That's the smell of fertile land. I can't wait to feel it in my hands.''

''Them two devil spawn,'' he said, pointing his finger at the mules, ''they smelling the river.'' He clicked encouragement to the mules. ''Go find it, boys.''

A few moments later Caleb breathed deeply as she had done. ''Me, I smell trees. They's all kinds of trees here, hardwoods and soft woods. We won't never lack for lumber."

He gave himself the pleasure of another sniff. "Soon as we get settled in, I'm felling some of them trees and building me a cabin all my own. And I'm putting a lock on the door. Ain't nobody coming in my place without they knock on the door first and I invite 'em in."

"Amen! My sentiments exactly."

Before they could plan further, the woods gave way to a clearing. It was a wide clearing, several acres' worth, and in the midst of it stood a small house built entirely of fieldstone.

Caleb stopped the wagon, though neither of them moved to get down. In a hushed stillness broken only by the clear whistled *bo ba* of a bobwhite quail, they watched as nature cast a magic spell upon the house. As the rising sun spread vibrant pink streaks across the dawn sky, it turned the stonework of the house from dark purple to violet, then from lavender to rose, and finally from pearl pink to gray.

When the magic was completed and the house stood out clearly against a background of thick, green trees, they both sighed softly.

"That's it, child. That's the lodge."

Twelve

July 1863

Letty sang to herself as she climbed the narrow stairway that led to the two small sleeping rooms.

> *"Froggy went a-courtin' and he
>   did ride, umhumm.
> Froggy went a-courtin' and he
>   did ride, umhumm.
> Umhumm, umhumm, umhumm."*

She knew only the first line, and she sang that offkey, but she was too content with her life to let those minor deficiencies bother her.

Grasping the handrail tightly, she ducked just before the stairway took a sharp left turn. It had taken her all the first week, and at least a half-dozen nasty bumps on the forehead, before she learned to duck, but now, after four weeks at the lodge, she did it without thinking.

Except for the bumps on the head, the stairs didn't bother her. They were her stairs, and she loved them, just as she loved everything at the lodge. From the moment she saw

it, it was home. She had envisioned some sort of crude
cabin—after all, it had been built as a hunting lodge—and
though it was far from elegant, it was much more than she
had hoped for.

The fieldstone had been laid well and caulked snugly,
and the shingled roof was still sound. There were windows
on either side of the sturdy front door and one in each
bedroom, and when she unlatched the shutters that covered
them, she discovered glazed panes, filthy but unbroken.

The great room downstairs served as both parlor and
kitchen; and in addition to a fireplace large enough to allow
a horse to stand up in it, there was a parson's bench, a pine
hutch, and a sturdy, rectangular table with six chairs—four
cane bottomed and two hide bottomed. The stairway leading to the small loft bedrooms was to the right of the front
door.

"Umhumm, umhumm," she sang.

She softened her song to a hum while she peeked inside
the smaller of the two bedrooms to see that all was well
with the occupant of the pecan crib. Satisfied that Fern was
still asleep, Letty went to her own room to return the chamber pot she had just taken to the privy. While in the room,
she heard the well crank squeak.

She went to the open window and leaned out. "Good
morning, Ca—I mean Othello."

"You got that right. It surely is a good morning. As fine
a morning as ever was."

Pulling the bucket up onto the side of the stone well, he
dipped a cup into the water, then drank deeply.

"You know what," he said, wiping his sleeve across his
mouth, "this water's tasting better every day. At first I
thought it a mite sulphury, but it seems to wet my whistle
sweeter with each morning."

Letty smiled her agreement. "How long before you'll be
ready for breakfast?"

"Pretty soon. This here bucket of water is for Jake and
Esau. They been fed already, but Bossie ain't been milked
yet, and she's hollering to beat the band. I'll be up soon as
I tend to her."

Later, as Letty and Caleb sat at the table, finishing their breakfast of grits, cornpone, and coffee, they planned the day's work.

The first few days after their arrival they had busied themselves with settling the animals and fowl and finding safe storage places for the food and seed they had brought with them. After that, they had worked on their individual homes.

While Letty cleaned and scrubbed the lodge, evicting more than one furry tenant, Caleb felled trees for his cabin. Though her house was now as neat and organized as she could make it, his home was still little more than a dirt floor surrounded by four walls and a roof, with holes where the door and windows should be.

"Are you planning to work on your cabin today?"

"Not today. I got plenty of time for that before cold weather gets here. It'll do me fine like it is for right now while it's still hot, and I can put the extras in a little at a time."

He drained his cup and held it out to her for a refill. "What we need to do today is start on the garden. We been careful so far, but the food we brought ain't going to last forever. If we don't get a crop in pretty soon, come fall we'll be cooking sorrow and eating regret."

More than a little fearful that he was right, Letty poured coffee from the enamel pot, filling his cup, then her own. With her elbows propped on the table, her cup cradled between her hands, she sipped the warm, fragrant brew and listened while Caleb mapped out his plan for their late-summer garden. Clearing a proper field in the now thick woods would take months, so for this first garden they planned to plow only the cleared area that surrounded the lodge, Caleb's cabin, and the small shed that served temporarily as the barn.

The area had been cleared of trees and underbrush several years ago as a fire buffer, and though some growth had returned, it was nothing like the dense forest land beyond. Their plan was to plant in every available inch of buffer land, then later, when there was more time, they would clear the land and snake off the timber between the house and the river.

"We'll get the peas, the okra, and the beans in first," he said, "since they'll come up right away. After we finish with that, we'll put in the sweet potatoes, the carrots, the collards, and the turnips."

She nodded her agreement. "Whatever you say. You just tell me what to do, and I'll do it."

He spoke almost apologetically. "Ain't nothing about this going to be easy, child. We got to protect the plow point, no matter what. We lose that plow point, we in big trouble. And to protect it, somebody got to take that old short-handled grubbing hoe and pull out any roots that might break the point."

Letty took a final sip of coffee and set her cup on the table. "I guess my name is Somebody. Since there are only two of us here, and one of us has never plowed before, I get the grubbing hoe."

Caleb turned his cup up and let the last drop of coffee slide into his mouth, then he stood and slid his chair under the table. "I'll go get Esau hitched up to the plow. We can get started soon as you get there."

After he left, Letty put the dishes in the deep tin wash bowl that sat on the hutch and poured boiling water over the two cups and plates. She didn't take time to wash them; instead, she went over to the fireplace and swung the big cooking pot toward her so she could stir the stew she had started earlier that morning. Satisfied their combined dinner and supper was coming along well, she pushed the crane back just enough so the pot was next to the fire but not directly over it, then she placed the wooden spoon in a dish on the mantel.

At the front door she lifted her gun belt off the gun rack, checked the Dragoon, then slipped her head and arm through the belt; she had learned the hard way to be prepared. Lastly, she picked up Fern, crib and all, and want outside to join Caleb.

It took less than half an hour to show Letty the difference between gardening and farming.

At White Pines she had worked in her herb garden for many years, and she had enjoyed the feel of the soil between her fingers while she fit the plants into the ground; she enjoyed the warmth of the sun on her shoulders while she weeded. There was such pleasure in being a creative participant in nature's cycle that she hadn't even minded the slightly sore muscles that came with the initial planting each season.

Nothing in Letty's experience in the garden, however, had prepared her for the backbreaking, bone-numbing labor involved in farming. After a morning of wresting roots from the earth with the heavy mattock, her wrists throbbed, her palms and fingers had begun to develop blisters, and her back ached so badly from the unrelieved stooping that she wondered if she would ever again walk upright.

"Whoa, Esau!" Caleb yelled. "Whoa, mule!"

Letty had never heard more welcome words. She had no idea why Caleb had stopped the mule, but whatever the reason, she blessed him and all the angels in Heaven for the respite. After relaxing her grip on the grubbing hoe and letting it drop to the ground, she put her hands on her knees and arched her back like a cat. It was all she could do not to cry out.

"Miss Letty?"

An uncertain quality in Caleb's voice made her straighten up and look at him. He was staring at something past her, and as she turned to see what it was, her right hand slid across her ribs until it touched the butt of the Dragoon.

"How do?" a nasally cracker voice greeted them. "Didn't know anybody was living here."

Letty crossed her left arm over her right, leaving her fingers touching the Dragoon at her side. The man who stood several yards away carried a rifle under his arm. The barrel rested across his forearm, with the muzzle pointed toward the ground, but Letty was ready to draw if he moved the weapon an inch. He didn't move it. He stood perfectly still while she took his measure.

A smallish man, he was probably no taller than five feet five, with deep-set blue eyes and a face full of scraggly beard. Like his beard, his hair was mousy brown and un-kempt, and his rough shirt and overalls were worn and caked with mud. He held a shabby felt hat in his hand, and while she stared at him, he turned slightly to his right and spat tobacco juice on the ground.

"Name's Jubal Morgan," he said. "Live over thataway a piece." He waved his hat in a westward direction.

"This here's my boy, Gideon." Having introduced his son, an eleven-year-old replica of himself, he prodded the lad on the shoulder until he remembered to remove his own hat.

Deciding the man was harmless, Letty moved her hand away from the Dragoon and pushed herself up off her knees. "Good morning, Mr. Morgan. I am Violet Bonner, and this is Othello Moor."

"Mizriz Bonner," he said. He nodded to Caleb and mumbled something polite-sounding but unintelligible.

The amenities over, he pointed to the string of seven or eight medium-sized fish the boy held. "Been fishing down at the river. We come over this way ever so often to have a go at catching Old Slippery, a big old granddaddy trout that has a hidey-hole on this side. We seen smoke coming out of your chimbley, but we figured it was some of them hunting folks. Didn't know anybody'd come here to live."

Letty swallowed before trying her new history on the strangers. "We've come from Savannah, hoping to escape the war. But this is our home now, for good and all."

Jubal Morgan nodded, then spat again. "Mighty fine-looking mule. Yes, sirree bobtail. Reckon a fella could do his plowing in less than two shakes with a mule as fine as that."

Letty looked behind her at the small amount of ground she and Caleb had covered in an entire morning and won-dered just how much better that hypothetical "fella" might have done. She was about to respond to the visitor's com-pliment to Esau when Fern claimed her attention with a series of soft, high-pitched, kitten noises.

Everyone turned toward the silver birch tree that shaded the mosquito-netted crib.

"You got a baby there, Mizriz Bonner?"

"Yes, a little girl."

Jubal Morgan's disheveled face crinkled into one big smile. "Well, I swan to goodness, Gideon. Mizriz Bonner's even got a little baby girl out here helping with the plowing."

Without another word, the man went over to the crib where he successfully stilled Fern's cries with a series of soft cooing and clicking noises. His son waited only long enough to scratch the top of his bare foot before he followed his father.

"We fixing to have a baby," the boy said after a quick peek inside the crib.

"How nice," Letty replied. "Are you hoping for a brother or a sister?"

He mumbled something, then reached down to scratch his foot again.

"Gideon's ma's been dead five years," Jubal Morgan answered. "Died of childbed fever."

He spat again. "It's my Patience that's in the family way. My little girl. She ain't hardly more than a baby herself, just seventeen last fall when she married Troup Jones. That's why I didn't let Troup take her away.

" 'Troup,' I says, 'I'll let you marry her, but you can't take her off, on account of she's my little girl.' So they got married, and Troup built them a room off the back of our cabin."

Gideon rubbed the top of his foot against the calf of his other leg and added his mite to the conversation. "Troup says Pa probably would've shot him if he'd've took Patience away."

Father and son both laughed loudly. Since this was obviously a family joke, Letty smiled politely. She didn't know what to make of the loquacious pair. She had never met anyone so talkative or so dirty. Having decided they were no threat to her or hers, her next concern was that one of these dirty crackers might try to touch the crib.

"Here," she said, "let me take the baby inside. She is probably hungry." While she scooped Fern up in her arms, she heard Gideon whisper something to his father.

"Mizriz Bonner," Jubal Morgan said. "Before you go, Gideon wants to know if you'd like this mess of fish we caught. It's only catfish, but they fry up real tasty."

After the meager meals they'd had the last four weeks, the thought of a plate of hot, succulent fish made Letty's mouth water. "Thank you, but, uh, I couldn't take your dinner."

"Oh, there's plenty more where these come from, ma'am. Besides, we caught them off your bank. They're probably yours by right."

Quickly, lest she embarrass them, Letty let her gaze scan father and son. They were slender, but neither of them looked underfed, and she and Caleb could use a change of diet. "You're sure?" she asked.

The boy nodded his head. "Yes'm."

"All right, Gideon. I'll take the fish and thank you, but only if you let me give you something to put on your foot. Unless I miss my guess, you've stepped in poison ivy, and I've got some sassafras bark ointment that will help soothe the itch."

Father and son looked at each other, and something passed between them, then Jubal Morgan stepped forward, his voice hushed, his eyes hopeful. "Ma'am, are you a granny woman?"

"A what, Mr. Morgan?"

"A granny woman."

He moved even closer, as if to get a better look at her. "We ain't had a granny woman in these parts since old Granny Turnipseed died six years ago."

"I see," Letty said, though she knew no more than when she had asked.

"Granny Turnipseed took care of my Sarah," the man said. "The first time was when our Patience was born, and the next was when Gideon here was born. And if Granny'd've been alive, my Sarah wouldn't've got the childbed fever that last lying-in. He lowered his voice. "Sarah wasn't delivering like she ought, and the pains had been going on for two days. When I heard tell there was a doctor staying at Mr. Finley's at the settlement, come with a party of men for some boar hunting, I got scared and fetched him.''

Jubal spat with exaggerated force. ''I never did hold with doctors at a lying-in. You let a doctor near a woman, and sure as shootin' she'll come down with childbed fever.''

He motioned for the boy to step away, then he lowered his voice almost to a whisper. ''I told Troup Jones I'd put a bullet in him for real if he let a doctor touch my little girl. But twix you and me, Mizriz Bonner, I been scared, scared something might go wrong with Patience, and nobody to help her if it did. She needs a granny woman.''

Letty nodded. ''How long before her confinement?''

Jubal Morgan let out a sigh that sounded as if he'd been holding his breath for months. ''It ain't long now, Mizriz Bonner.''

''Please,'' she said, already sick to death of her new name, ''call me Letty.''

Jubal's face crinkled into another one of those big smiles. ''Thank you, Miz Letty.'' He waved the boy back over, gave Letty the fish, then with surprisingly few words took his leave.

Having already stopped for the duration of Jubal Morgan's visit, Caleb suggested they take a rest.

''Just leave the catfish on the porch, child. Soon as I take Esau over to the shade and bring him some water, I'll come back and gut and scale them fish for you.'' Caleb's smile was almost as big as Jubal Morgan's. ''Catfish. Um, um, um! I can practically taste 'em already.''

Letty fed Fern then put her down on the far side of the room, away from the fire, and dished up plates of stew for Caleb and herself. They ate heartily of the stew and drank glasses of cool sweetmilk, but all they could talk about was the coming joys of fried catfish.

''Soon as we get the garden in,'' Caleb said, ''I'll have some time to catch us some fish. And do some hunting, too, now I got me a rifle.'' He took a long swallow of milk. ''Course, I'll have to do the hunting quiet like. Colored folk ain't supposed to have no guns. When I brought the rifle along with us, I didn't know there was anybody else living close by."

"Neither did I. I certainly didn't expect a settlement. Jubal Morgan mentioned a doctor staying at a Mr. Finley's. The place sounded like a boardinghouse for hunters. Whatever it is, I plan to stay clear of it. If there's one thing I don't want, it's a lot of people knowing where I am."

She had only just spoken the words when she heard the rumble of wagon wheels. "What on earth?"

Caleb's long legs got him to the window first. "It's Mr. Jubal," he said. "Young Gideon is with him, and two other folks."

Since the door stood open to let in fresh air, Letty stepped right out onto the porch and watched a slim, fresh-faced farm boy of about nineteen drive a swaybacked old mule almost up to the house. As soon as the wagon stopped, Jubal jumped down from the plank seat he shared with the young man, then he went around to the back to help a young girl out of the wagon bed.

The girl was short, hardly more than five feet, and she was large with child. The dress that hiked up over her round belly was freshly washed and ironed, and the matching poke bonnet, like the girl herself, was as neat as a pin. The round, freckled face Letty saw peaking from beneath the starched poke bonnet was pure Morgan, as were the deep-set blue eyes. Patience Morgan Jones was a cleaned-up version of Jubal and Gideon.

"Miz Letty," Jubal said formally, leading his daughter toward the porch, "this here's my girl, Patience. And that there"—he pointed toward the young man who still sat on the wagon—"is Troup Jones."

Patience smiled and dropped a curtsy, and Troup lifted his hat. Neither uttered a word.

"Troup ain't much of a talker," Jubal informed Letty pleasantly. "That's why him and my little girl get along so well."

Letty could well imagine that Jubal Morgan did enough talking for all of them, but she kept her opinion to herself. "Would you all care to come inside the house?"

Jubal refused for all of them, then began giving orders. "Gideon, you bring that stuff out of the wagon and set it on the porch till Miz Letty has time to worry with it. When you're done, come on around to the side with the rest of us."

He spat, then gave Patience a gentle nudge. "You go on with Miz Letty, sweet pea. She's fixing to tell you all them things your ma would have told you."

Letty felt the heat of embarrassment rush to her face, but Jubal seemed not to notice.

"Where's that Orthello fella?" he asked.

Caleb stepped out onto the porch. "Afternoon, Mr. Jubal."

"Ah, there you are, Orthello. Didn't see you at first. Been telling Troup Jones here about that fine-looking mule you got. Him and me decided to come over and have a closer look at it."

Letty watched all the males except Gideon stroll out to the silver birch tree where Esau waited patiently in the shade. With no polite way to get out of the chore Jubal had set her, she surrendered to the inevitable, took the young girl by the arm, and led her up the two steps of the porch and into the house.

The girl eased her unwieldy body into the chair Letty offered. "I apologize for intruding on your privacy, Mrs. Bonner, but when Pa takes hold of an idea, he's as hard to stop as a whirlwind."

Letty couldn't believe her ears. The girl's voice was completely free of the cracker that characterized her father's speech.

"Pa likes to think I'm still a little girl, with no knowledge of the body's natural functions. But I'm a farm girl, ma'am. I've watched animals give birth since I was this high. Also, my mother taught me everything she knew about the female body. Mother abhorred ignorance of all kinds."

Letty felt her eyes grow wide at the image of Jubal Morgan married to a woman who abhorred ignorance.

"I know what you're thinking, ma'am," the girl said

without a hint of apology. "The thing is, life can be hard for a woman who isn't handsome. My mother was a spinster with no one to take her part, and she wanted a home and children. Though she was a good bit older than Pa, he offered them to her. Pa's honest to the bone, Mrs. Bonner, and he never lies. Never. Those qualities were important to my mother. She never regretted accepting Pa's hand. Pa made sure she never regretted it."

Letty looked into the plain, sincere face beneath the cheap calico poke bonnet and knew a moment of true heart-piercing jealousy. She, Loretta Banks of White Pines Plantation, envied this girl whose father was a grubby, tobacco-chewing cracker. No, she corrected, she didn't envy the girl for having such a father. She envied her for having such *pride* in her father.

"Mrs. Bonner," Patience said, interrupting her thoughts, "even though I don't need you to explain about birthing, I am nonetheless overwhelmingly grateful that you are here. You are the answer to my prayers. Pa isn't the only one frightened about this birth. The bigger I get, the more fearful Troup becomes. And, if the truth be known, I'm a little worried myself. Now that you're here, though, I won't worry anymore."

Her smile gave her ordinary face an elfin charm. "At least, I'll *try* not to worry."

After Letty examined the mother-to-be, they sat at the table sipping glasses of cool sweetmilk and getting to know each other, with Letty thoroughly enjoying her visit with the girl who so perfectly suited her name. Exchanging ideas with a female she hadn't known all her life was a new experience for Letty, and one she wanted to repeat, but she began to feel guilty about enjoying her coze with Patience when she should be out helping Caleb with the plowing.

As soon as she could, without being rude, she stood up and put her chair under the table. "I need to see how Othello is doing. We have got to get our garden in before it is too late."

Patience eased herself out of the chair. "I'm sure they're doing fine, ma'am."

The significance of the girl's words didn't register with Letty until she stepped outside and discovered more than half the cleared land turned over in neat, plowed rows. While Caleb and Gideon wielded grubbing hoes, *down-pull-up, down-pull-up*, almost as though they were engaged in a contest, Troup Jones followed with the plow, handling it and the mule with ease, as though he'd invented the technique. While the others worked, Jubal Morgan sat on the ground beneath the silver birch, his back flush with the tree, his short legs stretched out before him, and his shabby felt hat pulled down over his face.

Not at all embarrassed to find her father asleep, Patience waddled over and tapped him on the head. "Pa, it's time to go. Miss Letty's got work to do, and I need to get home and get supper started."

Jubal Morgan stretched lazily before pushing his hat off his face and standing. Without the least trace of chagrin, he waved his hand toward the newly plowed rows. "See there, Miz Letty? I told you a fella could do his plowing in two shakes with a mule as fine as that."

Since her brain refused to provide her with a suitable reply, Letty was pleased that Jubal followed his observation with another on the pride a man could take in the accomplishment of a furrow well plowed. While he talked, he took his daughter's arm and escorted her back to the wagon, where he helped her settle herself comfortably in the back.

As he climbed up on the wagon seat, Letty remembered her manners. "Mr. Morgan, I really don't know how to thank you for the plowing. Such neighborliness is—"

"The plowing ain't neighborliness, Miz Letty. No, sirree bobtail. It's 'in kind' for helping my little girl. Us Morgans pay our debts up front." He leaned to the right and spat on the far side of the wagon. "That there next to the porch is neighborliness. Done by my little girl's own hand."

As Jubal Morgan gee-yupped his swaybacked old mule, Letty turned toward the porch. When she first came outside, she had been too interested in the plowing to notice the stuff on the ground, but now she wondered how she could have missed it. To the left of the steps was a small croker sack filled with peanuts, a woven basket of collard greens, another basket of dried peaches, a jar of honey, a freshly baked loaf of bread wrapped in a spotless white cloth, and a small block of salt.

Overcome by such kindness, she turned back around just before the wagon rolled out of sight. As it bumped and pitched across the rough ground, Patience raised her arm above her head and waved.

Letty returned the wave, marveling at the pleasure it gave her to know she had found a friend. No, she had found two friends—a soft-spoken, intelligent girl and a long-winded, tobacco-chewing, old cracker.

That evening, replete from a memorable dinner of fried catfish, collards, and slices of bread with honey, Letty and Caleb sat on the porch steps watching flocks of waterfowl they couldn't yet identify fly across the pink and orange sky.

Caleb sighed contentedly. "I believe the Lord saved the prettiest birds and the prettiest skies for down here on the Ochlockonee."

"They are beautiful."

Shielding her eyes from the fiery red ball that hadn't dropped all the way behind the thick trees, Letty watched an inverted vee of birds veer off to the left and then disappear from view.

When the birds were gone, she closed her eyes and inhaled slowly, enjoying the sweet perfume of wild jasmine combined with the aroma of freshly turned earth. "I believe the Lord also saved the best smells for the Ochlockonee."

"I know that's right."

After a spell of companionable silence, silence in which they watched the sun slip peacefully from sight, Caleb mapped out his plans for getting the seed into the ground the next day. "With all the good help we had today, if we can just get the right kind of weather, we might have enough to eat come fall. The crops—"

"Hello, the house!" a man's voice called from somewhere in the woods.

Letty stood and backed slowly to the doorway where she reached inside to the gun belt she had left hanging from the rack. With the Dragoon held behind her back, she rejoined Caleb just as a large, burly man materialized out of the gloaming, a brown-and-white-spotted hunting dog trailing at his heels. The man wore a rough shirt and overalls not unlike the clothes worn by Jubal Morgan, and like Jubal he carried a rifle in the crook of his arm. In his free hand he held a brace of grouse tied together at the feet.

"How do, ma'am?"

When Letty nodded, he held the grouse toward her. "These is fresh kilt," he said. "I brung 'em for the new granny woman."

Thirteen

"You might as well tell me, Caleb. I know something happened while you were at the settlement today. You've been quiet and withdrawn ever since you got back."

"It ain't nothing, child. I just got this upset in my guts, is all." As if to support his claim, he put his hand on his stomach.

Letty didn't believe for one minute that he had a stomachache. She had noticed a certain lack of spark in him all during supper. He had been even less talkative than usual, and he had avoided looking her in the eyes.

While pondering the question of what could be bothering him, she watched him bend forward, his arms extended, and let Fern wrap her chubby fingers around his thumbs. Caleb supported the toddler while she stood then put one plump, wobbly little foot in front of the other, yet for all he saw of her tottering efforts, he might as well have been in another world.

When he didn't praise the child, or go on about what he liked to call her "quickness," Letty knew something was definitely wrong. A thousand dire possibilities occurred to her, and in that instant Caleb's gut pain made a giant leap and began gnawing at *her* innards.

Pushing aside Fern's highchair, Letty left the mashed potatoes smeared on the seat and tray to harden as they would, and sat down in the closest chair. "All right, Caleb, what happened at the settlement? Were you hurt?"

"No. I just—" He seemed to reconsider what he'd been about to say. "Mr. Troup got into an argument."

Letty snorted. "Quit trying to fob me off. Troup Jones never utters five words at a time. How could a wooden post get into an argument?"

"It weren't none of Mr. Troup's doing. It was some of them newcomers started it."

Letty relaxed. *Nothing had happened to Caleb.*

With her mind relieved, she was free to take an interest in any gossip from the settlement. She leaned her elbows on the table and rested her chin in her palms. "What newcomers? Surely Troup didn't have an argument with one of the refugees."

"These ain't refugees. Leastways, they ain't like the families that's crowded into Mr. Finley's boardinghouse till the place like to bust open at the seams. The ones I'm talking about—half a dozen white men—just been hanging around the settlement the last couple of days. Mr. Finley say they claim to be here on official States' business. 'Looking for bummers,' they say, but the only thing I noticed any of 'em looking for was another jug of barleycorn."

"So they were drunk?"

He shrugged his shoulders. "Mayhap. Four of 'em was sitting out on the front porch of the boardinghouse playing cards, and the other two was lazing in them rockers Mr. Finley keeps out in front of the store. Mr. Finley say won't none of the refugee ladies come outside the boardinghouse anymore on account of them men being so common."

"I can believe that." Letty discovered a crumb she had left on the table and brushed it into her hand. "What I can't credit is Troup Jones getting mixed up with a bunch of trashy white men. I thought he had more sense."

"He does. Mr. Troup was just tying that old swayback mule of his to the hitching post, tending to his own business, when one of the men sitting in the rocker yells out to him, real rough like, wanting to know how old he was. When Mr. Troup don't pay him no mind, the man that done the yelling push his rocker back so hard it slam against the store wall. Then he swagger over to Mr. Troup like he got the good Lord's blessing to do anything he want to.

" 'I'm talking to you, Cracker,' he says. 'This here's official Confederate business. How come you ain't off fighting Yankees? Governor Brown says every able-bodied man twixt eighteen and thirty-five s'posed to be in the army of the Confederacy.' "

"Oh, dear. Did Troup answer him?"

Caleb shook his head. "He check the mule's harness like the man ain't even standing there. Then the man look Mr. Troup up and down like he some kind of dead vermin. 'You look able-bodied to me,' he says, 'so the only way you could stay out of this here war is if you was feeble-minded or you owned twenty niggers. You own twenty niggers, Cracker?' "

Letty closed her eyes for a moment. "And did Troup answer that question?"

"Most I ever heard him say at one sitting.

" 'I don't own nobody,' Mr. Troup say, 'and don't nobody own me. I work hard as I can . . . I don't expect nobody else to do it for me . . . and I ain't fixing to get myself killed just so some rich plantation owner that's too lazy to do his own work can keep buying people like they was mules.' "

Caleb reached down and swooped Fern up into his arms and walked over to the fireplace. "Then the white man gets right up in Mr. Troup's face and say . . ." He had to clear his throat. "He say, 'Niggers ain't the same as people, and they ain't nowhere near smart as mules.' "

Letty felt bile rise up in her throat. "And what did Troup say to that?" she asked quietly.

"Mr. Troup didn't say nothing else. I guess he done spoke his fill for one day. He just made a fist and, quick as lightning, socked that white man a good one right under the ribs. The man doubled up and fell over, and while he was rolling in the dirt, puking up barleycorn, Mr. Troup untied his mule, hopped up on it, and rode off.''

Letty wished Troup had kicked the man while he was writhing on the ground. She longed to kick the swine herself for putting that guarded look back into Caleb's eyes. She watched him as he stood there by the mantel, staring into the banked fire. His face was closed, and his eyes were wary in a way Letty hadn't seen since before they left White Pines.

''What else happened, Caleb? Did that man say something to you?''

He hugged Fern close for a moment, then he kissed her on top of her head and put her down on the floor to crawl around. ''Didn't much else happen.'' He retrieved a small gourd rattle from the mantel and put it in the child's hand. ''That was just about all.''

Letty willed herself to keep quiet.

Just about all.

That was as close as Caleb had ever come to telling her a lie. Something else had definitely happened, something that hurt him inside, yet he was such a private person, she knew he wouldn't tell her unless she kept after him. She wanted to help him, but she couldn't help if she didn't know what was wrong.

When Caleb stepped out onto the porch, Letty got up from the table and ran after him, inventing as she ran. ''Don't go to your cabin just yet. I need you to . . . uh . . . uh, to help me empty the bathtub.''

He paused, turning back to look at her. ''You finally used that tub I made you for your birthday?''

She smiled sheepishly. ''I had to. That old woman and the little boy who came just as you were leaving for the settlement had lice.''

''I guessed as much. Sure hope you didn't let that boy near Fern. You know cooties don't stand on ceremony. They'll crawl right off of one head and right on to the next.''

"Fern was upstairs asleep. They never even saw her. And thanks to you and my new granny room, I didn't have to bring them inside the house. I took them through the outside door. I was concerned about the lice, though, so after the woman and boy left, I filled my new tub with kettles of hot water, sprinkled in some spicebush to kill the vermin, and scrubbed myself from head to toe."

"You ready to go empty the tub now?"

She shook her head. "Let me put Fern to bed first. I don't want to worry about her getting into anything while we're hauling the tub out back."

Caleb grunted his agreement, then he folded his long legs beneath him and sat down on the steps to wait. He knew what she was doing; she thought if she wormed it out of him what happened at the settlement, they could somehow fix it. She meant well, but there wasn't any way of fixing what ailed him.

To keep his mind off the things he didn't want to remember, he pulled one leg up close to his chest and rested his chin on his knee, concentrating on the setting sun. The sun went down earlier these days, but there was still a good half hour of light left, more than enough to see by. He looked around him at all the familiar sights—all the things he loved: the tall, slender pine trees, the massive oaks, the dogwoods, the land that yielded crops almost all year long. It was good land. Land that made a man feel proud, feel like he belonged. *His* land.

"Damn him!" Caleb muttered between clenched teeth. "Damn that white trash!"

He jumped up as though propelled by some long-controlled inner spring that would not be held in check a moment longer. "Damn him to hell. Him and all his kind!"

Frustrated, Caleb dashed out into the yard, picked up a rock, then hurled it at a shiny, green-leafed turkey oak. He hit the tree square on, dislodging a shower of acorns. Still angry, he picked up another rock and hurled it after the first one.

"Damn him! Damn him! Damn him!"

He threw rocks as fast as he could find them and pick

them up, heedless of anything but his need to hit something. When he could no longer see for the tears that filled his eyes, he slumped to the ground, hugged his knees to his chest, and hid his face in the crook of his arm. His shoulders shook with the force of his sobs.

"Damn him! Damn him for making all those slave feelings come back."

The instant that white trash yelled at Mr. Troup, those old slave feelings had gripped Caleb's guts, twisting them inside his belly until he felt sick enough to puke. It was the tone of the man's voice. Caleb had reacted to that tone, just like in the old days. He'd stood there like a fence post, watching and trembling, unable to move while the man jeered at Mr. Troup. He might have stood there all afternoon if Mr. Finley hadn't come out of the store and yanked him by the sleeve.

"Othello," Mr. Finley said softly when Mr. Troup floored the stranger, "come in here quick before that fella catches his breath. No telling what he'll do if he sees you."

Caleb slipped into the store and crouched down behind the counter like Mr. Finley told him, staying as still as a scared rabbit. In a few seconds he heard the mule gallop past.

"Nigger lover!" the white man yelled at Mr. Troup's back. "You fixing to pay for this. I find you, I'll hog-tie you and haul you off to the army my own self."

Caleb heard the man stagger back to his companion and flop down hard into the rocker. "Gimme that jug!" he ordered.

For a full minute the only sound was the noise of a gullet opening and closing, then the man burped loudly.

"I'm fixing to get my horse and find me that nigger-loving cracker. Fixing to haul his ass to the army where them nigger-loving Yankees can shoot it off."

"Yeah," his companion added, "let the Yankees shoot him. Then, when they're done shooting crackers, they can take all the niggers they free back up North with them."

There was more gullet noise. The man burped again. "And any niggers the Yankees don't take with 'em, I'm shooting. From now on," he boasted, "I see any free nigger, he'll soon be a dead nigger."

Caleb had stayed hidden behind the counter until Mr. Finley said the coast was clear, then he'd gotten Esau and ridden back to the lodge like the hounds of hell were after him. All the while, he had felt sick to his stomach, sick that he'd hidden, and sick that a drunken, white-trash bully could rob him of the pride he'd felt ever since he'd become free. Pride he'd thought would be his forever.

The sobs finally quit shaking his shoulders, and the tears quit spotting his shirtsleeve, making it look as if he'd been out in the rain. But Caleb continued to sit there on the ground, his face hidden in his arm, his energy spent.

That was where Letty found him when she came back out onto the porch.

"What was wrong with the little boy with the lice?"

"With the little boy?" Letty shrugged her shoulders. "You mean besides having too many lice in his head and too little food in his stomach? For one thing, his mother is dead, and his father has been in the army for more than a year and could also be dead for all anybody knows. The old lady—his great-grandmother—is all the boy has left, and if I'm any judge of the situation, she won't live to see the winter."

"Life is hard," Caleb muttered, his voice wooden.

"There wasn't anything I could do to help her. I think she knew that before she came, but she came anyway. The boy said they walked six miles."

"Hope they home by now. It's fixing to rain."

Letty looked up into the sky that was almost dark. "I hope you are wrong. It has done nothing but rain since spring, and I've had enough rain to do me and then some."

"I ain't wrong."

"No," she said, "you never are."

For the last ten minutes, they had sat on the porch steps and talked quietly about everything except what was on both their minds—Caleb's tears.

Letty's hands still trembled from the panic that had

gripped her when she saw him sitting on the ground, his shirt wet with tears. Nothing had prepared her for that old feeling of helplessness as she witnessed his pain.

Why can I never help the people I love?

"Shh," Caleb said suddenly, though she hadn't been talking. "Somebody coming."

The fear in his voice made her jump up and hurry into the house for her gun. When she came back out onto the porch, she already had the Dragoon cocked and ready to fire. She heard the rustling of the grass and took aim.

"Miss Letty?" Gideon Morgan's high boyish voice called softly from behind a distant oak. "Miss Letty, if you've got that old Dragoon pointed at me, don't shoot."

"Gideon Morgan!" Caleb yelled, his voice a fine mixture of relief and anger. "You up to some devilment out there, boy?"

"Is anybody else around, Othello?"

"Ain't nobody but me and Miss Letty. You come on up here, boy, 'fore you get yourself shot."

In less than two minutes they were all inside the house with the door closed and a lamp lit so they could see each other. Letty let Caleb do the talking.

"All right now, boy, you better fess up. What you doing out here so late? You and me both know Mr. Jubal skin you alive if he find out you been running wild."

Gideon's eyes were bright with excitement. "Pa ain't back yet from hunting for that old wild boar." He shifted his weight from one bare foot to the other. "I, uh . . . Patience sent me over," he said quickly. "She wanted to know if Troup had come by here."

Letty and Caleb exchanged glances, their mutual disbelief needing no words.

"Boy, Miss Patience got too much sense to send you out alone with night coming on, unless it was for something mighty important. Now you start telling the truth this minute, or by the time I get through with you, you going to wish Miss Letty *had* shot you."

Gideon licked his lips. "But you don't know what's happened, Othello. You see, there are these men at the settlement, and they're looking for deserters and conscription dodgers. Troup was scared they might come after him, so he skedaddled.''

Caleb's face was stern. ''Mr. Troup never done that, and you know it.''

The boy had the grace to blush. ''Well, not *skedaddled* exactly, but he did go downriver a ways. He loaded his rifle and then wrapped some johnny cakes and streak o' lean in a clean rag. Said he'd be back in a few days, when those men left the area.''

Caleb laid his hand on the boy's shoulder. ''I know all about them men in town. Just like I know that wherever Mr. Troup went, he don't want you following him.''

''But I ain't following h—'' Gideon clamped his dirty hand over his mouth.

''I thought so. Now let's have the truth, boy. What you really doing out here?''

Gideon's chin jutted stubbornly.

Thinking it was time she intervened, Letty took the lad's dirty hand and led him over to the parson's bench. ''Gideon,'' she said, patting the bench, inviting him to sit beside her, ''we know you don't mean any harm, that you're just out for a lark of some kind, but don't you think this was a bad time for it? With your father gone, don't you imagine Troup was counting on you to be the man of the house, to stay at home and look after Patience and little Sarah?''

The stubborn chin relaxed. ''Yes'm,'' he said slowly. ''I reckon so.''

''Supposing those men from the settlement did come by your house. Patience would be there all alone.''

''Oh, they already been by. They—''

While Gideon studied a hole in the knee of his overalls, Letty stared at him, making him squirm on the bench. ''Enough now, Gideon. I want the truth.''

The boy exhaled noisily, his entire body slumping with the effort. ''I was hunting for the spy.''

''*The spy!*'' Letty and Caleb said at once.

Their surprise revived the boy's flagging spirits. He sat

up straight again, excitement lighting his deep-set blue eyes.

"He's a *Yankee* spy. A recognizing man."

"Recognizing?"

"Yes'm. That's somebody that goes out ahead of the army to scout out the enemy territory. Only, of course, this one was scouting Confederate territory, and we ain't the enemy."

"I believe you mean a reconnaissance man."

"Yes'm, that's what they called him."

"They? You mean the men from the settlement?"

"Yes'm. A gang of 'em came by our house a little while ago. At first Patience was scared, thinking they were after Troup, but they weren't interested in him. They were looking for the Yankee spy."

Letty stood up and looked down at the boy. She smiled to soften her words, hating to spoil his dream of adventure. "It's all foolishness, Gideon. Those men have been at the jug so long they are imagining things. There's nothing down here on the Ochlockonee for the Yankees to reconnoiter. Believe me, we're too far from anything of any importance to interest the Yankees."

"Begging your pardon, Miss Letty, but the men weren't drunk. One of them shot at the spy. Got him, too, he thinks. 'Cept the spy flew away before he could catch him."

"He flew?"

"Yes'm." Gideon's eyes became round as buttons. "And there's a hundred-dollar reward."

Caleb made a noise in his throat. "Now I know they was drunk. Ain't nobody fixing to pay a hundred dollars for no Yankee, spy or no spy."

"Oh, the reward ain't for the Yankee spy. The reward is for the balloon. The recognizing man was in one of those flying balloons."

Balloons? Letty couldn't get her breath; something seemed to be pressing down on her lungs. After a moment her knees gave way beneath her, and she flopped back down on the parson's bench.

A Yankee in a flying balloon. The words kept repeating

themselves in her brain, growing louder and louder, until she clamped her hands over her ears to shut out the noise. It didn't work; she still heard the voice in her head, even though Gideon continued with his story of the men who pursued the spy.

"The balloon must've been in trouble, on account of it was getting lower and lower and heading smack dab for the trees."

No, Letty thought. *I'm jumping to conclusions.* The Union Army must have dozens of balloons. And dozens of balloonists.

"The man's pretty sure the bullet hit the spy, but the balloon disappeared behind the trees before he could see for sure."

Balloon. Balloon. The words sounded louder and louder in Letty's head. *Balloon. Balloon. Thorn. Balloon. Thorn Bradley.*

Caleb pulled at the sodden shirt that clung to his back, then he kicked his heels into Esau's sides to encourage the mule to keep plodding through the unfamiliar woods. *I told her it was fixing to rain.*

Looking over his shoulder, he tugged angrily at Jake's leading rope. "Stay close, mule."

The mules didn't want to be here, but then, neither did Caleb. That Yankee didn't mean anything to him. He didn't care pea turkey about the Yankees or the Confederates. For all he cared, they could blow each other to kingdom come, and good riddance.

He glanced back at Miss Letty, who clung to Jake's harness. She looked like a drowned rat. He didn't say anything to her; it would have been a waste of breath. He'd already said all there was to say, and she hadn't heard a word of it. Even when he'd threatened to let her come out into the woods all by herself, she hadn't backed down. Trouble was, he wouldn't've let her come alone, and she knew it.

Calling himself a fool, he turned back around to watch where he was going. He still couldn't believe they were out here. Of all the bullheaded things he'd ever known her to do, this was the bullheadedest.

Why, he couldn't even remember that man she said had come visiting at White Pines. And even if he had remembered him, he didn't see any reason why they had to go looking for him. More than likely it was some other man anyhow. More than likely they were slogging through the woods on a wild-goose chase. And a wet wild-goose chase at that.

The rain that began as a light shower half an hour ago had turned into a typical autumn downpour, soaking not only man and mule, but also the leaves of the trees. As the waterlogged branches bent lower, they slapped the faces of both mules and riders, making the trip doubly difficult. Caleb ducked under a branch, then held it so it wouldn't rebound into Miss Letty's face.

He wished they would hurry up and find that blasted Yankee. The going was bad enough now, but if they didn't find the fella before they ran out of the pine thicket, instead of walking on this nice pine straw, the mules would be slipping in the mud.

Caleb remembered something he'd overheard Mr. Finley say about mud keeping the Yankees out of Atlanta. The heavy spring rains had turned the fields and roads north of Atlanta into muddy hog wallows, obliging the Yankee soldiers to cool their heels for weeks until they could move their mule wagons and cannons.

If mud could hold off a hundred thousand Yankees, mayhap it would slow down that gang of ruffians from the settlement. He sure hoped so, 'cause if those men caught him and Miss Letty helping a spy, they were as good as hung.

"Caleb," she called to him.

Turning his head, he cupped his hand around his ear so he could hear her.

"Do you know where we are?"

"I know where *we* are, but that ain't the same as knowing where that Yankee is. Near as I can figure from what

Gideon said, the man who saw the balloon was somewhere about—''

His words caught in his throat, for Esau had dug in his heels and nearly thrown him from the saddle. The instant he righted himself, he saw why the mule had balked. Even with no moonlight he could see it.

''Jehoshaphat!''

Caleb's heart tried to jump right out of his chest.

Just ahead was a creature as big as a room. It was batlike and blacker than the blackness of the night. The creature's body hovered three or four feet above the ground, while its wings, reaching from the branches of one pine to the branches of another, flapped back and forth in the gusty wind.

For several moments Caleb fought his desire to turn and gallop away. The creature looked hurt, and who could tell what an injured animal might—

''That's it!'' Miss Letty yelled.

Before he had time to realize what she meant, she slid off Jake's back and ran right up to that hovering monster; then she grabbed hold of its body and stuck her head inside it.

''He's not in the basket, Caleb. He must have fallen out.''

Glad he hadn't had time to make a fool of himself, Caleb got down off Esau and tied both mules to a tree branch. ''I'll circle around this way!'' he yelled. ''You go that way. We'll see can we find him.''

The search didn't take long. Caleb had gone only a few steps when he nearly tripped over something. It looked like a log, but when he tapped it with the toe of his boot, it groaned.

''Miss Letty!''

She was beside him in only seconds. Dropping to her knees next to the man, she turned him onto his back, then slowly ran her hands down his arms, his legs, and his body, checking him for injuries.

''I don't feel any broken bones, but he could be hurt inside. No matter what's wrong, though, I can't do anything here. I'll have to wait until we get him home.''

Caleb caught her arm. "Now hold on a minute! This could be anybody, anybody at all. Dark as it is, there ain't no way you could recognize him.''

"It's him.''

"You can't know that for positive. Only thing we know for sure is he's a Yankee. A *Yankee*. You know what that gang from the settlement would do if they caught us helping a Yankee? They'd lynch me right on the spot, and mayhap you alongside of me. And what about the folks around here that's got kin in the army? They'd be just as mad as the—''

"It's him, Caleb. It's Thorn Bradley. I don't have to see him to know.'' She tapped her chest. "I feel it in here, the same way I would if it were you or Fern.''

"But—''

She grabbed his hand and placed it on the Yankee's face. "Feel his face.''

"He got a scraggly beard and a mustache.''

"Never mind those, they're new. Feel his eyebrows, they'll be the same. They are thick, and they almost meet over his nose. And his nose is long and slender.''

Caleb wanted to pull his hand away; he didn't like feeling around on a man's face. "It don't prove nothing. Lots of folks got thin noses.''

"Feel his mouth. The lower lip. Thorn has a small scar at the left corner. Do you feel it?''

He did as she asked, then he pulled his hand away and wiped it on his britches. "They's a scar.''

Fourteen

Letty ran to open the door to the granny room, then hurried back to help Caleb lift Thorn Bradley off the mule.

"Stand aside," he said. "I'll do this faster by myself. We got to hurry if this crazy plan going to work."

She stepped back while Caleb untied the rope he'd used to secure Thorn to the saddle and slid him off Esau's back. He propped the injured man against the mule, then bent forward and let him fall across his back like a sack of flour. Without any help from her, he hauled Thorn the few yards to the granny room and laid him on the floor.

Letty closed the door behind them and lit the kerosene lamp. She had thought she was prepared for her first sight of Thorn Bradley, but when she turned from the lamp and saw his pale, almost bloodless face with its numerous cuts and bruises, she gasped.

"He ain't dead, child. I heard him groan."

Her heart in her throat, she knelt on the floor beside Thorn's still body and pressed her ear against his chest. "Yes, he's still alive."

"And we alive, too, but we won't be if we don't hurry. We ain't got no time to waste. You know what we got to do."

She nodded. "I know. Let's do it."

Without another word, Caleb reached for Thorn's boots. They were several sizes too large for his feet, so they slipped off easily. While he pulled off the boots, Letty unbuttoned Thorn's tunic and britches and began stripping the worn, blue uniform from his body. The material ripped in several places as she yanked and tugged at it, but it fared better than the rotted underdrawers which disintegrated at the first rough pull.

His skin was cold beneath her fingers. "I wish we had time to heat a kettle of water."

"Well, we ain't."

Caleb bent and slipped his arms beneath the injured man's arms. "Take his feet."

Letty did as she was told, and on the count of three they lifted Thorn and carried him over to the tub Letty had used that afternoon. The water still smelled of sweetbush, but it was icy cold, and when they set him down in it, Thorn gasped and opened his eyes.

He stared straight at her, then he blinked his lids and seemed to be trying to focus his eyes. "It's you," he said, his voice slurred. "I thought I was dream—" The effort was too much for him; his eyes drooped shut again.

He recognized me!

Though Letty's heart beat wildly with joy, her throat ached with unshed tears, and she couldn't have spoken at that moment if her life had depended on it. He hadn't forgotten. All those years, and he still remembered her.

Unable to endure the sweet agony of looking at his worn face, she moved away from the tub and went over to the shelves where she stored her dried herbs and supplies. From the nonmedicinal shelf she selected a jar of soapwort, a gourd sponge, and her scissors.

"Better bring some kerosene, too," Caleb said. "His clothes are alive with cooties."

He held the discarded uniform and boots at arm's distance while he crossed the room to the outside door. "I'll bury these things first, then I'll take care of Jake and Esau. When I get the mules dry and bedded down, I'll come back and help you take that Yankee out of the tub.''

"Thorn," she corrected. She poured kerosene into her palm and rubbed it into his matted hair. "This will all be for nothing if you slip and call him a Yan—"

Her words hung in the air, for Caleb had left the room and closed the door behind him.

While he was gone, Letty scrubbed Thorn with the sponge, trimmed his beard and mustache almost as well as a barber would have done, and cut his hair close to the scalp.

The bath finished, she spread a clean sheet on the floor, then when Caleb returned half an hour later, they lifted Thorn from the tub, laid him on the sheet, and wrapped it around him.

"Better dunk your feet in the water," she said. "We don't want mud tracks inside the house. Everything must look normal, as though we were home all evening."

Following her own advice, she lifted one booted foot and swirled it around in the filthy water until the mud came off, then she dunked the other boot. As soon as Caleb finished dunking his boots, they carried Thorn through the connecting door to the main room and up the stairs.

"Watch your head at the turn," she warned.

A grunt was Caleb's only answer, but he ducked just in time to avoid the low ceiling.

As soon as they laid Thorn on the bed in Letty's room, she removed the wet sheet and covered his naked body with a warm quilt.

She stared at the man beneath the quilt. He looked better than he had an hour ago, but he was so thin, at least twenty pounds lighter than when he and Andrew Holden had visited White Pines.

While she lit the candle that stood in an old pewter holder on the small bedside table, Caleb picked up the wet sheet and wadded it into a ball. "I'll use this to wipe the floor in the granny room, then I'll pull the door to and go on to my cabin. Unless there's trouble, you won't see me again till morning."

Letty nodded, unable to find words to thank him for what

he had done tonight, for the risks he had taken purely for her sake. Finally, needing to say something, she wished him sweet dreams. "And, Caleb?"

"Yes'm?"

"I've been thinking about what you said the other day about wanting to be buried on the knoll out back, beside that pink-blossomed bay tree."

"The one Mr. Jubal call the loblolly magnolia?"

"Yes, the loblolly. I was thinking that when you finish carving your marker, maybe you wouldn't mind carving one just like it for me. There's room for two next to that tree, and I can't think of anyone I'd rather spend eternity with than you."

He didn't look at her, but at the wet sheet in his hands. "Two markers ain't no more trouble than one. Come laying-by time, I'll find me a nice piece of wood that'll do for two."

He said no more, merely stepped outside the small bedroom and closed the door behind him.

Letty heard his footsteps on the stairs, then in a few moments she heard the connecting door to the granny room open and close. By the time she heard the outside door close, she had already stripped out of her muddy clothes, cleaned herself as thoroughly as possible at the washstand, then donned a heavy, flannel nightgown. The weather wasn't cool enough for flannel, but she didn't want to be wearing something as revealing as her summer linen gown if that gang from the settlement came by.

As she unfastened her braid and began brushing the thick, straight hair that reached to her waist, her attention was claimed by a slight movement from the bed. She looked over that way and discovered Thorn staring at her in the candlelight.

"Am I really here?" he muttered, his voice scarcely audible.

Relieved, Letty set the brush on the washstand and hurried over to the bed. "You're really here, Thorn. Though I can hardly believe it myself. Caleb and I found you and brought you home."

She laid her hand on his forehead. "You weren't seriously hurt in the fall, but you have a touch of fever. Unless I miss my guess, you've been sick for several days."

"Fall?" He moved his body slightly, as if to reassure himself that he could. The quilt slipped down off his shoulders. "How did I fall?"

"Shhh. Never mind about that now. For the moment, just rest and stay warm. Leave everything to me, and I'll have you well in no time."

While she readjusted the quilt, she allowed her fingers to linger for an instant against his firm neck. "Do you think you could drink a warm tisane?"

"I'd rather drink that," he said, looking at the thick hair that fell forward as she bent to tuck the quilt. Slipping his arm from beneath the cover, he caught a lock, wound it around his finger, then carried the hair to his face, breathing in its clean scent.

"It's been such a long time," he said. "I was afraid you would forget me."

He stared into her eyes, as if searching for something in their depths, then he tugged gently at her hair, pulling her face closer to his. Letty was certain he meant to kiss her, but fatigue got the better of him and his eyelids closed. In just a moment, though, he jerked them open again. "You're still here," he whispered, relief in his voice. "I was afraid you would be gone."

"I'm still here. I'm not going anyplace."

He sighed. "I'm afraid I'll wake up and find this is all a dream. That I'm back in . . ."

When his eyelids closed this time, they stayed shut, and in less than a minute the rumble of his slow, rhythmic breathing filled the room.

Recognizing the sound of healing sleep, Letty unwound her hair from Thorn's finger, then moved away from the bed. Confident now that she could leave him for a few minutes, she threw a large shawl around her shoulders, took the candle, and went downstairs to boil some water to make him an herbal tisane for when he woke again.

She rekindled the fire and had just poured a gourd of

water into the kettle when she heard the pounding of horses' hooves not far from the house. Her heart began to pound in rhythm with the hoofbeats. She thought she had prepared herself for the possibility of facing that mob of rough men, but when vague possibility became undeniable reality, she found herself clutching the edge of the table to keep her knees from buckling beneath her. Like her knees, her faith in her ability to act out the charade she had fabricated began to falter.

While the horses galloped up to the porch, she ran to the door to lift the Dragoon and holster off the peg. She dropped her shawl to the floor, slipped her arm and head through the holster, then retrieved the shawl and draped it around her in a way she hoped would conceal the bulge. With the feel of the weapon poking her ribs, some of her assurance returned, and she barely flinched when what sounded like a dozen pairs of boots reverberated on the porch.

"Y'all two go round yonder to the back," a gruff voice ordered. "Brady, you come with me. The rest of you men stay with the horses, and don't nobody do nothing till I say so."

"Why'ncha let Arlo go with you?" someone suggested, his tone mocking. "Maybe that cracker he had the run-in with today is inside the house. He'll be glad of a chance to settle the score with the fellow."

Several hoots and catcalls followed the man's suggestion. "Leastways he's been bellyaching about how he was going to settle the score. Ain'tcha, Arlo?"

"Grimley!" an angry voice yelled. "How 'bout I come put your lights out for you?"

"Yeah? You and what ten men?"

The challenge was no sooner issued than Letty heard the unmistakable sounds of a scuffle. The gruff-voiced man shouted above the commotion. "If y'all two good-for-nothings don't stop this fighting, I'm putting both your lights out!"

The silence that followed the threat lasted for several seconds before it was broken by a sledgehammer fist pounding at the lodge door. "Open up!" the gruff voice yelled.

Letty's heart became one with the pounding at the door. "Who is it?"

"Open the door! We're here on official business."

Knowing she had no choice but to comply, she took a deep breath and slid back the long, metal bolt. She had meant to open the door only a few inches, but when the man put his hand against the wood and pushed hard enough to let her know he was coming in with or without her consent, she stepped back and swung the door open all the way.

He was a big man—tall and heavyset—with a gamey, unwashed smell that made Letty want to clamp her hand over her nose. His hair was shaggy, and his clothes were rumpled and muddy. Since the small fire across the room and the candle on the hutch were the only sources of light, she couldn't see his face clearly. His features were a blur in the shadowed light, as were the features of the orange-haired man who followed him inside—the man he had called Brady.

Not that Letty needed to see Brady's face. She knew his features by heart. If the room had been pitch dark, she would have recognized him.

Brady. So, he was calling himself Brady now. She supposed it was as serviceable a name as Braithwaite.

Hoping to hide part of her face from view, Letty bent her head so her hair would swing forward, then she peeped through the concealing strands. Gone were the diamond pinky ring and the flashy gold-and-green suit, but the man standing in her doorway was, nonetheless, the man who had called himself Dozier Braithwaite—the man who had conspired to cheat her out of White Pines Plantation.

Remembered anger surged through her, but hard on the heels of that emotion was the realization that Braithwaite could expose her as well as Thorn. He could spoil the new life she had made for herself, reveal the truth of her identity, repudiate the lie she was even now rehearsing in her head. If he recognized her, he could ruin it all. *If he recognized her.*

She kept her head down, the hair obscuring her features.

Braithwaite stopped just inside the room, staring at her through the pale light and looking her over from the hair that hid her face to the hem of the nightgown that didn't quite cover her bare feet. She could almost feel his eyes examining her inch by inch.

"Begging your pardon, ma'am," he said in that phony drawl he still used, "but don't I know you?"

Quelling the desire to move over to the far corner of the room where the light didn't reach, she breathed deeply and tried to moisten her lips with a tongue that felt as dry as a cotton boll. "No, sir," she said in a drawl that outcrackered his own, "we ain't met. Me and the mister don't get to town much these days. Not since he took sick."

Braithwaite took a step closer. "I ain't often wrong, ma'am, and I never forget a face. I'd swear I've seen you somepl—"

"Never mind all that!" the large man bellowed. "We ain't come for no tea party. In case you've forgot, Brady, we're here looking for a Yankee."

Glad of any excuse to avoid Braithwaite's questions, Letty squealed dramatically. "A Yankee! All the saints in heaven, sir—tell me you're only funning. A Yankee? In these parts?"

The man stepped over to the stairs and searched the shadows behind them. "He was in one of them balloons. It come to earth not far from here, but all we found was the smashed up basket and a few sandbags. Since the balloon was too torn up to be used again, there won't be no reward for it, but we aim to find that Yankee just the same."

Letty pulled her shawl closer around her and let her voice tremble slightly. "And you think this Yankee could've found his way to my farm, mayhap be hiding here at the lodge?"

"Hiding or being hid."

The man strolled back over to her. "And if he's being hid, then them that's helping him are traitors." He leaned close to her, the putrid smell of his rotting teeth filling her nostrils, making her nauseated. "D'you know what happens to traitors?"

"They hang 'em," Braithwaite answered for her, his eyes open wide in his attempt to see her better.

"Brady's right," the man said, moving back a step. "They hang traitors. And sometimes they even hang the traitor's family and friends alongside of him . . . or her."

As though insulted, Letty stepped away as far as she dared and turned her shoulder to him. "You'll find no traitors here, sir. There's only me and my sick husband. I'd just come down to brew him a soothing draught when you—"

"Where's he at?"

"My husband? Why, he's abed. And I'll thank you not to go abothering him."

The man jerked his head toward the stairs, but before Braithwaite could obey the unspoken command, the door was thrown open. "What the—? Where'd you find them two?"

A man stepped inside the room. His gun was drawn and pointing at Caleb and Jubal Morgan.

Letty wanted to scream. Caleb knew the part he was to play, but the guileless, talkative Jubal could get all three of them hanged.

"We found this here nigger out back in a cabin," the man with the gun said, "but we can't get nothing out of him on account of he's loony as a bedbug. Don't even know what a Yankee is. Seems to think I'm fixing to yank out his teeth."

Caleb fell to his knees and raised his clasped hands in supplication toward Letty. "Please, mistress, don't let these gentlemens yank out my teeth. Othello ain't done nothing to get his teeth yanked out."

The big man put his foot on Caleb's back and pushed him aside. "Go on. Get out of here, you crazy old coot."

While Caleb scurried out on all fours, the big man approached Jubal. "And what about this one?"

"Found him snooping around in the woods out back of

the house. Ain't had much to say for hisself so far. Wouldn't tell us who he is or what he's doing here.''

Letty breathed a sigh of relief. Perhaps they still had a chance. If Jubal was keeping his mouth shut, he had his reasons for doing so. And he hadn't so much as batted an eye while Caleb performed his part in their charade. She would just have to brave it through and trust Jubal's innate intelligence.

She stamped her foot angrily. "I can tell you who he is and what he's adoing on my property. He's thieving white trash, that's who he is, and any time he knows my husband's abed sick, he comes asneaking over here to see what he can steal." As all eyes turned to Jubal, Letty edged a little farther away from the light.

"Now, Mizriz Bonner—"

"And don't you go atrying to cuzzin me with that hogwash about how it was weasels got my chickens that time. I know it was you. Just let me catch you redhanded one time, you piece of trash, and I'll do what these men are threatening to do to whoever is ahiding that Yankee soldier. I'll hang you to the nearest tree."

Not by so much as a raised eyebrow did Jubal react to her message about the threat of a hanging.

"Now, Mizriz Bonner, you ain't got no call to go scandalizing my name that way. I come over here neighborly like. My boy come home this evening with a young fern; says you give it to him to keep for a while. It was such a pretty fern that I come over to repay you by seeing if you needed my help with anything."

Letty almost fainted with relief. Before she could respond to Jubal's message, however, the big man stepped between them.

"You know anything about a Yankee soldier?" he asked.

Jubal pulled off his hat and looked up into the man's face. "No, sir. It's like I was telling Mizriz Bonner, I only come by neighborly like."

"Ha!" Letty scoffed. "You only came by because you thought you could grab something while I wasn't looking."

"Now, Mizriz Bonner, I done told you—"

"Throw this thief off my property," Letty ordered the man with the gun. "I don't even want to look at his face." Seizing the opportunity to move completely out of the light, she turned and flounced over to the far corner and sat down on the parson's bench.

The big man returned his attention to Braithwaite. "Get on upstairs and see what you find. And you," he said to the man who had brought Jubal in, "you go see what's through that door there."

While Braithwaite groped his way up the dark stairs, the other man went over to the granny room, pushed the door open, and peered inside. "It's too dark in there," he said. "I can't see a thing."

The big man jerked his head toward the hutch. "Take him that candle," he ordered Jubal.

Jubal took the candle to the man at the door. "I wouldn't go in there if I was you." His voice was hushed, breathy, as though he were telling a ghost story. "Never know what you might find in there."

The man at the door hesitated. Letty could almost feel the goose bumps on her own arms. Jubal took a giant step backward, then lowered his voice to just above a whisper. "The woman keeps potions and I don't know what all in there. Calls herself a healer, but there's folks hereabouts that call her something else."

Letty had no idea what Jubal had in mind; all they would find in the granny room were shelves of herbs and the wooden tub filled with dirty bathwater. If he had some plan, however, she was willing to follow his lead. She sat quietly and watched as the man with the candle reluctantly entered the room. Within seconds he was back at the door. He had dropped the candle in his haste.

"There's a coffin in there," he shrieked. "And there's some kind of dark liquid in it . . . with stuff floating all around." His voice almost failed him. "And some of the stuff looks like human hair." The man shuddered. "This here's a voodoo house, and I'm gettin' out while the gettin's good."

As the man ran to the front door and out into the damp night, Jubal turned his attention to the big man who stood next to the fireplace. "Did he say something about a coffin filled with liquid?"

When the man didn't answer, Jubal used that hushed, breathy voice again. "How can that be? Liquid'll seep out of a coffin. Leastways, it'll seep out of the kind of coffin made by God-fearing folks—folks that don't have no trek with potions and such like. 'Course—"

"Bra-dy!" The big man's voice cracked on the second syllable. "Get back down here."

Footsteps sounded in the darkness at the top of the stairs. "What d'you want? I ain't through searching around up here."

The big man walked over to the foot of the stairs, making certain his back was to the wall when he stopped. "You find that Yankee?"

Braithwaite came down several steps. "I found somebody, but I can't tell if he's a Yankee or not. He's lying under a quilt, and he's buck naked. I was looking to see if maybe they'd hid his uniform."

"Idiot. Can't you tell a soldier without he's wearing a uniform? Does he look like he lives in a house like this, or is he dirty and covered with lice and crabs?"

"He's clean, but—"

"Then get on down here. We're leaving."

The man glanced toward the granny room, then hurried to the front door. "Gimme my horse!" he yelled the moment his feet touched the porch.

Braithwaite tramped down the dark stairs, but just before he stepped outside, he peered into the dim corner where Letty sat on the settle. "You sure we ain't met before? Something about you puts me in mind of—"

"Brady! Get out here, you numbskull, or we're leaving without you."

As soon as Braithwaite stepped outside, Jubal closed the door and shot the bolt, then he let his thin body sag against the thick wood. Letty felt limp as a rag doll. Neither of them moved until the sound of the men's horses died in the distance, then Letty rushed forward and took Jubal's hands.

"You were wonderful! How can I ever thank you for what—"

"Save your thanks!" he said, pulling his hands free and stepping back. " 'Cause I ain't proud of this night's work." He looked at her with eyes that were both sad and angry. "I ain't much, Miz Letty, but I always been a man of my word. I never could abide a liar. And now I am one."

She didn't know what to say. "I'm sorry, Jubal."

"You've hid that Yankee," he said, ignoring her apology. "How come you done it, I don't even want to know, but hiding him makes you a traitor. I had to help you. I owe you that much for taking care of Patience and seeing our little Sarah was born healthy. But helping you makes me a traitor, too, and I take no pleasure in the fact."

He slipped the bolt and opened the front door.

"Jubal. Please don't go. Stay a minute and let me explain."

"Ain't nothing to explain. You're a headstrong woman, Miz Letty, and mostly I admire that in you, but this time you went too far." He stepped out onto the porch. "I reckon you had your reasons for what you done, but I don't like what I done."

As if needing to do something with his hands, he fished in his shirt pocket until he found his tobacco, then he bit off a chaw and put the plug back in his pocket. "Tomorrow morning I'll bring little Fern home to you. After that, you and me is quits. I don't never plan to set foot on your land again, and I'd appreciate it if you stayed off of mine."

"Please, Jubal. Don't . . ."

Her plea hung in the wet, night air as Jubal Morgan walked away, never once looking back.

Letty stood on the porch for a long time after Jubal left, too stunned and shaken by his words to do more than listen to the water drip off the eaves. The fact that she hadn't meant to involve him in this night's work did little to comfort her. Planned or not, the result was the same; he had come to her rescue as a friend, and now he was her friend no longer.

Feeling exhausted and very much alone, she went back inside the house and brewed the tisane. It had been less than an hour since she left Thorn asleep in her bed, but so much had happened in that hour that when she tiptoed back into her bedroom with the hot tisane, she was surprised to find him lying just as she had left him. His rhythmic breathing told her he still slept, unmindful of the drama that had taken place below.

She placed the candle on the washstand, then she laid her hand on his shoulder. His eyes opened instantly. "See if you can sit up. I've brought you something to drink. It will help ease your fever."

Obeying her, he sat up and let her hold the cup to his dry lips. While he drank thirstily of the aromatic brew, she began to tremble with reaction to all that had happened to her that evening.

Thorn put his hands over hers to hold the cup steady while he drained the last drops. "My poor girl," he whispered, caressing her fingers, "you're cold. Your hands are like ice." As though it were the most natural thing in the world, he lifted the edge of the quilt in invitation. "Come, get under here where it's warm."

Hesitating only a moment, Letty put the cup beside the candle, removed the shawl and Dragoon she still wore, and crawled under the quilt. She lay on her side, her back to him, careful not to touch him, but the rustling of the mattress told her he had moved even before she felt his knees crook behind hers and his arm pull her against his chest.

At first she stiffened, for the unfamiliar feel of a man's naked body pressed against hers unnerved her. Within a few moments, however, she heard his soft snores and felt his slow, even breath fan a wisp of hair at her temple, and eventually she relaxed. Like the cup she had held to his lips, his skin was warm. She snuggled against him, savoring his warmth, letting his protective arms soothe and comfort her.

She needed comforting. She had needed it for a long,

long time. For most of her life. She couldn't even remember the last time someone had held her close.

Actually, now that she put her mind to it, Letty recalled that time quite clearly; it had been almost seven years ago, in her herb garden. And the someone had been Thorn Bradley. At that time she had been inconsolable, but now, with the warmth of his body pressed against her back and his arm wrapped around her protectively, she welcomed consolation. For once in her life, she didn't feel quite so alone.

As she lay there watching the guttering candle make dancing images on the wall and the ceiling of her little bedroom, she gave herself up to the comfort of Thorn's arms. Her senses calmed, and her eyelids grew heavy and began to droop. She told herself to rest, to let go, that all was well. It had been a difficult evening, but the danger was passed, and nothing more could hurt her.

Later, Letty would remember that sleepy self-delusion.

Fifteen

Letty couldn't imagine what had dragged her from the warm, lovely cocoon of her dreams. It certainly wasn't the nasal *pee-yah* of the nightjar perched in the oak tree just outside her bedroom window. Birds never bothered her. Nor was it time to get up. The pink dawn light hadn't even begun to paint the black sky, and the room was pitch dark. Too sleepy to ponder the mystery of what had awakened her, she pulled the quilt back over her shoulder and tried to wiggle into the familiar groove that time and her body had molded into the middle of the mattress. She couldn't find the groove, something was in her way, something hard and immovable.

Suddenly wide awake, she was instantly aware of the warm body pressed against her back. Lost in the deep sleep brought on by her fatigue, she had forgotten about Thorn, forgotten that he had drawn her close then fallen asleep. He was even closer now, and at that moment the soft breath that tickled her temple had nothing to do with snores.

His arm still rested across her waist, but his hand no longer lay unmoving. To her surprise, his fingertips drew gentle, lazy circles around her belly button.

"My sweet love," he murmured softly. "You cannot

know how many times I have dreamed of holding you like this.''

While Thorn pressed his lips against her hair, Letty lay perfectly still, not daring to move.

"Umm," he whispered. "You smell so good. Like heaven itself. Have you any idea how I wanted to be with you?"

Letty didn't answer; she couldn't. Speech was impossible. It was difficult just drawing enough air into her lungs to breathe.

Raising up on his elbow, Thorn touched his lips to the side of her neck, then he let them linger there against her skin for what seemed like days, sending a slow, sweet warmth throughout her body.

"My beautiful angel," he said so softly she thought she might have imagined the words.

Letty knew she should move away. Leave the bed. Run from the room. But her legs and arms felt almost boneless, unable to do her bidding. The gentle pressure of his lips against her neck, his fingers making those lazy circles, they were doing strange things to her insides, liquefying her every muscle.

Slowly, coaxingly he turned her shoulder, urging it flat against the mattress so he could press his lips to the hollow of her throat. Though she knew she shouldn't, Letty turned without resisting, then she closed her eyes, wanting to savor the sweet sensation of his lips upon her flesh. After an eternity of sweet, tantalizing nibbles, his lips parted, and he touched her skin with the tip of his moist tongue.

At that unexpected touch, every inch of her flesh grew warm, and a pulse hammered beneath the spot his tongue had brought to life.

"I need you," he whispered. "I need to feel your arms around me." His voice was ragged. "I want to hold you, to love you. But I need you to respond . . . to love me, too."

Letty began to tremble in a way she had never trembled before. Her entire body tingled with life, and deep inside her a throbbing awareness begged her to respond to his need. She wanted to feel his lips touching her skin again, she wanted the touch of his tongue. She wanted, needed to feel his kisses upon her face, her mouth, her entire body.

"We'll go slow," he murmured. "I promise I won't hurt you. Please don't be afraid. I love you so much."

He loves me! Thorn loves me. She wasn't afraid; she was on fire.

He stopped making the circles on her belly and unfastened the top button of her gown. With each succeeding button, he left a kiss where the button had touched her chest. Letty was certain he could feel the pounding of her heart beneath his lips.

When all the buttons were freed, Thorn pushed the thick flannel aside and slowly slid his hand across her chest to caress her already taut breast. Waves of heat cursed through her with such force she thought surely her entire body would explode.

Unable to stand the sweet agony a moment longer, she turned to him, slid her arms around his waist, and pressed her trembling body against his. "Thorn," she murmured against his neck. "I love you. I have always loved you."

She heard him groan, and as he lowered his head and covered her mouth with his, she felt his body tremble as hers was trembling.

"My precious angel," he said against her mouth. "I can't believe you have come to me at last."

Later, when she lay in his arms, her head resting on his chest, the lingering thrill of his lovemaking still made her seem disconnected from her own body, almost as if she floated somewhere in another dimension. She could scarcely believe it had really happened, that Thorn had made love to her, and that all these years he had remembered her and loved her, as she had remembered and loved him.

But it had been real—the inexpressible joy of his weight upon her, then the wave after wave of pleasure that grew within her body until she thought she must call out or die of sheer happiness. Thorn had made love to her, and Letty had responded, loving him in return, just as he asked. Now she felt wonderful, even beautiful, and happier than she had ever been in her entire life.

Thorn touched his fingers to her chin and gently turned her face up to his, kissing her once again. This time it was a gentle kiss, as gentle as his other kisses had been fierce.

"My angel," he whispered.

He kissed her again then nestled her comfortably against his side. "I knew it could be like this."

Letty snuggled against him, unwilling to break the magical spell by talking. She had waited all her life for this, for someone to hold her close, someone to love her and cherish her, to call her his beloved, and she wanted to savor the feeling just a little longer.

"I knew I could make you love me," he murmured sleepily. ". . . knew I could make you respond to me as you did tonight."

Only half listening to his words, Letty nuzzled her face into the hollow of his shoulder, delighting in the male smell of his damp skin.

Once again Thorn's breathing was beginning to fall into its rhythmic pattern. He was almost asleep. "Your tears. They haunted my dreams. . . ." His words began to slur. "Not enough time before," he mumbled drowsily. "Your shyness on our wedding night . . . your distaste at my caresses. I . . ."

Letty lay very still, not even daring to breathe, while a perspiration that had nothing to do with the passion they had shared only minutes ago covered her bare skin. She strained her ears to hear his words, praying she had heard him wrong.

He drifted off for a moment, then he turned his head and buried his face in her hair. "Delia," he murmured groggily. "My beautiful Delia. My sweet bride."

His last words were like a knife—a dull knife that plunged cruelly into Letty's chest and gouged out her heart, cutting off her blood supply and making her colder than she had ever been before. The perspiration on her skin turned to ice, and she shivered uncontrollably.

Only moments ago she would have turned into Thorn's

arms for warmth, but now she lay rigid, like a slab of cold marble, waiting for the sound of his soft snores. When she was certain he was fast asleep, she eased out of his embrace, inched away from the bed they had shared so intimately, and tiptoed from the room.

With no place else to go, Letty crept through the darkness to Fern's bedroom. The tiny room was innocent of furniture except for a small pine dresser and a child's crib, so Letty lifted the quilt from the empty crib, wrapped the soft material around her naked body, and lay down on the bare, wooden floor.

While she lay there in the darkness, silent tears spilled out of the corners of her eyes and slid past her temples to be lost forever in her love-tousled hair. They were worthless tears, for they brought her no relief. They were as comfortless as they were silent, yet she could no more stop them than she could stop the jeering call of the lonely nightjar perched in the distant oak tree.

Cruel bird.

How he mocked her, deriding her for her stupidity. Where once he had cried out, *pee-yah, pee-yah,* now he taunted her with, *De-lia, De-lia.*

As soon as dawn's smudgy pink streaks appeared in the morning sky, a tired, bleary-eyed Letty tiptoed back into her own bedroom. The room was quiet. Except for Thorn's breathing, the only other sound came from outside, near the well, where a pair of clucking chickens scratched and pecked the soft earth.

While the early birds searched the muddy ground for bugs and worms, Letty searched for the flannel nightgown she had discarded with such abandon the night before. Spying the chaste garment peeping from beneath the bed, she snatched it up and stuffed it behind the washstand. Once that embarrassing reminder was out of sight, she lifted her work dress from its hook on the wall and tiptoed back out of the room.

She hadn't even glanced toward the man in the bed. She was afraid he might be awake, that he might be looking at her, and she didn't want to see the question in his eyes. She didn't want to answer that question. How could she tell him that his Delia wasn't here, had never been here? How could she admit that she was the woman he had made love to, the woman who had responded to him so wantonly?

Of course he never would have mistaken her for his wife if he hadn't still been out of his head. It was the fever. She realized that now. He was ill, probably hallucinating; that explained his behavior.

But how could she justify her own?

Mortification stuck in her throat like a fish bone, making tears well up in her eyes. Thorn would think she was a strumpet. Or worse yet, a desperate old maid who had taken advantage of his illness. A sob escaped her throat, for she couldn't bear to have him think of her that way.

Though it was no more than the truth, she admitted as she yanked the gray cotton dress over her head and began fastening the buttons up the front. All of it was true: She was an old maid, and she had acted like a strumpet first chance she got.

No point in lying to herself; she might as well face facts. If a thing looked like a mule and brayed like a mule, it wasn't a horse.

She pushed the last button through the buttonhole and wrenched the collar into place. Then, without giving a thought to the unbrushed tangles, she swung her hair over her right shoulder and began braiding it, pulling and jerking at the strands as though they weren't attached to her own head.

With a final tug that was more punishing than necessary, Letty tossed the heavy braid back over her shoulder. *An old maid's braid for an old maid strumpet.*

A lowering thought, yet surely only a strumpet would have acted the way she did last night. His Delia had obviously displayed more modesty. But then Delia was his bride and not a thirty-two-year-old spinster who was so starved for affection she would—

She stopped abruptly. *His bride.* Thorn was married. Her

eyes closed against the shame, and she braced herself against the wall to keep from falling. She had committed adultery! Heaven help her. Were there any commandments left that she hadn't broken?

What had gotten into her last night? Had some evil spirit taken possession of her body, bewitched her mind? She couldn't believe all the reckless things she had done. She had betrayed her own country, turned a good friend away forever, and risked not only her own life, but Caleb's as well. And for what? The object of her girlish fantasies. A man she hadn't seen in seven years.

A married man.

Sighing heavily, she pushed away from the wall and trudged down the stairs. She had behaved like a fool; she knew that now, yet she couldn't undo what she had done. It was too late. And though the fires of hell awaited her in the afterlife, she still had chores to do on this earth and a little girl who would be coming home soon.

Once she turned the bend in the stairs, several of those chores became readily apparent. The floor was covered with muddy boot prints, and the stench of wet horse flesh and unwashed male bodies permeated the room.

Wanting to expunge as much as she could of last night's insanity, Letty grabbed the water bucket and hurried out to the well. Caleb always drew her a bucket of water first thing each morning, then he would water and feed the stock until she called him to breakfast. This morning there was no sign of him.

She looked toward his cabin when she went outside, but she saw no smoke rising from his chimney. He must be sleeping late; heaven knew he deserved it after what she had asked of him last night. She wondered how she would ever make it up to him.

Plans for making amends filled her mind; otherwise, the instant she turned the corner of the house she would have seen the man who leaned against a limb of the sprawling live oak. As it was, she was already pulling the filled bucket up the well before she noticed the sun shining off the man's orange hair.

Startled, she jumped back and let go of the crank, re-
leasing the windlass. The rope whined as the bucket
plunged downward, and when it splashed into the water,
Letty jumped again.

The intruder set his hat on his head, slung his jacket over
his shoulder, then approached her at a leisurely pace.

"You!"

"Like I told you last night, I don't never forget a face.
And you remembered me, too, I'll be bound."

After a moment's panic, Letty regained her wits and
dredged up the drawl she had used last night. "Sure I remember you, sir. You were with them men who stopped
by here last night."

"Tsk, tsk, now, girlie. You can do better than that. I ain't
changed all that much. Of course, last time you saw me I
was living pretty high on the hog. I hadn't yet fallen on
these hard times."

Letty forced a smile to her lips. She would need to keep
her head. The man could still ruin her life and Fern's if he
revealed her identity. "Like I told you last night, me and
the mister don't—"

"You can stop the playacting, girlie. I know who you
really are. You threw me off some last night, with your hair
hanging down young-like, instead of old-maidish like you
used to wear it, but I kept pondering your face till I remembered."

To keep him from seeing how much his words frightened
her, Letty turned and began drawing the bucket out of the
well. The windlass groaned noisily as she turned the crank.

"Of course," he said, speaking above the noise, "I
would've kenned you sooner if I'd've known you were still
alive. A fella don't expect to have to recall a face that's
supposed to have burned up in a fire."

It was all she could do not to drop the bucket again. So
they thought she had died in the blaze that destroyed White
Pines. That fascinating possibility had never occurred to
her.

"That was a right smart trick you pulled, torching the
plantation."

Smiling as though they shared a secret, he winked and tapped his temple with his forefinger. "You got more in your *nous* box than me and old Maynard gave you credit for. Yes, ma'am. You're a real smart'un, you are. Fooled us all." The smile slid off his fleshy lips. "Of course, that fire came between me and Mr. DuBose Maynard, Esquire. And that wasn't so smart of you."

Braithwaite stepped closer to her, his cold, mud-brown eyes reminding her of a copperhead's. "Old Maynard took it hard when he found out that fine house he'd planned to live in wasn't nothing but a mound of smoldering ashes. Yes, sirree. Nearly drove me loony blathering on about all that European furniture and such going up in smoke."

Still feigning ignorance, Letty poured water from the well bucket into her smaller bucket then lifted it and turned toward the house. "I'm sure I don't know what you're talking about. Now if you'll excuse me, I have chores to do."

All semblance of friendliness gone, Braithwaite grabbed the bucket from her hand and tossed it aside, spilling water on her feet and down the front of her skirt. "Still think you're the grand lady giving orders, don't you, girlie girl?" He caught the braid that hung down her back and yanked her against his chest. "Think again."

The time for pretense had passed. Letty knew her best bet now was to brave it through, not let him know how much he frightened her. "What is it you want, Braithwaite?"

"That's more like it. We'll get farther, quicker, if you cooperate."

Though he still held her braid, his fingers thrust between the loose plaiting, Letty tried to push away from his chest. "As I said, what do you want?"

"Only what's mine. I want the three thousand in gold you cheated me out of."

She almost laughed. "*I* cheated *you*?"

Braithwaite yanked her hair painfully. "I told you that business came between me and old Maynard. He was all torn up about losing the house and the crops, but when he went to the bank and found out the tin box you'd had the clerk put in his safe was empty, he went crazy. Accused me of stealing the gold. He knew I used to do card tricks and juggling with a traveling show, and he claimed I'd switched boxes while no one was looking. He said it had to be me.''

The man's eyes flashed with anger. ''I told Maynard you'd taken the gold out somehow, but he wouldn't believe me. He said it couldn't have been you, because you were so stupid you didn't even know you'd been hoodwinked.''

The thought of the crooked lawyer's frustration pleased Letty immensely. Unfortunately she must have shown her pleasure, because Braithwaite yanked her hair again.

''He owed me. I did my part of the job—I got you to sell cheap—but Maynard wouldn't pay me. When I tried to take what was coming to me, he had me beaten up and hauled out of town. Swore he'd have me killed if I ever came back.'' A tic pulled at the corner of Braithwaite's left eye. ''Didn't even let me get my buggy and my trappings.

''But now I've found you, and you're fixing to give me what's owed me.'' To show he meant business, he pulled her head down and leaned into her face. His hot breath made her skin crawl. ''I want that three thousand in gold.''

For a split second she considered telling him he could have the money if he would go away and never come back, but just as she formed the first word, he gave her braid a vicious twist that forced her to her knees. ''You will do as I say, or else.''

The instant her knees touched the ground, a long-suppressed memory flooded her consciousness—a memory of another time she had been forced to her knees in submission. With that memory came a surge of hatred she thought she had buried with Abner Banks, a hatred so fierce it rendered her immune to pain. She wanted to kill Braithwaite for bringing that memory back.

''Take your hands off me, you filthy lout!''

Surprised, he let go of her hair and stepped back. Neither of them had any doubt why he had done it. His eyes wary and his mouth pouty, his was the face of a bully who had met his match.

His hesitancy lasted for only a few seconds, but that was long enough for Letty to get to her feet and run toward the porch. Her one thought was to make it to the front door where her Dragoon hung from the gun rack. What came next she neither knew nor cared.

And she would have reached the front door in plenty of time, if her wet skirt hadn't hampered her progress. As it was, she had only time enough to reach inside the door before Braithwaite's boots sounded on the porch. Unfortunately her hand encountered only the empty gun rack. Too late, she remembered dropping the gun belt and her shawl on the floor last night when she crawled into bed with Thorn Bradley.

"She-cat!" Dozier Braithwaite yelled as he grabbed the sleeve of her dress and yanked her back toward the porch. "You'll be sorry for trying to trick me again."

Surprising herself as much as him, she swung her fist with all her strength and hit him a stunning blow to the side of his head. He staggered backward. With nothing more in her thoughts than getting to the Dragoon, she ran toward the stairs.

She had made it up the first few steps, and had turned to the left, when she heard Braithwaite right behind her. Just as she felt his hands grip the back of her dress, she heard a thud. It was his head hitting the low ceiling. He hadn't known to duck.

"Damn!" He clutched his forehead for a moment, then he started toward her again. "I'll break your neck for that."

Letty had taken only one more step when a deafening explosion rocked the small area. Her eardrums rang as though someone had boxed her ears, and she fell to her knees. An instant later Dozier Braithwaite fell on top of her. Horrified, she pushed him with all her might. He rolled away without resisting, then he just lay there sprawled on the steps, not moving, not breathing, while blood oozed from a gaping hole in his back.

Letty didn't move, either; she couldn't. She lay there on the steps gasping for breath and staring at the lank, orange hair that fell across the dead man's face.

"Child?" Caleb's voice sounded so frightened Letty almost didn't recognize it.

To allay his fears, she dragged the hem of her skirt from beneath the dead body, clutched the handrail so she could pull herself to her feet, then stepped around the corner where Caleb could see her. "I'm all right. He didn't do—" Her voice died in her throat.

Caleb stood at the bottom of the stairs. In his hands he held Abner Banks's hunting rifle, still pointed at the dead man. An acrid-smelling smoke hung in the air above his head.

Letty could only stare, first at Caleb and then at the rifle. "You shot him." Her voice was even shakier than his. "Heaven help us! You shot a white man."

Her legs buckled beneath her, and she would have fallen if Caleb hadn't laid the rifle down on the floor and run up the stairs to help her. He took her trembling hands and led her slowly down the remainder of the steps.

"I had to do it, child. There wasn't no other way. I couldn't let him hurt you."

"I know." Her throat was so clogged with tears she could barely speak. She looked at the long, bony fingers entwined with her own. "But he was a white man. They . . . they'll hang you without a trial."

It being an unanswerable truth, Caleb said nothing. Like her, he stared at their entwined fingers.

Needing to sit down, they walked over to the parson's bench, then while they sat there, their hands joined as their lives had been joined for more than thirty years, Letty tried to think what to do. "I will tell whatever authority is interested that I shot Braithwaite. Being a woman, I might get off with a plea of self-defense. They—"

"No."

"But, I—"

"No," he repeated.

She tried to think of some argument that would sway him, but she looked into his stony face and knew there was none. Caleb would never let her say she killed the man. If she had done the shooting, he would have been willing to take the blame for her, but he would never let her do the same for him. In a land where chivalry was paid a nause-ating amount of lip service, with little substance behind it, in Caleb it was a reality. Gallantry was as much a part of him as the heart that beat inside his chest.

"I been thinking," he said. "Wouldn't nobody have to know the man was dead. Not if I toted him downriver someplace and buried him where nobody would ever find him."

"If *we* buried him," she corrected. "This mess is all my fault, and I'm not letting you clean it up alone."

"Your fault? Now how you figure that, child? Did you send that white trash an invite to come here and attack you?"

"As near as makes no difference, I did. It was me who decided to burn White Pines. And it was me who insisted on hiding Thorn Bradley. If I had listened to you, and not gone searching for Thorn, that gang of men might never have come to the lodge hunting for him."

Caleb looked at her, his eyes serious. "And you telling me you could've lived with that? You saying you could've left that Yankee out there to be captured and not cared pea turkey if he was taken to that awful prison camp we been hearing about?"

"Yes. No. I don't know. Maybe the men would have taken him to a hospi—"

In mid-sentence an idea came to Letty, making her drop Caleb's hand and stand up, her mind abuzz and her body suddenly alive with energy. "I've got it! I know what we'll do."

"I done told you, I'll bury—"

"No. This is better, believe me."

She went over to the steps and looked at the dead man, sizing him up from head to toe, her mind already ironing out any possible wrinkles in her plan. "What did you do with Thorn's Yankee uniform?"

"I stuffed it up my chimbley. I didn't have time to burn it yet."

"Thank goodness."

Without another word, Letty ran to open the door that led to the granny room, then she hurried back to the stairs. "Help me take this scalawag into the granny room. Then, while I clean up the mess on the steps, you go get the uniform out of your chimney." She picked up Braithwaite's feet as she talked. "And bring your razor when you come back. We'll need it."

Without a moment's hesitation, Caleb stepped over the body and grabbed Braithwaite beneath the arms. He, too, seemed suddenly energized. "What you fixing to do with that old raggedy uniform?"

"I am about to become a good citizen," she said, the irony of her plan almost making her laugh. "Those men were searching for the Yankee soldier who had been shot out of a balloon, and I think they deserve to find him."

Sixteen

Letty spread a length of osnaburg on the front porch so she could lay some herbs in the sun to dry. Since the weather had been so wet the past few weeks, she had little hope for these particular specimens, but laying herbs out to dry was something she did often. Anyone who knew her, and happened to come by, might be fooled into thinking she had nothing more important on her mind.

Actually she had a great deal more than herbs on her mind. She was worried sick about Caleb. He had gone to town to tell Mr. Finley about the Yankee he had found in the woods, and he hadn't returned yet. For her part, Letty would be glad when both Yankees—the real one and the substitute one—were gone from her life. She wanted to forget them both, along with the entire last twenty-four hours. But mostly she wanted Caleb to come home safely.

The extent of her worry was evident when she didn't hear Gideon until he was almost at the porch.

"Hey, Miss Letty," he called cheerfully. "I got something here for you." He turned his back so she could see Fern ensconced in a makeshift backpack.

"Patience says to tell you if you should happen not to want this little wildcat anymore, I can just bring her on back to our house. She says she'll be happy to raise her alongside little Sarah.''

Laughing for the first time in what seemed like ages, Letty dropped the corner of the thick cloth she had been spreading and went to lift the toddler from Gideon's back. ''Tell Patience it is a tempting offer, but I think I'll keep this particular little wildcat.''

She hugged the child close, planting noisy little kisses on the soft neck and cheeks, and reveling in the baby sweetness of the little body.

Fern allowed the caresses for a short time, then she squirmed to be put down.

''Told you she was a wildcat, Miss Letty. She may be only a year old, but she already knows what she wants and when she wants it.''

Letty set Fern on the ground, letting her crawl around in the familiar yard. ''Thank you for bringing her home, Gideon. And thank you again for taking care of her for me last night. I'm sorry you didn't get to have your adventure.''

The boy grinned all over his face. ''Guess what, Miss Letty? I found that Yankee spy after all!''

Letty choked on her own breath. By the time the paroxysm of coughing was over, the boy was well into his story.

''Don't know how I came to be so lucky this morning, when just about everything went wrong last night, but there he was, lying half hidden under that gnarly old buttonbush tree near the river.''

Gideon kissed his thumb, then touched it to his elbow for luck. ''If I'd've been ten feet the other side of the path, I'd've missed him.''

''And the Yankee,'' she asked hesitantly, ''was he hurt?''

''Deader'n a doornail,'' the boy answered cheerfully. ''I turned him over to be sure, but he was already getting stiff.''

The boy looked at the ground self-consciously. ''I tore his uniform coat. I must have done it when I turned him over; him being so heavyset. I didn't hear it rip, but it did, right up the back. Almost like I'd taken scissors and cut it.''

Letty looked away, not wanting the boy to see her face. He was too close to the facts for comfort.

"You would've thought I did it on purpose the way Mr. Finley took on.''

"Mr. Finley?''

"Yes'm. Him and a couple of those men that were hunting the Yankee last night came riding up almost as soon as I found the spy. Othello was with 'em. I didn't have a chance to say anything to him, though, on account of Mr. Finley was getting all over me like a wet shirt, saying I had no business being there.'' The boy's eyes flashed with anger. "And me the one that found that Yankee!''

As if only mildly interested, Letty said, "And what happened then?''

"They ran me off. Told me to bring Fern on home.''

Gideon's sense of ill use was evident in the set of his still-childish mouth. "When I get grown, I won't ever treat a boy with such rag manners. The least they could've done was let me have a button for a souvenir.''

"Quite true,'' Letty agreed. "Uh, you being the rightful finder of the Yankee, did you leave when they told you to?''

"No'm. I went off a ways, then I hid and watched. Those two men turned the Yankee over and looked at his back where he was shot. Then they went through his pockets. Mr. Finley argued with them, said he wouldn't stand for anybody robbing the dead, but they didn't pay him any mind. When they didn't find anything in the Yankee's pockets, they wiped their hands on their britches and said for Othello to bury him before he started stinking.''

"And did he?''

"No'm. Mr. Finley said Yankee or no Yankee, they'd give him a Christian burial. So Othello wrapped the spy up in some canvas and put him across old Esau's back to take him to the settlement.''

Letty's sigh of relief turned into a shudder.

"Don't you worry, Miss Letty. He wasn't stinking yet. Esau won't smell of dead man."

Like her, the boy sighed, only his sigh was one of contentment. "I'm just glad I was the one who found that Yankee spy. Finding him was the most exciting thing I ever did. Of course, it would have been more exciting if I could've seen him flying in his balloon. I bet that would have been something to remember."

Spreading his arms to either side, Gideon swooped around a delighted Fern in his imitation of a bird. "Yep, I sure wish I could have seen that balloon. The Yankee himself wasn't all that much to look at. Not like you would think a spy ought to look. Just a regular man with mud-brown eyes. And not a hair on his head! Bald as a hen egg. You would've thought his head had just been shaved."

After she settled Fern in for a nap, Letty got her scrub brush, a cake of lye soap, and a pail of water. Beginning with the stairs and working her way across the floor toward the door, she scrubbed away all the signs of last night's muddy visitors. Because she worked with a fierceness that surpassed her usual enthusiasm for the job, she was unaware of Thorn's presence until he cleared his throat.

At the sound, Letty gasped.

"Sorry, ma'am. I didn't mean to startle you."

He stuck one bare foot out from the cocoon he'd made of the quilt. "Guess these don't make as much noise without boots."

Embarrassed to realize that he was completely naked beneath the quilt, Letty looked at his foot, then forced herself to look at his face. It was still quite pale, but otherwise he looked well enough.

"When I woke up," he said, glancing around the room, "I thought I was at a field hospital."

"You're at my house. My farm, actually. Folks around here call it Lodge Farm."

Tossing the scrub brush into the bucket, Letty stood up and walked over to the hutch, where she washed her hands and arms in the dishpan. As she wiped her hands on the cloth that hung from a peg on the wall, she motioned for Thorn to come and sit at the table. "You are probably hungry."

"Yes, ma'am." Thorn pointed to the fireplace where the contents of an iron pot bubbled softly. "It was that smell that finally dragged me out of bed, and the best sleep I've had in months."

He gathered the quilt more securely around him, then stepped carefully across the wet floor. When he was seated, Letty ladled a bowl of rabbit stew from the pot and set it on the table in front of him. "I didn't make coffee this morning. Will sweetmilk do?"

"Milk?" He nodded. "I can't remember the last time I had fresh milk."

While Letty poured the milk from the tin bucket, then replaced the protective cloth, Thorn spooned large bites of stew into his mouth. He ate without stopping until the bowl was emptied and thoroughly scraped.

"There's plenty more," she offered.

Though he looked longingly at the pot, he shook his head. "Thank you, ma'am, but I can't take your supper."

Letty set the cup of milk down beside his hand, then took his empty bowl to the fireplace and refilled it. "We have enough. Eat."

He ate the second bowl more slowly, but with the same evident enjoyment.

"How long since you've had a meal?"

"I'm not sure," he said, draining his second cup of milk. "How long have I been here?"

"Since last night."

The entire memory of last night was so mortifying to Letty that she couldn't face him, so she turned away and busied herself at the hutch. It was pure torture for her, standing there waiting for him to ask her about what had passed between the two of them last night. When he spoke, however, his words had nothing to do with their lovemaking.

"How did I get here to . . . what did you call this place? Lodge Farm?"

"You don't remember?"

"No, ma'am. I remember the impact of the basket hitting the trees. Then the next thing I remember is waking up just a few minutes ago. In between is just a blur of crazy dreams. Several times I thought I was awake, but I guess I wasn't."

Crazy dreams. Letty didn't know whether to laugh or cry. *He didn't remember about last night.*

"Once I was positive the Rebs had me, because I dreamed I heard rifle fire just outside the bedroom door."

Letty turned quickly to look at him, her eyes wide with fear. What if he knew about Braithwaite? To her relief, he shrugged and smiled apologetically.

"That probably sounds absurd to you, ma'am, but most of what I dreamed was pretty far-fetched." He fingered an ancient nick in the wooden table, as if reticent to say more, and when he spoke again, his voice was only a whisper. "Mostly I dreamed about home."

After another long silence, Thorn lifted one thick eyebrow in that deprecating gesture she had remembered for years. "Being home with loved ones, that's a soldier's constant hallucination. It's probably just as well that I don't remember the hours I lost."

"Probably," she agreed, wishing the gods would grant her a similar, blessed amnesia.

After a time she reached across the table for the used bowl and cup. As she straightened up, she found him watching her, a smile pulling slightly at the corners of his mouth. Letty stared at his lips, her senses suddenly alive with the memory of his mouth on hers, and the passionate kisses they had shared the night before.

When she would have moved away, he stopped her by catching her hand and lifting it to his lips for the briefest of seconds. "Thank you, ma'am, for saving my life."

If he noticed that her hand trembled, he ignored it politely. "You said this place is called Lodge Farm. Please, ma'am, won't you tell me your name?"

•　　•　　•

Because of all the rain, the afternoon had been rather cool for September, and in consideration of his guest's recent fever, Caleb had lit the fire early. They sat close to the hearth, Caleb in one of his cane-bottom chairs, and Mr. Thorn, as his guest, occupying the braided leather rocker.

"I remember hitting a thick stand of trees," Mr. Thorn said. "But I don't remember much after that."

"That must be where me and Miss Letty found the balloon swinging in the trees. It was raining something fierce, and the wind was blowing, and in the dark that balloon looked like some big old monster." At the memory of his foolish fears, Caleb laughed, though it was a mistake anyone could have made.

Mr. Thorn laughed, too.

He had moved Mr. Thorn down to his cabin as soon as he got back from the settlement. He could tell Miss Letty felt uncomfortable having the man in her house, and he felt especially hospitable because everything had come out all right with that orange-headed trash. Nobody had looked too closely at the man in the Yankee uniform, and once Caleb had wrapped the body up good and tight in the canvas, nobody bothered to unwrap it for another look. He'd buried the man in Mr. Finley's family plot.

"Damn, I'm tired of rain. I swear, Othello, I've slogged through so much rain the past few months that I'm surprised I haven't grown duck feet. That's why I was on reconnaissance. I was looking for dry, passable roads."

"How come you crash?"

"In a balloon you have to get pretty close to the ground to see, and one of the dangers of being that close to the ground is getting caught in a wind current. I got caught. As luck would have it, I began to drift to the southeast, over enemy encampments. By throwing most of my ballast overboard, I managed to rise higher, out of firing range, but I also managed to get completely lost."

"I ain't never seen the ground from anyplace 'cept the ground, but I don't get lost much. How you reckon you come so far south?"

Thorn shrugged his shoulders. "These things just happen. I stayed aloft for several hours, letting the wind take me where it would, because I didn't know of a safe place to land. Of course, I knew I'd have to land while there was still enough light to see, so when the sun began to wester, I opened the valve and began my descent.''

"Is that when you crashed?"

"No. Everything went smoothly enough until just a few seconds before I reached ground. That's when somebody took a shot at me. The bullet whizzed so close, Othello, that I swear I felt the air stir next to my forehead." The smile that played on his face was half embarrassment and half relief. "I was as scared as I've ever been in my life.

"I tried to close the valve so the balloon would rise again, but it was too late. The next thing I knew, I was headed straight for that stand of trees you mentioned. I figured the next ten minutes would find me either dead or a Rebel prisoner."

While Caleb poked the fire, Thorn leaned back in the braided leather rocker, his legs stretched out in front of him on the old rag rug Minna had hooked twenty years ago. He had his eyes closed, but his face was anything but peaceful. Caleb guessed he was reliving that balloon crash.

"Lord, Othello, I'll never forget the sound of that ripping silk. It made my guts wrench.''

The next four weeks were fraught with anxiety for Letty. During the daylight hours she jumped at every outside noise, afraid someone would discover that she and Caleb were hiding the Yankee soldier. During the night hours she couldn't sleep for fear the next morning would be the one in which Thorn would awaken and recall every last detail of their lovemaking.

Worst of all, however, were the evenings when he moved about freely between Caleb's cabin and the lodge. It was the homey activities that took their toll upon Letty's heart: Thorn sharing supper with the family, Thorn relaxing before the fire, casting shadow puppets on the wall to entertain Fern, Thorn allowing the child to use him for a horsey. It was torment watching the easy camaraderie between him and Caleb, and each time Thorn swung Fern up into his arms or let her fall asleep on his lap, Letty was obliged to swallow the tears that burned the back of her throat—tears for what might have been.

When the four weeks ended, and Thorn and Caleb had finished building a canoe strong enough to withstand a long journey over rough waters, Caleb led him several miles down the Ochlockonee River and sent him on his way through the Florida panhandle to the Gulf of Mexico.

"I still don't like it," Letty said the night they left. "Even supposing there are Yankee ships in the Gulf, you can't be certain you will find one of them. And what happens while you are crossing Florida? You could run into a gang of Confederate deserters, or even a band of Seminole Indians. They are very fierce people, the Seminoles, and they don't like strangers."

"Mrs. Bonner," Thorn said, patting his stomach for emphasis, "after all the good food you've fed me these last four weeks, I feel strong enough to fight off a dozen bands of Seminole."

Letty wouldn't be teased out of her concern. "But we've had so much rain this year. The streams and creeks could be swollen the size of rivers. What if you get lost? What if you take a wrong turn?"

He and Caleb exchanged looks that spoke volumes, then he lifted Fern and swung her over his head. When he gave the child a farewell hug, then set her back on the floor, she held up her arms for more. Bending down, Thorn gently tousled her curls. "Goodbye, little one. Keep your mama company while Othello is gone, and don't let her worry about me getting lost."

Straightening, he held his hand out to Letty. "I won't lose my way, ma'am. I charted some of those waters several years ago when I was a surveyor. In fact, I traveled from a plantation just north of here—White Pines, I believe it was called—so my trip this time should be much the same route."

Letty put her hand in his, but her fingers trembled so badly she thought surely he would comment on it. He didn't. "That plantation," she said once she had her breathing under control, "perhaps I know the family. What were their names?"

Thorn raised that eyebrow. "Sorry, it was too long ago. I've forgotten. My only real memory of the place is the sweet smell of sugarcane being ground on a crisp, fall morning. And . . ." He looked down for a moment, as though trying to jog an elusive memory. ". . . and I seem to recall the smell of savory in bloom."

With that unwitting blow, he set the hat Caleb had given him on his head and pulled it down low on his forehead. "Rest assured, though, Mrs. Bonner, I won't forget Lodge Farm. And I will never forget your kindness to me. Never."

Having said all there was to say, he followed Caleb out onto the porch, then closed the door behind him.

As if turned to stone, Letty stood perfectly still, listening as Thorn and Caleb hoisted the canoe over their heads and walked around past the well to disappear into the woods. When there were no more human sounds, only the sounds of the fire crackling inside and an owl hooting somewhere in the vicinity of the barn, she sat down in the rocker by the fire and took Fern up on her lap.

"Self-deception," she told the child as though she related a bedtime story, "that is the real danger. It mocks us all. It's easy enough to tell when someone else is trying to fool you, but, oh, it's hard to recognize it when you fool yourself."

Later, after she took the sleeping child upstairs to her crib, then crawled into her own bed, Letty vowed never again to be the author of her own deception. She vowed she would stick to her original goal: to make a life for herself and Ocilla's baby.

Fern. Caleb. Lodge Farm. They were all she needed in her life. She didn't need or want anything else.

Just before she fell asleep, she made another vow, one she meant to keep, no matter how difficult. She vowed to erase Thorn Bradley, and her girlish fantasies, from her thoughts. Erase them forever.

The next day she had her first bout of morning sickness.

Seventeen

December 1864

Letty would always remember the winter of sixty-four as the winter of the refugees. They fled from General William Tecumseh Sherman and his army of sixty thousand as they marched from Atlanta to the sea. From November on, a steady stream of dazed refugees poured into the area. The crush of refugees, plus the illogical fear that the Yankees would abandon their planned march and decide instead to veer southwest and attack the small farms along the Ochlockonee, kept everyone's nerves on edge.

At first, though they had little enough in their own larders, farm families sent food to the settlement to help feed the homeless. As the number of refugees increased, however, the food disappeared with alarming speed. Finally, fearing for the welfare of their own families, the farmers stopped sharing.

Destitute and hungry, some refugees dug up fields in search of fall vegetables possibly overlooked, destroying the winter crops before they had a chance to grow. By Christmas—that season of peace on earth and good will toward one's fellow man—farm families were standing guard at night, pitchforks in hand, to protect their meager caches of sweet potatoes and turnips.

Toward the end of January, everyone Letty knew showed signs of weight loss. She, on the other hand, seemed to expand daily. While others complained of clothes hanging loosely on their bones, she was forced to leave too-snug buttons unfastened. In time, people noticed. Those who came to Lodge Farm for doctoring, as well as those who came to have Caleb mend already much-mended tools, stole furtive glimpses at her thickening waistline.

Though she looked them directly in the eyes, daring anyone to ask questions, she knew the scandal of her pregnancy would soon be common knowledge.

"It's only a matter of time, Caleb, before people begin to shun me."

"I reckon that'll separate the Christians from the Philistines then."

Letty chuckled. Caleb's head and shoulders were up the chimney, and his voice echoed from inside the fireplace, sounding much the way she had always imagined the voice of the burning bush on Mount Horeb. "You sound like the voice of—"

"Hand me that chisel, child. I found the problem. Grease and soot done built up around the damper, and that's why it ain't closing right."

She placed the tool in the palm of his hand, then watched it disappear up the chimney. Moments later chunks of solidified goo began sprinkling the hearth.

"It isn't as simple as Christians and Philistines," she said, returning to the topic of her public shame. "When we first came here and I presented myself as a respectable widow, the people accepted the legitimacy of my status and Fern's without question. This time they know better. They know I haven't got a husband, and I can't fault them for being scandalized."

Caleb withdrew from the chimney, debris in his hair and soot smudges on his face. His gentle brown eyes flashed with anger. "It don't matter none what you told people you was, and it don't matter what they know now. Folks hereabouts got plenty of reasons for taking your part, and they ain't got but one reason not to. Seems simple to me, Christians or Philistines.''

He leaned forward and knocked the grease chunks out of his hair. "And them that don't prove Christian better find someplace else to get their tools fixed and their mules shoed, 'cause I'm a free man, and I don't work for no Philistines. Not no more I don't.''

Unable to hide the tears his championing brought to her eyes, and unable to put into words how much his support meant to her, Letty snatched up the broom and began sweeping the debris from the hearth. Neither of them mentioned the topic again.

Later, while he built a fire in the freshly swept firebox, she sifted the last of their flour into a big bowl to make biscuits to go with the last of their streak o' lean. She pressed a well into the flour with her knuckles, added the lard and milk, and had just begun working her fingers through the mixture when she heard footsteps on the porch. An instant later someone pounded frantically at the door.

"Miz Letty! It's Jubal Morgan. Please, Miz Letty, open the door.''

Not having seen or heard from Jubal since the night he vowed never to cross her property again, she knew something was very wrong. She ran to the door, her fingers still coated with lard and flour.

"It's little Sarah,'' Jubal gasped the moment she opened the door. "She's burning up with fever, and Patience is afeared it's the influen—''

A sob caught in his throat, and he had to swallow before he could continue. As if suddenly remembering his manners, he snatched off his hat and wrung it between his hands. "Miz Letty, them fool things I said . . . please don't hold them against my family. You just got to come. It's our baby girl.''

An epidemic of influenza swept through the settlement and the small farms along the Ochlockonee, taking its toll on the poorly nourished population and banishing all Philistines. Letty's scandalous condition was forgotten as locals and refugees alike flocked to her door begging for help. No one asked if she had a husband; they asked only if she would please come. She always went.

Fourteen people died, six of them infants. It was a particularly virulent outbreak, hitting hardest at the very young and the very old, and doing most of its damage in the settlement where the refugees crowded together. The epidemic seemed to rage on forever, and by the time Letty pronounced her last patient free to venture from his bed, wild Dogwoods had opened their pure white blossoms to the warm, spring sky.

The news of General Lee's surrender at Appomattox Court House came on the heels of the epidemic. The news was received with sadness, but little weeping. People were all cried out.

By the end of May, word came of Jefferson Davis's capture and imprisonment, and with it the total and irrevocable fall of the Confederacy. Those refugees who had not already returned to their homes, or what was left of their homes, loaded their few belongings onto their backs and bid the Ochlockonee goodbye.

During the last week in June, Letty went into labor.

She scarcely noticed the first pain. In fact, she didn't classify it as pain, just a sort of buzzing discomfort in her lower back. As the day wore on, however, the buzzing became a dull ache that spread across her back, pushed at her hips, then moved around to the bottom of her swollen belly. Each time the dullness moved in the same pattern, and each successive time it felt a little more like pain.

Letty knew she was in labor. She had seen enough women go through it to recognize the symptoms. With the time drawing near, she brought the things she would need for the delivery from the granny room and stacked them on the table to check everything one last time.

Unfolding, then refolding the two yards of new oilcloth and the four yards of clean sheeting for herself and the baby, Letty placed them in a neat pile. Next to the material she set the pair of thick leather straps Caleb made for her last year—straps she buckled to the end of the bed to give laboring mothers something to hold to—and the wooden blocks she always carried to elevate the foot of the bed in case of uterine hemorrhage.

From her herb box, with its usual neatly stacked complement of bandages, herbs, salves, and the like, she removed clean scissors and twine to use on the umbilical cord. Lastly, she removed two vials: one of Squaw Vine, to shorten the ordeal, and one of Angelica, to help expel the afterbirth.

Letty touched each item, their familiarity soothing her. She knew they wouldn't soothe Patience, however. When the two women had gone over all these things several weeks ago, Patience's hands had shaken so badly she couldn't hold the twine to tie a practice knot.

"Oh, Letty, what if I do something wrong?"

"Silly goose," Letty said, trying to tease her out of her fear. "There's nothing to it. I'll do all the work. All you have to do is stand at the foot of the bed and catch the baby when it shoots out."

Patience had laughed, but she still looked nervous.

There really wasn't any reason to be nervous; they had worked it all out. As soon as Letty's labor started, Caleb was to take Fern over to the Morgans' to stay with Gideon and little Sarah, then bring Patience back to help with the delivery. *Nothing to it.*

Letty touched the items on the table one last time. When everything was laid out to her satisfaction, she stepped out onto the porch where Caleb had hung a large, tinny-sounding cow bell, just in case he wasn't within shouting distance when her time came. Grasping the rope attached to the clapper, she hit first one side of the bell and then the other. Before the second discordant clang had sounded, Caleb came running from the barn, his long legs covering the distance between the house and the barn at a speed worthy of a man twenty years younger.

He didn't bother asking if her time had come. "You hold on, child. It'll just take me a second to hitch old Esau to the wagon, then me and Fern'll be on our way. Miss Patience say she be watching for me every day, so I'll have her back here in two shakes.''

As it turned out, he took considerably longer than two shakes, and when he finally returned, he brought Fern back with him. The two-year-old was in his arms, her face hidden in his shoulder. Occasional shudders shook her small body, revealing a recent bout of crying. Caleb's face gave nothing away, but sweat glistened on his skin, giving it a satiny sheen, and great, damp rings stained his shirt beneath his armpits.

Letty stood next to the table, holding on to the edge of it while a spasm of pain racked her body. As soon as the spasm subsided, she looked toward the door. Unnerved by the rigid set of Caleb's face and the sweat on his clothes, she searched beyond him. The sun coming through the trees cast dappled shadows on the open door, but nothing else moved. There was no one behind Caleb.

Her mouth moved twice before the words came out. ''Caleb? Where is Patience?''

He shifted Fern to his other arm and gently patted her on the back. ''Shh, little one. We home now.''

A green bottle fly buzzed around the child's face trying to get to her damp eyes, but Caleb shooed the pest away with his hat. When he finally answered Letty's question, his voice was almost a whisper.

''I'd as leave cut off my arm as tell you this, child, but Miss Patience ain't coming. She got herself snakebit.''

Before Letty could say a word, another spasm shook her. She grabbed the table edge again and held on while the force of the spasm caused her to sway back and forth. She thought it would never subside, and it hurt so much worse than the last one. Each one seemed to hurt worse than the one before it. When the spasm finally ended, she realized Caleb was in the middle of an explanation.

''Gideon was sitting on the ground holding Miss Patience's hand, and crying almost as loud as little Sarah. He'd killed the snake—a fat, old copperhead—but he didn't know what else to do. The menfolk was gone hunting, and he was all alone. I carried Miss Patience into the house and put her on her bed.''

Letty forced her mind to concentrate on his words. ''Is she all right?''

''I think she will be. I scarified the wound with my Barlow knife, then I put her foot in a bucket of cold water while I found something to bind the ankle up with. I had to bring Fern home. I couldn't leave her there with—''

Letty lost the last of what he said because another wave of pain blotted out everything else. *Oh God. What am I to do without Patience?*

''Don't you start worrying, child,'' Caleb said. ''All the way home I was studying what was best to do, and I think I should go to the settlement and get Miz Finley. I know you set great store by lots of handwashing at birthings, and after Miss Patience, Miz Finley is the neatest white lady in these parts.''

Letty's breath was coming in gasps, but she managed to nod her head in approval of the revised plan.

''Just give me a few seconds to put Fern on her cot and shut the door where she can't get out of the room, then I'll go fetch Miz Finley.''

Caleb took the stairs two at a time. The sound of his footsteps was still echoing in the room when Letty felt a gush of warm liquid spill down her legs. With a sense of foreboding, she pulled up her wet skirt and felt between her legs. She touched the crown of the baby's head.

When Caleb came back down the stairs only moments later, he found Letty lying on the floor, her breath coming in short, ragged gasps, and her eyes glazed with pain.

''Caleb,'' she moaned between gasps. ''Help me. The baby is coming.''

Fear rooted him to the spot. He saw her lying in a pool of her own fluid, her dress pulled up to her thighs, and he couldn't move. She looked so . . . so helpless.

She made a keening noise, the likes of which he'd never heard before, then she grabbed her belly and rolled onto her side. Caleb felt like a trapped animal. He searched the

four corners of the room for someone—anyone other than
himself—who could help her.

"Caleb!" Letty called again, her voice on the edge of
panic. "Oh, God!"

"Oh, sweet Jesus," Caleb echoed, his voice almost as
panicked as hers.

He dragged his shirtsleeve across his sweat-stained face;
then, with legs as wobbly as a new colt's, he stumbled
across the room to the hutch. Quickly he began dipping
gourd after gourd of water from the bucket into the dishpan,
slopping half the liquid onto the floor in his haste.

"Caleb!"

"Hang on, child," he called over his shoulder, "I'm
acoming. Soon as I wash my hands."

Letty heard Caleb calling her, but his voice sounded
strange, as though he were down a well. She tried to answer
him, but her tongue wouldn't obey her, and she felt tired,
unbelievably tired.

"Open your eyes, child. Don't go to sleep yet. I want to
show you your son."

Though it seemed a Herculean task, Letty managed to
lift her heavy lids a fraction, just enough to see Caleb standing above her. With her somewhat distorted perception, his
face seemed composed solely of a wide, smiling mouth.
After concentrating all her energy, she brought his eyes, his
nose, and his chin into focus, then his shoulders, and finally
his arms. In his arms he held an incredibly small, incredibly
pink bundle wrapped up in yards and yards of uncut sheeting.

The bundle had blue eyes and feathery wisps of brown
hair.

"A son?" she whispered.

"That's right. We got us a boy. A fine, healthy man
child."

With the tip of his finger, Caleb traced the soft, pale
down above the baby's eyes—down that would one day be
thick, straight eyebrows. "The boy got your chin, Miss
Letty, and for that reason he looks a little like Fern did

when she was born. 'Cept for the chin, though, all the rest of him come from Mr. Thorn. Already he's the spitting image of his daddy.''

Caleb laid the baby in her arms so she could judge for herself, and as she pulled the sheeting away from the baby's face, her knuckles brushed his velvety cheek. Instantly the newborn turned his face toward her, his tiny mouth and tongue moving, searching instinctively at her touch.

An instinct as old as time stirred inside Letty, filling her with incredible joy, and as she gazed at the tiny miracle that had come from her body, tears spilled unchecked down her cheeks. Several months ago she had thought God was punishing her for her sin, but now she knew she had been mistaken. God hadn't punished her; He had given her a wonderful gift.

With infinite care, Caleb bent down and lifted the newborn from her arms. "I'm fixing to take this little man child upstairs and put him in his little crib. Soon as I get back from doing that, I'll tote you up to your bed so's you can rest.''

Letty watched him cradle the small bundle in his long, angular arms. "Come on, little Thorn,'' he crooned, "you got a proper bed waiting for you upstairs.''

"He's not a thorn,'' Letty corrected. "Thorns are sharp. If you get too close to them, they'll hurt you. That sweet angel could never hurt anyone.''

"I know that's right.''

A moment later Caleb climbed the stairs, crooning to the baby as he climbed and ducking at the turn without giving it a thought. "You hear what your mama say, little boy? Your mama say you ain't no thorn. She done already forgot all the pain you caused her getting yourself born.''

He paused at the top of the stairs and studied the tiny face that was so like the face of Thorn Bradley. "No,'' he said, "you ain't no thorn. You just a sweet little bramble.''

Eighteen

May 1877

"He's mean, Bram," Gideon said, leaning down from his handsome new bay gelding and lowering his voice so he wouldn't be overheard from the house. "You'd be smart to stay out of his way."

Letty heard the remark, but she stepped back inside the lodge before either of them saw her. She had no idea who Gideon was warning Bram about, but judging from the cut on her son's chin, and the slightly swollen bottom lip, the warning came a day late.

"I'm not afraid of Ezra Smithfield," Bram informed him with all the bravado of a boy still two weeks from his twelfth birthday.

"Dammit, boy," Gideon muttered through clenched teeth, "nobody said a thing about you being afraid. I'm just saying it's time you started using your head and keeping your fists in your pockets. It's one thing to take on the boys in the schoolyard, but it's something else when you start mixing it up with a troublemaker like Ezra."

Letty watched Gideon swing his slim leg over the bay's rump and step down beside Bram. Though the twenty-four-year-old Gideon's slender frame was rock hard and muscular, he was at a disadvantage when standing next to the boy who was already just an inch shy of six feet tall; still, he put his hand on Bram's shoulder.

"I know it's been hard on you," he said softly.

The boy turned his head away so that whatever he said was lost in the soft morning breeze. And though Letty strained her ears, she couldn't hear what he said.

Tears burned her own eyes. No one had to tell her why her son had been obliged to fight his way through the first few weeks of every new school year; she knew why. He had learned the word bastard before he had mastered his ABC's, and it hurt Letty that he had to pay for what was none of his doing.

Of course, no one ever spoke to *her* about the circumstances of Bram's birth, but she supposed it was unrealistic to expect schoolboys to appreciate the pain their name-calling would cause Bram.

It had surprised Letty last evening when her son came in with his face and knuckles already swelling, for he hadn't been in a fight for more than a year, probably because his last growth spurt had made him taller than his schoolmates. She hadn't asked him any questions about the latest fight; she had stopped asking years ago. No point in causing him further embarrassment.

Gideon rubbed the velvety nose of his new horse. "I know a little about the Smithfield family," he said, "from guiding hunters down the river to Mr. Finley's new camp. Old man Smithfield is sour on life. Or maybe life is sour on him, I don't know which it is.

"Anyway, his attempt to set up as a blacksmith failed, and according to folks that know, his farming never paid off. But he's a firm believer in not sparing the rod, and I'm not talking about the kind of lickings Pa used to give me when I'd get up to some lark. Preacher or no preacher, Smithfield canes hard, harder than even Ezra needs. Naturally, after one of those canings, Ezra turns around and takes his anger out on whoever's unlucky enough to be close at hand."

Gideon looked down at the toes of his thick boots, obviously embarrassed at his next words. "And it's not just Ezra the old man chastises. 'Owned his wife,' as the saying goes. After she died, Smithfield hired a colored woman to do the chores. Brought the woman up here to the settlement when he got the call to preach at the new church. Only he took a stick to her once too often, and she ran off. Miz Finley felt sorry for her and took her in, and now she's letting the woman stay in her shed until she can hitch a ride up to where she came from before she hired on with Smithfield."

Gideon ran his thumb along his freshly shaved jaw. "That's why Pa isn't going to church this morning. Says he won't sit under the same roof with a man that mistreats his womenfolk."

Bram stuffed his hands into the pockets of his good britches and hunched his shoulders. "Wish I didn't have to go. Ezra Smithfield's pa ain't got nothing to say that I want to hear."

Gideon gave the bill of Bram's cap a playful tug. "You'll survive. Don't know but what a little hellfire and brimstone might do you some good—might take some of the starch out of you."

He faked a punch to Bram's chin. "You just remember what I said and stay away from Ezra. I'd hate to have to bring your ugly carcass home in a wheelbarrow." He stroked his jaw again and grinned. "It might put me in bad with your sister."

Bram's groan of disgust, followed by Gideon's chuckle, told Letty that their serious conversation had come to an end and that she could join them now. "Good morning, Gideon," she called as she stepped out onto the porch once again. "Did you come over to ride to church with us?"

"No, ma'am, Miss Letty. I've done without church this long, reckon I can do without it a little while longer."

He gave Letty one of those teasing grins that ignited the devilment in his pale blue eyes. "After what Sarah's been telling me about that new dress of Fern's, I decided I'd better come over to see it for myself. If it's half as pretty as Sarah says, I may feel obliged to escort you ladies to church." He grinned again. "I brought a stick to beat the boys off with, but I—"

His softly indrawn breath told Letty that the object of his visit had just appeared. "Jehoshaphat!" he muttered. "A stick won't be enough. I'll need my gun."

Letty looked over her shoulder in time to see Fern pull the front door shut behind her. Although Fern had turned fourteen only a few days ago, her figure was already shapely enough to catch any male's eye, and the snug bodice of the ankle-length green-sprigged chambray showed her pretty curves to perfection. Her nut-brown hair hung down her back in a riot of soft curls, and threaded through the shiny tresses was a green grosgrain ribbon that exactly matched the dress. In her hand she carried a chip straw hat a shade darker than her creamy, ivory skin.

"You look very pretty," Letty said.

"Damned with faint praise," Gideon corrected, lifting the wide-brim gray hat off his head and making Fern a theatrical bow. "Believe me, you put the morning to shame."

Fern smiled in acknowledgment of the compliment, then she lifted her chin saucily. "And what about my dress?"

Because he was giving Letty a hand up into the wagon, Gideon was able to hide his teasing smile. "If I've told you once, Fern, I've told you a hundred times, I always like you in that dress."

"*Always!* I'll have you know, Gideon Morgan, that this is a brand-new dress."

Gideon's appraisal traveled slowly from the top of her head to the toes of her high-buttoned kid boots. "You know," he drawled, "I believe that *is* a new dress. Green, too."

Not completely satisfied with this form of notice, Fern informed him that when Waymon Spruell had sold her the chambray, he'd said the green was particularly becoming to her. "Waymon said it turned my eyes to aquamarines, jewels fit for a king's crown."

"Aquamarines," Gideon repeated, his voice edged with

disgust. "That's just the kind of fool remark that man-
milliner would say."

Putting his hands on either side of Fern's small waist,
Gideon lifted her up to sit next to Letty. "Take my advice
and don't pay Waymon any mind. Nobody else does."

Too angry to think of a fitting remark, Fern set her chip
straw hat on her head and busied herself with tying the
ribbons.

"See ya," Bram said to Gideon.

As her brother *gee-yupped* the mule, and the wagon began to roll, Fern looked straight ahead, determined not to
favor that infuriating Gideon Morgan with so much as a
wave.

Thanks to the newly graded road, the ride to the settlement
took only fifteen minutes, and during that time Fern forgot
her pique with Gideon and gave herself up to the excitement of the first service in their new church. Though to be
perfectly honest, she wasn't all that interested in hearing
Preacher Smithfield's sermon; all her excitement centered
around the covered-dish social following the service. It was
for the social that she had saved her new dress. She knew
she would be the center of a group of young people, a
number of whom were admirers.

As Bram passed the schoolhouse on the left, then turned
the wagon to the right and pulled into the shade of a tall
pecan tree, Waymon Spruell came running to the wagon to
help Fern down. He was followed closely by Willie Carr
and his cousin Titus, and all three of the young men com-
plimented her shamelessly, making her feel much better
after Gideon's lack of interest. As she strolled to the church
door, several older men doffed their hats and expressed
their desire to be thirty years younger, if only for the pleasure of paying her court.

Remembering those compliments kept Fern's thoughts
occupied for the first hour of Preacher Smithfield's sermon,
but as the morning wore on, and the sermon seemed to go
on forever, she began to grow antsy.

The preacher kept waving his long, skinny arms around

and shouting about sinners and hell and such, and each time
his voice rose to a crescendo, all the old biddies in the amen
corner would flutter their waxed palm fans and shout,
"Praise the Lord!"

After another twenty minutes of this, Fern decided if the
sermon didn't end soon, she might do some screaming of
her own, for her bottom felt sore from sitting too long on
that hard, backless bench. She was imagining how wonderful it would feel to stand up and stretch, and how mar-
velous a glass of cool lemonade would taste, when she felt
her mother stiffen beside her.

Sneaking a glance to her left, Fern saw Letty sitting rigid
as a poker and staring straight ahead, her chin jutting forward as if it was made out of stone.

Fern had no idea what had happened, only that Preacher
Smithfield had quit shouting. Now he was very nearly whis-
pering. His voice was so breathy it made her skin go all
goose-bumpy.

"Harlots," he said, the final letter of the hushed word
hissing into the far corners of the church. "Fornicators.
Magdalenes. Faithless wives. All shall burn in the eternal
fires of hell!"

Fern swallowed a lump that had suddenly risen in her
throat, for Preacher Smithfield was looking directly at her
mama when he said all those bad names.

Letty remained perfectly still. In fact, everybody was
still. Not a fan stirred. And nobody made a sound. It was
as if the entire amen corner had breathed in and forgotten
to breathe out. It was so quiet Fern could hear the horseflies
buzzing around the mules tied to the hitching post outside.

In the midst of the silence the preacher strode to the edge
of the pulpit. He stopped directly in front of where Fern
and her mother and brother sat, and with his left hand
clutching the Good Book to the lapels of his worn black
frock coat, he stretched his right arm out and pointed his
finger straight at Letty.

"Woe be unto the wicked!" he shouted. "For they shall
be found out and cast into the fiery pits of hell!"

Stunned to immobility, Fern could do nothing but stare.

She was wishing she could faint when Bram suddenly jumped to his feet, his hands clenched into fists as though he was fixing to fight somebody. Fern had never seen him look so angry. His face was so pinched up his eyebrows met in the middle as if they were one long growth.

"Mama," Bram said loud enough for everyone to hear, "can we go eat now? I'm starved."

Fern's face grew stove hot with embarrassment. Until Bram stood up, she hadn't known what the preacher was getting at. She knew that Bram got into fights a lot and that their mama never asked him what the fights were about, but until today she'd been able to ignore the implications— just as she ignored the whispers and the conversations that sometimes ended abruptly when she joined a group. She'd been able to ignore it all until today. Until today, when Bram stood up in front of everybody.

Fern was so mortified she just wanted to lie down and die.

But she didn't die. Life wasn't that kind.

While Preacher Smithfield stood there with his mouth hanging open, dumbfounded, as if he couldn't believe a boy who didn't even shave yet had interrupted the sermon, her mama stood up and took Bram's arm.

"I'm feeling a bit hungry myself, son," Letty said, "so I'm ready to leave whenever you are."

Fern heard the barn door open, but she didn't look down through the cracks in the hayloft to see who had come in. She'd seen all the people she could stand for one day— maybe forever. She definitely never wanted to go to the settlement again. The story of what happened in church was probably being retold in every house from the Ochlockonee to the Florida border.

All Fern wanted was to get away from this horrible place and never come back. She wanted to go someplace where they knew how to appreciate a young lady of good breeding. After all, *she* was a de Bonheur of Savannah, not a . . . a . . . She couldn't even say the word in her head.

"Fern," Othello called from just below her, "come on

down, sugar. The company's all gone home.''

Fern didn't answer him. Instead she picked up the Bible she hadn't touched since she'd brought it from the house a couple of hours ago, and pretended to be engrossed in its pages.

''You up there, sugar?''

''Go away, Othello. I want to be alone.''

He didn't go away, of course. He never did anything she told him to, and within seconds she heard the creak of the ladder that led to the loft. Almost immediately she saw his gray head appear in the opening of the trap door.

Grasping the top of the ladder for support, he swung his long legs from the rung onto the loft floor. ''Whew. That climb gets harder every year.''

''Then you shouldn't have climbed it. I told you to go away.'' Fern held the Bible close to her face so she didn't have to look at him. ''I'm reading and I want to be alone.''

She heard Othello's smothered laugh. ''That'll sure please Miss Letty—you reading, I mean. Surprise her some, too, mayhap.''

Fern turned her back on him, but he ignored it and sat down beside her on the bale of hay. When she yanked the edge of her skirt from beneath his leg, he made a *humph* sound in his throat.

''You always telling Miss Letty she treat you like a baby. Mayhap today be a good time to start showing her how grown up you can be. You acting like you seven, 'stead of fourteen.''

Fern turned toward him so he could see how heartbroken she was. She could feel the tears starting and she knew the effect tears had on her eyes. A young man who once stayed at Mr. Finley's told her they reminded him of dew-kissed pansies.

''Save your tears,'' Othello said. ''I been watching you spill them things for years. They ain't going to work on me today.''

He stared at her until she couldn't take it any longer, then she swiped the tears away with the back of her hand

and tossed the Bible onto the hey-strewn floor. "This was the worst day of my entire life!"

"Um-hmm. I reckon it was. Miss Letty and Bram probably didn't like it much, either."

"Bram. Oh, yes. Dear, wonderful Bram. Take his part like you always do." She sniffed, then dabbed her nose with the edge of her sleeve. "I'm sure Bram made a beeline to your cabin to tell you what a *hero* he was and what a *ninny* I was."

"I don't recall either of them words coming up."

Feeling her cheeks grow warm with remembered embarrassment, Fern told Othello how her mama and Bram had walked out on the sermon. "They were halfway to the church door before Mama remembered me.

" 'Come along, Fern,' she calls over her shoulder, 'we're leaving now.' "

Fern balled her hands into fists. "And no matter what Bram may have told you about me wanting to go to the social, I wasn't fixing to stay there."

"Course you weren't, sugar."

"She's my mama, too."

Othello reached over and gently opened Fern's clenched fists. "Bram didn't say nothing to nobody. Soon as he brought the wagon to the barn, he lit out for the woods. Didn't even unhitch the mule. Ain't nobody seen hide nor hair of him since then. All I know about this morning is what Miss Patience told me when she got here."

"Yes, she and Sarah followed us home in their wagon. Only not at the crazy, break-your-neck pace Bram drove. Miss Patience was on her feet before Mama and Bram even got to the door of the church. And in spite of what everybody says about her being so smart, Othello, I don't believe Miss Patience even knew what was going on. You won't believe the silly thing she said."

"What she say, sugar?"

"At the top of her voice, Miss Patience yelled, 'Wait up, Letty. Don't you dare start eating without me and Sarah. I've got a jar of scuppernong preserves in my basket that I want your opinion on.' "

Othello pulled a faded bandanna from his back pocket and wiped his eyes. His voice was husky. "Miss Patience makes a mighty fine scuppernong preserve, and that's a fact. Always has. And she makes a dang sight better Christian than a dozen finger-pointing preachers."

"But you missed the point, Othello. We didn't eat the preserves or anything else. We came straight home."

"I know, sugar. I was just thinking out loud."

Neither of them spoke for several minutes. Finally Fern stood and walked over to the loft door for a breath of fresh air. While she gazed past the zigzagging split-rail fence that bordered the freshly graded Lodge Farm road, she noticed a dust cloud rising in the distance.

"Another wagon is coming," she said. "And I thought everybody and his dog had already been here. You'd think people would have sense enough to leave us alone instead of trekking up and down our road like flocks of migrating mallards."

Fern heard the crackle of hay as Othello walked over to the trapdoor. "If them *mallards* stay too long, sugar, you can come on down to my cabin. I reckon you must be right hungry by now."

She shook her head. "I'll stay here, Othello. I don't think I'll ever want to eat again."

Sometime later, however, when the grumbling in her stomach convinced Fern that she had been a little hasty in refusing the offer of food, she climbed down the ladder and walked down the short footpath to Othello's cabin. The toe of her boot had just touched the smooth boulder used as a stepping stone to the porch when she heard voices inside the cabin.

"Hold still, boy," Othello ordered. "This all the witch hazel I got. Either I can put what's left of it on your cuts, or you can keep squirming like a hound dog with worms and make me spill it all on the floor. You choose."

Bram made a hissing sound. "I can't help it. It burns like fire!"

"I know that's right. I 'spect Miss Letty got some balm

up at the house that don't hardly sting at all. You want to go up there and let her tend to them cuts?''

''No, sir.''

''Then hold still. If a boy's wooden-headed enough to go looking for a fight with a fella that outweighs him a good thirty pounds, he oughtn't to fuss about a few little dabs of witch hazel.''

Fern knew full well that her brother would never tell her about the fight, so she backed away from the porch and tiptoed around to the window to peep inside. Bram sat in a cane-bottom chair beside the maple table, and Othello sat just in front of him, a shallow wash pan at his elbow.

Blood dribbled out of Bram's nose, and a purple goose egg decorated his forehead just above his left eyebrow. While Fern watched quietly, Othello stanched the blood, then dropped the rag he'd used into the wash pan. After he turned Bram's head toward the light and dabbed one last cut with witch hazel, Othello got up, walked over to the unlit fireplace, then sat down in his favorite rocking chair.

For a full minute the only sound was the rocker moving back and forth over the hard wood floor. ''Did you whip him?'' Othello asked.

''No, sir. Ezra did most of the whipping. And he'll probably want to have another go at me once he sees what I carved on the hitching post in front of the church. But I don't care.''

''You telling me you used that bone-handle knife I give you for Christmas to go carving up folks' hitching posts?''

Bram nodded, then laughed softly. ''I carved a poem about Ezra liking to kiss farm animals.''

When Othello did not join in the laughter, Bram returned to the matter at hand. ''I knew I couldn't beat him when I took the first swing. Actually, it was my only swing. But I drew his cork for him. You should have seen him, Othello. Old Ezra bled like a stuck pig.''

Othello rocked some more. ''So if you knew you couldn't whip him, how come you to go looking for him?''

''Because I couldn't call out his daddy.'' Bram hit the table with his fist, making Fern jump. ''But I take an oath,

Othello, if his old man ever points his finger at Mama like that again, preacher or no preacher, I'll go after him.''

"Well, now, wouldn't that be a fine sight, a boy beating up on a preacher. I reckon that would make your mama real proud."

Bram got up from the table, covered the room in a half dozen long strides, then threw himself down on the walnut bedstead. He lay on his back with his arm draped across his eyes, and for a moment Fern thought he might be crying. When he spoke, however, she knew she'd been mistaken.

"Sometimes I just want to run away from here and never come back."

"Don't you go talking foolishness, boy. You don't know it, but the world's a hard place—a mighty hard place. Here on the Ochlockonee, folks need your mama and her doctoring, so you and me get treated tolerable. The folks that live in the places you talking 'bout running away to, they don't need no granny woman. They'd do you dirt just for the devilment of it, just to pass a lazy Saturday afternoon."

Nothing was said for a while, and Fern thought they had finished. She was just about to tiptoe back around to the door when Bram turned over on his side and propped himself up on his elbow.

"Othello?"

"Um-hmm."

"Will you tell me about my father?"

The rocker stopped, and the stillness that followed was like the air just before a lightning storm. Finally Othello said, "I reckon you ought to ask Miss Letty about things like that."

"It wouldn't do me any good."

Bram studied the white quilt beneath him, running his finger around the green stem and red petals of one of its half dozen flowers. "Fern used to ask Mama questions about her father all the time, and the only thing Mama would say was his name and where he came from." Bram's voice sounded husky. "And she was *married* to Fern's daddy."

Othello took time to form his reply. "Son. Your mama and me, we got some bad memories. And when the memories is bad, folks don't like to talk about them. You understand what I'm saying?"

"I guess so. But I don't even know my own father's name."

The floorboards creaked as the rocker moved back and forth once again. "That all you want to know? Just his name?"

"If that's all you're willing to tell me. I already know what he looks like. Like me."

The rocker stopped abruptly. "How you know that?"

Bram chuckled. "I definitely didn't get these wild eyebrows from Mama. Of course, Fern doesn't look all that much like Mama, either."

It was Othello's turn to chuckle. "I don't know 'bout that. Sometimes when Fern gets to acting mule-headed, that chin of hers juts out just like Miss Letty's does. Two peas in a pod, I'd say."

They both laughed, and Fern was torn between staying hidden so she could listen and going inside to give them both a piece of her mind. She decided to listen a bit longer. Maybe Othello would say something about her own father; there was so much she wanted to know. She'd given up asking her mama.

"You're right, son." Othello spoke so softly Fern almost didn't hear his next words. "You're the spittin' image of Mr. Thorn. Thornton Bradley, that was his name. And he come from up North, a place called Connecticut."

Bram mouthed the name silently. "Did Mama know him long?"

"She met him before we moved down here to the Ochlockonee. That was several years before Fern was born. He was doing surveying back then."

"Did you like him?" Bram asked, his voice hesitant.

Othello nodded. "Mr. Thorn was a private man. Didn't talk much 'bout hisself. But him and me got along fine. We even built a boat together once."

The room was very quiet for a while, then Othello continued. He spoke deliberately, as though he wanted to be certain that Bram heard every word. "What I just told you is all I know 'bout Mr. Thornton Bradley. 'Cept for this one last thing. You ain't got no cause to be ashamed of having him for a daddy." Othello cleared his throat. "And I know he would have been proud to have you for a son."

This time, when Bram put his arm across his eyes, he did cry.

Fern felt tears fill her own eyes, though they had nothing to do with her brother's pain. She cried for herself and for her own father, Monsieur Verne de Bonheur. If her father had lived, he would have been proud, more than proud, to have her for his daughter. Fern knew it was the truth; knew it as surely as she knew her own name. Nobody needed to tell her.

But she wished somebody had.

Nineteen

Letty hadn't been to the settlement since the day before the sermon, more than two weeks ago, but this morning necessity sent her in that direction. After enduring two breakfasts of reboiled coffee grounds, she decided that a woman could live just so long without a decent cup of coffee. With a fresh supply of beans in mind, she made up her own shopping list, then stopped by Caleb's cabin to ask if he needed anything. Ignoring both Caleb's offer to go in her place and Bram's silent disapproval as he hitched the mule to the wagon, Letty set out for Finley's Mercantile.

The mule, having traveled the same route for years, plodded his way toward the settlement, needing no guidance from the driver, and leaving Letty free to wool-gather to her heart's content. As woman, wagon, and mule approached the outskirts of the settlement, however, Letty was roused from her reverie by a movement to the left of the road. To her surprise, she saw the door to the small jail swing open as someone moved about inside the wooden structure. A pail of water, a thick square of brown soap, and several scrub rags lay on the ground just outside the door.

The jail, barely distinguishable from a two-hole privy,

stood as the settlement's warning to lawbreakers that they would not go unpunished.

Shortly after the war, when thousands of soldiers were released from the army and let loose on the roads to return to their homes, or to whatever nefarious careers they had followed before the war, the people of the settlement thought it wise to protect themselves from any would-be criminals. To this end, the farmers and businessmen elected a justice of the peace and collected money to build a jail. Mr. Finley was, of course, the logical choice for justice of the peace, and his first official act following the election was to use the small sum of allocated money to build an equally small jail.

The jail had been used a dozen or so times in as many years, mostly to house the occasional drunk while he slept off the effects of too much corn liquor. On one occasion, five or six years back, a horse thief had been apprehended and locked in the cramped jail until a circuit judge could be summoned.

Letty remembered the event quite well. For the better part of a month, no one talked of anything else. The settlement had been abuzz with excitement, awaiting the coming of the judge and the trial. On the day following the judge's arrival, a jury of local men was selected, then the trial was held on the porch of Finley's Mercantile so that as many of the locals as wished to could witness the procedure.

Letty had refused to attend the trial, but her refusal put her in the minority. Before a street packed with men, women, and children, the accused was tried and found guilty of horse thieving. Later, while the judge joined two local couples in the bonds of matrimony, the convicted man was chained to a wagon, using manacles rather hurriedly wrought by Caleb.

Drawing parallels to those two different types of shacklings supplied Jubal Morgan with an oft-repeated story—a story whose humor was strengthened by the fact that when the horse thief was driven the forty miles to Cairo, Georgia, where he was then transported by rail to an appropriate prison, one of the new bridegrooms jumped at the chance to help drive the wagon.

After the horse thief's month-long incarceration, the small jail had needed to be fumigated for bedbugs, after which it was thoroughly scrubbed and later whitewashed. Following that one incident, only an occasional scrub was deemed necessary to make the premises fit enough for the habitation of drunks. Judging from the pail and rags sitting beside the door, Letty assumed that someone was about to give the cramped enclosure one of those infrequent scrubs.

That someone was a woman. A colored woman. And though the scrubbing wasn't of particular interest to Letty, the scrubber was. She was a stranger in a place where everyone knew everyone else.

Unable to curb her curiosity, Letty stared at the woman who emerged from the jail. Because she balanced a chamber pot on her hip, she was obliged to watch where she placed her bare feet, lest she trip and spill the chamber's fetid contents. She was dressed in an ankle-length, faded blue calico skirt covered by a much-mended white apron, and her head was neatly wrapped in a bright red bandanna.

Though Letty could see neither the woman's face nor the color of her hair, she could tell from the looseness of the ample bosom and the broadness of the hips that the woman was no longer young.

Strange, Letty thought with a sudden, throat-tightening sadness, *but the woman reminds me of Verona.*

It was an absurd idea, of course. Verona would be quite old by now if she was still alive. The woman scrubbing the jail was probably no more than fifty, younger than the cook had been the last time Letty saw her.

Letty swallowed the lump in her throat. Even now, fourteen years later, recalling the day Verona, Priam, Sudy, and all the other slaves were loaded on wagons and driven away from White Pines Plantation made Letty feel as though someone had punched his fist through her heart.

Pushing the unsettling memory from her mind, she decided that the woman in the bright red bandanna must be the maid-of-all-work who had come to the settlement with

Preacher Smithfield. The one who had taken refuge with Mrs. Finley; the one who had run away from the preacher and his too-ready rod.

As the mule *clip-clopped* slowly past the jail and turned onto the main street of the settlement, Letty was forced to return her attention to the wagon. Within seconds she halted the animal beside the hitching post in front of Finley's Mercantile, but before she could climb down from the wagon, Waymon Spruell stepped out of the store, bounded off the low porch, and hurried to assist her.

"Morning, Miss Letty," the young clerk greeted, his hand supporting her elbow as she alit. "And how is everyone at Lodge Farm this fine morning?"

Letty had no trouble guessing who the young man meant by *everyone*. "All the inhabitants at the lodge are just fine, thank you, Waymon. And how is your mother fairing?"

"Mother is in fine fettle, ma'am. That potion you gave her seems to be doing the trick. I'll tell her you asked about her." The amenities completed, the young man left Letty's side and busied himself with the tethering of the mule. "Uh, ma'am?" he began when Letty would have passed him by and stepped up onto the porch.

"Yes, Waymon?"

"If you should be wishing to call on anyone—say, Miz Finley—I'd be happy to take your shopping list and fill it for you while you visit."

Unaccustomed to such service, Letty raised her eyebrows in question. "*Should* I visit Mrs. Finley for some reason? Is she ill?"

"No, ma'am. Miz Finley's not ailing." The young man adjusted the plain garter that held his shirtsleeve to a reasonable length just above his slender wrist bone. "Leastways, she's not ailing that I know anything about. It's just . . ."

Letty placed her hand on the young man's hand to keep him from mutilating his sleeve garter. "What is it, Waymon? What's wrong?"

Thwarted in his destruction of the garter, he adjusted the top button of his collarless shirt as though it was suddenly too tight to allow him sufficient breath. "The thing is, Miss Letty, there's someone inside the store at the moment, and I just thought you'd be more comfortable if you came back later."

Turning to stare through the open door of the store, Letty saw someone in the dimness. A tall, skinny man leaned against the scrubbed pine counter, a small stack of provisions at his elbow. Today he wore baggy overalls and an old felt hat of indistinguishable color, but even without his worn black frock coat she recognized Preacher Smithfield.

He was watching her, a smirk on his face.

Feeling her anger rise at Smithfield's insolent challenge, Letty stepped up onto the porch. "Since when, Waymon Spruell, is Finley's Mercantile too small to accommodate more than one customer at a time? I'm out of coffee, and I'd appreciate it if you would weigh me up a pound of your freshest beans." She stared directly at Smithfield. "As soon as you finish with this customer, of course."

Waymon hurried to his spot behind the counter and began toting up the preacher's purchases. "That'll be two dollars and twelve cents," he said, his voice cracking nervously on the final word.

"Put it on my account," Smithfield said, still not taking his eyes off Letty.

The man had not removed his hat when Letty entered the store, and she supposed he thought the obvious discourtesy would throw her into a fit of the vapors. She almost laughed out loud. She had learned rudeness at the hands of a master; nothing this ignorant lout could do would shake her composure.

The clerk pulled the green store ledger toward him, dipped his stylus into the ink pot, then began listing the preacher's purchases. While the scrape of his pen filled the silence, Letty moved over to the fabric table to examine the latest shipment of goods.

"Did you bring a croker sack, Preacher? Or shall I bundle these things for you? Wrapping is two cents extra."

"No sack," he answered. "You can wrap 'em. Wrap 'em up good. I got plenty of time."

While her back was to the two men, Letty heard Waymon push the ledger back across the counter, then turn to pull a length of brown wrapping paper from the roll attached to the shelf behind him. In his nervousness he must have yanked too hard, for the metal bar pulled free of the recessed slots, and the large roll of paper fell to the floor with a loud thud.

To Letty's disgust, she jumped.

"You oughta get that thing fixed, Spruell," Smithfield advised, a sneer in his voice. "Somebody could get hurt."

"Yes, sir."

"A good blacksmith oughta look at that bar. The thing probably needs replacing. Course," he added slowly, "I understand the folks around here depend on some Nigra for their smithing."

"Yes, sir," Waymon said. "Othello Moor. Othello's been the only blacksmith in these parts for as long as I can remember."

"You don't say so?"

"Yes, sir. He's a real good worker, Othello is."

"Is he now?"

Smithfield hooked his thumbs inside the bib of his overalls and leaned back against the counter, as though he had all day to discuss the matter. "I heard tell of a Nigra blacksmith once, somewhere downriver a ways. So folks said, *he* was a pretty good worker, too. Thing was, seems he got too uppity."

Something in Smithfield's tone sent warning shivers up Letty's spine. She'd misjudged the lout. There was something he could do to shake her composure; he could threaten the people she loved.

"Yep," he continued, "the way I heard it, this Nigra got too big for his britches, and some citizens had to string him up. Hung him from the rafters of his own blacksmith shed, they did, and—"

"You slimy piece of trash!"

Letty covered the distance between them in only seconds, stopping just in front of Smithfield. One look at the stubborn set of her chin and the man stepped back.

"You listen to me, *Preacher*, and you listen good. Nobody threatens me and mine. Nobody! And if you ever repeat that story you just told, if you ever even mention Othello's name, I'll put a bullet through your sanctimonious gizzard. So help me God!"

Having said her piece, Letty turned and walked out of the store, leaving the two men to stare after her; the younger man with his jaw hanging limp in shock, and the preacher with his eyes blazing with hatred.

"Trollop," the preacher muttered when speech finally returned to him. Thinking to give voice to a list of further suitable names, he hurried to the doorway. To add to his anger, Letty had already climbed onto the wagon and *gee-yupped* the mule, her speed churning the dust beneath the wagon wheels.

Frustrated, Smithfield stepped out onto the porch to yell after her. But as he did so, he saw her drive past the colored woman who used to work for him. The colored woman was walking in the middle of the road, and as the wagon passed her, the woman dropped the bucket and rags she carried and jumped back as though she'd just seen a ghost. Then, to Smithfield's surprise, the woman began yelling like a crazy person and waving her arms above her head.

"Wait!" the woman yelled. "Miss Letty! Wait up. Don't you know me? It's me. It's Sudy!"

Twenty

"Whoa, mule! Whoa."

Letty yanked twice at the reins before the mule came to a stop. Still not believing her ears, she turned to look at the woman who ran toward her, her faded calico skirts flying and her ebony face streaming with tears.

"Miss Letty!" the woman gasped as she drew close to the wagon. "Tell me I ain't dreaming. Tell me you ain't dead like Mr. DuBose say you was."

Dozens of thoughts raced through Letty's brain, not the least of which was the havoc this woman could wreak in all their lives. The harm she could do to Fern. But as Letty looked into the tired face that was different, and yet so familiar, she felt a sea of memories wash over her—memories of Verona, Sudy's mother, who had been practically a mother to Letty. And memories of Sudy nursing Fern, giving sustenance to Ocilla's newborn babe as freely and unselfishly as she gave it to her own son.

Unable to stop herself, Letty climbed down from the wagon and folded Sudy in her arms.

They embraced until Sudy's sobs eased and her body ceased its shaking, then Letty stepped back to have a look at this person from her past—the past she had thought long buried. "I saw you earlier," she said, "cleaning the jail. But I had no idea it was you. I still can't believe it. How on earth did you get so far south of White Pines?"

Sudy swiped her rolled-up sleeve across her tear-streaked face. "It happened after the fire. When Mr. DuBose Maynard find out he don't have no fields of cotton to pick, nor no fine house to live in, he tell the work boss he ain't got no need for slaves what's eating their heads off at his expense. So quicker'n you can say it, he send everybody to the auction block."

Letty gasped. "Everyone? Even Priam and Verona?"

Sudy nodded. "Mr. DuBose say sell everybody."

"That bastard! Do you have any idea what became of Priam and your mother?"

"No'm." Sudy wiped her eyes with the hem of her apron. "I never heard nothing from my mammy again. Reckon she dead by now."

Letty had difficulty swallowing. "And Henry? What about your son?"

"Me and Henry, we stayed together. I give the work boss that gold watch of Marse Abner's—that watch you give me for Henry—so he make sure me and my boy don't get split up. We went to a plantation a day's ride south of White Pines. We was lucky, I reckon. Old Missy, she pretty good to me, so after the war we just stay around there. But Old Missy, she die of the smallpox, and pretty soon her grandson say we got to get off'n the place. Ain't no more work for me there."

"So where is Henry now? He can't be more than fifteen—surely you didn't leave him when you went to work for Preacher Smithfield."

"*Preacher!* The *devil*, you mean." Sudy spat on the ground, as though she'd tasted something nasty, and the red clay made the spittle look like blood. "I didn't go to work for that man and I didn't leave my boy. Henry leave me. But only temporary like."

"Temporary?"

"Yes'm. He big and tall, my Henry, big like a man. So when he hear they opening a syrup factory in Cairo, and

hiring colored men to grind the cane and such, he go to
Cairo to see 'bout getting one of them jobs. He 'sposed to
send for me soon as he get a place, but the weeks pass,
and I ain't heard nothing.''

The concern in Sudy's dark brown eyes was replaced by
the light of contempt as she continued. ''After a spell, I
decide I better go find my boy, and that's how come I meet
up with the preacher. I was walking to Cairo when that
devil pass me by on the road. He axed me where I was
going, then he say for me to get on the back of his wagon.
He fixing to give me a ride to the syrup factory.''

Sudy spat again. ''But he lied. Next thing I know, I on
his miserable 'scuse for a farm, doing all the chores and
getting whupped for my trouble. And he never give me one
penny for all I done around that place.''

Letty clicked her tongue sympathetically, but her mind
was running at full speed. Maybe, just maybe, if she tread
carefully, she could still avoid catastrophe. ''So that's what
you want, then, Sudy, to get to Cairo?''

''Yes'm. That's all I want, to go find my boy.'' Sudy
looked expectantly into Letty's face. ''My mammy used to
say a body could near 'bout see the wheels turning in your
head when you was thinking, Miss Letty. I see 'em turning
now, and I sure hope you studying on how I can get to
Cairo.''

When Letty nodded, Sudy began to cry again. ''The Lord
done answered my prayers. Thank you, Sweet Jesus.''

Letty patted Sudy's shoulder and told her to dry her eyes.
''I believe I heard someone say that you were staying at
Mrs. Finley's.''

''Yes'm. Miz Finley took me in when I run away from
the preacher. She give me a pallet in her wash shed till I
can find me a ride to Cairo. She be happy to hear you fixing
to help me get—''

''No!''

As Sudy's eyes grew wide with surprise, Letty forced
herself to speak softly. ''What I meant, Sudy, was don't
say anything to Mrs. Finley. Not just yet. It might be best

if we kept this conversation between us for the time being. Can you do that?''

Sudy nodded enthusiastically. ''I won't tell nobody. Not till you say so. You can trust me, Miss Letty. You remember when you axed me not to tell nobody 'bout that baby of Ocilla's—that little Cinnamon Fern? Well, I never told a living soul. Not never.''

Letty's knees almost buckled under her. She struggled to keep her voice from revealing the trembling inside her body. ''That was good of you, Sudy. Now I know I can trust you to keep this new secret to yourself. I'll tell Mrs. Finley everything she needs to know when the time comes.''

''What time is that, Miss Letty?''

''When the wagon comes to take you to Cairo.''

Deciding that speed was of the essence, Letty determined to get Sudy away from the settlement as quickly as possible. She wished she could get her away that instant, but the only place she could take her was the lodge, and that was out of the question. The less Sudy knew of the inhabitants of Lodge Farm, the better for all their sakes.

''I'll send the wagon tomorrow. Can you be ready to leave at first light?''

''Yes, ma'am!'' Sudy's smile lit her face, making it appear young again, and reminding Letty of the Sudy she had known years ago.

Rapidly running the list of possible drivers through her mind, and arriving at the only safe choice—Gideon Morgan—Letty told Sudy to be expecting a young man. ''And, Sudy.''

''Yes'm?''

''The driver will explain everything to Mrs. Finley. You just let him do all the talking. Also, he'll have a little money for you, to help you get settled in Cairo.''

Sudy's tears started again. ''Miss Letty, you always was good to me. Don't know how I can show my 'preciation for all this.''

''You can do one thing for me, Sudy.''

''Anything. You just tell me what it is, and I'll do it.''

Letty reached up to her lips and pantomimed turning a key, a gesture she hadn't used in years. "Please remember that all the secrets we've shared through the years must remain just that—secrets."

Following Letty's lead, Sudy raised her hand to her own lips and turned the imaginary key. "Like I told you before, Miss Letty, I won't tell nobody nothing. Not if my life depended on it."

The promise made, the two women hugged once again then bid each other farewell. While Sudy picked up the bucket and rags she had dropped, then ran toward Finley's Guest House, Letty climbed aboard the wagon, *gee-yupped* the mule, and hurried toward Lodge Farm.

Everyone seemed in a rush to leave. Everyone, that is, except the man who stood on the porch of Finley's Mercantile. He remained as if rooted to the spot. Resting his thumbs inside the bib of his baggy overalls, Preacher Smithfield pondered the exchange he'd just witnessed between that ungrateful colored woman and the Bonner harlot. He had no idea how the two had come to know each other well enough to be on hugging terms, but he meant to find out. Sure as sweet heaven was above and fiery hell was below, he meant to find out.

Letty hadn't slept a wink all night. She had tossed and turned for hours, unable to chase from her thoughts the fear that someone at Finley's Guest House might inadvertently lure Sudy into telling all she knew about White Pines Plantation and Fern's birth. To add to Letty's worries, Caleb had ridden over to the Morgan farm shortly after supper to hire Gideon to drive Sudy to Cairo, and though the cock had already crowed for first light, Caleb still hadn't returned.

With a feeling of impending doom, Letty gave up all attempts at sleep. Tossing back the light cover, she rose and dressed herself, then tiptoeing so as not to wake Fern, she went downstairs to wait. She had just filled the enamel-coated coffeepot with water and set it on the cooking plate when Caleb arrived. He knocked softly then pushed the door open and entered the quiet room.

"Where have you been?" she asked more sharply than she meant to.

"You sleep any, child?"

"No, I haven't slept! How could I when you didn't come back? What kept you?"

Caleb walked over to the new Stewart's cookstove that stood in the middle of the fireplace; cautiously he touched his finger to the lid of the enamel pot to check on the progress of the coffee. "Gideon ain't home," he said calmly. "Gone down the river, guiding a couple of men from the guest house for some boar hunting. Been gone for two, three days."

Knowing the futility of trying to push Caleb into telling a story at a quicker speed, Letty gritted her teeth and resisted the urge to throw something at her lifelong friend.

"Mr. Troup fixing to do the driving," he said finally. "He on his way to get Sudy now."

A loud sigh was all Letty could muster. Thank God! For her peace of mind, Troup Jones was an even better choice than Gideon. Gideon Morgan was sociable and liable to say more than he should; while a saint would be tempted to curse trying to get information out of the Morgan son-in-law. Troup would probably drive to Cairo and back without saying more than "hello" and "goodbye" to anyone.

Caleb settled himself into the rocking chair next to the ladder that led to Bram's sleeping loft. "The reason I'm late is 'cause Mr. Troup had a busted shaft on his wagon. I stayed to help him fix it, then him and me sat talking till time to go."

Talking? Letty could just imagine the flow of conversation between those two wooden posts. "Did you tell him how we knew Sudy?"

"Didn't tell him nothing, child."

"Then how did you convince him to take her all the way to Cairo?"

"Didn't have to convince him. I just told him Sudy was a colored woman that fell on hard times on account of that preacher. When I say that, Mr. Troup say do I need *him* to drive the poor woman someplace. Owes me a favor; or so he says. Me, I think he just did it 'cause it needed doing. He the only man I know that's worthy of Miss Patience.''

Relieved beyond measure, Letty sat down at the table and buried her face in her hands. When she spoke, her voice was little more than a whisper. "I was so frightened.''

"I know, child.''

"What were you frightened of, Mama?''

Letty and Caleb both turned at once, surprised to see Bram leaning over the banister from his sleeping loft, his bony knees showing beneath the outgrown nightshirt. Caleb was the first to recover. "Your mama ain't afraid of nothing, boy. Don't you know that by now?''

"Yes, sir. But she said—''

"I'm afraid I've run out of eggs," Letty interrupted, her composure regained, "and I'm ready for my breakfast. So if you've had enough sleep for one night, young man, how about putting those constantly growing feet of yours into some shoes and going out to the coop for me? A half dozen should do me. I'm making griddle cakes.''

Bram's expression said he wasn't fooled, but he didn't pursue the matter. Retreating into his private area, he returned a minute later with his britches pulled on over his nightshirt and his bare feet stuffed into his boots. Like the boy he still was, he stepped on only two rungs of the ladder, then jumped down the rest of the way. The entire floor shook when he landed.

Letty and Caleb both sighed when he closed the door behind him.

After the eggs were fetched, and the griddle cakes cooked and eaten, Bram and Fern went to dress for school while Letty and Caleb remained at the table, enjoying a second cup of coffee. Caleb had just dropped a cube of sugar into his cup when he heard horsemen coming down the road. Horsemen followed by a mule and wagon.

"Mama," Fern called from the top of the stairs, "somebody's coming.''

Expecting the early-morning arrivals to be in need of

medical attention, Letty left her coffee on the table and went through to the granny room to wait there. When the knock sounded, however, it was at the front door.

Opening the door slowly, Caleb found Mr. Finley standing on the porch, a small croker sack in his hand. The morning sun, radiating with all the glory of a June day, shone mercilessly on the old gentleman's face, revealing deep lines Caleb had never noticed before. He touched his forehead in polite salute to the old man.

"Morning, Mr. Finley."

"Othello," Mr. Finley said, his voice sounding sad, and almost as old as his face looked. "I'm afraid I've come here in my capacity as justice of the peace."

At a loss as to what he should reply, Caleb looked past Mr. Finley to the other three horsemen, one of whom was Preacher Smithfield. Beyond the horsemen he spied Troup Jones. Troup sat in his wagon, his gaze riveted to the reins resting loosely in his hands.

The wagon was empty.

"Mr. Troup?"

"Never mind about him," Mr. Finley said. "I've got to ask you a couple of questions. You want to step out here on the porch?"

While Caleb did as he was bid and stepped outside, Mr. Finley reached inside the croker sack and withdrew something wrapped in a piece of white sheeting. With unsteady hands, the old man opened the cloth. Inside the folds lay a bone-handled pocketknife, the blade extended. The blade of the knife was stained, and at the sight of it, Caleb's heart almost stopped. The stain was blood.

"You ever see this knife before, Othello?"

Caleb looked at Troup Jones, but Troup's eyes remained downcast.

"I made it," Caleb said. "Carved the bone myself. Fact is, I made three of them knives. One I kept for me, and the other two I give for Christmas gifts."

Mr. Finley nodded. "That's what Troup Jones told us. I understand you gave one of the knives to him."

"Yes, sir. I give one of them knives to Mr. Troup."

Mr. Finley rewrapped the bloodied knife and returned it to the croker sack. "You want to empty your pockets for me, Othello?"

Wishing for all the world that he didn't have to do so, Caleb turned his pockets out. Several pennies fell to the porch floor, their soft plinks sounding loud in the silence. A crumpled bandanna quietly followed the pennies. A final item hit the floor with a decided thud. It was a bone-handled pocketknife.

Mr. Finley put his foot on the closed knife as if to hold it in place. "Troup!" he yelled. "Show us your knife."

Looking as though he wished he were anywhere but there, Troup Jones reached into his back pocket and pulled out his knife. It was identical to the knife on the floor and the bloodied one now lying in the croker sack.

"Now, Othello," Mr. Finley said, "you told us you made three of those knives. Troup's got his knife in his hand, and yours is there on the floor. You want to tell us who the other one belongs to?"

Caleb heard footsteps behind him. "It's my knife," Bram said.

Almost the instant the words were out of Bram's mouth, Letty pushed past her son and stepped out onto the porch. "What is this all about, Mr. Finley?"

"Murder!" Preacher Smithfield yelled, raising his fist into the air as if importuning heaven to witness his words. "Murder," he repeated. "Another of the Lord's Commandments broken! Another sin laid at the feet of—"

"Quiet!" Mr. Finley ordered, anger making his voice firmer than it had sounded since he arrived. "I'll thank you to let me do my job, Preacher. When I need you, I'll say it loud enough for you to hear from back there."

A suspicion too horrible to contemplate made Letty grab Caleb's arm for support. "Who?" she whispered. "Who was murdered?"

"Miss Letty," Mr. Finley said, his words only slightly louder than hers, "do you know a colored woman by the name of Sudy Banks?"

Letty couldn't draw enough air into her lungs to answer the question.

"Of course she knows her!" Smithfield yelled. "I saw them together with my own eyes."

"*I* know Sudy Banks," Caleb said.

Mr. Finley shook his head. "I didn't ask you, Othello. I know where you were around midnight. Troup Jones says you were with him." He paused for only a moment. "Miss Letty, you mind telling me where you were at that time?"

"I was here," Letty answered softly. "Here at the lodge. I went up to bed some time around nine."

"Can anyone vouch for that?"

Letty looked from Mr. Finley's embarrassed face to Caleb's wooden one. She shook her head. "No. The children were asleep by the time I went up."

"Then I'm afraid I have no choice. I got to do my duty." Mr. Finley cleared his throat. "As justice of the peace, I arrest you, Letty Bonner, for the stabbing murder of Sudy Banks."

Twenty-one

"It's my fault, Othello. I must have lost the knife the day I had that fight with Ezra Smithfield."

Bram sat on the steps that led to Fern's and his mama's bedrooms, his elbows propped on his knees and his hands balled into impotent fists. His still boyish face was strained with the effort to contain his frustration.

"You remember I told you how I used the knife to carve that stuff on the hitching post? Well, I haven't seen it since that day. I didn't tell you I'd lost it, on account of I felt so bad about losing the gift you made me for Christmas."

"Don't none of that help your mama."

"But don't you see? Someone must have found my knife. And whoever found it, that's who murdered that woman."

Caleb didn't reply. He leaned against the doorjamb, staring past the split-rail fence to the road beyond, as if hoping the wagon that took Letty away would suddenly materialize and bring her back home where she belonged.

For a time, the only sound in the room was Fern's soft crying. Since the wagon left, she had sat at the table with her face hidden in the crook of her folded arm. When her sobs lessened to only an occasional hiccough, she raised her head and looked toward Caleb. Tears soaked her cheeks, her arms, and the table beneath her arms. "How could they do that? How could they just take Mama off that way?" She put her hand to her mouth to still her quivering lips. "I'll never speak to Mr. Jones again as long as I live. I hate him!"

"Hush, sugar. Mr. Troup just give Miss Letty a ride in his wagon, is all. He do what any gentleman do." Caleb tried to keep his voice steady. "You remember that horse thief? You rather see Miss Letty walk to town like that thief, with her hands tied together, being pulled by a rope behind Mr. Finley's horse?"

Fern's watery moan answered Caleb's question.

Unable to contain his outrage, Bram jumped up and pounded his fist against the wall. "But they locked that thief up. Surely you aren't saying they're fixing to put Mama in . . . in the jail?"

"Use your brains, boy! They arrested her. Where you think they fixing to take her? To Finley's Guest House?"

"I . . . I guess I didn't think."

When Fern moaned again, Bram turned and kicked the banister, once, twice, three times, until one of the spindles shattered and pieces of it fell to the floor. Unfortunately the senseless destruction made little difference to his feelings of anger and frustration, and it made Fern cry even louder.

Ashamed of his outburst, Bram walked over to the table and sat down on the bench. Awkwardly he laid his arm across Fern's shoulders, not certain how she would react. When she turned and pressed her damp face into his chest, however, something suspiciously like a sob went through the boy, and he put both arms around her and consoled her until all her tears were shed.

"Othello," Bram said some time later, "what do we do now?"

"Do?" Caleb pushed away from the door. "I'm fixing to do what I do every morning. I'm fixing to water the mule and the cows and give 'em their fodder. By now I 'spect they thinking I done forgot 'em. After that," he added, his voice determined, "once I get the chickens fed,

I'm hitching the mule to the wagon and going to see Miss Letty. Y'all can come if you want to.''

"Yes!" Fern and Bram spoke at the same time.

"I'll feed the chickens," Bram offered.

"And while y'all do that," Fern said, "I'll go upstairs and get Mama's pillow and a blanket. And maybe a wash-rag and some soap. You know how Mama is about clean-liness. She'll probably want her hairbrush, too."

"That a good notion, sugar."

"And get her bedside candle," Bram added, "and re-member to put in plenty of matches. Tonight, when it gets dark, Mama will—" His voice broke.

The three of them stood very still and quiet for a few moments, each lost in his own private thoughts. Finally Caleb said, "Let's go," and they all moved at once to fulfill their appointed tasks. While Fern grabbed a basket, then sped upstairs, the two males headed toward the barn. Within the half hour they were all in the wagon driving toward the settlement.

The fifteen-minute ride was completed in a silence over-shadowed with dread; each of them afraid, not knowing what to expect. But as soon as they spied the small jail, and the man sitting in the grass, his long legs stretched out on the ground and his back propped against the side of the wooden building, they all spoke at once.

"It's Troup Jones!" Bram said.

"He didn't leave Mama alone," Fern added, her voice weak with relief.

"He surely didn't," was Caleb's only comment, but the smile on his face expressed more than words ever could have.

While Caleb deftly guided the mule beneath a shade tree not too close to the Morgans' wagon, Troup Jones got up and walked over to help Fern down. After the two men nodded to each other, Caleb hurried over to the little build-ing and scratched softly at the padlocked door. "It's me, child."

"Caleb." Letty's voice was muffled behind the wooden door. "Thank God."

Caleb was forced to take a couple of deep breaths before he could say anything. This was even more difficult than he'd imagined. "Child, I—"

"Mama? It's me and Fern."

"We brought you some things, Mama." Though Fern tried to keep her tone light, her voice began to quiver. "I packed everything in a basket."

"Where's the window?" Bram asked, his own voice none too steady. "I don't see any window!"

"It's around back," Letty answered, her voice sounding stronger as she became mother and protector once again. "But whatever you brought will have to wait until Mr. Finley returns to unlock the door. The window is really just a couple of slits near the roof."

"Can you see out, Mama?"

"There's a ledge for sleeping, son. If I stand on that I can see a little bit."

Bram and Fern both rushed around to the back of the building and began waving their arms above their heads.

"I see you, children."

His height giving him an advantage, Bram drew close and slipped his fingers through one of the slits. "Mama," he whispered.

Letty laid her cheek against her son's rough fingers, but only for a moment. She told him to take his sister back around to the front. "I need to speak with Othello, son. Do you think I might have a private word with him?"

"Yes, ma'am. I'll tell him to come around here, and me and Fern will go back over to the wagon with Mr. Jones."

Like Bram, Caleb slipped his bony fingers through the slit, and Letty grasped them gratefully. "Caleb," she said, her voice hushed, "it doesn't look good for me. There's more than the knife pointing to my guilt. Mr. Finley says someone—he wouldn't say who—has given signed testimony against me. The testimony mentions White Pines and accuses me of killing Sudy to keep her from revealing the lies I've told about my past. My unnamed accuser claims that Sudy told him my secrets, and that those secrets, once revealed, will prove that I am capable of murder.

"And," she added, "Waymon Spruell has also been mentioned as a further witness against me."

"Mr. Waymon?"

"He gave corroborating testimony regarding my violent nature."

"What Mr. Waymon know about anything? He just a clerk in the store."

"He heard me threaten to put a bullet through Preacher Smithfield's gizzard."

"Oh."

"*Oh* is right. That one piece of testimony will be the truth. And it just might get me hung."

"Don't say that!"

"We might as well face the facts."

"Not that one, child. Don't you let me hear you talking about nothing like that."

As if he had said something funny, Letty laughed, although the sadness in the sound made Caleb flinch. "It's a grand joke on me," she said, "that after all the sins I've committed, I'm probably going to be punished for the one thing I didn't do."

For a while they said nothing more, then much as the children had asked him earlier, Caleb asked, "What we fixing to do now?"

"I wish I knew."

"We got to do something, child."

"Mr. Finley said he would send someone to the Cairo train depot to telegraph for a circuit judge to be sent to the settlement. That could take anywhere from two weeks to a month. Meanwhile, I stay here in the jail. Afterward? Who knows?"

Their private talk was interrupted by the dramatic arrival of Jubal Morgan and Patience Jones. Father and daughter burst onto the scene, riding double on Gideon's spirited new bay gelding and holding on to the horse for dear life. Jubal's old gray hat was pulled down low to keep it from blowing off his head, and Patience's skirts flew all about, exposing the tops of her boots and several inches of thick cotton stocking. Fortunately for their safety, Troup Jones

was agile enough to catch the gelding's bit and force the
animal to submit long enough for his wife and father-in-
law to dismount.

"Miss Letty," Jubal yelled the instant he slid off the
sweat-speckled horse, "you in there?"

"I'm here, Jubal."

The feisty little man quick-stepped over to the jail.
"Howdy, Orthello," he greeted. "Troup sent word that
Miss Letty'd been arrested, but I wouldn't believe it, not
till I seen it with my own two eyes."

" 'Fraid it's the truth, Mr. Jubal."

Jubal shook his head in disbelief. "What's this world
coming to, putting a woman in jail? Tobias Finley must be
crazy, the old coot. But don't you go to worrying, Orthello,
'cause my Patience has got a idea how to get Miss Letty
out of there."

Two days later, at the Cairo train depot, Caleb pushed a
sheet of paper across a scarred wooden counter toward the
telegraph operator. The paper was creased and yellowed
with age. "I want to send a telegram," Caleb said, "to this
address." When the operator picked up the first paper,
Caleb set a second sheet on the counter. "This here's the
message."

The telegrapher counted out the words of the message,
written in Patience Jones's neat hand. "You got a lot of
words here," he said, "and a telegram this size will cost
you a heap. 'Fore I can send the dispatch, I got to see your
money. Set it there on the counter."

Ignoring the man's rudeness, Caleb removed a thin
leather pouch from his pocket and set a twenty-dollar gold
piece on the counter. The brilliance of the shiny coin
rivaled the afternoon sun's bright rays.

"I doggit!" the telegrapher exclaimed. "Is that thing
real? I disremember when I last seen such."

"Othello?" Troup Jones called from the wagon. "Is
everything all right?"

"It's fine, Mr. Troup. The gentleman just ciphering the
charge."

After tasting the coin for authenticity, the operator went over to the telegraph machine and began clicking out the message. A full forty minutes passed before notice came back that the message was received in New Haven and would be forwarded to the proper person.

While the telegrapher counted out the change from the gold piece, Caleb wiped his sweaty hands down the sides of his britches. *It's done. Please, Lord, let it be the right thing.*

Caleb breathed deeply to steady his thoughts, knowing it was too late for doubts now. Right or not, the telegram was sent. Miss Letty would probably be madder than a wet hen when she found out, but he'd had to do something to help her. He couldn't just stand by and let her be hung for murder. And he couldn't think of anyone else who would know how to contact that lawyer from Charleston.

Scooping up the copper and silver coins from the counter, Caleb dropped the change into the leather pouch, then he carefully refolded the yellowed paper and returned it to his pocket. Patting the pocket that held the folded paper, Caleb mumbled, "You told me to let you know if I ever needed anything. Well, I need something now. I need it bad. And, Mr. Thorn Bradley, I surely do hope you remember your promise."

Twenty-two

"We fixing to bury her at the lodge," Caleb said. "But only if you ain't got no objections. Miss Letty say don't do nothing till I talk to you."

Henry Banks wiped the backs of his large hands across his sodden cheeks. Though still a boy, Henry was at least six feet tall and easily mistaken for a man; that is, until he turned his trusting brown eyes on a person. Puppy eyes, Caleb called them. For that's what Henry was, an overgrown puppy, and just as guileless.

They had found the lad outside Cairo, living in a miserable shanty, in the midst of a cluster of equally miserable shanties situated between a weed-choked hill and a shallow, sluggish creek. The arrival of the wagon and the two strangers had created such a stir among the suspicious shanty dwellers that Henry suggested they talk in the road at the top of the hill.

"I built the coffin myself," Caleb said. "Made it smooth and snug, then I took it to the settlement and brought Sudy back in it. She in our icehouse now, waiting for the burying."

"Sweet Jesus take my mammy home," Henry whispered, the softly spoken words almost a prayer.

"Amen," Caleb echoed, a bit taken aback by the boy's sincere piety.

"Mr. Moor," he said, "if you please, tell Miss Letty I say the Lord surely bless her for all she done for my mammy. Mammy tell me time out of mind how Miss Letty save her life and mine, too, and how Miss Letty give her a gold watch for me, for when I a grown man."

The boy stuffed his big hands into the pockets of his overalls, overalls held together more by patches than by their original material. His puppy eyes looked directly into Caleb's. "And I'd take it kindly in you, sir, if you was to say a Christian prayer when you lowers my mammy into the ground."

Caleb nodded. "I surely do that, Henry."

"And, Mr. Moor?"

"Yes."

"Tell Miss Letty can't nobody make me believe she done murder. And tell her I be prayin' for her deliverance."

With that, the boy stepped back politely to let the two men know he didn't mean to keep them standing in the dusty road any longer. "I 'preciate it, Mr. Moor, you coming all this way to bring me word of my mammy's passing." He touched his forehead to Troup Jones. "And I thank you, too, sir."

Their goodbyes said, Troup Jones and Caleb climbed up on the wagon, while the boy turned to walk back down the hill.

"Gee-yup!" Troup called to the mule. The animal obeyed, and the wagon wheels began to roll.

They had traveled perhaps a dozen yards when Caleb said something to Troup, who immediately pulled back on the reins. "Whoa, mule."

Even before the wagon quit moving, Caleb turned and called after the boy. "Henry?"

Henry sped back up the hill, his bare feet kicking up the red dust. "Yes, sir?"

"How come you not working at the syrup factory?"

"It was all a hum. The jobs was all taken 'fore I got here."

"How you been living, then?"

"Best way I can, mostly. Somebody give me a yard job now and then, or ax me to clean they henhouse and such like."

While Caleb wrestled with his thoughts, the boy waited quietly, his eyes downcast, trying to hide the ray of hope that radiated through him. Caleb was reminded once again of a trusting puppy.

Finally Caleb pointed toward the shanties. "You got any belongings back at that place you living?"

The boy shook his head. "No, sir. I ain't got nothing. I had two dollars saved up once, 'sposed to be my going-home money, but somebody took it while I at the privy. Took my shoes, too."

Caleb felt he had no choice. He jerked his head toward the back of the wagon. "Reckon it be best if you was to say the prayer over Sudy your own self. If you want to do that, then hop up on the wagon. After the burying is done, if you want me to, I'll bring you back to Cairo."

The trip back to the Ochlockonee took another two days, and because Caleb knew that Troup was anxious to get home after his long absence, he suggested they take the back route to the lodge, avoiding the settlement and the jail. Caleb had every intention of getting Henry settled in the cabin, then driving immediately to the jail to visit Letty. That plan was sidetracked, however, when he noticed the door to the granny room standing ajar.

"Somebody in there?" he called, pausing just outside the door.

"It's me, Caleb."

Letty stepped out of the dimness of the room into the sunlight. "Sorry if I startled you."

Caleb's jaw hung open in surprise. "Child, I—" He stopped, unable to speak above the fear he'd been holding at bay.

Letty reached out and laid a slightly shaky hand on his forearm, squeezing it in greeting. "You don't have to say anything. I know you were worried about me."

None too steady himself, he placed his hand over hers. "I couldn't do nothing to help."

"I didn't think anyone could. I felt helpless myself. Especially when I thought I would have to spend the night in that awful place."

Still unable to cope with the relief he felt, Caleb asked, "How come you here? Did Mr. Finley find the real murderer?"

"No. Not yet. I'm home because Patience found a way to get me out of jail, at least for a while."

He shook his head in dismay. "Miss Patience got a lot in her *nous* box, I always say that, but I don't see how anybody—"

"I know, I couldn't believe it myself." A smile lit Letty's face. "Really, it was the drollest thing. The way Jubal tells it, Patience marched up to the front of Finley's Guest House and called Mr. Finley's name, practically challenging him to come speak with her. Of course, by the time he came outside, a number of his paying guests had gathered on the veranda to see what all the commotion was about.

" 'How can I help you?' Mr. Finley asked.

" 'I believe, sir, there is a female in the jailhouse.'

" 'Yes, ma'am,' he said. 'I regret to say, there is.'

"Then, according to Jubal, Patience asked loudly, 'Is it true that drunken men are often housed in that same jail?'

" 'Yes, ma'am,' he answered, 'that is occasionally necessary.' "

Letty raised her eyebrows in a theatrical manner. "Naturally, such shocking information caused Patience to grow faint. As you can well imagine."

"I can't imagine no such of a thing!" Caleb corrected. "Miss Patience ain't the swooning type. She didn't even swoon that time the copperhead bit her on the leg."

A smile pulled at the corners of Letty's mouth. "Oh, but that was a different circumstance altogether. In this instance, Patience most definitely grew faint. And when a couple of Mr. Finley's paying guests offered to bring her one of those bentwood chairs from the veranda, she declined nobly, asking rather that the gentlemen consider her feelings, much as they would honor the tender sensibilities of their own mothers and sisters.''

'' 'For I want nothing more,' Patience insisted, 'than what any other God-fearing woman would want. I want to preserve decency. And to that end, I wish assurance from our duly elected justice of the peace that should any drunken men need constraining, the female now residing in the jail would not be forced to remain there alongside an unrelated male.' ''

Caleb chuckled. ''Mr. Finley been bested, and that's a fact. What he say then?''

''What could he say? He assured Patience, and his paying guests, that he wouldn't *dream* of housing the two sexes together in such an unseemly manner. And when prodded further, he agreed that should any drunken men need constraining, he would personally release the female in question from the jailhouse, until such time as the inebriate was no longer a threat to the peace of the settlement.''

''Since you here,'' Caleb said, ''I reckon one of them drunken men needed constraining.''

''Oh, yes. A steady stream of drunks began showing up at the settlement, each acting disorderly and needing to be jailed.'' Letty smiled, but at the same time her eyes appeared suspiciously moist. ''The first to be arrested was Jubal Morgan.''

Caleb's mouth fell open again. ''Mr. Jubal? Why, he dead set against hard liquor. He a regular bull alligator on the subject. You trying to tell me he been drinking?''

Letty shook her head, and suddenly the tears overran her eyes. ''Our dear friend was only playing a part. He doused his hands with corn liquor, then he stumbled around making a nuisance of himself until Mr. Finley was forced to arrest him or lose face before his guests. I, of course, was released until the jail was empty again.''

Caleb cleared his throat. ''Mr. Jubal still in the jail?''

''No,'' she answered softly. ''Every eight hours, another man stumbles into the settlement to be arrested. When the new man goes in, the other man, now sober, goes home.

Mostly they are men whose families I've doctored over the years.''

"And Mr. Finley sitting still for all this?"

She nodded. "I think he is relieved to have an excuse to let me remain at home. I gave him my word that I would present myself in town the moment the circuit judge arrived.''

Quiet for a time, letting this latest development sink in, Caleb finally said, "So, he done sent someone to Cairo to telegraph for the judge?"

"Yes. And speaking of Cairo," she said, her tone implying that she didn't want to dwell on the subject of the judge, "did you find Henry?"

Caleb gasped. "Lordy, I plum forgot about Henry."

Stepping back out of the doorway of the granny room, he waved toward the boy who leaned against the turkey oak that shaded the front yard. "Come on over here, boy, and meet Miss Letty."

Henry joined them, his already battered straw hat crushed in his hands, his eyes downcast respectfully. "How do, Miss Letty."

Smiling, Letty stepped over to the boy who was such a bittersweet reminder of both his grandmother and his mother. Gently she reached up and put her hands on either side of his whiskerless face. "Henry," she whispered. "The last time I saw you, you were a little baby. And look at you now. You are practically a grown man."

"Yes'm." Though embarrassed, the boy let her look her fill of his face. "My mammy say all the time that I grow like a weed."

The mention of Sudy reminded all of them why Henry had been sought out, but Letty was the first to speak. "We're very sorry for your loss, Henry."

"Yes'm," he answered softly.

Caleb cleared his throat as if to disturb the uncomfortable silence that had fallen, and Letty let her hands drop from the boy's face and stepped back.

"The boy come to see his mammy buried proper."

"Yes, sir," he agreed politely, then he turned his gaze

back to Letty. "Mr. Moor say he built a snug coffin for Mammy, then bring her here. I surely do 'preciate all he done. And I 'bliged to you, ma'am, for letting him put the coffin in the icehouse for keeping. Now I be able to kiss Mammy goodbye."

A quick look passed between Letty and Caleb.

"You didn't tell him?" Letty asked, her throat suddenly tight from combined grief and regret.

"I told the boy Sudy been murdered. That's all. At that time I didn't know I'd be bringing him here."

Henry shifted his weight from one bare foot to the other. "Ain't no call to fret on my account, ma'am. Mr. Moor, he tell me Mammy stabbed, so I know she didn't die peaceful. All the same, I want to tell her goodbye."

Letty felt as if her heart would break. "We had planned to bury Sudy on the knoll out back. It is the spot we selected as our family resting place. Except for the songs of the birds, it is quiet there, and on the crest of the knoll there is a wonderful old loblolly Magnolia that spreads its limbs like protective arms. If Othello took you to the knoll now and let you have some time alone, don't you think maybe that would be enough? You could take as long as you wanted. You could say a prayer or just listen to the peace of the place. Maybe that would help you feel you had said a proper goodbye to your mother."

Nervously Henry rolled and unrolled the brim of his straw hat. His forehead was wrinkled, a question in his eyes. Despite his man's height and bulk, he was still a young boy, afraid to ask the question, and even more afraid to hear the answer. "Don't mean no disrespect," he said finally, his voice shaky, "but how come y'all don't want me to see my mammy?"

Wishing she didn't have to hurt the boy further, but unable to look into those trusting eyes and lie, Letty answered him truthfully, quietly. "I'm sorry if we misled you, Henry. Sudy was stabbed, that's true, but the knife wound didn't kill her. She was staying in the Finleys' wash house, and that's where she was murdered. Someone—I don't know who it was, nor why he was there—took a long-handle washing paddle and—'' Letty swallowed to ease the tightness in her throat. ''I'm so sorry, Henry, but someone beat your mother to death.''

The circuit judge arrived on a Friday afternoon, exactly twenty-six days after the telegram was sent summoning him to officiate at the trial of an accused murderer at the Ochlockonee settlement. Sharing the hired coach on which the judge arrived were two strangers to the district. One of the strangers was a portly gentleman with thinning, blond hair; the other was a tall, well-built man with dark brown hair, slightly silvered at the temples, and thick, black eyebrows.

A room at Finley's Guest House had been held for the judge. The best the house had to offer, the spacious room was located on the second floor, overlooking the peaceful back garden with its rows of pink and purple portulaca and its fragrant cape jasmine. Fortunately rooms were found for the other two travelers as well. Since it was the middle of July, however, and the height of the fishing season, these last two rooms were situated on the attic floor and faced the hot, dusty street.

Shortly after the judge's arrival, Mr. Finley sent a message to Lodge Farm instructing Letty to come to the settlement first thing Monday morning, Saturday being a busy day at the Mercantile, and the Sabbath being ineligible for the business of jury selection. No mention was made of the two strangers, although their debarkation had caused even more of a commotion than the judge's.

Why his arrival should provoke such a dramatic response was a mystery to Thorn Bradley, especially since these people were complete strangers to him and had no reason for their sudden and unexplainable dislike. And dislike him they did. There was no mistaking the truth. Their host had been the first to react oddly.

While Thorn was busy signing the leather-bound registry book that sat on a claw-footed table in the corner of the small foyer, Mr. Finley hurried down the carpeted stairs to greet his guests. ''Judge Wooten,'' he said, almost as if the dyspeptic little man with the dusty stovepipe hat and the nubby carpetbag were an old friend, "a pleasure to see you again, Your Honor."

Ignoring the judge's rather cranky reply, their host turned and warmly pumped Andrew Holden's hand, assuring Drew that all the comforts of the establishment were at his disposal. "You need only ask, sir. Our house is your house."

Expecting a similar speech from their host, Thorn replaced the stylus, closed the inkwell, then turned from the registry, his hand outstretched. To his surprise, his reception was far different from that of the other two guests.

At first Mr. Finley merely stared, as though trying to place him. Then, in the middle of asking if they had perhaps met before, the old gentleman suddenly gasped. Thorn withdrew his untouched hand as he watched the expression in Mr. Finley's eyes go directly from recognition to disbelief, then from disbelief to anger.

Before their host could regain his composure, the soft rustle of skirts announced the arrival of his good wife, who bustled into the foyer to add her welcome to that of her husband. Upon spying Thorn, however, the plump, gray-haired lady stopped dead in her tracks, and the ready smile died on her lips. After staring at the new arrival long enough to accept the testimony of her eyes, the elderly lady turned her nose up and sniffed as if she'd discovered a dead mouse in the larder. Without voicing a single word to anyone, Mrs. Finley turned sharply, her skirts swishing crisply as though to underscore her outrage, and exited the room.

Neither Drew nor Thorn could explain the elderly couple's reactions. Once they were in the privacy of their adjoining rooms, Drew offered the suggestion that perhaps their host and hostess harbored a grudge against Yankees.

"The war ended twelve years ago, Drew."

"True, dear boy, but one must never underestimate the tenacity of a grudge. It has been the motivating factor behind many an evil deed. As a lawyer, I've dealt with grudges that outlived the original parties involved. Grudges that were passed down, like the house and the furniture, to succeeding generations."

"Yes," Thorn said, distracted by his thoughts. Talk of grudges reminded him of his father-in-law and the hatred that vitriolic old man had held for him—a hatred he had carried to his grave.

Ten years after Delia had walked into the icy waters of the Atlantic Ocean, killing both herself and her unborn child, the old man had still blamed Thorn for her death. With his last angry breath, he accused his son-in-law of not loving Delia enough, of being unsympathetic to her sensitive nature and her bouts of depression, thereby leading her to end her life rather than live it with her husband.

". . . So try not to alienate them, dear boy."

Thorn snapped out of his unpleasant reverie. "I'm sorry, Drew, I missed the first part of what you said."

"I was just reminding you that the telegram stated that it was *my* help this Mrs. Bonner needed. You may be a wizard at those steam engines of yours, but you have no legal training. I daresay that is why your presence was not asked for and probably not expected. Judging from your initial reception here in town, I have to wonder if it was wise for you to come. No matter how illogical their reasons, if the locals take you in dislike, it could undermine my defense of your friend."

Pondering this logic for a moment, Thorn agreed. "Your point is taken. For Mrs. Bonner's sake, I'll try to keep myself out of sight as much as possible."

"And perhaps keep your acquaintance with the lady to yourself as well?"

When Thorn nodded, Andrew Holden glanced at his reflection in the looking glass above the washstand, then he gave a tug to the elegant striped waistcoat that refused to stay in place over his ever-widening middle. Sighing with resignation, he turned and strolled to the door connecting the two rooms. "I have been invited by our host to join him and the judge on the veranda for a cool drink. I trust you will not be offended if I do not ask you to accompany me?"

"Not at all." Thorn gave a seemingly negligent wave of his hand. "Enjoy your drink."

The moment the connecting door clicked shut, Thorn's indifferent posture vanished. With purposeful movements, he tossed his leather valise onto the hobnail counterpane and began to unbuckle the straps. After withdrawing a large roll of greenbacks from beneath a stack of fresh linens, he removed a number of bills from the roll, transferred them to the inside pocket of his blue coat, then retrieved his wide-brim, gray felt hat from the peg beside the hall door.

Mindful of at least one part of his promise—to stay out of sight as much as possible—Thorn shut the door behind him then hurried down the hall to the back stairs. His destination was the footpath that would lead him through the back garden and beyond it to the stable yard.

Having spotted the discretely placed notice in the foyer informing guests that a horse and buggy were available for hire, and with at least two hours of daylight remaining, Thorn saw no reason not to drive to Lodge Farm right away. Once he'd satisfied himself that the inhabitants were in no immediate danger, he would heed Drew's advice and keep his acquaintance with Othello and Mrs. Bonner a secret.

No, not Mrs. Bonner. He had never liked remembering her by that name. *Just Letty.* It was a simple name; honest, forthright, like the woman herself.

Thorn's pulse quickened at the thought of seeing her again; and Othello, too, of course. He was anxious to see both his friends.

Of course, Drew was right. Othello's telegram had not asked him to travel all the way from Connecticut to Georgia. The request had been for him to contact Drew and ask Drew to come help Letty. Be that as it may, Thorn had come, too. He had been unable to stop himself. From the moment the telegram arrived, he had been more or less obsessed with the idea of returning to Lodge Farm.

He couldn't make Drew understand this pull he felt toward the place. Not surprising. How could he explain it to someone else, when he didn't understand it himself? They had saved his life, Letty and Othello, even risked their own lives in the saving of his, yet this need in him to see them, and Lodge Farm, went beyond mere gratitude.

Somehow, deep within him, Thorn knew that his life had changed while he had been hidden at the lodge. Something had happened to him during those days and weeks. Something that still puzzled him. He had known peace there, a sense that he had come home. Yet how could that be, especially when all those days and weeks had been spent wanting nothing so much as to return to his real home, and to his bride? To Delia.

Delia.

He had loved Delia so much at that time. He had lain in Letty's bed, and later the bed in Othello's cabin, and longed for his bride, for his Delia. He had never loved her so much as he had loved her when he was at Lodge Farm. Strange, but only now did Thorn realize how odd that was. Delia had seemed so real there. So close. So giving.

In his dream she had loved him as no one had ever loved him before. Even though she had been inexperienced and shy, she had responded to him unselfishly, freely, showing him the passion and warmth he had always longed for. That love had literally dragged him from the jaws of death.

After all these years, Thorn could still recall that dream, a dream that had been more real than life itself. Even now, the memory of it made him weak with longing. When he had awakened the next day, all he had asked of heaven was to let him survive the war and return to his bride. He had ached to hold her in his arms as he had held her in that dream.

But dreams are not reality. He discovered that fact as soon as he returned to New Haven. The woman in his dreams did not exist. Any illusions he'd had about a shared love between him and Delia vanished the first time he tried to take his bride in his arms.

Shaking his head to force those sad, frustrating memories back to the past where they belonged, Thorn hurried toward the stable where he found a likely horse and buggy for hire. With the stable lad's assurance that he couldn't miss the turnoff to Lodge Farm, Thorn drove through the settlement with its half dozen wooden buildings.

He held the horse to a canter until they moved beyond the small schoolhouse and the church that looked newly completed, then once they passed an odd little structure that resembled nothing so much as an oversized privy, Thorn let the horse have its head. In slightly more than fifteen minutes, he made a right turn onto the Lodge Farm road. Immediately he reined in the horse to look around him at the place that had never been far from his thoughts.

It had changed.

The gray stone house looked much the same, as did the sturdy barn, but the farm was neater, more prosperous-looking, with its graded road and the split-rail fence that zigzagged along the side of the road, beginning at the turn-off and coming to a stop at a grapevine-covered arch.

The arch, situated about fifteen feet from the low front porch of the house, was a latticed overhang almost obliterated by green-leafed vines, the vines thickly entwined and heavy with bunches of lush, yellow-skin scuppernongs. Beneath the arch, shaded by the scuppernong vines, were two open-slat benches, one on either side, constructed, Thorn supposed, for the comfort of those people who came for Letty's doctoring skills.

The granny room! How strongly he remembered the tangy aromas of the granny room.

Thorn felt a smile pull at his lips as he recalled that aroma. Over the years, the mingled spicy-sweet bouquets of the different herbs had become a part of Letty, clinging to her clothes, her hair, her skin. Each time she passed by him, the perfume of her filled his nostrils. All in all, it was a clean, womanly smell, a fragrance that was Letty's alone.

As was her voice. He remembered Letty's quiet voice, hushed by the thick log walls of the granny room, as she spoke soothing words to people he never saw. People who remained strangers always, because their presence was an ever-present threat to his safety.

Yes, he told himself, the place had changed. And yet, as he grew accustomed to the differences that time and hard work had wrought, he realized that it was still the same.

The swift beating of his heart told him that Lodge Farm had not changed.

But would it welcome him again?

The benches beneath the arch were unoccupied at the moment, but Thorn decided not to approach the house immediately. Suddenly reluctant to thrust himself unannounced upon a woman who might not even remember him, he decided to go in search of Othello instead.

He felt certain that the neat, bark-strewn path to the left would lead to the blacksmith shop, and beyond that to Othello's cabin. But in order to take the buggy down that path, he needed to back the horse several feet. "No point in tipping over," he muttered, "and becoming Letty's patient once again."

"Were you talking to me?" asked a voice from the other side of the fence.

Startled by the sudden noise, the horse tried to bolt, but after a few moments struggle, Thorn had the animal back under control.

"I was talking to myself," Thorn replied once he'd located the dark-haired youth whose blue-gray eyes seemed to be looking icy daggers at him, "but only because I had no idea that anyone else was within hearing."

On the other side of the rail fence, a lad stood just in front of a neatly tended herb garden. At first glance, the lad's pose appeared careless, with a scythe balanced lengthwise across his shoulders, one hand circling the handle, the other hand resting on the shaft, near the well-honed blade, but on closer inspection he looked anything but relaxed. Defensively he surveyed Thorn's blue coat, the neatly tied cravat, and the tan britches.

"Are you the judge?" the boy asked, his tone as belligerent as his stares.

"No. I have no connection at all with the legal profession."

Visibly relieved by the negative reply, the boy exhaled loudly. Relaxing his rigid posture, he swung the scythe from his shoulders and propped it against the split-rail fence. "We've been expecting a judge," he said by way of apologizing for his rudeness. "You're wearing town clothes, so I thought maybe you were him."

"I am not. Most of yesterday and this morning, however, I shared a stagecoach with a Judge Wooten. When I left the settlement twenty minutes ago, the judge was ensconced on the guest house veranda, sipping a cool drink."

"I hope he chokes!"

Suppressing a smile, Thorn flicked the reins slightly, encouraging the horse to close the thirty-yard gap that separated him from the boy. He wanted to get a closer look, for there was something familiar about the lad. Though why there should be, he couldn't say, as he was acquainted with no one here at the farm except Letty, Othello, and the little girl, Fern.

On closer view, Thorn realized that the lad was younger than he'd estimated. At a distance he'd been misled by the boy's height. *He's probably no more than twelve. When I was here before, chances are he wasn't even born.*

Yet, as he continued to observe the lad, the feeling kept teasing Thorn's brain that he should recognize him. Scanning the youthful profile from the dark brows, down the slender nose, to the stubbornly square chin, Thorn suddenly thought he saw the connection. "I know that chin," he said, smiling to soften any sting in the words. "My guess is you're related to Mrs. Letty Bonner."

The boy nodded. "I'm her son. I'm Bram Bonner."

"Happy to meet you, Bram. I'm an old friend of—" Thorn stopped, suddenly struck by the implausibility of the boy bearing the Bonner name. Letty Bonner was a widow. She had been a widow for more than a year when he knew her, so for her to have a son who bore her name, she would have had to . . .

Thorn turned his head so that the wide brim of his hat concealed his face and his speculations. Mere seconds later, when he'd schooled his expression, he once again looked at Bram. A hint of color stole up the boy's neck, and the Bonner chin thrust forward pugnaciously, as though Bram had guessed the train Thorn's thoughts had taken. Hoping to dispel any embarrassment he'd caused the lad, he climbed down from the buggy.

"I knew your mother many years ago," he said. "She's a wonderful woman."

As he walked toward Bram, his hand outstretched, Thorn saw a change come over the boy. Now Bram stared at him much as the Finleys had done when he'd checked into the guest house. But where the elderly couple's eyes had been filled with indignant recognition, Bram's eyes registered something akin to awe.

"My name is—"

"I know who you are," Bram said breathlessly.

Thorn's eyebrow lifted slightly. "You do?"

"Yes, sir. You're Mr. Thornton Bradley. And you live in Connecticut. Several years ago you built a boat here, then you sailed it down the Ochlockonee to Florida and the Gulf of Mexico."

Startled by this recitation of his personal history, Thorn asked, "How do you know all this?"

The boy looked him squarely in the eyes. "Othello told me."

"Did he, now. And why would Othello wish to apprise you of my time here at Lodge Farm?"

"I wanted to know," the boy said. "I wanted to know because you're my daddy."

Twenty-three

"But, I tell you, Othello, it's preposterous!"

Thorn slapped his palm against the scrubbed pine table then stood abruptly, knocking the cane-bottom chair over in his haste. The cabin was too small to pace, as he would have liked to do, so he walked instead to the window and looked out. That was a mistake. The boy—Bram Bonner—stood some distance away, tossing pine cones at the smooth bark of a crepe myrtle tree and carefully avoiding looking in the direction of the cabin. Like a puppy who longs to come inside, but is afraid he might receive a kick for his trouble, Bram waited.

Thorn's anger cooled at the sight of the boy. Human nature having proved unkind so often in his own life, it wasn't hard for him to imagine the number of fights the lad must have been in as a result of his name. Shoving his hands into the pockets of his tan britches, Thorn continued to stare at the boy. "He's a fine-looking lad," he said quietly, "but I'm not his father. Not that I blame Letty for saying that I was. She probably never expected to see me again. All the same, I'm afraid it was a lie."

He heard the rocking chair creak as Othello stood. Then seconds later he heard a sound he hadn't heard since his war years, a sound that strikes fear into every soldier's heart. It was the soft click of a hammer being pulled back. Instantly Thorn wheeled. He couldn't believe the testimony of his own eyes. Othello stood beside the unlit fireplace, a hunting rifle in his hands.

The rifle was aimed straight at Thorn's heart.

"You got zactly one minute to get out of my house," Othello said, his voice thick with mingled hurt and anger. "Then you got zactly two minutes to get off the place. After that, if you ever set foot on this farm again, I shoot you down like I shoot a weasel caught in the henhouse."

"Othello, what did—"

"Miss Letty don't lie 'bout something like that. But that ain't none of your nevermind. Not no more it ain't. So you just go on and git while the gittin's good." He waved the rifle, motioning Thorn toward the door. "And don't you go saying nothing to that boy, neither. Not a word. Bram got enough to bear without being denied to his face."

Moving slowly and cautiously, Thorn righted the cane-bottom chair he'd knocked over, then sat down in it.

Othello brought the rifle close to his cheek, sighting down the barrel. "I told you to get on out of here!"

Thorn didn't move from the chair. "I apologize, Othello. There's no one in the world whose word I would believe before yours. And there's no one I admire more than I admire Miss Letty. I can't say it any plainer than that. It's just . . ."

Othello didn't put the gun away, but he did rest it over his arm, the barrel pointed toward the floor. "Just what?"

"Just that I don't understand how it could be true. How could I father a child and not know it? I don't even remember being alone with Letty." He put his elbows on the table, then rested his forehead in the heels of his hands. When he spoke, his voice was muffled. "It doesn't make any sense."

The rocking chair creaked again as Othello sat back down. "That's zackly what I said to Miss Letty when she drag me out in the pouring rain to go looking for some Yankee soldier I didn't know and didn't care nothing 'bout.

'This is crazy,' I told her. 'Don't make no sense.' "

For a while, the only sound was the soft swaying of the rocking chair. "Me, I didn't even remember who you was. And truth to tell, I wouldn't't've gone after you if I had've remembered. But Miss Letty plum certain it was you out there hurt. Soon as she heard 'bout 'em shooting some Yankee soldier out of a balloon, she made up her mind it was you. She near 'bout fret herself sick, scared one of them bummers fixing to get they hands on you before she could find you. I couldn't stop her from going looking for you, so I went along to keep her safe."

For just a moment, Thorn wondered if his friend had him confused with someone else. "Are you talking about *me?*"

"Who you think I'm talking 'bout?" Othello spoke sharply, as though infuriated with Thorn's inability to understand. "You think Miss Letty just go rambling through the woods every so often looking for any stray Yankee soldiers she can find? Use your *nous* box. She born and raised right here in Georgia. Why would she risk getting herself hung as a traitor for some Yankee she didn't even know?"

Thorn shook his head. "I can't imagine, and that's the truth."

He ran his hands through his hair, as though trying to clear his brain; things were getting less clear by the minute. "I never asked why before. I guess I was too grateful to have been rescued to question my fate." He looked across the room at Othello. "So why was I the one she saved? Why me?"

"Mayhap it's 'cause you the one that come to the plantation that time."

"What plantation?"

"White Pines, that's what."

The rocking chair stopped, and Othello leaned forward. In the silence, brown eyes watched startled, blue-gray eyes. "You remember White Pines, I can see it in your eyes. Miss Letty remember it, too. She risk everything to find you in them woods and bring you back to the lodge to doctor you back to life. She done it all 'cause you the one that offered to take her and little Ocilla away on your boat. She didn't never forget that. And she didn't never forget you.''

Letty read the message from Mr. Finley for the fifth time. *Monday,* it said. The trial would start on Monday. Fingers trembling, she crumpled the note and stuffed it deep inside her apron pocket, then she looked around her, searching for something to do—some job that would keep her too busy to think about Monday.

There was nothing. The chores had all been done.

In the twenty-six days she had been waiting for word of the trial, she had baked so many loaves of bread that she'd had to give most of them away before they spoiled. She had scrubbed the lodge cleaner than it had been in years, and she had darned, washed, and ironed every article of clothing in the house.

Knowing she would scream without something to keep her from dwelling on the trial and its possible outcome, she went to the granny room. There, too, everything was as clean as could be.

The small cot that sat beneath the window was freshly made up, with the sheet tucked snugly around the husk mattress, and the thin quilt folded catty-corner so it could be drawn across a patient if needed. The tall stool sat beneath the worktable; both scrubbed with white oak bark and wild alum root just this morning. The sharp smell of the disinfectant still permeated the air, even with the granny room door open.

The wooden herb boxes all shone, as did the freshly wiped shelves. The two tin basins were cleaned and hung on their nails for ready use. The long, narrow blade had been sharpened on the draw-shave knife she used to shave medicinal bark from trees, and the double handles cleaned and rubbed with oil. All her tools and instruments were spotless and in their proper places.

With nothing else to do, Letty decided to grind some comfrey root. She liked to keep a good supply ground and ready for use when someone came in with a broken bone.

Over the years, she had worked out a system. She would pour the ground comfrey root into a basin, mix in the water to make it into a paste, then turn immediately to set the broken bone. During the setting, the patient often passed out for a short time, and while they were unconscious, Letty would work quickly, spreading the paste on the injured limb. With any luck, the paste would be set rock hard by the time the patient was conscious and ready to sit up.

Having found a job that needed doing, Letty set an earthen bowl on the worktable, then took a bundle of pungent, gray-green stalks from a box on one of the shelves. With an economy of motion resulting from years of experience, she began to pulverize the comfrey root. Lost in the rhythmic, scraping sounds the grinding stone made against the sides of the bowl, she didn't hear the soft knock at the granny room door.

"Letty," a deep, masculine voice said, "we need to talk."

Startled, she jumped back, sending the bowl skidding across the table and over the edge. The bowl, the grinding stone, the comfrey root, all fell unheeded to the floor.

Even after a dozen years, Letty instantly recognized that voice. Myriad conflicting emotions chased one another through her brain as she turned to look at the man who stood just inside the doorway. He was older, there was no denying the truth, but if anything, he was even more handsome than she remembered.

Wordlessly Thorn stared, his eyes scanning her from head to toe, as if looking for the clue to some riddle long unsolved. Unnerved by his scrutiny, Letty reached to the nape of her neck where her trembling fingers captured a lock of hair that had fallen free from its braided coronet. Unfortunately, tucking the strand back into place became an almost impossible feat, simply because Thorn watched her every move.

Neither of them spoke, and the silence seemed to stretch between them, growing more taut with each passing second. When Letty could stand it no longer, she tried to speak, but the word came out little more than a whisper.

"Thorn."

The name had no sooner left her lips than Letty's thoughts flew to her son, to their son. Her heart pounded with such force it threatened to burst out of her body; all the while her insides turned to jelly at the thought of what Thorn's sudden appearance would do to Bram. Not to mention the havoc it would wreak upon her chances at the trial.

"Why are you here?" she asked once her throat relaxed sufficiently to speak.

"I heard about the trial. I came to help."

"To help?" Letty didn't know whether to laugh or cry. "More than likely, you've come just in time to get me hung."

That accusation being unanswerable, Thorn said, "I didn't come alone. I brought Drew with me."

For the first time, Letty smiled. "Drew? But how did Drew know?"

"Othello sent me a telegram saying you were in serious trouble. In the wire he asked if I knew how to find Drew."

"Othello sent *you* a telegram? I don't underst—"

"At the time," Thorn continued, ignoring Letty's interruption, "I had no idea how Othello, or you, knew Drew, but that was unimportant. The only thing that mattered was that you needed help. So the next day after the wire arrived, I caught a packet down to Charleston."

Concentrating on only the first part of his speech, Letty said, "What do you mean, 'At the time'?"

"Drew was in the middle of a trial, so I had to wait almost a week in Charleston before we could leave. After the trial, we caught the first train west, then at the final train stop we hired a coach. We arrived about an hour ago."

"You said, 'At the time,' " Letty repeated.

Thorn stopped for a moment, as if measuring his next words. "Drew believes he is defending a stranger. I told him I needed his legal skills to help an old friend of mine, a Mrs. Bonner. Of course, I had no way of knowing that *my* old friend was also *his* old friend, Miss Loretta Banks of White Pines."

Letty felt her knees grow week. *Was the entire story of*

White Pines to come crashing down upon her? First Sudy, and now Thorn and Drew. With unsteady hands, she pulled out the stool and sat down before she fell down.

"Years ago," she said, her words hushed, "you told me you didn't remember anything about White Pines."

"And I didn't remember it. Not consciously, at any rate. Not until today. I went by Othello's cabin before I came here; he told me the whole story."

"He never!" Anger suddenly stiffened Letty's spine. "Othello would never betray me."

"You're right. He never would." Thorn stepped away from the doorway, tossing his hat onto the table as he moved closer.

"Othello merely helped me to remember a few facts, Letty. But he wouldn't have said a word, not if I hadn't met Bram." He said no more, certain that last fact would explain it all.

It did.

Letty felt cold, as if all the blood had left her body. "What did you say to Bram? What did you tell him?"

Thorn shook his head, a hint of anger in his eyes. "What did *I* tell *him*? I told him nothing. But you can imagine my shock when the boy informed me that I was his daddy."

Suddenly this was all too much for Letty, so she hid her face in her hands. With her face covered, she didn't know that Thorn had stepped around the table, not until he knelt beside her and tugged her hands away from her face.

"He's a fine boy, Letty. A boy any man would be proud to have for a son. I only wish you had told me. I wish I'd known about him sooner."

"And what about your bride?" The word felt dry and choking in Letty's throat. "Would she have wanted to know about my son, too?"

"My wife died more than ten years ago. She . . . it happened within four months of my return home."

Filled with remorse, Letty tried to apologize. "I'm truly sorry. I know how much you loved Delia."

The soft hiss of Thorn's indrawn breath told Letty she

had madè a mistake. "And just how would you know that?"

Where Letty had been cold only moments ago, now her entire body became flushed with heat.

"How did you know about my bride?" he asked. "How did you know about Delia?" Thorn still held Letty's wrists in his hands, and now he gave them a slight pull. "Answer me."

Feeling like a cornered animal, Letty wished she were a possum so she could close her eyes and play dead. "You . . . you told us about her."

"No," he said slowly, "I never mentioned my wife to anyone. It was a point with me to keep my private life completely private. I never even said her name, except perhaps in my dreams."

The moment the words were out, Thorn looked as though he'd just been punched in the stomach. "My dream," he said softly. "Oh, God. Oh, God, Letty."

With his hands still gripping her wrists, Thorn stood, pulling Letty to her feet as well. Then, as if the words were torn from him, he asked, "Were you in my dream, Letty?"

Letty felt as though her lungs had forgotten how to function. Focusing on the knot of his cravat, she said, "I . . . I don't know what you're talking about."

"No?"

Thorn grasped the side of her neck with his right hand, then he put his thumb under her chin and forced her to look up at him. Slowly he searched her eyes for the truth. "I think you know very well what I'm talking about."

She tried to turn her face, but the pressure of his thumb stopped her. "Take your hands off me!"

"Were you the woman in my dream, Letty?"

When she closed her eyes so he couldn't see her thoughts, he spun her in his arm so that her back was against his chest, his right arm clamped across her shoulders holding her in place. Then, like a man possessed, he yanked the hair clip that held her braided coronet in place and began unbraiding her hair.

"How dare you! Let me go!"

Letty tried to pull away from him, but he twined his strong fingers through her hair and held tightly.

When she grew still, he began once again to free her hair from the braid. "I have to know," he said.

As soon as the thick braid was undone, he shook the hair so that it spilled over her shoulders and down her back. Then, before she realized his intention, he spun her around, locked his arm around her waist, and lifted her off the ground.

The crackling of the husk-filled mattress filled her ears as Thorn fell back on the cot, pulling her down on top of him. With her hair hanging down like a thick curtain on either side of her face, Letty tried to push away from him, but he held her fast. "Be still," he said. Then, his voice no more than a husky whisper, he added, "Please, Letty."

Unable to refuse his whispered request, Letty grew still.

Slowly Thorn turned his head back and forth, feeling the texture of Letty's hair as the silky strands drifted across his face like gentle waves lapping then receding from the banks of the river. With each movement, he breathed deeply, filling his senses with the scent that was hers alone.

Finally, as though all his questions had been answered, he crushed her body against his and buried his face in the side of her neck. He moaned softly, and the sound, plus the feel of his strong arms around her, awakened memories Letty thought she had buried years ago.

Unable to stop herself, she turned her face to his, wanting his kiss as she had never wanted anything in her life.

But he didn't kiss her.

He looked at her for a long, long time, his eyes filled with an emotion she couldn't read, then he shifted his weight and turned on his side so that she was no longer on top of him. Disentangling himself from her skirts and her long tresses, he rolled away from her, then stood up, leaving her alone on the cot.

At the granny room door he stopped and leaned his shoulder against the sturdy wooden frame. For several minutes he merely stared out at the trees in the distance. "It was you," he said finally, the words so soft Letty wasn't certain she had heard them. "All this time, it was you."

Letty lay on the cot where he had left her, her body rigid with embarrassment. *How he must despise me for letting him think he had made love to his wife.*

"Such a waste," he said.

"What?"

"I'm sorry, Letty. I hope that someday you can forgive me."

Before she had time to ask him what she was to forgive him for, he pushed away from the door, snatched his hat from the table, and strode away.

Drew came to see her the next morning. Thorn had apprised him of Letty's true identity the night before, so he wasn't as shocked as he might have been. Still, he had some personal catching up to do before they got down to the business of the trial. The scuppernong arch offered both shade and privacy for their conversation.

"I told Thorn to stay out of sight," Drew informed her in answer to her shyly asked question as to his whereabouts. "The old couple at the guest house seemed to take him in aversion, and I was afraid they might not be the only ones to do so. I didn't want him influencing the jury unfavorably. He agreed, as I knew he would, that we shouldn't risk any possible anti-Yankee feelings spilling over to work against you."

"So he won't be coming here today?"

"Not if I can help it."

Drew cleared his throat, an obvious segue. "But enough about Thorn. We need to discuss you and your future, so let's get down to cases. I've read the sworn statement of this Preacher Smithfield, and—"

"Smithfield! I knew this was his doing!"

Overwhelmed by a feeling of rage at the man's twisted need to prove his superiority, Letty stamped her foot, causing an overripe scuppernong to fall onto the bench beside her. Taking her anger out on the fruit, she picked up the swollen grape and threw it with all her strength. Unfortunately, the childish act did little to ease her frustration.

"This is retribution, Drew. It's Smithfield-style retribution."

"Can you prove that?" he asked, his voice as calm as hers was agitated.

"No, I can't. But all my instincts say it's true. By the preacher's reckoning, I am an abomination—a sinner who goes unpunished—and a flaunter of the laws of the Lord. I think he believes it is his mission to see the wicked receive their just deserts. And in addition to his religious fervor, it is quite possible that the man bears me a grudge, that he blames me for causing him to lose face before his parishioners."

"Be that as it may, Miss Loretta, this Smithfield swears that the Negress, Sudy, told him some pretty sordid stories about the goings-on at White Pines. Secrets you would not want known. Secrets for which you would do murder."

"He's lying, Drew. There are no *sordid* stories. Of course, we all have things in our lives we wish to keep private. Sudy grew up at White Pines, so she had firsthand knowledge of one of those private things. But only one. And she promised me she would never divulge my secret. I believed her then, and I have not lost faith in her."

Drew gave her a cold, penetrating stare—a technique, she had no doubt, that proved most effective in the courtroom. "I notice, Miss Loretta, that you did not deny being a murderess."

For just a moment, Letty's heart seemed to stop beating. How could she deny being a murderess? She had, after all, done murder. But that was long ago. And though she was prepared to pay for that sin in the hereafter, she had no intention of paying for someone else's crime in the here and now.

"I did not kill Sudy," she said.

Drew reached forward and patted her hand. "I believe you. Do you have any idea who did?"

"How could I? All I know for certain is that Sudy was afraid of Preacher Smithfield. She said he whipped her, and I didn't doubt it for a minute. He has a history of being heavy-handed with his discipline. She also called him a devil and a liar, and for that reason I do not believe she told him anything about me and my life at White Pines. At least, not of her own free will.''

Drew remained quiet for some time, and Letty supposed he was considering her story. It was difficult to tell, for he had learned to school his features well. ''It is fortunate,'' he said finally, ''that we do not have to prove who committed the murder, only that you did not. If we can discredit Smithfield's testimony, then all we need concern ourselves with is the knife found at the scene of the crime. It belonged to your son, I believe.''

''Yes. The knife belonged to Bram.''

Letty looked into Drew's face. This time she didn't try to read his thoughts, she knew what was coming.

''You must prepare yourself, Miss Loretta, for what may come up during this trial. Secrets, no matter how long buried, have a way of surfacing.'' He let his words sink in. ''And now,'' he said, ''I believe it is time I met Thorn's son.''

Twenty-four

The number of men, women, and children who gathered four years ago for the trial of the horse thief was nothing compared to the throng who gathered Monday morning to witness the trial of the local granny woman, Mrs. Letty Bonner. Once again, the trial was being held on the porch of Finley's Mercantile, so that all who wished could attend. But unlike the former trial, which had about it an air of excitement bordering on frivolity, this trial involved a valued member of the community, and because of that, a certain hushed formality prevailed.

By the time the foursome from Lodge Farm arrived at the settlement, the morning dew had surrendered to the on-slaught of the July sun, and waxed palm fans were already stirring up much needed breezes in the crowd. As Drew escorted Letty to the porch of the Mercantile, and to the cane-bottom chair designated as the defendant's seat, he tried to ease some of her nervousness by joking that at least she got to sit in the shade.

"Yes," she agreed, the calmness of her voice belying the panic that gnawed at her insides like rats at a wheel of cheese, "before the day is up, half those people sitting in the sun will wish they could swap places with me. And for my part,'' she added, ''I would gladly make the exchange.''

Drew smiled, but Letty could tell his mind was already fixed on his part in the day's proceedings.

Within five minutes of Letty's arrival, Judge Vernon P. Wooten threaded his way through the congestion of assorted chairs, stools, and overturned barrels occupied by the spectators. When he reached the porch, he took his place behind the bench, which was, in this instance, the claw-footed table borrowed from the foyer of Finley's Guest House. Letty had no trouble guessing the purpose for the chair placed to the right of the judge's table. That chair was for the comfort of those who would testify against her.

Afraid she would lose her composure if she looked at the supportive faces of Jubal, Patience, and Sarah, who sat on the front row, or the worried faces of Fern and Bram, who had been given places on the veranda of Finley's Guest House, Letty concentrated on the crocheted curtains that billowed in the open windows of the second and third floors of the guest house. For just a moment she thought she spotted a tall, dark-haired man at one of the attic windows. But before she could determine if it was Thorn who stood vigil, Judge Wooten pounded the table with his gavel and declared the court in session.

The name of every adult white male present was put into a hat, and the jury was selected by drawing names from that hat. Since neither Andrew Holden, lawyer for the defense, nor Tobias Finley, justice of the peace and prosecutor, voiced any objections to the twelve men chosen, the jury took their seats on the front row, and the trial began.

The prosecutor called his first witness, Waymon Spruell, clerk at Finley's Mercantile. Waymon testified, albeit reluctantly, that he had heard Mrs. Letty Bonner threaten to put a bullet through Preacher Smithfield's gizzard.

''Evidence,'' the prosecutor stated, ''of the quick temper of the accused.''

''Objection,'' Drew said, ''summation on prosecution's part.''

''Sustained,'' Judge Wooten decreed. ''Mr. Finley, the

jury will determine for itself whether or not the accused has
a quick temper.''

''Beg pardon, Your Honor.''

No one, other than Letty, seemed to notice the relieved
look on Mr. Finley's face. She silently thanked her old
friend, however, for he had managed to insert the words
quick temper into the proceedings, in lieu of the original
accusation of *violent temper.* ''I have no more questions
for this witness,'' he said.

Andrew Holden, on cross examination, asked Waymon
only one question. ''Did you, Mr. Spruell, ever hear Mrs.
Bonner threaten harm to the Negress, Sudy Banks?''

''No, sir,'' Waymon answered happily, ''I never did.
And furthermore, nobody can make me believe she did that
Nigra harm, on account of Miss Letty wouldn't hurt a fly.''

Since that speech was greeted with ''Hear, hear'' by a
number of spectators, Judge Wooten was obliged to pound
his gavel and shout, ''I will have order in my court!''

When the spectators settled down, Drew said he had no
more questions for the witness.

''Mr. Finley,'' Judge Wooten instructed, ''call your next
witness.''

''The prosecution calls Preacher Willard Smithfield.''

In his role as witness, the preacher had chosen to wear
his Sunday clothes. His old black frock coat had been
brushed and sponged, and a freshly starched collar was but-
toned to his shirt. In his hand he carried his own dog-eared
Bible, choosing to take his oath of ''truth and nothing but
the truth'' on that Testament rather than the one provided
by the court.

''Preacher Smithfield,'' Mr. Finley began, ''I have here
in my hands an affidavit, sworn to and signed by you, at-
testing to a certain conversation you had with the murdered
woman, Sudy Banks. As it was on the authority of this
affidavit that the accused was brought to trial, is there anything you would like to add to or retract from your statement before I offer it in evidence?''

Smithfield placed his Bible over his heart. ''No call to

add, and no need to retract. It's all the truth, pure and simple."

"Very well," Mr. Finley said, placing the paper on the table, "then will you tell the jury in your own words what Sudy Banks revealed to you?"

"You mean the secrets that got her killed?"

A general stirring in the crowd caused the judge to demand silence. "Just repeat what you said in the affidavit," he instructed.

"Well," Smithfield began, "the Nigra—Sudy Banks, she called herself—worked for me when I lived downriver, before I got the call to the new church here in the settlement. She did woman's work: cleaning, cooking, a little light gardening, that sort of thing. Nothing too taxing. I don't remember exactly how long she was with us, but her, me, and Ezra all got along fine as five pence. Naturally, when me and my boy moved up here, Sudy decided to come along with us."

Smithfield shifted his chair an inch or two to the left to enable him to look directly at the gentlemen of the jury. "Of course, we're all acquainted with the fickleness of Eve's daughters—never mind what color they are—so it wasn't surprising that soon as we got settled in, Sudy started saying as how she was missing her boy. Henry, I believe she called him. Well, when she said she wanted to go to Cairo to find her boy, I told her if she went I'd have to get me another gal to do her work. Sudy said her mind was made up, so I said for her to go on and get. But her and me parted ways friendly like."

"Mr. Finley," the judge said, his patience obviously tried, "is there a point to this witness's story? If there is, please see that he gets to it before nightfall."

"Yes, Your Honor."

Mr. Finley stepped forward to take control of the testimony again. "Preacher Smithfield, you heard the judge. You are here to give evidence regarding what you swore to in your affidavit, so please get to the point."

Smithfield turned in his chair and glared at Letty. "The point," he said, "is that the defendant is a liar. Everything about her is a lie. Even her name. She calls herself a widow from Savannah, when she is, in fact, from a plantation called White Pines. And her name is Letty Banks. *Miss* Letty Banks.''

Letty looked beyond the crowd to the veranda where Fern sat in one of the rocking chairs reserved for the Finleys' paying guests. Remembering how shocked the young girl had been at the disclosure of Bram's bastardy, Letty needed to see how she was taking this revelation.

Not well, obviously. Bram stood just behind Fern, his hand on her shoulder. Letty could see the girl's face—it was ashen with shock.

I must not react. Drew warned me that the truth about my supposed widowhood might come out. And he warned me not to lose control of my emotions.

Raising his voice above the whispers of the crowd, the preacher continued. ''Sudy was one of the White Pines slaves, and she knew Letty Banks from the day she was born. Same as she knew Letty Banks's sister.'' He paused, waiting until he was certain he had every ear. ''A mulatto sister,'' he added triumphantly. ''A mulatto who lived right there in the main house, wearing silk dresses and eating off fine china, while thousands of hardworking, God-fearing white men went hungry and—''

''Objection, Your Honor!''

Drew was on his feet immediately. ''The affidavit contained no testimony about what was worn or eaten by any of the inhabitants of White Pines. Furthermore, my client cannot be held accountable for the actions of her father. If the prosecution is basing its case on the assumption that my client would commit murder only to conceal the fact that her father sired a mulatto, then half the ladies who lived on plantations would be—''

''Enough,'' Judge Wooten ordered. ''Your objection regarding the affidavit is sustained. Everything else is overruled. And let me caution you, counselor, that since you will have your turn to cross-examine the witness, I want no further orations disguised as objections. Do I make myself clear?''

"Yes, Your Honor. I beg the court's pardon."

"Mr. Finley, you may continue with this witness."

"Thank you, Your Honor."

"Preacher Smithfield, since you must restrict your testimony to the affidavit, I ask you, did the woman known as Sudy Banks give you this information about Miss Letty living at White Pines?"

Smithfield kissed his Bible. "She did."

Mr. Finley nodded, then stepped off the porch to take his seat. "I have no more questions. Your witness, Mr. Holden."

Drew approached the porch slowly. "Mr. Smithfield," he began, "you stated in the affidavit . . . Here," he said, retrieving the paper from the table, "let me refresh your memory. You said, 'The Nigra told me that if she wanted to, she could tell some sordid stories about Miss Letty. Stories that Miss Letty would probably kill to keep secret.' "

Drew set the paper back on the table. "This story of the mulatto child on the plantation, is this the *sordid* secret to which you refer?"

"I—"

Drew continued quickly, not letting Smithfield answer his question. "Of course, as a preacher of the Gospel, you must find the licentious behavior on the part of some former slaveholders totally reprehensible."

"Yes, and—"

"But I assure you, Mr. Smithfield, that this kind of shameful activity was repeated on hundreds, perhaps thousands of plantations throughout the South. And while polite society may have turned a blind eye to the all-too-frequent instances of mulattos, quadroons, and octoroons who bore a striking resemblance to their masters, I assure you their existence was most definitely not a secret."

Smithfield had tried several times to interrupt, and now his face was red with the effort. "There was more than one secret!" he yelled. "Just like there was more than one mulatto."

"Your Honor," Drew interrupted quickly, obviously

wanting to quash any further revelations, "the answer is nonresponsive. Please instruct the witness to keep his comments to the testimony of the affidavit."

Smithfield didn't wait for the judge's ruling. "But it wasn't only her pa acting licentious," he said, "it was her, too. It was Letty Banks, too. She—"

Judge Wooten pounded the table with his gavel. "The witness will be quiet, or I will have him—"

"The Lord's truth shall be heard!" Smithfield yelled, ignoring the judge's warning. Then, jumping to his feet, he spread his arms wide, as if imploring the crowd. "Hear me! Those of you who are God-fearing, righteous folk, pay me heed! That Jezebel, that lying harlot who came here claiming to be a widow, has foisted her own mulatto child upon you. And it was to hide that secret that she murdered Sudy Banks."

In the hush that followed, Letty stood, her hands balled into fists. If there had been a way to do so, she would have committed murder gladly at that moment. "You lying snake! Sudy never told you any such tale. You made it up, all of it, to serve your own ends."

"There is my proof," Smithfield declared, pointing toward the veranda. "There is the mulatto girl herself."

Everyone turned to see where the preacher pointed. What they saw was Fern, standing beside the rocking chair she had just abandoned, and trembling so badly that without Bram's supporting arm, she would have fallen. When she began to cry, Bram put her behind him to shield her from the stares of the crowd.

"Weep!" Smithfield bellowed. "Gnash your teeth, you daughter of Satan. It will do you no good. For you are evil begotten, and as doomed to burn in the eternal fires of hell as the slut who spawned you and the nigger who sired you."

Waving the Bible above his head, the preacher yelled jubilantly, "Sin is discovered! Truth is uncovered! Praise the Lord!"

The crowd was stunned to silence, and into that silence a tall, dark-haired stranger spoke. After the preacher's rant-

ings, the stranger's calm words sounded like the voice of
reason. "If I were you," warned the man who stood in the
doorway of Finley's Guest House, "I would be careful
about invoking the name of the Almighty. I read someplace
that the Lord has His own way of dealing with those who
bear false witness."

"Order!" Judge Wooten demanded. "This has all gone
far enough. You," he said, pointing to the man who had
just spoken, "if you have anything pertinent to say to this
court, step forward and let's hear it."

Thorn Bradley walked to the edge of the veranda. "As
you can see," he said, holding his empty hands toward the
crowd, "I have no Bible with me. But I swear by everything I hold dear that the preposterous story you have just
heard is a lie. The truth of my own testimony rests in the
fact that *I* am the father of Bram and Fern Bonner."

Letty sat like a stone image, her chin raised defiantly and
her gaze concentrated on some undefined point above the
heads of the crowd. Distractedly, as if this were all hap-
pening to someone else, she listened to Thorn's testimony.
It was a story of young love thwarted; a story that sounded
suspiciously as though it had been lifted from the pages of
Shakespeare.

"So you are telling us," Drew prompted, "that Miss
Letty's father would not consent to the match."

"No, sir. Talk of war was rife, and I was a Yankee.
Abner Banks turned a deaf ear to my plea. I begged Letty
to come away with me on my boat, but she wouldn't dis-
obey her father. Before I left White Pines, Letty and I . . .
what I mean is we . . ."

"Speak up," Judge Wooten ordered.

"I held her in my arms," Thorn said. "We lay together
in her herb garden. Need I say more?"

Drew cleared his throat dramatically. "And it is your
sworn statement, sir, that the fruit of that, uh, *liaison* in the
garden is the young woman known as Fern Bonner?"

"I declare that Fern is my daughter," he said. "But by
the time I had word of her, the war was on and I was

already an officer in the United States Army.''

"And you never saw the child?''

"Only once,'' Thorn said, "when she was about this high.'' He held his hand about a foot and a half above the ground. "That is, of course, when Letty and I . . . uh . . .''

"Never mind,'' Drew interrupted. "We are all aware that you have a son. The likeness is most striking. But these good men of the jury might wonder why you did not marry Miss Letty at that time and give the children your name.''

"It was wartime, and I was a Yankee. Letty was always loyal to the Cause. She wouldn't marry me. And though I begged her to come North with me, to my home in Connecticut, where she and our daughter would be safe from the ravages of war, she refused to abandon the people of the settlement who needed her. As usual, she put the needs of her friends and neighbors before her own safety.''

As Thorn continued, several woman in the crowd resorted to their handkerchiefs. "Letty is a proud woman— some might even call her bullheaded—and she lives her life by her own code of ethics, apologizing to no one and paying little heed to what others might think of her. That is why it is preposterous to suggest that she would kill someone merely to conceal the fact that her father once sired a mulatto child.''

Why, Letty wondered, was Thorn perjuring himself? He could have stayed behind the curtain that billowed in the window of his attic room. No one would have blamed him for disclaiming any knowledge of Letty. So why had he come forward? Why?

"I have no more questions,'' Drew said, bringing Letty's thoughts back to the trial.

"Me, neither,'' Mr. Finley added.

"Well, I have!'' Smithfield yelled from the back of the crowd. "Who shall sin against the Lord and not be smitten down? If there be harlots and fornicators among you, whither shall—''

"I will not have these proceedings disrupted further!'' Judge Wooten declared. "Someone take that man out of here!''

Almost before the words were out, Gideon Morgan and Troup Jones rushed to do the judge's bidding. They caught Smithfield by his arms and more or less dragged him away. As the threesome disappeared behind the guest house, Letty heard Smithfield denouncing Troup and Gideon as minions of the devil.

When order was restored once again, the judge called for the summations. The prosecutor's was brief. "I reiterate the testimony of my two witnesses," Mr. Finley said. "According to my first witness, Miss Letty has a quick temper. And according to the affidavit of my second witness, Miss Letty wished to keep a secret of certain things that happened while she lived at White Pines Plantation. Considering this evidence, I trust the gentlemen of the jury to reach the proper verdict."

Mr. Finley bowed politely to the judge, to the opposing counsel, and to the jury. Then he sat down.

"Gentlemen of the jury," Drew began. "On the subject of Miss Letty's quick temper, I feel compelled to confess that several times this afternoon I, myself, have felt the urge to put a bullet through Mr. Willard Smithfield's gizzard."

When the laughter in the crowd subsided, Drew got to the matter of the affidavit. "You will remember that when Mr. Smithfield first took the stand, he was asked if he wished to add anything to or retract anything from his original statement. At that time, he placed his Bible over his heart and said, 'No call to add, and no need to retract.' "

Drew paused, allowing time for the jury to recall the action and the words. "I suggest to you, gentlemen, that Smithfield invented that last, scurrilous lie when he discovered that the evidence of the affidavit was insufficient to convince anyone of Miss Letty's need to conceal her past.

"And I further suggest that it is preposterous to imagine that Miss Letty—a person you all know as a healer, dedicated to alleviating pain—would take a wash paddle and cruelly bludgeon a helpless Nigra woman to death. If there is someone in this community who is known for his over-zealousness when laying on the rod, I remind you, gentlemen of the jury, that person is not Letty Bonner."

Twenty-five

Letty returned the dipper to the pail she had set next to the beautifully carved wooden cross bearing Sudy's name, then she knelt beside the still-convex grave to pack the damp earth more solidly around one of the petunias. It was late in the season to be transplanting petunias, Letty knew that, but they were the only flowers she had in bloom at the moment. And they were red.

Red. The color alone painted a memory sharp with the aromas of fried chicken and bubbly sweet potatoes and vivid with warm sunshine and blue sky. A memory that caused a tightness in Letty's chest, for she felt again a small hand in hers; Ocilla's hand. Her eyes now moist, Letty recalled the morning she and Ocilla had walked down to the cookhouse to ask Verona about material for Sudy's birthday present.

"Sudy's a plumb fool about red," Verona had said, "been that way since she was a baby. She probably pitch a hissy fit if she knowed I could've chose red for her birthday dress and didn't."

Using the backs of her muddy hands, Letty brushed away the tears. She remembered something else Verona had told her that day, that two gentlemen were coming to visit Abner

Banks. At the time, Letty had assumed the visitors would come and go without making the least difference in her orderly if restricted life. How wrong she had been. Thorn Bradley came to White Pines that day, and from the moment she looked into his eyes, he took possession of her heart.

Try as she would, Letty had never been able to forget him. Then yesterday, as she had listened to his testimony—testimony he swore was the truth when, in fact, it was a quixotic story invented to shield her and Fern from Springfield's half-truths—she had decided to give up the struggle. Forgetting Thorn was an impossible task.

As long as she lived, Thorn Bradley would be in her thoughts, because she loved him. It was that simple. It had always been that simple.

Not that she believed for one second that Thorn returned her feelings, no matter what he had said on the witness stand about their being star-crossed lovers. He had proved his wish to distance himself from her when he vanished as soon as the trial ended.

After Drew's summation, the jury had needed less than five minutes to come to their decision. Upon returning from their short deliberation inside Finley's Mercantile, they had pronounced Letty, "Not guilty." But when she had looked for Thorn among the crowd of well-wishers all trying to get close enough to assure her that they had never believed in her guilt, Thorn was gone. She hadn't seen him since.

"And you probably never will," she told herself. "So quit moping around like a lovesick girl and finish those flowers."

Suddenly aware that she wasn't alone, Letty turned slowly to look behind her. As if the mere thinking of his name had caused him to materialize, Thorn stood at the base of the knoll. He held his hat in his hand, and a soft breeze lifted a lock of his dark hair and let it fall across his forehead. Heat rose to Letty's face as she realized how badly she yearned to go to him and brush the errant strand back into place. Just to let her fingers touch his face and . . .

"Hello, Letty," he said, his voice soft in deference to the new grave.

She didn't respond, she couldn't, but he didn't seem to notice.

"Othello told me you were here planting flowers," he said. "I stopped at the lodge first, but there was no one at home."

Finding her voice, Letty told him that Bram and Fern had gone berry picking. "They went with Gideon and his niece, Sarah, so they probably won't get home before suppertime."

"That's good." After that enigmatic remark, he said nothing more for a while, then he asked if he could join her.

As Letty watched Thorn climb the knoll, the young girl who still lived inside her found pleasure in the athletic grace that was so much a part of him. Beneath the finely woven material of his tan britches, the strong muscles of his thighs bunched and relaxed tantalizingly as he moved, putting her in mind of a tawny panther she had surprised years ago down near the river's edge.

"The bay has grown," he said when he was beside her.

"What?"

He pointed to the tree with its green, leathery leaves. "The sweetbay. It's grown ten feet since I saw it last."

She nodded. "Folks around here call these trees loblolly magnolias." Then, as though an amusing notion had just occurred to her, Letty smiled. "I guess the bay and I are both loblollies, both going by names we've no legitimate claim to."

"No," he corrected. "If you're a loblolly, it's because you're firmly rooted, and strong, and supportive, and . . ." Pausing, he reached up and broke off one of the fragrant blossoms that hadn't quite faded under the July sun, then he held the blossom to his nose and inhaled. "And like the loblolly," he added softly, reaching down and tucking the blossom into her braid, "you always smell wonderful."

Afraid he would see how breathless she was at his

slightest touch, Letty busied herself gathering the dipper and pail.

Thorn extended his hand. "Here, let me help you up."

"No, no," she said, pushing to her feet before he could touch her again, "my hands are muddy."

"We've shared mud before," he said. "Many years ago, in your herb garden at White Pines."

Remembering that he had told every last person in the settlement that he and Letty had conceived a child while in her herb garden, she turned away, her entire body warm with embarrassment. "About Fern," she began, "I appreciate your motive for saying that she was your daughter, but—"

"May we speak of that another day?"

More than happy to leave that subject, Letty asked him if he had come to tell her the news of Preacher Springfield's arrest. "For I must inform you that Drew was here early this morning. He told me how the preacher had taken his anger out on his son, half killing the boy. And how Ezra, dazed and bleeding, had stumbled to the guest house to tell Mr. Finley that he had found Bram's knife the Sunday the boys had fought, and that his father had taken the knife with him the night Sudy was killed."

Thorn reached over and took the pail from Letty's hands, and by common consent they left the knoll and walked across the pasture toward the lodge. "Drew told me he had come to take his leave of you before returning to Charleston. I am here, among other reasons, to tell you that the new trial will be held tomorrow. Judge Wooten hopes to complete it in one day, so he can be on his way to the next stop on his itinerary."

Letty walked briskly to keep pace with Thorn's long stride. "If you've come to see if I plan to attend the trial, I assure you I do not. I have had enough of trials and judges to last me for a lifetime."

"I hope not," Thorn said, "for Judge Wooten has agreed to marry us this evening, after he finishes his supper. I am ordered to have you at the guest house no later than seven o'clock for the wedding. Mr. and Mrs. Finley have agreed to stand as our witnesses."

Her mind reeling from the shock of his words, Letty tripped on a stick hidden in the grass, prompting Thorn to wrap his arm around her waist. As if she had approved the move, he gathered her close against his chest.

"I assure you, that is quite unnecessary," she said, not altogether clear herself whether she meant the wedding or his heart-stopping embrace.

"It is to me," he murmured.

Letty attempted to extricate herself from his muscular arms, but each time she tried to push away, he tightened his hold. "This is ridiculous," she said, finally ceasing to struggle.

"What is?" he asked, his mouth so close to her ear that his warm breath caressed her sensitive lobe, sending shivers of delight down her spine to secret places whose joys she tried not to remember.

"A wedding," she replied. "It is out of the question." Even to her own ears, the tone of her answer lacked the conviction she had meant to put into the words. Trying again, she said more resolutely, "If you have some quixotic notion that my honor needs protecting, let me assure you everyone within twenty miles of the settlement knows that I bore a child out of wedlock. That's twelve-year-old news.

"And as my friend Jubal would say, 'The mule is gone; no point in fixing the barn door at this late date.' "

"But you must consider," Thorn said, his words low and soft, almost hypnotizing, "the possibility that I might want desperately to recapture the mule. What then?" Tracing his forefinger slowly across the fullness of Letty's lips, he asked, "What if it is the one mule in the world meant for me? And ponder further the fact that I have been lonely all my life, not knowing where to find my one special mule."

"Honest?" she asked breathlessly, not at all put off by the unlover-like comparison to a beast of burden known for its unmanageable nature. "You're not just making that up out of some misguided sense of chivalry?"

Encouraged by the wistfulness in her tone, he smoothed

his hands down her back and over the curve of her hips, fitting the length of her body snugly against his before enfolding her once again in his arms. "For years I thought I had made *you* up. Or, rather, dreamed you up."

"You did?"

He nodded, the action putting his lips in contact with her forehead. For several wonderful moments he let his lips explore the texture of her skin. "My mother loved me," he said, "but she died when I was a child. After her death, there was no love in my life."

"But what about your wife? Your Delia? When you were wounded, you spoke of her in your dreams. I-I always thought you loved her."

He shook his head. "I loved the idea of her. She was beautiful and mysterious. Not like anyone else I had ever known. It was only after my return from the war that I saw the real person. Delia was a very complicated young woman. Troubled and very unhappy. I was never her husband in the true sense, nor even her friend. She would not allow it. She was unable to give love or let anyone love her, and very soon my only feelings for her were those of concern and compassion."

"Poor young woman," Letty said. "And poor Thorn."

He kissed her forehead. "Yours is such a tender heart. You can even find sympathy for a girl you never knew."

"Yes," Letty said, "and for the young man who once cared for her, the man who had no love in his life."

"Not for a long time," he said. "Not until the night I held a wonderful, giving, beautiful woman in my arms."

He crushed her to him. "God, Letty, the time we've wasted. I never forgot this place, nor the feeling of completeness I knew here. Now I know it wasn't the land that made me feel whole. It was you. I can't let you go. Not now. Not when I know that you are real. You must marry me."

Her heart nearly bursting from her chest, Letty wanted to believe that what he said was true. Oh, how she wanted to believe it. But he had lied so well on the witness stand.

What if he was doing so again, just to protect her? "Are you certain you want to get married?"

"Get married? No. Marry *you*, however, that's an altogether different matter. I love you, Letty Bonner. I think I have loved you for as long as I've known you, only I was too much of a fool to realize it."

"You love me?"

He answered her question by bending his head and kissing her, his mouth warm with tenderness.

Deserting her lips for only a moment, he pressed soft kisses onto her eyes, then with the tip of his tongue he teased the warm, sensitive pulse points in her neck. Letty felt as if her senses had caught fire, while her spirit sang with a joy she had only dreamed of. When he captured her mouth once again, deepening the kiss until she felt her knees grow week, Letty moaned with pleasure.

"Say it," he urged hoarsely. "Say you will marry me."

Wrapping her arms around his neck, Letty tried to pull his face back down so that she could kiss him again. "Must we talk now?" she asked, her voice half pleading.

"Yes," he whispered, his mouth no more than a quarter inch from hers. "I must get your promise now, while you're all soft and warm and pliable in my arms."

"Please," she whispered, and he couldn't resist the softness of her voice or her lips. But before he lost himself in her warmth, he said once again, "Say you'll be mine."

"But what of the people here who depend upon me? I know you were inventing a story when you told the judge that I wouldn't leave the people here who need me, but it's true. I couldn't go away. And what about your life, Thorn? You have a home, a business, friends. And you—"

He stopped her words by kissing her once again, a gesture she responded to with enthusiasm. When he ended the kiss, a teasing light in his eyes stole her breath away. "I had to stop you," he said. "I was afraid you were about to cap your argument by saying you wouldn't marry a Yankee. That's the one thing I can't change. My home I can sell, my shipping line will run itself, and the only people who matter to me live here at Lodge Farm. Now will you please put me out of my misery and say you'll marry me?''

The teasing light was in her eyes now as she moved against him, very much like a cat begging to be stroked. ''If I say yes, will you then end *my* misery?''

Groaning, he crushed her to him. ''Oh, yes, my sweet girl.''

''Then I say yes, too.''

''You'll marry me?''

''Yes.''

With a cry of exultation, he kissed her deeply, thirstily, and as they kissed, Thorn lifted Letty in his arms and carried her to the shelter of a grove of turkey oaks where he lowered her gently to the soft, sweet-smelling grass.

In the distance, meadowlarks whistled their clear, mellow notes, and the soft breeze made music of the rustling leaves. While in the privacy of their shaded bower, Thorn made love to Letty . . . slowly, gently, reverently, giving to her and receiving in return all the love the two of them had held in their hearts for so long. Heart to heart, soul to soul, they gave and received, finding the love they had both only dreamed of.

And the reality was better, far better than the dream.